I0613256

Wrath
of
Empire

Other science fiction by Ian S. Bott

The Shayla Carver universe

Ghosts of Innocence

Master assassin Shayla Carver has killed many times. That's what assassins do, nothing to lose sleep over, but this mission is different ... she's never killed a whole planet before.

The Ashes of Home

Shayla Carver, master assassin (retired) and planetary governor, is exiled and tasked with rebuilding her home planet. But deadly ghosts from her past haunt her, and even her own survival is the least of Shayla's worries.

Standalone stories

Tiamat's Nest

The virtual world comes alive and reaches out into the real world with deadly results. University professor and devout technophobe, Charles Hawthorne, confronts technology full on to end the hidden threat to humanity.

The Long Dark

Trapped in the lengthening nights of Elysium. Abandoned by the last convoy south. Alone with her teenage son. Anna never thought she would die this way, but a fight for survival unexpectedly becomes a battle for the future of the entire colony.

Wrath of Empire

Ian S. Bott

Dark Sky Press

This book is a work of fiction. All characters in this book are ficti-tious, and any resemblance to actual persons, living or dead, is purely coincidental.

Copyright © 2023 by Ian S. Bott

All rights reserved. No part of this publication may be reproduced, distributed, or transmitted in any form or by any means, or stored in a database or retrieval system, without the prior written permission of the publisher.

Published by Dark Sky Press, an imprint of Ian S. Bott, Writer and Artist
Visit our website at www.iansbott.com

Book Design by Jim Bisakowski
Cover illustration by Ian S. Bott

ISBN **978-1-7774021-2-9**

Printed in the United States of America

First Edition: May 2023
10 9 8 7 6 5 4 3 2 1

To readers who enjoyed *Ghosts of Innocence*
and *The Ashes of Home*
See how the journey begins

Chapter 1

Year 8067, late autumn

"Is it wrong that I don't feel sad?"

The question startled Chalwen back to the here-and-now. She'd been scanning the tree line and peering into shadows, alert for anything out of place, when she'd let her attention wander. A stand of thousand-year-old Veshi oaks spread their gnarled canopy over a walkway leading deeper into the imperial family graveyard. The play of light and shade had distracted Chalwen, an unforgivable lapse in a bodyguard.

The many layers of security surrounding the hectic days of the official state funeral surely made this the safest place on the planet. All the same, Chalwen cursed under her breath and carried out a hurried situation check.

Prince Julian still gazed at the plain memorial where the family had just interred the ashes of Empress Florence. He tilted his head as if in thought, studying the simple inscription carved into the rough stone. Chalwen struggled to read his mood while checking the positions of the guards maintaining a watchful cordon at the edge of the clearing. Everyone was on edge this evening, but Julian seemed more distracted than upset.

"Your grandmother was ... a complicated person," Chalwen murmured.

"I didn't really know her."

Was that sadness in his voice? Regret? Fear, even?

"I'd hoped she'd teach me more about statecraft, and, you know, emperor stuff."

"Your tutors teach you all that, though, don't they?"

"Politics, and history, and etiquette and elocution ..." Julian shook his head. "Don't get me wrong, I love Doctor Vicky but *she's* never had to raise taxes or meet another Head of Family or send the fleet to go stamp out a rebellion. It's *different*. I'll have to learn one day, and Father's always too busy to bother with me."

Chalwen shuddered, then reminded herself that Julian was only nine years old. He was only aware of the last few years of Florence's rule, not the bloody century that preceded them. "It's never a bad thing to think ahead. Today, you're only a step away from the Skamensis throne."

"Why today? Father's been emperor for a year now. Grandmother already gave him the throne, so surely her death changes nothing."

It changes everything, Chalwen wanted to scream. But it would take years for Julian to navigate the maze of conflicting powers that made up the empire. "True enough, but while Florence lived, in many people's minds she was still an empress. If anything happened to your father, she could have resumed the throne."

"Could that really have happened?"

Chalwen pondered the question. "In theory, if your uncle Ivan didn't beat her to it. But she's no longer here to stop him. You're right. As next in line, you do need to prepare yourself." *More than you can know.* Chalwen shuddered again. If anything *had* happened to Emperor Paul, Ivan had little hope of wresting power from a still-formidable Florence. But young and inexperienced Julian? Another matter entirely.

"I know Father's sad." Julian screwed his face. "I honestly can't tell what Mother's thinking. Josie and Flossie can't stop bawling their eyes out, of course."

Of course, Chalwen thought. Of all Paul's children they'd had the closest relationship with their sweetly tyrannical grandmother.

Empress Florence had continued a long line of brutal oppression with imaginative savagery, only softening in her later years with the births of twins Josephine and young Florence, two years Julian's junior.

Something had changed her then, ending in her declaring Paul her successor rather than the elder Ivan.

Could a last minute change of heart really make up for decades of iron rule?

From the corners of her eyes, Chalwen noted the six members of Julian's escort falling in around them as they started towards the shadowed avenue leading back to the residence. Steel-grey clouds chased the last few rays of sun, and a damp chill seeped through the gardens from the ocean beyond the clifftop wall.

"To answer your question, no, it's not wrong."

———•◦•———

In the entrance lobby, Chalwen went ahead and nodded a wary greeting to Tobias Bertolini, the head of household security at Cravel Braz. "I commend the Crown Prince to the care of the household guard."

The rest of Julian's personal guard followed as far as the sheltered portico, and stationed themselves at a discreet distance. Protocols over jurisdiction were tricky and jealously guarded. Outside, Chalwen was grudgingly allowed to dictate terms for Julian's safety. Indoors, the household guard took over, though Chalwen herself insisted on accompanying the Crown Prince. Tobias twitched one corner of his mouth in a sneer, but otherwise made no move to either acknowledge or impede Chalwen. That seemed to be about the best Chalwen could expect in this snooty company.

Chalwen felt at home in the Mosaic Palace at the heart of the capital in Prandis. She'd spent much of her life there and knew the people, the factions, the intrigues. Beyond the capital was another world. Each of the imperial residences across Magentis had its own atmosphere. Warm and homely or cold and businesslike, forward-looking or aggressively conservative, humane or cruel, each household carried with it the accumulated baggage of past occupants. This ancient pile at Cravel Braz, though one of the minor palaces, had been Florence's favored retreat. The buildings and grounds were steeped in the uncompromising strictures of iron rule. The stones oozed a weight of history too deep to fathom. In Florence's absence, this was now most emphatically Ivan's turf.

Their footsteps clacked on worn flagstones of the hallway leading from the grand entrance hall into the massive rotunda that lay at the heart of the palace. Chalwen took her place just behind Julian, and relaxed fractionally as the household guard took station around them. At least they were now under cover.

An intense buzz of conversation came from the open doorway to the family sitting room on their right. Julian glanced at Chalwen over his shoulder and rolled his eyes.

"You know damned well I won't nominate Amelia van Buren." The Emperor's voice carried into the hallway, low but insistent. "She would cheerfully criminalize half the population for simply breathing the wrong way."

Aah, Chalwen thought, that same argument simmering still. The Assembly had been tied up in knots for months trying to settle on a candidate for the head of the Imperial Judiciary.

"And there is nothing that will persuade me to back Jefferin Marx." Chalwen's scalp crawled at the venom in Ivan's tone. "If you hold to your current path you'll face humiliation in the Assembly."

The two most powerful men in the empire stood on either side of a log fire crackling in a hearth wide enough to roast a boar. An open bottle sat on the table to one side of the fireplace. A rare vintage of Dragon's Breath, if Chalwen judged correctly from the dusty label. A fitting toast to the late Empress.

"Then we need some other way out of this impasse." Paul turned as Julian crossed the threshold. "I think a change of subject is in order. Julian will learn about Assembly intrigues all too soon. Let's not burden him before his time."

Julian, Chalwen and the guards paused just inside room and gave brief bows to Paul, before fanning out on either side joining the Emperor's and Grand Duke's retinues.

"Why would the call of duty be seen as a burden?" Boyish tones vanished as Julian straightened his back under the mantle of Crown Prince. "This argument has dragged on long enough, don't you think? Neither of you is going to budge, so you're at a deadlock."

Ivan quirked an eyebrow at Julian. "I'm glad *someone* in this family sees sense. Do you have an equally sensible suggestion to offer?"

Chalwen's shoulders bunched at the mocking tone, but Julian seemed unfazed.

"Find another candidate."

Past Ivan's shoulder, Chalwen noticed a brief flicker of a smile cross Paul's lips. What was he up to? Had this exchange been prearranged?

"The Supreme Judge is a lifetime appointment," Paul said. "Not something to be proposed lightly."

"But you're each backing people you like and taking your followers with you. As long as you do that, you'll never get a consensus in the Assembly."

Ivan's eyes narrowed as he gave Julian an appraising stare. Whatever Julian and Paul were up to, the inexperienced youngster risked overplaying it. Ivan would sniff out collusion in an eyeblink. "So who would *you* recommend, then?"

Chalwen's breath hitched.

"How would I know?" Julian's eyes lit on the table with the bottle. He smiled hopefully at his father, who gave a stern shake of his head. Julian's shoulders slumped. "All I know is that you've got a list of good judges. Any one of them could *do* the job, but there's no one you'll both like, so find the one you both least *dislike*."

Chalwen released her breath. If this innocence was an act, even she couldn't detect it.

———•◆•———

By the time Julian took leave of his father and uncle, a gaping hole gnawed at Chalwen's insides. Once she'd escorted Julian to his quarters and handed over to the night shift, she'd be free to get a meal in the barracks.

At the entrance to Julian's sitting room, Marcus Tyee, Julian's personal aide, greeted them. "I'm sure the Crown Prince is tired and hungry after this long day." His nasal tones and flapping hands as he shooed Julian through to the dressing room reminded Chalwen of a broody hen.

She grunted and glanced either side of the door, tensing. The room temperature seemed to have dropped a few degrees, despite the fire in the grate.

Marcus must have noticed her unease. "The guard is changing. The next shift will be here momentarily."

The hairs on the back of Chalwen's neck still prickled. "And you were here at the change?"

"Of course. I was happy to keep watch over the quarters for a few minutes."

Some of the tension eased from her shoulders. Despite disarming appearances, Marcus had proved himself to be sharp and competent and utterly devoted to Julian. Chalwen had once seen him humiliate a would-be mugger in the back alleys of Prandis Braz, with lightning-fast surgically-precise knife work that left his assailant unhurt but almost naked. The mugger was last seen hurdling trash cans to escape, with shreds of tunic and pants and dignity hanging off him in tatters. Chalwen had been laughing too hard to assist.

The premises were in safe enough hands, but this was unforgivably lax of the household guard. She scanned the room for anything else amiss.

"Curried meatballs! My favorite."

Chalwen started. The table in the middle of the sitting room lay empty. There should have been a tray of food there for Julian, and she'd just been about to call the kitchens to chase them up, but the cry of delight had come from the bedroom next door. It took a precious second for the implications to sink in, then she raced to the door calling out, "Julian, wait!"

Too late. A pained groan greeted her as she burst through the bedroom door, and she glimpsed movement in the corner of her eye. As she thumbed her lapel transmitter, the sound of retching came from the bathroom beyond. "Chikadee down. Medic to nest."

She repeated the message in the few seconds it took her to cross the room. Dammit! Where were the household guards? Julian stood over the hand basin rinsing off his face. He looked pale and shaky, but he was on his feet.

Chalwen whirled at a sound behind her. Her beam pistol was out of its holster and trained on the door before she recognized Colonel Simon bin Mellin, head of the imperial bodyguard, and Chalwen's commanding officer.

"Lieutenant ap Gwynodd. Seems the Emperor will need a new heir." He scrawled notes on his notepad.

Chalwen frowned, steadied her breathing and lowered her weapon. Simon had got here way too fast. He must have been waiting. Another drill.

Simon confirmed it with a code word, officially ending the emergency. All the same, she kept her weapon drawn and ready while approaching voices and running feet sounded in the corridor outside. She didn't holster it until the medic had pronounced the Crown Prince healthy, and given him a tonic to settle his stomach.

"Yuck!" said Julian. "That tasted disgusting."

Chalwen wasn't sure if he was talking about the tainted food or the tonic. Simon hovered nearby all the while, alert, judging her performance. She'd already failed the most important test by allowing her charge to poison himself, but even though this was clearly a drill she didn't allow herself to relax too soon.

Back in the sitting room, and with Julian picking tentatively at a fresh platter which Chalwen had checked carefully, Simon barked, "Lieutenant ap Gwynodd, how did the assassin slip past your guard this time?"

Chalwen eyed the offending tray on the sideboard. "The chain of custody was broken. This is not the tray that was checked and signed off in the kitchen. It doesn't carry the proper seal. A good imitation, but it was swapped somewhere en route. This attempt would never have had a chance if I'd got to it first."

"And yet, the assassin knew that by placing the tray in the bedroom rather than the living room, on a night of formal mourning, it would be found first by a half-starved youngster before you had a chance to check it."

"More important, I think, is that someone had access here to make a swap."

Simon huffed. "Defense in depth, Lieutenant. Never rely on just one safeguard. Report to my office for a formal reprimand."

"That's not fair, Colonel," Julian protested. "I was the one too impatient to notice."

Simon's eyes never wavered, and Chalwen returned his gaze as she said, "Your safety is in my hands, Magister. If you died by your own actions, the fault would still be mine for failing to train you properly. We will review food safety procedures tomorrow."

Assuming I'm still here tomorrow.

———•◆•———

Once the night guard had arrived and been briefed on the security situation, Chalwen left the imperial family quarters with gnawing hunger temporarily masked by gnawing dread. A hidden stairwell led down into the labyrinth of service corridors beneath the residence. Guards stood at key intersections and patrolled the subterranean acres, on high alert. The apparent attempt on Julian's life had made everyone jumpy. There would be a thorough debriefing. Lessons would be hammered home in true imperial fashion.

Had they been told yet that it was only a drill? Maybe not. Chalwen was not about to enlighten them. Where in Space were you all half an hour ago? The thought tasted bitter.

She emerged in the cramped warren of guard offices and ready rooms alongside the main entrance hall. As the head of the imperial bodyguard, the colonel and his immediate staff merited their own offices here. Chalwen was too low on the food chain to warrant such courtesy.

She knocked, entered, saluted and stood at attention.

Colonel Simon bin Mellin lounged behind his desk. He studied his notepad for several long seconds before glancing up at Chalwen. "Relax, Lieutenant. Despite what I said upstairs, you had little chance of detecting this plot in time."

For a moment, Chalwen stared at him. Then the weight of this failure on top of so many others overtook her. "You have a knack for setting me up to fail." The words slipped out unbidden. The reality was starting to set in that Julian was safe, there had been no danger. She stiffened herself before her legs could give way in delayed reaction and relief. She just had to swallow her pride and take whatever reprimand was coming.

But instead of the expected reaming-out for addressing a superior officer with disrespectful snark, Simon shook his head. "You are being set up to *learn*, so that you'll have a fighting chance of saving a life when the real time comes. And the Crown Prince himself needs to learn that this is no game."

He opened a drawer and plonked a bottle and two glasses on the desk. "At ease, Lieutenant." He motioned her to the chair opposite.

She sat, but left her glass untouched. "How can I be at ease? Someone was able to tamper with the Crown Prince's supper tray. Was there inside help?"

"My agent used only the resources available to a trained infiltrator. Members of the household staff were misled, but not knowingly turned to treachery."

Chalwen was sure she'd never get to meet this mysterious agent. Or agents. Why assume Simon only used the one? "So, it was down to procedural lapses then." Frustration threatened to boil over. "I have no jurisdiction over the staff or guards here. The perimeter I can establish is only as good as the local organization."

Simon glared at Chalwen. "Here, then, is the real lesson today. Don't let yourself be limited by the official lines of jurisdiction."

"I don't see how a lowly lieutenant can overrule a household head! Tobias keeps tight rein on this residence and his staff ignore me entirely."

"You've allowed yourself to be compromised by a petty empire-builder."

Chalwen gaped at Simon's brusque assessment.

"But," he continued, "ask yourself this. Who do you owe allegiance to? Tobias? Or Julian?"

"You know the answer to that." Chalwen sighed.

"More to the point, you know what needs to be done to secure the Crown Prince's safety. Don't even ask permission, just do it. Act with enough confidence and bullies like Tobias will back down."

Chalwen pondered his words and reviewed this evening's events. It occurred to her that whoever Simon contracted to carry out these mock infiltrations was taking an awful risk. With trigger-happy guards on the prowl, the game could easily turn deadly. There had to be some safeguards in place. "Who knew about the drill?"

"On household staff? Only Tobias."

The lapse in security in Julian's quarters disturbed her. It was as if some members of the household guard had gone out of their way to make it easy for an assassin. "Would he have invoked any recognition protocols, to avoid accidents?"

"And inadvertently tipped someone off, you mean? It's possible." It was Simon's turn to pause in thought. "Regardless, the drill is as much for the local security as for Julian's own bodyguard." Simon speared her with another glare.

So why was the local security conspicuously absent? Tobias had shown her nothing but contempt during their stay. She could understand him wanting the mock attempt to succeed to show her up, but that didn't make sense. It would reflect just as badly on his own staff as on her.

Another thought disturbed her even more. Maybe Tobias himself wouldn't have sabotaged the cordon around Julian, but what if something he'd let slip *had* tipped off someone else that there was an intruder on the prowl? *What if someone had thought this was a genuine attempt, not a drill?*

A chill seeped down her spine. Once more, Simon's words haunted her. She'd been too ready to cede responsibility to the local security. "Trust no one," she murmured.

"Chalwen." She startled at the unaccustomed familiarity, and the sudden earnestness in Simon's voice. "I know I've been hounding you hard, but I need you to be sharp. With the old Empress gone, these are dangerous and uncertain times. The Crown Prince will need all the help he can get if he's to survive long enough to take the throne."

Chalwen glared around the windowless confines of the palace communications office, and wrinkled her nose at a nearby catering trolley piled high with mess trays and food scraps. This room would have been a clamor in the wake of last night's drill, as a flurry of alarms were raised then stand-down orders confirmed and issued, but the only evidence this morning was the wreckage of late-night sustenance waiting for a kitchen porter to wheel it away.

She turned her glare back to the sergeant barring her way. "A secure office. Screened from eavesdropping. And an intercept-proof line to Imperial Security headquarters. Yes." She spoke slowly, as if to a dim-witted child.

The sergeant appeared too dim-witted even to spot the sarcasm. Although seated at his desk, he still contrived to look down his nose at Chalwen. "You do realize this kind of request is not to be made lightly. You'll be in all sorts of trouble if you're caught misusing imperial channels."

He seemed eager to give the impression that he was doing Chalwen a great favor by heading her off as if she didn't know what she was doing. She read the dismissive contempt in his manner. More of Tobias Bertolini's influence. More of the old-world snobbery that pervaded this whole damnable palace. The two comms techs in the far corner of the room looked away hastily when Chalwen glanced their way. One of them didn't bother to hide the smirk on her face as she turned back to her screens. You're a fraud, their manner yelled. You don't know what you're doing, and have no business here.

And they're right, a small voice insisted. Humiliation lingered from the failed drill last night. Everyone was talking about it. Talk in the staff corridors hushed as she approached, and her shoulder blades tingled under accusing stares as she passed.

Rallying her courage, Chalwen counted slowly to three before pointing to the authorization slip she'd sent from her notepad to the sergeant's desk. "Unless you're disputing the authenticity of this document"—the sergeant started to splutter a denial—"then you'll understand that this is not a request, it's an *order*." She put as much ice into her tone as she could muster. "You do realize there are penalties for impeding the Emperor's work."

They locked eyes, unblinking, until the sergeant's gaze wavered. "Hmmph. No need to get shirty," he muttered. "Just doing my job."

He tapped briefly on his desktop and jerked his chin at the nearer comms tech, who no longer smirked. With a scowl, she led Chalwen down a short hall and pushed open a door.

The brashly-lit room smelled of lemon floor polish with a hint of ozone and burnt rubber. Chalwen closed the door and engaged the room's standard surveillance countermeasures. The line to the capital city was already active by the time she took her seat at the desk. The surface glowed in readiness. No more messing around with officious assholes; electronic systems followed their programming and didn't argue back.

She picked up a stylus and wrote out the access code for Second Lieutenant Henri Chargon, a senior data analyst in the Bureau of Counterintelligence.

Technically speaking, this wasn't a counterintelligence matter. Equally, Chalwen had no business speaking to a data analyst there. Thankfully, the authorization documents she carried discouraged unwanted questions.

She and Henri were part of an unofficial network established by Emperor Paul, long before he became emperor, to resist the worst policies of Empress Florence. People like them, high enough up the food chain to be useful, not high enough to attract attention, formed a covert collaboration within the official machinery of government. The Hidden Light. Although, Chalwen mused, now that Paul *was* emperor and they were acting on his orders, that probably made them official now.

But still covert.

A face came into focus on the desktop. Brown eyes framed in shoulder-length black hair gazed at her. The middle of the night in Cravel, it would be late evening in Prandis, and yet Henri looked calm and alert and as inscrutably unflappable as ever.

And he was waiting for her to initiate the conversation. He wouldn't say anything until he knew the security situation at her end.

"I have some data points to add to your collection." The manner of the communications staff in the office nagged at her. Surely it was inconceivable, and yet ... "Henri, you have better tools at your end. I asked for a secure and *private* line."

She knew better than to openly voice her concerns, but she and Henri had worked together long enough now. Henri hummed a quiet tune. "Seems like you've brought some baggage with you." That confirmed her suspicions. "Give me a few minutes to lighten the load."

The line went silent for a while, leaving Chalwen to her own dark thoughts. She carried a writ signed by the Emperor allowing her to commandeer at will any means of communication. The writ should command unquestioning obedience, and yet the sergeant out there had questioned it. Not only that, but his staff then had the nerve to eavesdrop. They must believe themselves to be in a position of power to think they could get away with acts that came very close to treason. Grand Duke Ivan's grip here was strong indeed.

"Okay, we're now as private as we can be." There was a hint of laughter in Henri's voice. "It's amazing what an invitation to a fact-finding meeting with Defense of the Realm can do for one's peace of mind."

Defense of the Realm? And presumably Henri meant their Internal Investigations agency. He really had brought the big guns to bear.

Quickly, Chalwen outlined her suspicions about local staff aiding the would-be assassin. "I don't have the time or resources to launch a full-scale investigation here," she concluded, "but it seems to me there should be some kind of follow-up. Is there anything you can do?"

"No need. I didn't just make empty threats to your friends about a DOR visit, I piggy-backed on one already on its way. I know you don't always see eye-to-eye with Colonel bin Merrin, but he's already filed a preliminary report on last evening's exercise and voiced his own concerns. Seems he reached much the same conclusion."

A sudden thought struck Chalwen. "Henri, did you have any inkling that there would be a drill like this going on?"

"Could I have warned you? No, I could not."

That was his 'If I tell you, I'll have to kill you afterwards' tone. Chalwen changed tack. "Do we bring this to Sea Breeze?"

There was a long silence. Eventually, Henri said, "I don't think it would be anything more than he already suspects."

"What? I'm talking about traitors, on his own staff."

"Every corner of the empire, including the palaces, is infested with mixed allegiances. At any moment, given the right conditions, any one of those allegiances could turn their hands against the current emperor and in favor of another potential heir. This is nothing new."

More silence.

"But we can at least add to our files on individuals to be watched."

Take out an enemy and another would simply take his place. Better to keep him where you can see him. Chalwen much preferred direct action, but Henri and his office knew what they were doing.

Chalwen emerged from the office and glared at the sergeant at his desk. His cheeks flushed and he refused to make eye contact. Behind him, Tobias Bertolini loomed. He looked up from a notepad in his hand as the door clicked closed behind Chalwen. He looked pale and shaken. Hiding her smile, she suspected she'd have no more trouble from him.

In the weightlessness of the vast weapon bay, Commander Gregor Pavlenko hung from a guide stanchion and swiveled in a slow three-sixty. The skin on his forehead crinkled in the dry heat, and his eyes pricked. Where he gripped the stanchion, his palms reddened. He should have worn goggles and gloves for this environment, but he wouldn't be here long enough to suffer more than discomfort.

Sounds of machinery surrounded him, voices, the clash of metal on metal, but it all seemed to come from a distance, as if heard through a long pipe. Beneath his feet, the barrel of *Wrath of Empire's* plasma cannon stretched into the distance, obscured by a bewildering multi-colored maze of machinery. Two thousand feet long, this cannon was the signature weapon of imperial *Sword*-class battleships. This one weapon was bulkier than the whole of most warships, and could level a city with a single blast.

Gregor had no practical need to be here. In fact, he could watch progress on the overhaul far better from his station in the operations room, but from time to time he needed to see the weapon up close. Watching people crawling like ants over its surface brought home the true size of his responsibility. This was military overkill on an arrogant scale. No one should hold such power without a generous dose of humility and fear. In his five years as *Wrath of Empire's* senior weapons engineer, he'd never yet had to point it at anything other than military targets. He prayed, as he did every time he reported for duty, that he never would.

The moment of introspection passed. He steadied himself against the stanchion and pushed off towards the nearest airlock. Outside the weapon bay, and once more in the ship's artificial gravity, he shrugged on a jacket against the relative chill and headed back to the twilight world of the combat operations room.

Gregor settled into his seat and nodded thanks as an orderly placed a cup of unsweetened tea on the desk to one side. He sipped the bitter brew and cleared his mind, then turned his attention to the spread of consoles that surrounded his command post.

One by one, stations reported in. Maintenance crews cleaned pipes and nozzles, reattached wires the width of human hairs and jumper cables thicker than his forearm, replaced worn parts, closed hatches and tightened fastenings.

The plasma cannon was ancient technology, and so simple in concept—rip apart atoms of feedstock to create a star-hot plasma, and belch it out in magnetically-confined parcels of destruction. Even after all these millennia it remained the most powerful weapon in regular use. Technically, it ranked second to the quark bomb, but nobody counted that. Attempts to assemble quark bombs had a ninety percent failure rate, along with lost lives and irradiated continents. They were not practical weapons of war.

Even so, the plasma cannon still needed a small industrial city's worth of power generation, containment systems, cooling systems, and all the attendant controls and sensors. It had been mastered by the navies of the six Families and used by many Freeworlds and brigand outworlds, but only the Skamensis navy had successfully scaled it up to this level.

"You've been to see Violet again, haven't you?" Lieutenant Una Spelze, Gregor's most senior weapons specialist, plonked herself down at the next station.

He gave a non-committal grunt.

"You always get that faraway look in your eyes." She grinned. "It's kinda cute, you know."

"There's nothing cute about taking your responsibility seriously." Gregor glanced once more at the flickering lights of the dashboard. Progress was good, but they'd be at it for hours yet.

He swiveled in his seat and gazed across the room to where a small army of intruders crawled behind and under his familiar battle consoles, wrestling a snake pit of wiring harnesses out from open floor panels and knitting them into the fabric of his world. In some sense, he felt violated, but he brushed off the feeling. This was the empire's new toy. New levels of automation to bring a clinical calculation to battle decisions. Progress. He'd better get used to it.

Following the line of his gaze, Una said, "The techs report they're close to finished hooking their control lines in."

"So," Gregor whispered, "it'll have its finger on the trigger for real soon."

"With loads of safeties and aborts in between." Una's voice was light, but the set of her shoulders said otherwise.

———————

A bitter wind whipped at Grand Duke Ivan Skamensis, laced with salt damp driven off the heaving grey seas below the cliffs. Sharp hoof-beats on the hard-packed clifftop trail clattered above the endless hiss and rumble of thundering surf. Yellow gorse blossom glowed in morning sun.

Ivan's bodyguard kept a loose formation around him as they crossed the main road leading into the tiny town of Cravel Braz, and he spurred his horse into a canter. He angled inland away from the road, and cut across country, a desolate windswept moor of rough grass and stands of gorse. The chill air cleared Ivan's senses of the cloying fug of woodsmoke and cooking that permeated the palace. With the official mourning ceremonies over, the whole palace seemed hell-bent on making up for the week of deprivation with cozy warmth and comfort food.

As they slowed and climbed, the town huddled in the valley to their right overlooked by the walled palace grounds on the headland. Beyond the town, the stone pier of a tiny fishing harbor braced itself against the restless expanse of the Bay of Jorka.

Which came first, the town or the palace? Every time Ivan climbed these uplands and took in the inhospitable expanse of rolling hills, he toyed with the same question. Was the palace built here because of the town? But then, what ruler would build an imposing home in such a desolate and isolated backwater? Or did the town grow up around the palace? That made even less sense, unless the site once held more importance than was now apparent. Maybe because the question seemed to have no answer, pondering its paradox brought on a meditative calm, something Ivan was badly in need of right now.

He reined in his horse and turned to survey the buildings. Sun winked off distant windows under lowering clouds. All he knew for sure was that town and palace had been here for thousands of years, and the origins had been long lost to even the most astute historians. The palace still showed traces of ancient fortifications that hinted at a genuinely defensive purpose in times past. And the name itself offered a clue. Cravel Braz, styling itself as a city, was far too grand an aspiration for the half square mile of buildings laid out in the distance. It hinted at forgotten glories.

There now remained an isolated retreat that suited the ascetically-minded. And the weight of history attracted people who valued tradition, which made yesterday's mock assassination so puzzling.

The drill itself wasn't what troubled Ivan. That was accepted practice, unpredictable, any time, any place. His unease stemmed from the manner in which the assassination had technically succeeded. From what little Ivan could glean, the operative must have had inside help, or at least a remarkable number of people turning a blind eye to suspicious events. If not active collaboration, there had at least been some *will* for the Crown Prince to die.

Tobias had remained tight-lipped about the whole affair, and Ivan doubted he had anything to do with it. He would have known about the drill, for sure, but Ivan was sure he'd have done nothing to interfere one way or another.

Back to the question of tradition. That bugged Ivan. Why would a household so steeped in tradition, so loyal to the Skamensis family, abet an apparent plot against one of its own?

As Ivan gazed at the huddles of rooftops, it all looked so peaceful. The scene revealed nothing of the deadly intrigues simmering behind those walls. Everything looked as it must have done for a thousand years, and would no doubt look for another thousand. Human lifetimes were so fleeting when held against the stately wheeling of planets and continents.

Perspective. That's what Ivan gained on these rides into the wilds. And then he smiled. The realization had washed over him so gently, like a sea mist, so obvious that it must have always been there waiting to be acknowledged. He'd just been too caught up in the immediacy of politics.

Adherence to tradition was a matter of perspective. When people thought of support for the empire, they naturally assumed that meant support for the current emperor. But the tradition in Cravel went far deeper. The individual on the throne meant nothing. What mattered was continuity of the Family, and adherence to a set of standards. And of all the Family alive today, in the eyes of the people of Cravel at least, those values resided in Ivan, not in Paul or the Crown Prince.

Ivan felt knots ease from his shoulders as he led the formation of riders onto a path that would bring them back down the valley to the town. It all made sense now, although it gave rise to more worries. If he'd reached this conclusion, so would others. He hoped this incident wouldn't prompt people to look too closely at staff loyalties across all the imperial residences. That could cause Ivan no end of bother.

The town of Cravel might be small, but it catered well to royalty and their guests. Only a few were privileged to stay at the palace itself. The residence lacked the extensive staterooms that graced the likes of the Mosaic Palace at Prandis, or the Palace of Butterflies at Henriss Garden. To make up for that lack, the town itself boasted numerous inns and two large hotels to rival the luxury of a planetary capital.

Ivan and his escort turned onto a riding trail that wound towards the back of town between   stands of spruce on one side, and rough pasture on the other. The trail led to a large riding ring and stable block that backed onto The Crown, a favored watering hole of the emperor's guests.

The stable master greeted them as they dismounted, and led their horses away. Ivan strode through the courtyard and a gate that led into a formal garden. Up stairs to an ornate verandah, empty of clientele in this late season.

A concierge stood waiting inside, where warmth and the scent of summer flowers enveloped Ivan. "Your usual rooms are ready for you and your guests, Magister Summis."

Wordlessly, Ivan strode through a grand hallway and down a side passage to a private suite of rooms. He was pleased to find his lunch guests already assembling, drinks in hand. "Please excuse my absence a while longer," he called out. "I will freshen up after my ride before joining you."

A door led to a private hall and dressing room. It took a matter of moments to strip off his outer clothing and change into indoor finery. He turned to find an attendant in hotel livery waiting for him. The attendant brushed and tied back Ivan's windswept hair with swift and expert movements. Time was of the essence. His guests wouldn't miss him for maybe twenty minutes, but he'd better emerge looking like he'd spent that time preening himself.

The attendant silently opened a hidden panel at the back of the room and led Ivan down a service staircase. A few turns and more stairs later, and they emerged in a bright lit parking garage. "Hotel surveillance has been taken care of, Magister. Your movements will not be observed."

His guide led him to a nondescript ground car, a gyro-stabilized two-wheeler, silver grey and slightly dusty. The windows of the rounded central cabin were tinted a deep blue, giving no hint of the interior.

Although the vehicle showed no signs of life, as Ivan approached the near door swung open. He stepped onto the running board and looked in. The unpromising shell belied the luxury inside. Deep brown calfskin couches faced each other across a low crystal-topped table. All was trimmed in silky smooth and exquisitely expensive true-ebony.

If the interior was unexpected, Ivan barely managed to hide his surprise at the craft's single occupant. The cryptic invitation, that had led to the charade of his morning ride and lunch party, had given little away. Code words hinted at the purpose of the meeting, nothing specific about the person behind it. He turned his hesitation into a polite nod of greeting and swung himself smoothly on board. "Honorina Philip. I didn't realize you were here in person. Cravel Braz is somewhat out of your way and ... parochial, compared to your usual surroundings." His mind raced as he sat. He'd expected to meet a go-between, but for Honorina to put herself out like this was serious business. The door snicked shut behind him with an ominous weight and finality.

The mountain of flesh opposite him regarded him through heavy-lidded eyes, half-hidden in a nest of walnut wrinkles. Waist-length white hair glowed in the buttery light of the cabin. Honorina's blank stare gave the impression of mental vacancy, but Ivan knew this was the sharpest and most dangerous person in civilized space.

"Cravel is a seat of royalty. It has a discreet charm of its own. Besides"—Honorina waved a languid hand—"I bring my comforts with me."

"As well as a renowned flair for both secrecy and theatrics. A curious combination."

"I'm sure we'd have been as comfortable upstairs, but here I can assure us both of the utmost privacy."

Ivan frowned. "Your presence on Magentis could hardly have gone unnoticed."

"It's true, I represented the Philip Drayson Coolidge Defense Conglomerate at the funeral, and paid my respects to the Emperor in Prandis. However this day I have business here in Cravel."

Business? There was nothing in Cravel Braz that could possibly interest a senior partner in one of the largest interplanetary arms dealers, except ... Ivan hazarded a guess. "Is the Emperor's stance on diplomacy causing anxiety to the Conglomerate?"

Honorina reclined, allowing the deep upholstery to cradle her bulk. "My partners are getting nervous at the Emperor's attitude towards the Maestro project. Of course I will make my humble petition to him, but I don't expect to sway him from his course."

Ivan schooled the sickening emptiness in his stomach. He had a feeling he knew which direction this conversation was heading. He waited with polite interest.

"My petition to the Emperor is of course nothing more than a pretext. I am here to sway *you*, Grand Duke."

The words sounded almost benevolent, but Ivan suddenly had the uncomfortable sensation of prey in the crosshairs. There were few people in the known worlds with the power to rival an emperor's. Honorina Philip was one such.

And she had no patience with weakness. At least they were on common ground there. Ivan reminded himself who *he* was, and allowed a shard of ice to enter his voice. "Maestro is important to me. That is all your partners need to know."

"Specifics, Ivan. With so many trillions at stake, I need to convince my partners that Family Skamensis is serious. I can guarantee there will be other interested buyers if the Emperor backs down."

Oh, really? We were already into the territory of threats? "We are paying you for exclusivity," Ivan growled.

"But only as long as the project proceeds."

A fair observation that deserved an answer. "The Emperor has a voice, but so do procurement lawyers, and certain reliable politicians of the Assembly." Ivan was already calculating how much he could afford to reveal of the reach of his network. "He will find he is not in a position to back down. And of course the Admiralty itself is a slow-moving bureaucracy. It can strike like a cobra in times of war, but grind like a glacier when it comes to implementing a direction that runs contrary to its own interests."

———•◦•———

The following morning, Chalwen called her squad leaders together in an empty office in the heart of the guard house. Boots clacked on stone floors outside, and metallic clangs and crashes echoed from the kitchens next door. It was early still, and the household was stretching and waking.

"New rules of engagement. The full bodyguard accompanies the Crown Prince everywhere, just like in Prandis."

"Even inside?" That was Skinner, the leader of Opal Squad.

"Just like in Prandis." Chalwen repeated. "And the advance team clears the way ahead of us."

The advance team leader chuckled. "Magister Bertolini won't be happy."

Chalwen smiled at the overblown honorific.

"What about the household guard?" Javarro, the Ruby Squad leader, asked.

"Screw 'em." Chalwen's tone was brittle as glass. "I'm done with pussyfooting around people's sensibilities and friggin' turf envy. Just ignore the household guard. We're not asking their permission to do our jobs."

Through the remaining days in Cravel Braz, the tension in the residence crackled like a desert thunderstorm. People here had tacitly colluded in an assassination attempt. Chalwen was sure of it. She seethed at the thought, and some of her mood must be showing in her expression. Servants bowed their heads and avoided her gaze. House guards and even high-and-mighty Tobias Bertolini snapped to attention when she approached, and responded to the smallest demand with crisp efficiency.

None of them dared interfere with her team.

Thank Space for small mercies.

As days passed, Chalwen couldn't rid herself of the feeling that she trod in enemy territory. And, the realization came gradually as if she was avoiding facing the implications, what about the other branches of the imperial household? What about the Mosaic Palace itself? What treachery might lie beneath the displays of deference, the smooth-running bureaucracy, the thousand-year-old ceremonial gloss?

It was unthinkable, yet here she was thinking it. The solid ground she walked on felt like it had suddenly shown itself to be eggshell thin. The tapestry of friendships and rivalries that she'd taken for granted took on new and ominous meaning.

At last, the time came for them to return to the capital city. At the foot of the ramp into the cruiser Chalwen shivered in the gale sweeping across the landing field. She gazed back to where the forbidding walls of the residence dominated the headland cliffs.

Behind her, the advance team inspected the craft while the pilot completed her pre-flight checks. Chalwen received the all clear, and signaled to the duty squad leader to bring Julian and his small staff out from the field office.

A chill down Chalwen's spine had nothing to do with the weather. Who could be trusted in Prandis? Who *there* might want to harm the Prince, or any others of the Family?

Chapter 3

Year 8068, winter

Commander Gregor Pavlenko entered an authorization code, unlocking the sealed instructions glowing on the desk surface in front of him. He was conscious of dozens of pairs of eyes fixed on him from across the battleship's combat operations room.

He took in the main points at a glance, then turned to face Lieutenant Una Spelze. Her anxiety showed, one foot tapping the floor. Gregor was nervous too, this test would take them into uncharted waters, but neither of them could afford to show it. He glanced at the foot. She swallowed and stilled the movement.

"Primary objectives: training camps, supply depots, and off-world comms infrastructure." He addressed Una, but his words carried above the surrounding hum of the warship to the far reaches of the room. "One hundred and twenty in total. Some hidden, locations known approximately. Some close to civilian populations. Ancillary goals include priorities for certain key objectives, and minimal collateral."

Someone at the back of the room gave a low whistle.

"Yep," said Gregor. "This is a tricky one, and this time Maestro is being given sole command. Be interesting to see what our new baby makes of it."

Still only a speck in the distance, the target planet circled the faintly glowing cinder of its dying star. Tactical schematics painted a simulated picture of teeming cities, factory complexes, and military installations onto the barren world.

Around the room, technicians started laying bets on what would be the ship's first move.

Gregor transferred the package of instructions into the battle system. His fists clenched in the endless pause while the First Officer, unseen on the ship's command deck hundreds of feet away, authenticated and loaded a complementary package. The two packages dovetailed into one seamless whole, a recipe for destruction on an unimaginable scale.

A large segment of the battle system's display abruptly dimmed. The displays were still live, still showing information, but they were now cut off from human control. Secondary stations around the room allowed the crew to deal with the warship's defense, but the offensive power of the battleship was no longer in their hands.

Gregor shivered and resisted the urge to scratch at the sensation of insects crawling through his harsh buzz cut. The thought of turning battle control fully over to automated systems gave him the creeps. He eyed the kill switch glowing on the desk in front of him.

Without warning, and with breathtaking speed, *Wrath of Empire* closed in on the planet.

"It's going for the fast kill. Comms and defense." Una's voice at his shoulder sounded rueful.

A faint click on the desk beside him. Without looking away from the display Gregor swept the five franc coin into his pocket. "Of course it is. Any time you know you've got the firepower on your side—which we do—fast is better. Hit hard, precise. Less room for messiness."

Wrath of Empire swept around the planet, lacing the surface with glowing tracks of sun fire. Now the attack was underway, all banter stopped. The operations room became a tightly-controlled hubbub of jargon as the crew watched over the vast machine in their care.

Gregor raised his eyebrows at the rate of fire as blast after blast hammered the target, but Maestro clearly knew the operational limits to within a percentage point. And, Gregor knew, the battle system was receiving real-time telemetry and could adjust on the fly if anything showed signs of wear. The human crew had a whole bank of monitoring stations collating data from thousands of feeds, and years of experience taught them how far they could push the weapon. But human judgment carried with it a margin of caution. Maestro had no such reservations and danced a fine line on the edge of disaster. Gregor wondered what the maintenance cost would be after this punishment.

It seemed that Una was having similar thoughts. "Wonder if Maestro knows all the weapon's quirks?"

Gregor grunted, and pointed to a handful of readings. None of them alarming in isolation, but taken together they spelled trouble.

"Hit the abort," Una hissed.

Gregor shook his head. "The techs need to see it work, and they need to see if it fails. Better now than in battle."

Moments later, a minor overload in one of the plasma feeds turned into a cascade of failures too fast for Maestro to correct. Gregor punched the abort before too much damage could be done. "Point made," he whispered.

With a deep sigh of relief, he watched the crew run through the system shut down and start a damage assessment. A live fire drill was nerve-wracking, even against an uninhabited planet and with all other ships withdrawn to a safe distance.

Beside him at her station, Una chewed her lip, scowling at the displays in front of her. "It was doing well until then, but Maestro took us right over that land battery there."

Gregor studied the decision logs, tracing the inner workings of the system's probability calculus. "Risk deemed acceptable. All known intelligence on that battery says our shields could take it for long enough to cross its line of fire."

"Taking out imaginary targets painted onto an empty ball of rock is one thing," Una muttered. "Wonder how it'll behave when the target starts firing back."

"But it took out the targets quicker and more cleanly than we could have done under manual control. See how it made best use of the cool down time between shots to move on to its next objective."

"What about that town?" Una pointed.

"Interesting call. Must have weighed speed or risk ahead of civilian casualties."

"Or completeness. Two objectives with only approximate locations. Chose a broad blast to cover the odds. Town happened to be in the way."

Gregor felt queasy. "The mission parameters were only to *minimize*, not *eliminate*, collateral. I doubt a human in charge would have played it that way, but *Maestro* did. That'll give the analysts at Admiralty something to chew on." And would they even care, Gregor wondered. Elimination was absolute, with anything above zero being unacceptable, but the moment you lifted the bar *above* zero who decided how to calculate an acceptable price?

The door to the operations room burst open and the Maestro project manager stormed through, followed by a posse of techs and analysts.

They all gave ground, subconsciously forming an impromptu honor guard for Jules Okwanda, the senior executive from the contract team, who stalked into the room like someone used to dominance and ownership. "What the hell did you abort for?"

Gregor eyed the man coldly. "Your product just fried our primary weapon. Right now we're not a battleship, we're an expensive cruise liner."

The project manager stared bug-eyed at the bank of screens behind Gregor. "Those are the tactical logs! My team will take those for analysis."

"The mission logs remain the property of the imperial navy. You'll get a redacted copy after we've cleansed them of restricted data." Gregor's words were addressed to the project manager, but the message was directed to Okwanda.

At first sight, Jules Okwanda wasn't someone to be taken seriously. Short and round, almost dwarfish in stature, he could easily be overlooked in a crowd if it weren't for his brilliant orange hair. Short-cropped, sharply-shaved patterns stood stark against midnight scalp. What he lacked in stature he made up for in attitude. And he had the corporate power to back up his innate belligerence.

The two men locked eyes. Gregor didn't flinch. It didn't matter that he was right. To Jules Okwanda, right and wrong didn't enter the equation. All that mattered was what you could get away with, and closer to civilization an executive of the Philip Drayson Coolidge company could get away with murder. But out here, beyond the reach of any comms relay, two weeks from the nearest contact with civilization and political and underworld connections, the officers of His Imperial Majesty's navy held the upper hand.

Gregor didn't flinch, but he'd been careful to stay on the right side of regulations and to keep his tone matter-of-fact. It didn't pay to antagonize people unnecessarily. After all, even the navy made port in civilization sometimes.

Okwanda gave a tight smile. "Of course. I trust there will be no undue delay. We have much to learn from this exercise and my team is on a tight schedule to make this system operational." He bobbed his head and left, followed by his retinue.

"After we've worked out how much to bill your company for the damage you caused," Una muttered under her breath, once the team of contractors was out of earshot.

She turned back to her console and checked off as stations around the room reported in. "Shut down and cool off will take another half an hour. Preliminary damage reports suggest we've got two days of maintenance ahead of us."

"Around the clock?"

Una grimaced and nodded.

"Look on the bright side, that will give the contractors time to finish installation in *Fire* and *Scepter*, ready for combined maneuvers."

"Oh, goody." Una gave Gregor a sidelong stare. "This system gives me the creeps, and don't tell me you haven't felt it too. Are you sure they haven't buried a generalized AI in there?"

An involuntary shiver wracked Gregor. The thought had occurred to him, more than once. More troubling was the question of whether any of them would even know. Imperial techs had audited the code, and he'd seen the classified reports, but who really knew how general intelligence arose in the first place? It wasn't buried in a line of code, he was sure of that, so would they recognize it when they saw it?

He squashed that nightmare thought and stuck to the official line. "Every part of Maestro has been picked apart. It's an impressive piece of work, but it's still a specialist tool. Good in its line of work. Totally oblivious to anything beyond that."

"Okay," Una whispered, "the question is, with a fleet of *Swords* to scare the crap out of anyone in the way, why do we need to shave a few seconds off a clean-up job that humans can do almost as well?"

"Admiralty's orders." Gregor shrugged. "We don't get to question the whys and wherefores. We just get to test these new systems, try to break them ... then put them into commission."

That wasn't the whole story, Gregor knew. With so much firepower under their fingertips, the power to wipe out whole populations, human hands might hesitate at the last second. That firepower had been put to the test from time to time in the nine-hundred-year history of the imperial *Swords*. And people's willingness to commit cold-blooded genocide had been tested too. The weak link in the chain.

When it came down to it, an automated system would never hesitate to follow orders.

———•—•———

The guards' mess hall in the basement of the main barracks rang with the clatter of cutlery and shouted conversations. Despite the crush of bodies, a wash of cool dry air dispelled the afternoon mugginess. Winter in the capital city brought humidity with little relief from the sub-tropical heat.

Chalwen loaded her mess tray at the serving counter, carbs and protein in quantity, all steeped in a ferociously hot sauce. Even though she usually dined at her desk or in the small canteen at the guard house next to the imperial residence, Chalwen was no stranger to the bustling mess hall. She enjoyed the change from the limited fare at the canteen, and the mess hall provided one of the best sources of gossip.

Since returning to the Mosaic Palace, Chalwen had tuned in to the Prandis rumor mill, sounding out attitudes and loyalties. The picture was troubling. Nobody would openly criticize the Emperor of course, and many people honestly supported him. That open support made her job harder, driving any words of dissent underground. But pry gently and persistently in the right places, and there were indeed hints of dissatisfaction. Surely Imperial Security was aware of this? Maybe they were. The undercurrent was just that, nothing more than hints of contrary opinions, nothing actionable let alone treasonous. And they were so prevalent it would be impossible to keep watch on everyone who held distaste for some policy or other.

And yet, Chalwen had an uneasy feeling there were depths of division she hadn't come close to seeing.

She nodded greetings to a few acquaintances, then sat near one end of a half-full table. She hoped to pick up unguarded gossip about the events at Cravel Braz, but being at the center of those events she'd found most people were reluctant to talk openly with her. She figured her best strategy this evening was to eavesdrop on nearby conversations.

Her pointed concentration on her food gave the impression she was lost in a world of her own. She tuned her attention to the chatter around her. A group of rookies at the table behind bitched about the aches and pains of a hard morning's training, and a long night on watch still to come. Somewhere to one side, a sergeant was looking forward to a spell of home leave. A more serious group speculated on what the Emperor would do about a local uprising on a distant farming world.

All disappointingly mundane. Details of Julian's mock assassination weren't common knowledge, but she knew rumors had preceded their return to the Palace in the capital. Even seeing who was talking about it, never mind what they were saying, might give some clues about the factions in the household.

A squat and burly lieutenant plonked himself down opposite her. Chalwen's scalp crawled at the sudden tension in the room. Further down the table, people hastily finished their mouthfuls and picked up trays, some still half full.

"Lieutenant Bresk." Chalwen tried to keep the irritation out of her voice. "Always a pleasure."

The head of Grand Duke Ivan's bodyguard smirked.

Shadows on the edge of Chalwen's vision confirmed her suspicion that he wouldn't be alone. The chair to her left scraped and creaked as Corporal Arnie Stokes, another of Ivan's bodyguards, settled himself. A whisper of movement to her right, and there was Sergeant Heather van Buren.

Small and wiry, a member of the regular palace guard rather than the elite bodyguard, she was nevertheless the one Chalwen needed to watch out for. She had a reputation for sly nastiness, and Chalwen had seen her in training.

"Lieutenant ap Gwynodd," Lieutenant Bresk murmured with a conspiratorial smile, "I hear you lost a member of the Royal Family out at Cravel."

Chalwen tried to ignore him and picked at her food. Her attempt to sound out the palace grapevine had just been thwarted. Of course Ivan's staff would all be well aware of what had happened, that was hardly a startling finding. They were all best buddies with Tobias Bertolini and his haughty crew. Now, the best she could hope for was to escape this trap without too much damage.

"Oh, that's not fair, Lieutenant." The wiry sergeant's tone was sympathetic. "I understand the Crown Prince actually survived the good lieutenant's lapse in care."

"Beg pardon, Sergeant van Buren, I do indeed stand corrected." Lieutenant Bresk's voice oozed gracious condescension. "Mind, the young prince is such a serious lad it's sometimes hard to tell if he's still breathing."

"An easy mistake to make, to be sure."

Chalwen clamped her jaw shut. They wanted to provoke her, and it was getting close to treasonous talk, but this crew played this game too well to let themselves be overheard.

"I say, Sergeant, be a good sport and pass the condiments for Lieutenant ap Gwynodd."

"At once, Lieutenant," the sergeant said briskly. "I was forgetting she must be used to a much superior level of service, being the guard to the *heir*, after all."

Beside her, the brawny corporal huffed.

"Hush there, Corporal," the sergeant said. "I know some find it hard to credit, but the Crown Prince is indeed the lawful heir rather than the Grand Duke."

Chalwen assessed her options. She could try to leave, but she was certain they had contingencies in mind to stop her. There was only one way this conversation was going to end. It was just a matter of who threw the first punch.

Corporal Stokes must have decided he needed to contribute to the baiting. "Can't see him making it long enough to fill his father's shoes."

At last! The opening Chalwen was looking for. "Close your mouth, Corporal," she said amiably, "you just halved the average intelligence in the room."

"Careful, ap Gwynodd," Bresk growled. "That's my corporal you're talking to." Oh, yes. He saw the weak link here. Corporal Stokes had a notoriously short fuze.

"I'm just saying, Lieutenant, that Corporal Stokes has the intelligence of an amoeba."

She took note of the movement beside her as the corporal started to stand, but outwardly she kept her attention on the lieutenant opposite.

"Easy, Stokes," he barked. "The lieutenant is going to apologize."

It was Chalwen's turn to smirk, directing her best look of disdain at the simmering volcano alongside her. "Please accept my deepest apologies, I mis-spoke and I fully retract my statement. The good corporal *doesn't* have the intelligence of an amoeba."

Chalwen was ready for the swing. She ducked beneath it and caught the corporal's elbow, helping it on its way as she stood. Carried by his own momentum, the corporal staggered and tangled his feet in his chair.

He managed to stay upright, just, and faced Chalwen again. His face was beet red and a vein throbbed in his temple. With a snarl he took a more measured lunge. Chalwen twisted and deflected most of the blow across her chest while landing her palm squarely across his nose.

Blood sprayed.

Chalwen stepped away from the table to give herself room, and to keep Sergeant van Buren in sight. Corporal Stokes shook his head and wiped the back of his hand across his mouth. The sergeant stood, appearing relaxed. A faint smile touched her lips.

The corporal closed again and suddenly Chalwen's arms were pinned by her sides. She cursed her stupidity. She'd been paying too much attention to the obvious opponents in front of her. She should have remembered these brutes always ran in packs.

She gasped and tried to double up as a meaty fist buried itself in her gut. Another blow dimmed her vision, but she managed to see that others in the mess had stepped in to even up the odds. She squinted at the position of the arms pinning her and took a guess, slamming her head back with all her strength. A splitting pain in the back of her head told her she'd connected. The arms loosened. She was free.

But not for long. Against her struggles, more arms held her down. Across from her, three burly guards were subduing the furious corporal.

All struggles stopped as Colonel bin Merrin's voice cut through the bedlam. "Someone here has some explaining to do!"

———————

Eyes front, back straight, Chalwen stood in front of the colonel's desk. The closed door blocked speculative chatter and curious stares from the outer office. Lieutenant Bresk and his crew, together with numerous witnesses, had been and gone, Bresk giving Chalwen a surly glare as he left.

"Another brawl, Lieutenant?" The colonel sounded resigned rather than angry. "Any explanation this time?"

"None, Sir." Chalwen knew better than to try to lay blame. It was an unwritten rule. You didn't rat out your colleagues, no matter how much you loathed them. You just planned your revenge at a later date.

"Bresk and his crew admit that Stokes threw the first punch, but they insist that you provoked him."

And Chalwen was sure none of the dozens of witnesses would be saying anything different. "Sir, I cannot argue with that description of events." They may be thugs, but they also honored the rules. At least they admitted to the first blow, and that was the best division of blame that Chalwen could hope for.

"Another reprimand on your file. Watch your step." The colonel was going through the motions. He knew the rules too, written and unwritten, and had expected nothing different.

He frowned. "I assume Bresk and company must be watching their weight these days."

"Sir?"

"Why else would they go to the mess and sit down without any food?" Chalwen felt her mood lighten. The colonel had to follow protocol but he'd just told her that he knew exactly what had happened this evening.

"I guess they just wanted the company, Sir."

The colonel nodded. "Work on your situational awareness, Lieutenant. I don't expect to hear of you being taken from behind again. Dismissed."

As she left the colonel's office and shut the door on her own tiny cubbyhole in the guard house, Chalwen stopped and smacked her forehead with her palm.

Stupid!

Stupid, stupid, stupid! How had she missed that detail? The colonel had spotted it, yet even after he'd pointed it out, it took her this long to see the significance. No food. That hadn't been a chance encounter. They had entered the mess hall and walked *past* the serving line, already knowing she would be there and knowing what they intended to do.

Were they trying to intimidate her, or provoke her to get her busted from guard duty? Was this a result of her guarded inquiries?

And who was 'they'?

One thing Chalwen was sure of. If someone was so determined to see her gone, someone saw her as a threat.

That, she could live with.

Chapter 4

Gregor glanced at Una Spelze. "Well," he said.

"Well, indeed." She sat back and folded her arms with a thoughtful look on her face. "The creepiness factor just ramped up tenfold, but I confess to being impressed."

"Yeah ... to both. Maestro kept the plasma feeds inside working parameters this time. Did the contract techs program that in, or did Maestro learn?" Gregor's scalp crawled. Machine learning was nothing new, but it was the first step along a dangerous and forbidden path.

"Huh. You think that's weird? What's really bugging me is"—Una leafed through the pack of mission commands they'd just executed—"I don't see *anything* in here that talks about how the objectives were going to be divided up between the ships."

"And we loaded the *entire* mission parameters into Maestro. Presumably the other units fed the same orders into their systems."

Una checked the orders against the mission log. "This is it. *Fire*, *Scepter* and us carried this out between us. Perfectly co-ordinated, no conflicts, no overlap. But how? And now I think about it, I don't recall anything in the installation specs about hooking Maestro into comms. It has secondary drive, primary offense, and enough sensors and telemetry to sink a troop carrier, but no comms."

"Could it have a separate comms circuit, maybe?"

"I'll dig into it. If the engineers installed something like that without us knowing about it, I'll be well pissed."

Gregor stood and stretched. "You okay to wrap things up here?"

" 'Course. You don't have to ask. You've got to face all the brass and eggheads for the debriefing. Rather you than me."

With an exaggerated sigh, Gregor darkened his console and left the combat operations room. Double blast doors, sealed during battle stations, opened as he approached. Military police on either side saluted.

Corridors, broad and almost empty of human traffic compared to passageways on most warships, stretched into the distance, broken at intervals by the sills of open blast doors. The most noticeable features, and something Gregor still found hard to get used to even after six years serving on *Swords*, were the straight and clean lines. The ubiquitous comms and control panels, emergency lockers and damage control stations, were set flush with the partitions, and there was a glaring absence of protruding machinery. The maze of pipes and cable runs that made up the guts of a warship had been banished out of sight, behind access hatches and in dedicated service corridors criss-crossing the ship. After his years of experience on board smaller warships, the lavish use of space felt obscene.

With a ground-eating stride, Gregor traversed corridors and companionways until he reached his cabin. There, he showered quickly and exchanged working overalls for his service uniform.

After more corridors and levels, he reached the battleship's main command complex. Heavily-guarded blast doors opened out into a labyrinth within the labyrinth. Here, the ever-present machine hum seemed quieter, the air warmer and suffused with a whiff of burnt plastic. Guards stood at every corner. To one side, doors opened into the main command deck. A cacophony of sound—conversations, commands and responses—enveloped Gregor as he hurried past. More doors led into the warren of operations rooms, briefing and conference rooms, as well as bridge crew ready rooms that surrounded the command deck.

He stopped at the threshold to a small briefing room and saluted. Captain Borodina waved him in.

Alongside the captain, the only other occupant was Jules Okwanda. The captains of *Fire of Revenge* and *Scepter of Truth* looked on from the briefing room wall screens, along with Gregor's weapons counterparts from the other two *Swords*.

At Gregor's puzzled look, Captain Borodina said, "Your official reports will be collected in due course. This is an informal debriefing. First impressions from this morning's exercise." She gestured around her. "This is it for this meeting, Commander."

Gregor nodded and closed the door behind him. Faint clicks and a brief whine told him the room had been sealed against intrusion. For an already-secure briefing room in the heart of a secure command complex, this seemed to be taking secrecy to a paranoid level.

"I've assured the captains here that we can all speak openly," Jules said.

Gregor wondered at the arrogance of an assurance like that. Who was really in charge here?

"Today we had our first test of combined operations," Jules continued. "As the senior officers closest to the action, I'm seeking your honest and unfiltered opinions. None of the official verbiage that the written briefings will contain."

After an awkward silence, Gregor offered his earlier thought down in the operations room. "What we saw today was ... impressive."

The weapons officer from *Scepter of Truth* sneered. "It handled a tightly-specified mission more efficiently than we could accomplish through the normal command structure. But in a highly controlled setting and within a limited sphere of operations. How will it behave in full battle conditions?"

Jules seemed unfazed at her open skepticism. "We must always keep in mind the purpose of Maestro. The niche it's designed to occupy."

"Whatever." She gave Gregor a wry smile. "At least it was programmed with bigger safety margins this time. After what happened to your main weapon in the early tests ... let's just say, our kit is held together by prayers and plastic wrap compared to *Wrath's*."

"Maestro will never become a general purpose tactical command system." An impatient edge crept into Jules's voice. "It's a specialist. It carries out and optimizes set piece engagements with predetermined objectives." He paused to catch his breath. "Yes, it has a large repertoire of tactical responses to handle dynamic and unpredictable conditions, but the clear advantage it has over human command is its ability to keep those overall objectives firmly in its sights."

Under some circumstances, that focus could be a virtue. To Gregor it also sounded cold and ruthless. He suppressed a shiver, and decided to probe at the question that had disconcerted him and Una this morning. "It's one matter to co-ordinate movements between three ships. Does that scale up to a whole fleet?"

Jules smirked. It seemed Gregor had inadvertently steered the conversation back onto preferred territory. Jules held a secret that he was dying to share.

Gregor pushed harder. "I mean, won't the comms load increase exponentially as you add ships to the network?"

Jules glanced at Captain Borodina, who nodded. She said, "What you're about to hear is classified, of course, but I'm sure secrecy won't last long once the system has seen battle."

"But the longer we allow our competitors to chase down blind alleys, the better." Jules seemed uncharacteristically cheerful after the morning's successful trial. "To answer your question, Commander, comms will not be an issue."

"You've found a way to scale up the network?"

"No. I mean there is no comms load to increase, because there is no communication between units."

Gregor stared, inwardly re-evaluating what he'd witnessed today.

"Ship to ship communications would be a weak point," Jules continued. "Easy to attack. The moment an enemy sees a fleet maneuvering in concert, the first thing they do is throw up interference. Then where would we be?"

A fair point, Gregor thought. He'd wondered about that himself, but he was so convinced there was sophisticated ship-to-ship co-ordination happening he'd assumed the issue of interference had been addressed.

"No. Each unit is acting independently. It has its tactical objectives, but decisions are being made dynamically in real time, and Maestro constantly monitors conditions and adjusts accordingly."

Gregor thought back to the test attack this morning. The three *Swords* had seemed to act as a single unit, weaving around the planet in a ballet of destruction. It looked like they'd been carefully orchestrated. "So the ships act as a team, but with no explicit central control."

"It does help if all the units have the same programming and the same objectives. Maestro is programmed to assess the movements of other units, regardless of whether or not they're other Maestro vessels, and judge whether or not they are acting in concert. If it assigns a high probability, then it will optimize its attack patterns for greatest efficiency assuming the other units are also doing the same and reaching the same conclusions."

"Clever. And if they aren't?"

"As long as another unit is acting to further our ship's objectives, it will let them get on with it and choose the next objective to work on."

"And if another unit isn't?"

"Well, that depends. If it simply isn't contributing, then Maestro will ignore it. But if it obstructs, or even acts in a hostile manner, let's just say I would personally choose to be elsewhere."

The ground car slowed in the early evening crush of people on the streets of Prandis Braz, and turned into an unmarked portico set back from the bustling sidewalk. The understated architecture was in the classical tradition, all polished steel and armored polymer, shielding visitors from the world outside.

Grand Duke Ivan Skamensis stepped from the car and strode up the steps with barely a glance at the escort vehicles of his personal guard. They weren't needed here. Inside the ancient halls and chambers of the Acacia Club he was as safe as in his own quarters in the Mosaic Palace two miles away.

They wouldn't be admitted to these halls, anyway. Not even for him. Only the highest ranking members of the empire's elite could pass through these doors, despite the absence of any visible security. Anyone fit to be invited as one of the club's guests would have already been implanted with an imperial passkey. Unbreakable security, identity assured without question. The club knew *exactly* who entered its premises, and had a range of measures to deter gatecrashers.

It was rumored they even had their own morgue and crematorium in the basement. Ivan had no reason to doubt the rumors.

Cool, fresh air greeted Ivan as he stepped into the grand lobby, his feet soundless on centuries-old Monsk carpet. Pillared halls led away ahead, left and right. Figures moved in the distance. Voices chattered behind. More members arriving.

"Ivan." A stately woman glided past giving a polite nod.

And inside these walls, he was simply 'Ivan'. Titles and honorifics were meaningless here.

A liveried attendant approached with a tray bearing a tumbler of chilled Almay di Barras Semillon. Ivan took the glass with a nod. Someone had anticipated his needs.

"Guests are asking after you in the Palm Room, Sire."

Ivan sipped his wine, eyes closed. He had a few minutes to spare, and it never hurt to keep his contacts fresh. Who knew what snippets of information he might pick up? He acknowledged the message and turned down the nearest hall.

As he ventured into the heart of the club, the hall grew busier. Ivan weaved between groups of well-heeled patrons, exchanging pleasantries along the way.

The double doors to the Palm Room lay open at the end of the hall, a popular meeting place adjoining the club's largest and most formal dining room. Typical for the time of evening, the chatter of dozens of voices drifted into the hallway as he crossed the threshold.

"And here's the man himself!"

It seemed Ivan had entered in the middle of a conversation at a remarkably convenient point. The timing felt staged.

"If anyone can explain the Emperor's fit of madness, that would be Ivan."

He paused by a glass-topped bar table and picked a piece of candied trout from a platter. "And what particular madness might you be talking about, Miranda?"

The thin lipped merchant looked taken aback. "Surely it's obvious? I understand he's pressing ahead with bringing his register of financial interests to the Assembly."

Before answering, Ivan scanned the room. Small knots of people drifted closer. Nobles, company owners, an ambassador. He spotted an Assembly Member near the back but taking a keen interest in the conversation. So that's what lay behind the message left with the doorman.

Some interested parties were desperate to hear his stand on Paul's legislation.

"Well, he has his own values and standards to abide by. With that view in mind, I see no evidence of madness."

"He's setting himself up to fail." Miranda gave a flicker of a glance towards the Assembly Member. "Wouldn't you say that pursuing a futile goal is evidence enough?"

"Progress will always suffer setbacks. Nothing worth doing happens without a struggle."

Miranda huffed. "Don't you oppose the transparency bill?"

"Your source should practice more nuance. I have no objections to transparency in itself." Ivan gazed around the circle of faces. "I've always said that legitimately-acquired wealth and position is a sign of competence, and fitness to rule. If someone uses their wealth to steer the policies of the empire, then why hide it?"

A mischievous impulse took hold of Ivan. He glanced sidelong at the intense young Assembly Member. "For example, if you, Miranda, were to invest in the successful campaign of, say, Alistair, there's nothing wrong with that in my view."

Miranda reddened, while Alistair spluttered, "This is all *hypothetical* of course!"

"Of course," Ivan said blandly after just the right length of a pause. "And if the source of your backing were to be public knowledge, then everyone would know exactly what to expect. A vote for tariffs on the import of Benga wheat and other staples from dom Calvino space would now be predictable behavior, simply a wise investment paying off, instead of a source of scandalous speculation."

Ivan studied the play of light in the depths of his glass while he let that thought sink in.

"So, I don't object to transparency *per se*. Let's say, I have my misgivings. Transparency is often the first step towards control and restriction. Once funding can be traced, what's to stop people disapproving of wealth pulling the strings? I can foresee caps on campaign donations, then moves to eliminate patronage altogether from the Assembly elections."

With his free hand, Ivan flicked an imaginary piece of lint from the Skamensis Family crest on the breast of his tunic. "Of course, such

questions are of no interest to me. I have no elections to face or campaigns to fund. However—"

The sudden sharpness in his tone stilled the remaining voices
in this part of the room. Ivan was aware of heightened scrutiny even
among more distant groups that feigned disinterest. He let the silence
deepen a few heartbeats.

"There are factors dearer to my heart that work in its favor. I mentioned *legitimately*-acquired wealth. You all know my opinions on the
proceeds of crime and vice. Moves towards transparency would greatly
limit the influence of the criminal elements that stain our empire."

Through the subservient murmurs of assent, Ivan took note of a few
sour faces and hastily-concealed reluctance. He filed the names away
for future reference.

"So"—Ivan gazed up at the ceiling—"I find myself uncharacteristically ambivalent. On this matter, I am not taking a position. Let the
Assembly vote with its conscience."

"And let them lay bare their morality for the world to see." A petite
woman slid to Ivan's side and took his arm in a grip that belied her
seventy-nine years. "Are you dining tonight? You are most welcome to
join my party."

"Sadly not, Josie. I'm paying a courtesy visit, all too brief I'm afraid.
Now, if you'll excuse me, I have other matters to attend to this evening."

The veteran Assembly Member relinquished her grip with good
grace. "Another time, then."

Ivan chose a roundabout path from the Palm Room to his private
suite. He needed a few minutes' solitude to process what had only just
occurred to him. He'd not given much thought to Paul's latest piece
of legislation. As he'd told the assembled club members, he had mixed
feelings about it, and he had more important things to attend to. But
that lack of thought now bothered him. What was his brother up to?
The bill had precisely zero chance of being passed. The Assembly and
its committees were just going through the motions, and Paul would be
well aware of that.

It was nothing more than a smokescreen, Ivan now realized. It held
the attention of the media, the legislators, and the commerce barons
who felt threatened. So what was the real work going on behind that
screen? The more Ivan thought about it, the more troubled he grew.

Whatever the outcome in the Assembly, with his proposals Paul risked antagonizing many powerful people, and he held too fragile a grip on the empire to be making more enemies. But the Emperor knew that too ...

Ivan missed a step and stumbled on the richly-patterned carpet. He brusquely waved away the nearest guests who'd noticed his awkwardness. Inwardly he cursed himself for being blinded for so long. Given its political cost, the smokescreen had to be hiding something of paramount importance to Paul, and Ivan hadn't a clue where to start looking.

He regained his composure. Right now he had an important guest to meet, though now he wondered if even this interview was nothing more than another smokescreen. No. Surely not. This next matter was as important to Ivan as it was to Paul.

Ivan pushed open the door to his suite.

The single occupant rose and turned to meet him.

It was true, Ivan mused. People could easily mistake them for siblings with their similar lanky frames and thin faces. Walnut skin and black hair typical of native Prandiskis were hardly remarkable, but hazel eyes narrowed appraisingly were almost a mirror of Ivan's own, an unusual feature on this continent. The slightly older man facing him lacked Ivan's full lips, and his hair was already thinning, but yes, they could be related.

"Ivan."

"Abraham." The greetings were cautious.

As the host, Ivan offered the usual courtesies of refreshments, comfortable seats, and polite small talk, but he could tell that his guest was as impatient as he was with meaningless formalities. Ivan came swiftly to the point. "I'm sure the Emperor has already made some overtures regarding a potential offer."

"And I'm equally sure you know I can't discuss any such dealings."

"Of course not." Ivan's tone was conciliatory. "I didn't invite you here to pry into any dealings with my brother. However, I'm sure you're aware of the difficulty we've been having settling on a candidate to put to the Assembly."

Abraham Crode narrowed his eyes and gave a humorless smile. "So, straight to the heart of the matter. The Emperor can court whomever he wants, but any discussions are pointless without also gaining the support of the Grand Duke."

"And vice versa." Ivan nodded gravely.

Abraham huffed. "My record and qualifications are public knowledge. If those don't stand scrutiny, I'm not in the business of begging
for your support."

Ivan should have felt insulted, but the words were matter-of-fact.
And surprising. All the other hopefuls had fallen over themselves to
make watertight cases for their appointment. "You have no ambition
towards the highest judicial office in the empire?"

"I have no ambition to sell myself as anything other than that which
I am."

"And yet you need to sell yourself to gain my support."

Abraham took a sip of his drink and set the tumbler back on the
side table with precise movements. "I hate to find myself correcting
someone of such high nobility, but you're wrong. I have no such need.
If I'm the right person then make the appointment. If I'm not, then I
wouldn't wish to accept the position."

The silence lengthened. Abraham held Ivan's gaze with no sign of
discomfort. Before the pause could become awkward, Ivan said, "I wish
more people could speak with such refreshing honesty." Except that
this conversation was going nowhere. It seemed that directness was the
order of the day. "I've studied your judgments. You are, if I may charac-
terize you with such crude brevity, highly conservative."

Abraham inclined his head. "I think that would be a fair, if over-sim-
plified, summary. But I think innate conservatism is a prerequisite for my
profession."

"How so?"

"The law today is founded on judgments past. Thousands of years of
case history. That ship does not change course easily."

"So what happens when the dictates of history conflict with today's
needs, or, say, the needs of a pressing crisis facing the empire?"

"You mean would I be tempted to bend the law in favor of current
expediency? That's a dangerous precedent. Besides, who decides which
interests are the overriding ones?" Abraham gave Ivan a sharp look.

"That, I'm sure, would be up to you."

"You do realize, the most I can offer is to apply the law to the best of
my abilities, without favor." Abraham emphasized the last words.

Ivan snorted. "The law is a tangled mess of logic, often contradictory, and tripping up over itself with unintended consequences as people find new ways to honor the letter while tossing the spirit to the desert wind."

The words and contemptuous tone were meant to provoke a response. Ivan studied Abraham carefully, but he seemed unfazed by this dismissive assessment of his craft.

In fact he laughed. "Of course it is, Ivan. If not, how would lawyers and judges earn a living?" Abraham must have decided that the interview was at an end, because he abruptly stood. "Now, if you'll excuse me, I understand they're serving a particularly fine guinea fowl in The Library this evening."

Alone in his suite, Ivan called for food to be brought and settled at his desk with a scroll laid out in front of him.

Abraham couldn't be bought. His own words and manner this evening simply confirmed what Ivan had learned, and not just from passive observation. Various temptations had crossed the judge's path in recent weeks, to sway judgments away from their proper course. All had failed. But, as Abraham had acknowledged, the law often left a lot of interpretation to the judge. Maybe he couldn't be bought, but he certainly could be influenced.

That would have to be good enough.

Ivan sighed. It may not be quite the outcome he would have preferred, but an honest judge was better than the stalemate he and the Emperor found themselves at.

The impasse over the judicial appointment neatly highlighted the precarious balance in the empire. People imagined the Emperor to be all-powerful, but in reality he only held the throne while he enjoyed enough backing from the legion of economic, political, and military interests that formed the real foundation of the imperium.

Many of those interests had thrived under Empress Florence and resented the more liberal policies under Paul. Many would gladly back Ivan, but he knew it wasn't that simple. His brother attracted strong support of his own, including a grassroots popularity that couldn't be dismissed. The empire was divided, a state of affairs that dismayed Ivan deeply.

His mind wandered back to the question of what Paul was hiding. Something big. Something Ivan needed to ferret out.

He picked up a stylus and made a series of coded annotations on the scroll in neat, flowing script.

It was three months to the Crown Prince's tenth anniversary. Ivan could hardly be away from the capital for such a signifiant milestone, but the moment the festivities were done he was due a break. A working break, admittedly, paying an official visit to the worlds of his ducal fiefdom. A noble's duty was never done, and Ivan took duty seriously, but this was as close to leisure as he allowed himself.

He'd have to leave the ferreting to Bernie Fischer, his Private Secretary. Another covert task for Bernie's extensive network of spies. Bernie could handle one more assignment. In fact, he relished the chance to sniff trails of deceit and to weave his own webs to befuddle the competition.

Ivan's notes added to a dense patchwork of lists and charts and calendars spread across the scroll, a summary of his working life, both official, lawful, and otherwise. He checked the progress of each line of work, confirming that nothing was coming to a head that would keep him on Magentis. Bernie was competent, and far more than just a Private Secretary. In fact, he was the architect and captain of many of the ventures on Ivan's scroll, as well as those not committed to any form of written or electronic record. They were in good hands.

Satisfied, Ivan turned at last to his supper.

Chapter 5

"You wanted to see me, Captain?" Gregor Pavlenko burned with curiosity at the unexpected summons. The arrival in-system of the destroyer *Sparrowhawk* had the whole ship buzzing with anticipation. News from the outside world. Messages from families. And, Gregor assumed, orders from the Admiralty.

Within an hour of *Sparrowhawk's* arrival, he was standing at attention in the doorway to the captain's day cabin, with its broad windows overlooking the battleship's main command deck. The timing couldn't be a coincidence.

"At ease, Commander. Close the door." Captain Ivanka Borodina's brown eyes smoldered. Her mouth, though rarely graced with a smile, pressed in an unusually tight line.

As soon as Gregor complied, the captain shuttered the windows and tapped a series of commands on her desktop. Faint clicks behind him told Gregor the doors into the day cabin had been secured, and presumably electronic countermeasures had also been engaged.

"You have news from Magentis."

"Along with more mundane communications, *Sparrowhawk* carried a highly encrypted document. The Emperor has issued a directive that work on Maestro is to cease."

"Does that mean we're done here?" Gregor found it hard to believe, after the staggering investment the navy must have already poured into the project.

"The hell it does," the captain snarled.

Gregor's mind reeled. He locked eyes with the captain and forced himself to think. Pieces clicked into place. He barked a short laugh. "Do we have an explicit order to stand down?"

"Not as such. I have an Information Briefing from Admiralty advising me that the Emperor has directed *them* to halt work on Maestro." A faint, humorless smile failed to soften Captain Borodina's angular features.

Gregor swallowed. "So, we ourselves have not been issued any orders." Under normal circumstances, the Emperor's smallest wish would be indistinguishable from a direct order. Someone at Admiralty was stalling, but how could they expect to get away with such obstruction? They must have high level backing to dare such a thing.

"From what little detail the Briefing contains, I understand that lawyers and policy analysts at Admiralty are working out how best to implement the Emperor's directive. As far as we're concerned, we have an army of weapons engineers on contract. As long as we're paying them, I expect them to work."

"Any idea how the Admiralty can stall the Emperor's directive like this?"

"The Briefing was naturally light on detail."

"They can't openly admit they're stalling."

"Quite." The captain poured herself a glass of tea from a pot on her desk. "They are giving the earnest appearance of working diligently through a series of obstacles."

"Of their own invention."

"Not entirely. Or at least, not all recent. I think someone may have anticipated interference somewhere along the way. Right now it's in murky legal territory. Until the contractor acknowledges that the contract has been legally terminated, they are obliged to continue working."

"Meanwhile," Gregor mused, "we're in deep space, three weeks away from the nearest inhabited world, and hardly less than that from the nearest comms relay. Any further updates from Magentis will take a month or more to arrive."

"And that is dependent on a ship ferrying messages out to us from within range of the nearest comms point."

It seemed that the captain was waiting for Gregor to say something more. He decided to address the obvious question. "If the Admiralty hasn't directly ordered us to return, why would they bother to advise us of the directive?"

"On the surface, by doing so they can claim they are not simply ignoring the Emperor."

"They've taken the first, albeit ineffective, step." Gregor nodded. "And the subtext is—"

"Accelerate the testing and stay out of comms reach until we're done. The Emperor can't cancel a completed project."

"You could have simply given me a new deadline without mentioning the new information. There's more to be said, isn't there."

"Two things." Captain Borodina smiled again, and this time there was genuine humor in her eyes. "I need you to be alert to any rumors circulating aboard ship about the project. Imperial Security have their official office on board, plus whatever undercover spies they've managed to plant. They will have received parallel information about the Emperor's wishes and when they realize work is proceeding they'll do their best to report back."

"Of course they are working under the same communications constraints that we are."

"Exactly, which brings me to my second point. They can't communicate to or from us if nobody outside this task force knows where to find us."

"You're moving us to another target planet. What will stop *Sparrowhawk* from reporting our new location?"

"They will ... eventually. They're coming with us when we relocate, and they will then return to Skamensis space and report in."

"Which buys us—what?—a few more weeks?"

"Hopefully enough to complete testing to the point of signing off acceptance."

"I'll get the project team to compress the schedule and also work out how much substance can be deferred to remediation and warranty post sign-off."

The captain nodded approval. "You get the idea. And I'll need a memo from you advising me why a new test site is needed. Some deficiency in the location we're using."

It was Gregor's turn to smile, although that was for show. Inside, he was churning with conflicting emotions about this turn of events. "I can do better than that. What if we need not just one, but a series of sites to test the system under variety of physical conditions?"

Captain Borodina stared blankly at Gregor for so long he wondered if he'd made an error of judgment, or—worse—if she suspected something. Then she threw her head back and laughed. "I knew I promoted you for a reason! Make it happen, Commander."

———————

Nobody knew all the labyrinth of hidden passages and concealed entrances that riddled the imperial quarters at the heart of the Mosaic Palace. Even Chalwen understood there were limits to her knowledge, but few people knew these passages better. In the early years of The Hidden Light, she and Henri, Paul and his elder brother Lorenzo, had mapped out a multitude of ways to leave and enter and meet unseen.

Senior members of the bodyguard, of course, knew many of the residence's secrets buried in the thickness of the walls. They had to, to keep their charges safe. So evading your own bodyguard took skill and cunning, qualities Emperor Paul possessed in good measure along with years of practice. Seemed he felt the need to put that practice to the test.

By the light of a glowtube strapped to her forehead, Chalwen climbed the last few rungs of a ladder and felt for the hidden switch at the edge of the hatch above her head. The switch simply announced her presence. The hatch could only be opened from the other side. After a few anxious seconds waiting, a barely audible click sounded and the hatch swung up.

The room above lit up as Chalwen climbed through the opening, momentarily dazzling her. Her eyes adjusted, and she turned to face Paul who perched on a camp stool near one wall of the tiny chamber.

For a moment, Chalwen stood, disoriented, unsure who she was greeting: her emperor, or her long-standing comrade in arms.

Paul broke the awkward silence. "Bring back memories?" His face creased in a broad grin as he stood and swept Chalwen into a hug like friends greeting for the first time in years.

Memories, yes, too many that she'd prefer to stay buried. "If we'd ever been caught, you might have been lucky enough to face a quick death at the end of a beam rifle. The rest of us would have burned for treason." She shuddered. "I thought the days for tricks like this were long gone. If you want to talk to me, you only have to summon me to your office."

"And have to explain to three dozen guards, secretaries, and minor functionaries what would warrant a personal and private audience with a lieutenant in the imperial bodyguard?" Paul snorted.

"Fair comment, and this isn't Light business either?"

"No." Paul sat again and gestured Chalwen to another folding camp chair beside him. "This is personal."

Chalwen sat and leaned back against bare stone. Machinery hummed on the far side of the wall.

Paul seemed lost in thought, then he said, "Julian is growing up."

"Faster than any nine-year-old should." The words slipped out before she could think them through.

Paul smiled sadly at the admonition in Chalwen's voice. "True enough. His tutors push him as hard as he can cope. He needs to mature ahead of his years."

"He's a quick study. I can vouch for that."

"You're concerned for his wellbeing, I understand that, and I'm not just talking about his physical safety."

Chalwen shrugged. "Do you get to talk to him about his training? Does he understand the pressure he's under?"

"Even the Emperor sometimes has the chance to be a father. Just not often enough." His voice hardened. "He is the heir to the throne, and that call of duty trumps any wish for a normal childhood. But it's not Julian I'm concerned about today."

He locked eyes with Chalwen. Her stomach lurched.

"I read enough reports on what happens around me and my staff. And I talk to my officers in the palace and the guard house."

Here it comes, thought Chalwen. "Including the colonel? My end-of-term report must make dismal reading."

"Including the colonel." Paul nodded. "I know how deeply you doubt yourself."

So that's what this was about. All the drills the colonel imposed on her team, all the mock assassinations and abductions she failed to prevent. And her complaints about impossible assignments had finally found their way back to the Emperor.

No, Paul surely wouldn't trouble himself with petty details. She knew him better than that. This went deeper. She swallowed, building up the courage to bring deep-seated fears out into the open.

"Sometimes ..." Chalwen struggled to find the words. "Sometimes I wonder why I'm here. "

Paul cocked an eyebrow.

"You got me fast-tracked into the bodyguard. You appointed me when there were others far better suited ..."

Paul held up his hand. "Look at us. Both still in our thirties. Still young, yet with so much water under the bridge. In my view, simply surviving the last fifteen years warrants an A-plus on your report."

Chalwen studied him, searching for signs of sarcasm.

"You need more faith in yourself. Think of what we've done in that time."

"The two of us, Lorenzo, and Henri." Chalwen chuckled, feeling some of the tension drain away. "Quite a mixed bag."

How did we ever get together, she wondered? Two sons of an empress, and two friends low in the palace hierarchy. The start of it all was lost to her in the dizzying kaleidoscope of events since.

"Quite a team, you mean. Lorenzo was always the backbone, the fixer and quartermaster."

"And Henri could weasel us past any closed doors, and you saved our lives countless times with quick reflexes and a quick draw with a beam pistol." Chalwen sobered. "And I kinda tagged along for the ride."

"Tagged along?" Paul looked aghast. "You were in the driving seat. You could always sense trouble brewing. Things off key."

"The canary in the coal mine," she whispered.

"Remember Cendithor?"

Chalwen closed her eyes. A strategic outpost out in the Cutler Drift, far from Magentis and close to the Firenzi border. Too fiercely independent for Empress Florence's liking.

"We knew Florence was up to something," Paul continued.

A hot blush crept up her cheeks. "Come on. I just saw guards posted where a protective detail had no business being, and they carried wide-angle stunners. Weapons for crowd control, not for taking down a threat in a crowd. They were expecting a riot."

"Exactly. Florence's chance to declare the planetary assembly unfit to govern and install her own puppets. But thanks to you, when her staged protest stormed the assembly room, they found it empty. The members met at the winter palace instead to approve a bilateral pact with their nearest Firenzi neighbors."

Chalwen grimaced. "Florence was pissed, but there was nothing she could do openly to nix a legally-constituted planetary government's vote."

"And another buffer in place between us and the Firenzi. Another safeguard against an all-out assault by either party."

Okay, but ... "Paul, why are you bringing this up? You didn't ask me here to chew over old war stories."

"You think that maybe you don't belong at the head of a bodyguard. Maybe you didn't earn it. Maybe I gave you your position, insisted on it, in fact, over quite vocal objections, because of our past together?"

Chalwen nodded.

"You're right. Of course I did. You are here because of our past, but not from favoritism." Paul leaned in close, his eyes blazing with determination. "Julian is surrounded by guards, hand-picked and well-trained. Your squads are filled with people who are better shots than you, faster in combat, stronger, sharper-eyed, any quality you care to mention ..."

"Way to make a girl feel good about herself!"

"They're good at all that so *you* don't need to be. You bring something to the squad far more valuable. That sixth sense, that will pick up on threats before they have a chance to take form."

Paul clapped a hand on Chalwen's shoulder, and heaved himself to his feet.

"You're here because I can think of no person I'd rather have protecting my eldest son."

As one of the senior officers on board *Wrath of Empire*, Gregor was entitled to a cabin all to himself. He'd served on everything from frigates to cruisers and battleships. One feature they'd all shared: lack of elbow room. Even an officer's cabin was cramped, with little room for anything but a bed, closet, desk, maybe a wash basin on the larger ships. If you drew the short straw, you sacrificed some of your precious headroom to intruding pipes, cable runs, or vent trunks.

Not so on the *Swords*. These craft dwarfed the next largest class of battleship. The ship's frame was built to house the two-thousand-foot-long plasma cannon plus all the attendant machinery and power plants, together with the scaled-up drive, shielding, and secondary armament. Crew accommodation, fitting between and around machinery spaces, scaled up to match.

Gregor closed the door behind him to what would be a comfortable suite on a passenger liner. He crossed to his desk and checked for electronic intrusions before settling down with his elbows on the desk and his face buried in his hands. If anyone should be spying, his posture would hopefully be seen as someone at the end of another exhausting day. In truth, Gregor was afraid for anyone to see the roiling emotions flickering through his eyes once he let his guard down.

He'd just witnessed evidence of treason. Some office, right at the top of the navy hierarchy, had dared to sideline a clear instruction from the Emperor. His own captain appeared perfectly comfortable with this, which hinted at a far-reaching support for the old military aggression of Empress Florence.

And he was now complicit in that defiance.

But he had to be. He had to maintain his cover.

That thought steadied him. He sighed and stretched. The best anyone—especially the Emperor—could ask was that he do his duty to the best of his ability.

The difficulty was that duty sometimes led to conflicting loyalties.

No, that wasn't quite true. He knew exactly where his loyalty lay, but sometimes he had to act in ways that appeared in conflict in order to win the longer game.

A glance at the desktop display told him he had half an hour before dressing for the formal wardroom dinner this evening. Time enough to compose himself properly and rebuild the self-confidence that had been shattered by the captain's treasonous orders.

He was not a professional undercover agent. He had no training in this kind of work. He was simply a career navy man, a weapons specialist and now a senior officer. The quandary for him was that he had faith in Emperor Paul's judgment and methods, which put him in an uncomfortable minority on board a deeply traditional ship like *Wrath*.

A samovar steamed on a sideboard behind him, prepared earlier by his orderly. Gregor stood to pour himself a cup of tea, and sweetened it with honey. He hoped the trembling in his fingers wasn't noticeable. He'd barely managed to stay in character when the captain dropped her bombshell. He'd recovered and proposed measures that would help her towards her goal, but it went so deeply against the grain to do so.

He needed to report this. But how?

He couldn't send a message simply as Commander Gregor Pavlenko. Any such message would be intercepted and deleted. He might be silenced openly on some trumped-up charge, or, more likely, meet with a fatal accident. Warships were dangerous environments even when they weren't at war.

The more obvious path was to report discreetly to the Imperial Security office on board. They were better placed to get a message out unmolested, but the end result was likely to be just as terminal for Gregor. There was no guarantee that the entire ImpSec office was loyal to Emperor Paul, and Gregor was well aware that the security officials themselves were being watched around the clock. No one could make an approach without Captain Borodina being aware of it. It was all part of the games captains played with their on-board chaperones.

The easiest path under normal circumstances was to make use of the covert tools installed on his notepad, tools that neither Captain Borodina nor ImpSec were aware of, and talk to his cell in The Hidden Light. From there, word would find its way back to the Emperor.

The trouble was that those tools only worked when the shipboard comms had a direct connection to a relay node in the interstellar network. That same constraint also ruled out the other lines of communication. Until the captain released a vessel to make the weeks-long journey back to civilization, no messages were getting out at all.

Gregor would have to get creative.

Feeling like an infiltrator behind enemy lines, Gregor took his seat at the dining table. Formal dinners in the wardroom of a capital ship were always glittering affairs. Best porcelain, crystal, and silver was on display. Evening dress uniforms were the order of the day as the senior members of the company enjoyed food and drink to rival an imperial state banquet.

To mark the successful completion of phase one multi-unit trials, the captains and the most senior officers of all three *Swords* and the support fleet were present, including the captain of *Sparrowhawk* who doubtless was wondering when she'd be allowed to return to civilized space with a progress report.

Also present, looking uncomfortably out of place amongst the military finery, were Jules Okwanda and the senior members of the contract team.

"I hope to see more of you in our wardroom over the coming weeks," Captain Boridina announced as she welcomed and introduced the visiting officers. "We still have a long way to go, and we'll be working all the more closely through the next stages of the project."

Sadly, Gregor's appetite this evening wasn't up to the challenge. He picked at his food, his mind still turning over the captain's orders and pondering his conflict of interest. His ears pricked up when he heard his name.

"Commander Pavlenko has advised me that we need a new target planet for the next rounds of tests."

Gregor looked up, startled. He hadn't expected to be put on the spot like that, and he hadn't yet decided how to explain the need for a move. He covered his confusion with another small mouthful of food while he thought. "We originally chose the system we're in for its simplicity," he improvised. "One rocky planet, and not a lot else."

He dabbed his mouth with a folded napkin while his mind mapped out a plausible line of thinking. "There's so much complexity with the whole battle system, we felt the need to limit the variables at play and examine the system's response to a clean environment that we had full control over."

He looked around the table, especially catching the eyes of the visiting senior officers. He had a feeling this was the audience the captain was most keen to bring onside. "I think you can all appreciate just how close to realistic combat that is."

Knowing nods and a ripple of laughter told him he'd judged correctly.

"Given the outstanding success of trials so far, and in consultation with the project team, we need to push the boundaries into more realistic scenarios."

Captain Borodina said, "This means we'll shortly be moving our base of operations."

"Where to?" asked *Scepter of Truth*'s weapons officer.

Gregor glanced at his captain for a hint of how she wanted to play this. To his surprise, Jules Okwanda came to the rescue.

"That's the thing," Jules said. "Now we've got a good sense of Maestro's capabilities in these early scenarios, we're revising our original plans to be more ambitious. My team will work with Commander Pavlenko to identify candidate sites from deep space surveys."

Gregor wondered if the captain had briefed Jules already on the need to stay out of contact. Did the fiery PDC executive know of the Emperor's orders?

The captain of *Sparrowhawk* looked sharply at Captain Borodina. "My orders were to return with regular updates. Will you have chosen a new test site before I need to return?"

"You're attached as liaison to this squadron, under my command. While we're on the move, *Sparrowhawk* stays with us. Once we've settled on a location you can report back to Admiralty without fear of not finding us again."

The destroyer's captain looked ready to protest, but after a glance at the smug expressions of the other battle group's captains her mouth pressed in a thin line. She nodded and turned her attention back to her dinner.

Chapter 6

G regor Pavlenko pored over Admiralty charts covering a span three hundred light years from their current position across the galactic north of Skamensis space.

A mess tray sat half-empty alongside him. From time to time, the aroma of garlic and turmeric tempted him to take another mouthful, but for the most part he sat, absorbed in his research. The lights of the large conference room had been dimmed, and sound deadening around the room's edges screened out all noise other than the background hum of the warship, the soft rush of ventilation, and the occasional creak of a chair and the scratch of a stylus on notepad.

Reams of data scrolled over the desk in front of him. Each of the quarter million stars in this region of space was listed, many with nothing more than an Imperial Survey designator and a brief annotation of star type. That still left tens of thousands with more detailed information about planetary composition from deep sky surveys, and even some visits, over the course of thousands of years.

As he refined his search, the constellation of lights scattered across the conference room desktop dwindled. The most promising, he flagged and sent the co-ordinates over to the two other occupants of the room.

Gregor only knew them as Tamara and Zach. Up to now, they had been working behind the scenes, closeted away in the suite of rooms given over to the contract project team. He'd not been properly introduced and didn't have a clear picture of their roles on the project. The most he'd gleaned was that Tamara was someone senior on the testing team, and Zach had something to do with battle tactics. What was clear to him, however, was that these two must be very senior in the Philip Drayson Coolidge hierarchy. Even the surly project manager deferred to them. Gregor guessed they reported directly to firebrand Jules Okwanda.

Also clear to Gregor, these two knew about his and the captain's delaying tactics to keep the small fleet out of contact for as long as possible. The real reasons for the move from their current test site were not common knowledge, but Tamara and Zach conferred and openly discussed how to justify the criteria they were feeding to Gregor. Between them they constructed a credible web of fiction that would stand scrutiny in front of an Imperial Board of Inquiry. Gregor hoped it would never come to that.

Gregor squinted at the latest request from Tamara. He'd scouted out a variety of conditions at their request—multi-planet systems, rings and moons around gas giants, dust fields and dense rings of asteroids—but this one seemed a stretch. "A blue supergiant? Are you serious?"

"The ionization will virtually blind all but short range sensors," Zach explained. "We need to see how Maestro will handle a multi-unit operation with limited sensory input."

"You could simulate sensor loss very easily." Gregor seemed to have taken on the role of devil's advocate. Most people would by now be showing some exasperation at his constant poking at their logic, but Tamara and Zach seemed to relish the challenge.

"With that line of reasoning," Tamara said, "we could have simply played war games entirely in simulation from the comfort of a laboratory on Magentis."

"We did all of that before we began installing anything on a real warship," added Zach. "You've already seen how different it is testing systems in the field."

Tamara glanced at Zach, "Of course, we'll write all that up in more formal technical language—"

"Read: corporate bullshit," said Zach with a smirk.

Gregor sighed. "You'll want some sort of preamble to explain why these test plans weren't listed in the original timetable. If an inquiry team does start digging, one of the first things they'll ask is why we changed tack mid-program. Why weren't all these reasons apparent at the outset?"

It was Tamara's turn to grin. "Justifying departures from original plans is one of my specialities."

Gregor felt this revealed far more about the corporate profit-driven culture than she intended. He turned back to his tables of data. "Okay, blue supergiants coming up," he muttered.

———◆◆———

Chalwen's attention roved, restless, across walls and rooflines, crowded courtyards and shadowed corners on the half-mile walk from the imperial family quarters to the Assembly Room sitting just inside the grounds of the Mosaic Palace. Teams of guards discreetly gave the all-clear at each hand-off point in a well-practiced dance as the security cordon spread a protective web of flesh and steel and electronic surveillance.

Julian's personal tutor, Doctor Vicky Sharma, bore the brunt of the youngster's inquisitive chatter, quite at home fielding questions and quizzing him in turn about the buildings, their history, and the legislative process.

Emperor Paul had always been careful to shield his eldest son from the political scrum, until now. Maybe, Chalwen mused, the death of Empress Florence had finally opened him up to the need to prepare the Crown Prince for the duties to come. Interesting that Julian had reached that same conclusion ahead of Paul. Or maybe Paul had simply been putting off the inevitable. Either way, Julian's schedule had gotten busier in the last three months with invitations to see the machinery of government in action, and this new busyness placed extra burdens on Chalwen and her team.

This was Julian's first visit to a formal sitting of the Assembly, and he was visiting in style. Even though this outing formed a part of his schooling, what nine-year-old boy wouldn't be excited by a field trip and escape from the confines of his study?

All the same, his mood was a shadow of the boyish exuberance he might have displayed even a year ago. In the last months, Chalwen had noticed a marked change, a maturity, in his outward conduct, and his questioning had taken on a more penetrating depth than any nine-year-old had a right to wield. Many of Julian's formal lessons took place behind closed doors without even his escort present. As a result Chalwen had little insight into Doctor Vicky's methods, but she had no doubt the tutor was coaching the Crown Prince in far more than purely academic knowledge.

They passed the back of the Office of Deliberation and into the shadow of the Assembly Room itself. Chalwen's official duties had never taken her into the precincts of the Legislative Assembly. She'd sat a few times in the public viewing galleries in off-duty hours, but she'd never before entered from the palace side through the Green Gallery.

Seen from the air, the Green Gallery resembled nothing more than a lean-to propping up one side of the Assembly building. Until the scale of the building hit you.

From inside, the gallery was lofty and airy, filled with light from the transparent roof seventy feet overhead.

The tiled floor sported some of the mosaics that characterized so many rooms and halls in the palace, but these were understated in comparison. Pale golds and creams swirled in abstract patterns which seemed to lead the eye to the features that gave this gallery its name.

Waist-high retaining walls formed a series of raised beds down either side. The beds were lush with stands of dense foliage, species from every corner of the empire. Chalwen longed to linger here and admire some of the rarer specimens, but she wrestled her awareness back to the job in hand and shivered at the multitude of hiding places for hidden threats.

Voices in her microscopic earpiece confirmed that her team had already swept the area, and they'd been preceded by the Emperor's own bodyguard.

In between the beds, water features played, breathing life and fresh-ness into the cavernous space. This gallery was reserved exclusively for the Emperor and a few privileged guests, a cool and restful refuge from both the humid heat outside—a typical Prandis day as winter turned to spring—and the raucous arguments and endless heckling of the Assembly itself.

Their small company emerged at the back of a private box set in among the public and media galleries at the western end of the Assembly Room. High partitions behind and to either side screened them from nearby view, but the hubbub of conversation hit Chalwen like a physical blow.

In front of them, banked rows of seats and carved rosewood desks stepped down to the main floor of the Assembly Room, curving around on either side to enclose three sides of the floor. At the far end, a dais held desks for the Assembly officials, and beyond that, the imperial throne. At a rough count, Chalwen reckoned three-quarters of the seats were occupied. This was a busy session.

She kept half an ear on the questions and answers between Julian and Doctor Vicky as the tutor pointed out various Assembly Members and talked about their worlds. Chalwen smiled to herself. Julian was getting an education by stealth. There was nothing like seeing people in the flesh to bring the vastness of the empire to life.

A sense of expectation built up as the Clerk of the Floor, surrounded by a small army of junior clerks, emerged from the officials' dressing room and made her way across the dais. In full ceremonial regalia, the white-haired Clerk was unhurried, and paused here and there to speak to guards and officials. Her retinue settled at their desks on the lowest level of the stepped dais while the Clerk herself took a seat two steps down from the imperial throne. She folded her robes across her legs and took a sip from the crystal glass at her side.

The atmosphere in the vast chamber went from casual and noisy to intensely businesslike in a heartbeat when the Sergeant at Arms strode across the dais and grounded his ceremonial spear at a slant by his side.

Two seconds of silence, then, "His Imperial Excellency, the Essence of Unity, Emperor Paul Skamensis." The Sergeant at Arms didn't bellow, didn't even raise his voice, but his words carried clearly across three acres of enclosed space.

With a rustle of movement, three hundred people in front of them, and countless more unseen in the public galleries alongside and behind, rose as one.

The Emperor strode onto the dais, aloof and regal in his robes of office. With a theatrical flourish he swept his robes around him and sat.

"Be seated," the Sergeant at Arms said. He bowed first to the Emperor, then to the Clerk, and backed away from center stage to his station at one side.

The Emperor cleared his throat. Julian's eyes were fixed on his father a hundred yards away at the far end of the chamber.

"I call this session of the Assembly to order." Paul's voice resonated through the room. "Madame Clerk, please proceed."

The Clerk stood and intoned a brief prayer to the Essence of Unity. As she sat, the stiff formality of the occasion evaporated. The Emperor lounged back and stretched his legs out. Across the room, Assembly Members settled themselves more comfortably. Chalwen spotted one in the row below them prop his feet up on his desk.

An usher hurried forward with a small table which he set in front of the Clerk. She consulted the scroll stretched out on its surface. "I see tabled a pro-forma Bill, folio eighty sixty-eight dash one thirty-three. To whit, a draft proposal to establish a public register of financial interests in Assembly Members' campaigns and official operations."

Doctor Vicky murmured to Julian, "Straight to the one we're here to see. This is what your father is trying to get passed."

The Clerk paused and looked around the chamber. "Is there a Member willing to bring this Bill to the floor of the Assembly?"

"If this is Father's Bill," Julian asked, "why doesn't he bring it up himself?"

The tutor leaned closer. Chalwen's fingers twitched in reflex at someone so close to Julian. "Remember, the Assembly advises the Emperor. He can't really advise himself, can he? So when he wants something done through the Assembly, he has to get one of the Members to bring it forward on his behalf."

Chalwen tore her attention away from Julian and his tutor. As far as she knew, this Bill faced insurmountable opposition. Who would be brave or stupid enough to table it?

"Could he actually sign his own law, though?" Julian's whisper sounded like a shout next to her in the expectant hush. "Without the Assembly?"

"In theory, he has the constitutional power. The Assembly is technically only advisory, he's the one who signs things into law. But it's very dangerous for an emperor to bypass the proper channels. It would set a bad precedent."

Meaning, Chalwen thought, it would get up some powerful people's noses just on principle. And if you had to resort to those tactics, it meant you'd already lost too much support. From there it would be a short step to either abdication or an assassin's blade.

The taut silence was broken at last by movement over to one side, and a sigh like rustling leaves that swept over the room. Aah, that made sense. Josie Kang, the Member from Derrin's high-tech manufacturing quarter, stood and bowed to the Clerk. Secure enough in her constituency not to worry about popularity, and enough of an independent to curry favor with either Ivan or the Emperor with impartiality. And, as far as Chalwen knew, honest enough not to be worried by the proposed legislation. Especially when she knew it had practically zero chance of actually making it onto the statute books.

She wondered what Paul might have promised Josie in return for her support.

"Do I hear any objections?" The Clerk paused little more than a heartbeat. "None heard. Folio eighty sixty-eight dash one thirty-three is moved to the Committee of the Auditor Fiscal for formal drafting."

When the Clerk moved on to the next order of business, Julian looked at at his tutor. "Huh? Is that it?"

"For now." There was a hint of laughter in Doctor Vicky's voice. "It means that people will work on the wording of the Bill now. The real test is when it finally comes back for a vote."

Chalwen added, "This step is nothing more than a formality. Nobody in their right mind will object to sending the Bill to committee, not with the Emperor watching."

———— ◆ ————

"Feeder three's tripping out again." Una's voice was a frustrated growl.

"Maybe Maestro did more damage than we thought." Gregor frowned in thought. A part of him was working on the very real problem of the dodgy plasma feed that had always given them trouble, but a major part of him was struggling to contain his excitement. He'd just solved his communication problem. There were still risks, but he'd never get a better chance.

"Lieutenant Spelze," he announced briskly, "work up a rota and schedule for a full overhaul on feeder three. Inside and out. It's time we got to the bottom of this malfunction."

"Full overhaul? Will take a couple of days, Commander. And by 'outside' I assume you mean EVA?" She stopped just short of voicing her doubts. Crawling around the outside of the hull was usually something you left to the shipyards.

"Could be a blockage in one of the blow-off vents." Gregor could still see the question marks in Una's eyes. "PDC are being billed to rectify damage from their system. I'll let the accountants wrangle the details, but I would say this came into scope."

───

Once he was sure the EVA team had cleared the airlock, Gregor suited up in the upper hangar ready room. He checked there was no one else nearby, and unlocked a cabinet at the end of the row of kit lockers. Inside, he'd stashed a low-power beacon with a memory device attached. The whole unit was no larger than a small backpack.

Gregor secured his helmet and entered the airlock. All cycles of the ship's airlocks were routinely logged, which is why he needed an excuse to be out on the hull. "Deck Control," he said. "Comms check. Commander Gregor Pavlenko joining the repair crew topside."

"Comms check confirmed," a bored voice announced. "You are clear to exit, Commander."

Not a murmur of suspicion. Gregor thanked Eternal Unity that he'd always made a habit of mucking in when his crews were in the thick of dirty or dangerous work. He cycled the lock and opened the outer hatch. Midnight black showed through the opening, dusted with brilliant pinpricks of stars. Gregor eased his head above the coaming and scanned the artificial horizon of the warship's upper carapace. Lights in the distance illuminated a small forest of vent housings and access hatches atop feeder three.

Gregor clipped a safety line to the nearest of a network of guide rails criss-crossing the hull. He hauled himself, now weightless, out of the airlock and to one side. Casually, he launched the beacon into space and away from the tell-tale shaft of light from the airlock. It would drift, inert, away from the warship, too small to alert the sensors.

He'd set a timer to wake up the beacon a week from now, long after they'd be gone from this system, and before anyone came looking for them. The memory unit contained an encrypted message to The

Hidden Light and co-ordinates of the forty candidate sites they'd picked out. A lot of systems to search, but the best he could do.

Maybe the fleet would be intercepted before they signed off the Maestro project, and maybe it wouldn't. The fleet might be out of contact for months yet, but at least the Emperor would be alerted to the Admiralty's defiance.

Chapter 7

Year 8068, spring

Afternoon sun baked the ten acres of the inner gardens behind the imperial family quarters. Paths wound between lush beds and stands of shade-giving palms. The far wall and the bulk of the residence building shimmered in the distance.

Under the spread of one of the garden's ancient pavilions, the air was mercifully cool. Refrigeration machinery in the high eaves spread its balm on the crowd gathered between the pinkstone pillars of the open sides.

In the center of the pavilion, the entire Skamensis Family gathered. An assassin's dream and a bodyguard's nightmare.

Emperor Paul sat beside a refreshments table with Lady Miriam alongside. Four of their children paid dutiful attention while Ivan, inscrutable as ever, lurked in the background. But pride of place today was given to Crown Prince Julian Skamensis, on his tenth birthday. He sat slightly apart. From over his shoulder, Chalwen scowled protectively at the line of well-wishers straggling across the floor of the pavilion and around the perimeter.

At Julian's gesture of dismissal, a second cousin, a weasely man and a known supporter of Empress Florence's old ways, bowed and turned aside followed by his wife and single sullen child. He'd been all charm and smiles presenting a ceremonial short sword in a tooled and jeweled scabbard. Chalwen already had the weapon checked carefully for traps, poisons, and hidden electronics. She doubted a guest would make such an overt move, but it was her job to be paranoid.

The voice of the senior usher cut through the background murmur of fifty conversations. "Supreme Judge Abraham Crode."

Chalwen hid a start of surprise. So, the Assembly had finally voted on the judicial proposal. She'd been so caught up in security arrangements these past few days, she was out of touch with less important goings-on in the outside world.

Crode stepped forward and bowed. "Crown Prince, please accept my congratulations and best wishes on your anniversary."

He was empty-handed, which was not unusual. Many people came with gifts too large to carry. At the latest tally, Julian was now the proud owner of an airbike, a fountain to be installed in one of the famous plazas at Henriss Garden, a tapestry of dragons in flight, and a bed carved from Evenian lemonwood.

"On this decennial occasion"—Crode straightened and gestured towards the wall behind the pavilion—"you'll find a small and unworthy token in the household stables."

Julian's eyes lit up. He looked over at Paul, who smiled back.

"A genetically-scaled Arabian Black," Crode continued. "I picked him out myself. A perfect size and temperament for a young but experienced rider."

With a visible effort, Julian collected himself. "My thanks, Justice Crode." He glanced over to his family at the table. "Uncle Ivan, you must take me riding with you now I have a proper mount of my own."

Ivan and Paul exchanged glances. For a moment, Chalwen could have sworn she saw a slight softening of the Grand Duke's features, but dismissed it as her imagination.

"I'm sure a few gallops in the Meadow would be in order, to start off with." Ivan bowed his head to the Emperor. "With your permission, Brother."

Paul smiled and acknowledged with a casual wave of his hand. Remembering his place, Julian had already turned his attention back to the guest standing patiently in front of him.

"Justice Crode, I believe congratulations of your own are in order, on your recently-confirmed appointment."

"My thanks, Magister." Abraham Crode gave a bow a fraction lower than was strictly necessary. "I look forward to serving the empire in whatever way my poor abilities permit."

"I'm glad my father and uncle were able to come to an agreement at last. Their arguing was starting to curdle the milk."

Crode leaned forward and lowered his voice to a stage whisper. "I rather get the feeling that I merely represented the least offensive choice to both parties. Hardly an auspicious endorsement."

Chalwen glanced sidelong in surprise, but Crode's face crinkled good naturedly.

"Justice Crode, I'm sure anyone they considered was more than qualified for the role."

"You honor me, Magister."

"I understand my father had to choose between outstanding candidates with nothing more than preferences and ideologies to separate them."

Chalwen did a double-take. Where did a sentence like *that* come from? She could definitely see the hands of Doctor Vicky and maybe Marcus Tyee in the Crown Prince's poise.

It seemed Julian's words had surprised Justice Crode, too. He blinked and straightened. "Indeed, Magister."

"It seems strange that preferences can get so much in the way of things that should be straightforward."

Abraham coughed into his hand. "Excuse me, Magister, I fear there's nothing *straightforward* about judicial appointments."

"I mean, isn't it your job to apply the law, regardless of any preferences? So why would they matter to anyone?"

"Indeed, Magister." Abraham laughed, but his eyes held a calculating glint. "I hope you remember these words in years to come when the time comes for you to appoint my own successor."

———◦•◦———

The unsigned card on Ivan's desk bore a simple message: *A keepsake for the proud uncle.*

With the ceremonial gift-giving over, Ivan sought brief refuge in his office, taking every opportunity to review his affairs before the imminent departure to his fief worlds. He'd soon need to bathe and change for the more intimate family gathering this evening, but the card and gift-wrapped package waiting on his desk derailed all other thoughts. Ivan unwrapped the package to reveal a true-ebony trinket box inlaid with sea jade. His fingertips brushed the lid, shivering at the exquisite silken feel.

He snatched his hand away. He needed no note to identify the sender of the gift. True-ebony, fabulously expensive signature of Honorina Philip. But the real message lay in the sea jade, a mineral found only on Alfano in di Brugui space.

Alfano. Still rebuilding its prosperity after a calamity that had rocked the six Families nearly two decades ago.

Ivan squeezed his eyes shut and swallowed. This skeleton still haunted him.

In a bid to disrupt di Brugui expansions towards his own fiefdom on the outskirts of Skamensis space, the younger Ivan, under the tutelage of Empress Florence, struck a deal with Honorina Philip to smuggle arms to a workers' uprising on Alfano. From a military perspective, the move had worked well.

Too well.

Of course he should have realized Honorina would play both sides and arm the terrified planetary elite with even more advanced weapons. The ensuing bloodbath had cost millions of lives and laid waste to a continent.

The lives mattered little compared with the damage to Ivan's reputation if his involvement ever became known. Grand Duke Ivan Skamensis supporting a peasants' rebellion? Even though the catastrophe lay years in the past, his own political support would evaporate overnight.

Honorina had held this secret over Ivan's head ever since. It mostly lay unspoken between them, but the choice of an exquisite mineral found only on that ravaged world had to be a subtle reminder.

Ivan's racing thoughts unwrapped more layers of meaning in the bizarre gift. He had no conceivable use for such a box, but the subtext hinted at secrets being kept safe ... or not, given the ornamental rather than functional nature of the box. Beyond that, the note showed Honorina was well aware of the close relationship between the Crown Prince and the Grand Duke, and the defense conglomerate had sent an emissary with an antique hunting bow as a gift for Julian. Were they hinting they were prepared to arm the youngster against his uncle if the need arose?

Real or imagined? Was he overthinking things? Who knew, where Honorina was concerned? The threat was clear enough, though, and she had to be referring to the Maestro project that Paul had ordered stopped. For Honorina to play this card right now, the project must be vitally important to the conglomerate.

Ivan acknowledged a discreet knock at the door. Two servants entered, bowed, then glided silently across the study to the quarters beyond to begin drawing Ivan's bath.

Duty called.

He glanced one last time at the precious box and anger flashed red through his mind. Honorina's reminder was superfluous to the point of insulting. Emperor Paul's best efforts to reverse track would come to nothing. Ivan's own people in the Admiralty would tie Paul's orders up in knots, but they were only one line of defense. The project was unstoppable. The best lawyers and engineers had made sure of that.

Did Honorina not understand that Maestro was important to Ivan, too? One day, a suitable opportunity would present itself and Ivan would take the throne. The empire would stand strong and proud again, and he needed a battle fleet with the most advanced capabilities. A fleet that would send a message to the other Families, along with the countless brigands and insurrectionists infesting the outworlds. They would kneel and tremble. They would know their place!

Chapter 8

W arm orange light of Eta Capilani bathed the veldt of Devonia and lit rustling grasses like a miles-wide brush fire. It was a sight that Ivan never tired of. Scrubby knots of jewel bush and majestic outposts of acacia and baobab cast shade. On the heat-hazed horizon, ramparts of the Outer Cascades floated like a bruise on the sky.

Devonia, Ivan's ducal fief, and these grassy plains in particular, felt more like home than anywhere on the teeming imperial capital world three hundred light years distant. Towering on an outcrop overlooking the plains, Greyspire was his retreat within a retreat. As imperial residences went, Greyspire was small and intimate. It comfortably housed Ivan and his entourage, with a few spare suites for when Ivan needed to woo influential guests on his own demesne away from ImpSec's prying spyware.

Of course, Ivan had a choice of palaces and lodges scattered across the planet, but Greyspire, set in a million square miles of untouched wilderness, had always been his favorite. Somewhere to invite the most privileged of his inner circle.

A low rumble in the distance announced visitors. Ivan glanced to where a dark speck slowed and traversed the landscape on an approved flight path that offered no direct line of attack. It sometimes amused him to wonder exactly how fast the hidden defenses would spring into action if a craft should deviate from the safe corridor across his private and *almost* untouched wilderness.

His head of household, a powerful and unsmiling woman in her sixties, approached.

"That will be Scipio Firenzi and his staff." Ivan squinted against the midday glare and made out a second craft approaching a mile back from the first. From what he knew of Scipio, the Firenzi heir would be piloting the lead vehicle in person, and pushing the speed limit on the permitted approach. "Bring Lord Scipio here to the mid terrace, and have a table set out for a light luncheon."

He didn't need to mention showing Scipio's entourage to the guest quarters and introducing his bodyguard to the local head of security. Stukker knew her job, and no detail escaped her impassive gaze. She bowed her head and headed back indoors.

The air cruiser disappeared from view behind the slope of the ridge, to where a landing field and hangars nestled in the curve of the steep outcrop.

Not for the first time, Ivan found himself wondering at the risk he was taking inviting the Firenzi noble here. Although Ivan went to great lengths to control the flow of information in and around his personal fiefdom, a visit like this wouldn't go unnoticed by the all-seeing Imperial Security. There were bound to be spies, even here in Greyspire. But Ivan had been careful over the years to cultivate a persona of gaming and hunting, of entertaining nobles, politicians, and business moguls. A visit like this couldn't go unremarked, but at least it was arguably unremarkable.

As long as ImpSec never caught wind of the real reasons for this visit. On that matter even Ivan was in the dark, at least in terms of specifics. Scipio's office had contacted Ivan's office asking to meet to discuss a business proposal. The bland wording fooled no one even as it gave nothing away. On one level, everything to Ivan was business, but they did have common interests. They were both in the business of succession—taking the helm of their respective Families and eliminating anything standing in their way.

Scipio wanted an alliance.

Maybe in hindsight it was a logical move, but Ivan was surprised to realize he'd never considered the possibility. He strolled to the edge of the terrace and rested his hands on the thick but almost invisibly transparent balustrade.

A dust cloud in the middle distance marked the passage of a large herd, most likely gazelle at this time of season. Ivan's fingers twitched at the thought. He longed to be out there, stalking, selecting his kill, but today he had game to stalk closer at hand. He'd had little direct dealing with Scipio, half-brother to Josef, the Firenzi patriarch. They'd crossed paths a number of times, at state functions, at trade negotiations, or across the table at ritualized cessations of hostilities arguing the terms for the return of assets seized from one Family by the other. More of the latter during Empress Florence's rule, more of the first two since Emperor Paul took the throne.

The two men had common ground. Both were ambitious and ruthless, direct and uncompromising, hardworking and unsentimental. They both loved rough outdoor pursuits and fine luxuries in equal measure. But Scipio had always appeared to Ivan to be something of a thug and an oaf, intellectually challenged, not someone to be taken too seriously. Maybe Ivan had misjudged. This meeting would be interesting.

A faint scuff of feet behind. Ivan turned and studied the younger man as he strode purposefully from the shadowed doorway and across the terrace.

Although he lacked Ivan's height by a full head, Scipio's stocky frame and bearing exuded power. He stopped five paces away and bobbed his head. "Magister."

The greeting was polite but perfunctory, falling just short of insult. Scipio's tone made it clear he didn't normally defer to anyone, and he was following form as a matter of choice, not necessity. The self-assurance was good, as long as he knew his place.

Ivan locked eyes with Scipio a few moments longer. With his pale skin and red hair, he couldn't be comfortable out here in the full glare of sub-tropical sun. Beads of sweat formed on his forehead, but he gave no signs of distress. His grey eyes were hard and calculating.

"My Lord Scipio, welcome to Greyspire."

The Firenzi noble cocked his head towards the main body of the building, which rose like a fluted teacup from the center of the terrace. "Now I see it up close, I wonder at the name. It looks grey from a distance, but from here the steel and glass are distinctly blue."

"A trick of the light." Ivan gestured to the sky. "The orange tint washes out the blue, especially from a distance."

Scipio turned slowly, taking in the unspoiled panorama. "What I've heard about this place hardly does it justice. You really have chosen to isolate yourself here, haven't you?"

"That is very much by choice. This is a place for quiet and reflection, though rest assured urban comforts are only an hour's suborbital hop away."

Scipio grunted.

"I don't know how the local time compares to the shipboard schedule you've been keeping, but it's lunchtime here and I assumed some form of refreshment would be welcome." Ivan gestured to where servants were setting up a canopy over a table near the edge of the terrace.

"Afterwards, my staff will show you your quarters. You have a fully-equipped office with secure comms onto the external net. You're also welcome to use the recreation and viewing facilities on this and the upper levels."

"You must have more use for quiet and reflection than I ever did. What do you do for fun out here?"

Ivan gave a tight smile. "Distractions are mostly of the outdoor variety. Game on this continent is varied and plentiful. I can arrange a proper hunt if that would be to your liking. But perhaps a ride this afternoon to loosen shipbound joints?"

As dusk fell, Ivan ushered Scipio onto the dining terrace, a broad paved circle perched on the edge of the promontory next to Greyspire's main tower. The first stars shone in a moonless sky, silhouetting the bulk of the tower behind them. Ivan led the way to a table under the eaves of an open-sided shelter that spanned most of the terrace. Warmth from a blazing fire pit at the heart of the shelter dispelled the deepening night chill.

"Greyspire is a place for informal dining. Everything we eat tonight has been killed or grown wild on this estate."

Servants filed from the main house and placed covered trays on ceramic warming hobs set into the tabletop.

As soon as the dishes were laid on the table, Ivan dismissed the servants and his security detail.

Scipio looked at him questioningly, then nodded to his own bodyguard. "Stand down until called for."

Scipio's squad captain looked troubled. "Sire, that goes against—"

"All your training, standing instructions, and instincts," Ivan interrupted smoothly. "I know. Just ask yourself this, Captain. If I wished your master harm, here in the heart of my home territory, how would you expect to stop me?"

The captain opened his mouth, then closed it again.

"Exactly," Ivan said. "Although it makes people uncomfortable to admit it, personal bodyguards are little more than ceremonial show in a place like this."

"Which begs a question, Magister. With your own guard dismissed, what if my master now wished *you* harm?"

Scipio raised an eyebrow. Ivan laughed. He recognized the calculating iron in the captain's voice. This man had seen active service, had seen and probably committed unspeakable acts without a qualm. And he was not awed by aristocratic rank or title. Either this was a fluke, or Scipio knew how to choose his staff wisely.

"Have no fear, Captain. My own guard is not so distant as you might think, and nor will you be." Ivan noticed that Scipio was still gazing at him and had made no move to admonish the guard. A faint smile played at the edges of Scipio's mouth. Had the pair of them been testing him? The thought amused Ivan and also cheered him. He needed allies with competence, self-confidence, and a calculating self-interest.

Scipio stirred and waved the captain away. "I'm sure the Grand Duke's head of household will show you where you can stand watch and await further instructions."

Ivan glanced towards the main house and gave a tiny nod for the benefit of Lieutenant Shan Bresk and a pair of marksmen concealed behind cunningly-hidden embrasures. The signal allowed a slight relaxation, preliminary skirmishes over, tests administered and passed.

Once they were alone on the terrace, with nothing more than the crackling fire for company, Ivan lifted the lid off a soup tureen. "A chowder of bluegill and yam, if I'm not mistaken, seasoned with local turmeric and cream from the milk of wild mountain goats." He gestured. "With no servants to overhear, the downside is you'll have to serve yourself."

While Scipio filled a bowl and busied himself slicing a crisp baguette still warm from the oven, Ivan placed his notepad on the table and made a few annotations. The air on the terrace seemed to thicken, and the teeming insect noises dimmed. "Visual and acoustic dampening. Along with electronic countermeasures, we are now effectively alone."

Scipio pursed his lips and nodded approvingly. Ivan ladled soup into his own bowl and sipped.

At last, Scipio said, "The soup is excellent. And I believe we both have information to share that needs to remain between us. So how can you be certain I'm not recording it?"

"Of course you are," Ivan snorted. "Even if we solemnly promised that no record of this meeting would be made, I'm quite sure neither one of us would believe the other. So it seems better all round to acknowledge that we both have our own records of this meeting, to hold as collateral."

Scipio shrugged and drew a scroll from an inner pocket of his tunic, which he unrolled on the table.

"And as the host," Ivan continued, "with the home advantage if this meeting turns sour, I'll start by offering some collateral in good faith."

They ate in silence for a few minutes while Ivan marshaled his thoughts. He was also curious to see how the notoriously fiery Scipio managed his patience.

At last, Ivan placed his spoon on the plate alongside the bowl and nudged it to a precise perpendicular with the table edge. "How much is your Special Service aware of plans within the Imperial Admiralty for an automated battle command system?"

Scipio dabbed his lips with a napkin. "Enough rumors to be sure something along those lines was in progress. Not enough to tell us much about its capabilities, other than being reasonably confident that no treaties were being breached trying to solve generalized AI."

"Trying to *re*-solve generalized intelligence," Ivan said quietly. "That particular genie came out of its bottle once, and once too often."

"Solve, re-solve, either way the techniques were lost and no one in their right minds would try to recreate it." Scipio looked sharply at Ivan.

"But why ask? Our intelligence, scant though it is, was clear that the Emperor had stopped all work on this battle system."

"That is what all official records will indicate." Ivan met Scipio's startled look. "At least, they will show that the Emperor made his wishes known, and that his loyal servants have diligently sought to implement those wishes."

"But the work is still going on." Scipio's face whitened. "Do you honestly believe such systems will give you a decisive edge in battle? Should Family Firenzi be worried?"

"Not for a moment, and no more than usual. To me, the value in preserving the project is more economic and political than military."

"So, which conglomerate are you trying to keep sweet with such a lucrative contract?" At Ivan's pointed stare Scipio laughed and said, "A question too far. I understand. I was just hoping to fill a gap in our intelligence. These arms merchants take secrecy to a level that makes governments look inept. Okay. I suppose I need to place myself in equal jeopardy."

"Assuming you can match my furtive guilt."

Scipio sobered and said, "I think I can. Dear brother Josef has been taking me more and more into his confidence as hopes of a direct heir dwindle."

"That's always baffled me," Ivan admitted. "With the Firenzi gift for all matters medical, shouldn't fertility be a minor technicality?"

Scipio gave a sly smile. "The Firenzi are indeed gifted in medicines and drugs, including subtle and *undetectable* barriers to conception."

Ivan stared, then chuckled. He began to sense depth and subtlety in Scipio's scheming to rival Ivan's own. Within seconds, the two of them were laughing so hard, tears streamed down their cheeks.

Ivan sobered first. He lifted the lid from the next dish. "Come, Scipio, I don't want to get on the wrong side of my chef by neglecting this feast."

Scipio sniffed. "A wild rice risotto ... venison?"

"Aged in the deep cellars beneath this rock. The meat should fall apart in your mouth."

"As if it will have the chance. This outdoor air does wonders for the appetite."

"Don't stand on ceremony!" Ivan passed Scipio a serving spoon. "Of course, we haven't yet touched on the real reason for your visit."

Scipio hesitated, loaded spoon half-way between tureen and plate, then he shrugged and took a few more spoonfuls. "I think our exchange of dirty linen is enough show of good faith. Each of us has enough knowledge to ruin the other if either of us steps out of line."

"You have something to propose that's even more damning?"

"Yes. There are developments—*secretive* developments—within the Families that could bring big changes to our political landscape. To be honest, I was hesitant to bring this matter up at all. I felt I needed to handle it with care and discretion, but for all I know you're already apprised of what's going on and I risk looking foolish."

Ivan kept his expression politely encouraging while he served food for himself, but his mind churned behind the mask. Whatever Scipio had on his mind must surely involve the Emperor somehow. Nothing else seemed to warrant the precautions he'd taken up to now, and Scipio wasn't the kind of man to scare easily. Was it an assassination, or some other plot? Ivan practiced patience.

"But then, whether you're already in the know or whether this will come as news to you, I sense that we might hold similar views and might want to pool our resources in steering events to our mutual benefit."

Ah, there was yet another layer of defense before Scipio would release his secrets. "And you're looking for me to agree to a coalition before you've revealed what we're collaborating on?" Ivan raised his eyebrows.

"Of course not. Not quite, anyway. But before I say anything more, I do need to know that you're at least not averse to the idea."

"So, *in principle*, would I consider partnering you in a venture that we consider mutually beneficial?"

"Exactly."

"Hmm." Ivan poured himself a glass of wine and sipped. Scipio, he noticed, had stayed with water throughout the meal. He was not known for his temperance, so he was being careful to keep a clear head. So, he *could* exercise discipline when he felt the need. Ivan nodded. "We've not had close dealings before, but I've seen enough of your reputation and ways of working to be confident in a joint venture. Providing the benefits are as mutual as you suggest."

"Very well. I'll lay the rest out and we'll see if we have common ground. As I said earlier, Josef is taking me into his confidence as the only viable heir. That's the only reason I ever got an inkling of this."

So this is back to Josef? Ivan reassessed his earlier musings. One thing he was sure of, Josef wouldn't stoop to assassination. Josef was too honorable, and he and Paul were too closely aligned in their thinking.

"Even now, I'm not privy to all the discussions, but it seems your brother has been busy behind the scenes."

"I'm normally a patient man, but you've got me hooked. Spit it out."

"The Families are preparing for a Conclave."

A Conclave? Ivan sat back, struggling to control his expression, all good cheer evaporated.

Did the Emperor really hope to unite the six Families in peace? A noble quest, oft-lauded by the hard-of-thinking. Ivan was neither for nor against outright war, but diplomatic and military tensions kept the ruling Families strong, as vital to society as vigorous exercise to a healthy body. Paul would see the empire's strength atrophy.

More dark thoughts crossed Ivan's mind. He couldn't begin to imagine Honorina's reaction to this new threat to company profits.

Scipio leaned back in his chair and regarded Ivan with a smug smile. "From your expression, I gather this *is* news to you. I had wondered how big a circle was involved on the Emperor's side."

The unstated conclusion dropped like a lead weight between them. Not only had Paul undertaken the arrangements without advising Ivan, a deliberate and troubling omission in itself, but preparations had been so secretive that Ivan's network had caught no whiff of anything amiss.

And the more Ivan thought about it, the deeper the implications became. Bringing the Families together would be a logistical and diplomatic nightmare. How *could* something so far-reaching have escaped his notice? Unless ...

"Do you have any knowledge of how far progressed these arrangements are?"

"I believe all the Families have been approached, but they're not all committed. Yet."

"But no outright rejections." It was a statement. Without all six Families at the table, it couldn't be a true Conclave.

"You probably need time to absorb this. And, as you said, it would be a high crime to let this marvelous food go to waste."

That was true on both counts. Once Ivan had recovered from the initial shock of Scipio's announcement his appetite returned in full measure. The news would take time to absorb, even longer to verify. Then there was the matter of what to do about it.

Scipio's assessment of progress didn't sound like much to the layman, but to bring all the Families to the stage where they were even considering a meeting at the same table was a monumental achievement in itself. Up until a few minutes ago, Ivan would have been sure he had spies throughout Paul's organization. Clearly not. Paul must have set up an entirely separate network. That intelligence alone made this house visit worthwhile. Maybe the shortcoming it revealed would have angered a lesser man, but to Ivan it was simply data to be filed and manipulated. Only a fool would ever assume his knowledge was complete, so Ivan was gratified rather than angered to have a chance to extend his own boundaries.

Meanwhile, the two nobles picked their way through dish after dish, and talked amiably about war and trade, politics and sport. Ivan found himself uncharacteristically eager to sing the praises of his wilderness retreat. Aside from riding and stalking, salt flats a hundred miles to the west offered world-class land-yacht racing where Ivan had arranged to meet some of Devonia's like-minded aristocracy.

Finally, Ivan felt the time had come to bring the conversation back to the main purpose of Scipio's visit. There were still loose ends to tie off.

"What is your view in all this? A brokered peace could be very lucrative for those Families positioned to take advantage of it."

"Peace is overrated." Scipio snorted. "Conflict drives industry, drives innovation, and channels wealth in the right direction."

"So, you would be looking for ways to ensure the Conclave failed?"

"I think I just made my own position clear. I'm taking a huge risk discussing this so openly, but this is why I wouldn't entrust this conversation to even secure comms channels. Any talk of putting a spike into those proceedings is a clear case of treason. Not something to be taken lightly."

That much was true. Their motives were very different, but in this matter at least they shared a common aim. Scipio saw opportunities for wealth and power in endless skirmishes. Ivan wanted to rule an ordered world where people knew their place and knew their duty. On the surface, he should be as much in favor of lasting peace as Scipio was against it, but Ivan had long ago come to a deep if rather sad realization. Populations paid more heed to their leaders and protectors, and willingly surrendered more power, when there were wolves at the gates.

It had also occurred to Ivan that a failed Conclave, especially after it became public knowledge, would seriously weaken Paul as emperor.

It seemed that during the course of the meal he'd made up his mind. He smiled. "I'm in."

As was his habit, Gregor Pavlenko checked his suite for electronic surveillance and opened the hidden tools on his notepad.

Maestro had been officially signed off a month ago. A mountain of work still remained, but with some crafty rearranging of project deliverables they'd met the legal conditions to declare the contract fulfilled. The PDC staff were happy. Never mind that several critical stages still lay ahead of them, labeled as warranty work, that would all happen out of sight of the contract accountants back at Admiralty.

Gregor felt sick at his own part in the deception, but he'd had no alternative. He'd done what he could to alert the Light of what was going on. Other than that, he was in no position to stall the project. Anything to arouse suspicion would have seen him removed from his post, and the work would have continued anyway.

Now they'd finally returned to Skamensis space and had normal comms running. They were back in touch with civilization.

Gregor hoped the message he'd left with that beacon might have been found. At best, he hoped there might already be orders waiting for them when they returned to comms contact, ordering a dismantling of the work. Once the Emperor knew about Maestro and intervened, once it was out in the open, Gregor would be able to advise how to prevent the system from becoming properly operational.

No such luck.

Barring that, each day Gregor checked the covert channels hoping for word from The Hidden Light. Even though the Emperor might have his reasons for not moving openly, surely he'd want a report on how far the work had progressed.

But that channel was silent, too. There had been meetings, lots of activity while Gregor had been out of touch. There was much to catch up on, but nothing related to Maestro.

Gregor poured a cup of tea and settled down to read. An uneasy feeling tickled the back of his mind. He couldn't pinpoint it, but he couldn't ignore it. He scanned his suite again. No intrusions detected. On an impulse, he scanned the notepad itself. It appeared to be clean, but ImpSec could bury anything they wanted without his knowledge.

He turned to the tools the Light had installed for him. These were far from ordinary. Possibly designed by some techs at ImpSec, but working in hidden corners that the regular spooks wouldn't think to look.

He froze. There were unidentified routines lurking in the depths under layers of obscurity. He was under hidden surveillance.

Normally, he'd be confident that the use of his specialized comms couldn't be spied on, but this didn't look like run-of-the-mill monitoring. Something had prompted the on-board security office to be watching him. Even his link to The Hidden Light had to be regarded as compromised.

He was on his own.

———————

"A new business opportunity has presented itself rather unexpectedly." Even with the security surrounding him in Greyspire, security commissioned directly by Ivan through trusted sources a healthy arm's length from ImpSec, Ivan was careful with his words. Those words were traveling the comms exnet where ImpSec was anything but arm's length away.

The meeting with Scipio played over and over in Ivan's mind. It presented great threats and even greater opportunities. But to pursue any of them needed the skills of his trusted fixer, currently three hundred light years away on Magentis.

"And I take it there is some sensitivity involved," Bernie Fischer replied. "A meeting in person is required?"

"You have the idea." Ivan briefly regretted his decision to leave Bernie behind at the capital. But then, most of his secretive dealings were best handled from there, and Ivan hadn't considered that Scipio would drop such a bombshell. He'd thought the Firenzi noble might be currying favor or genuinely making a business proposition. Something relatively innocuous. But not this.

Bernie sucked his teeth. "Would I also be correct to assume you're staying out in Devonia space? Wait, let me guess, urgency is also an issue."

Ivan gave a dry laugh. "You're on a roll today, Bernie. I have too many important and highly visible engagements out here, so, yes, I intend to keep to my schedule. A week from now I'll set off for Sethridge, then Tigris and Bexel. You have my schedule."

"Already ahead of you, boss."

Bernie hummed to himself a few moments while Ivan let the massage chair in his inner office sooth some of the tension out of his shoulders. Beyond the windows of the darkened office, the moonless sky of Devonia was a glorious blaze of starlight dramatically cut through by the inky depths of the Twin Sisters nebula.

Bernie cleared his throat. "Let's hope *one* unexpected happening is our quota for the month. Barring more surprises, everything at this end is ticking along nicely and I can manage affairs as well from a cabin as from an office."

"If it helps," said Ivan, "I'll speak to the Admiralty and line up a fast scout for you."

"So, say, twenty-five light years a day? Maybe twenty-eight? I can intercept you between Sethridge and Tigris. If the urgency is real I suggest a mid-space rendezvous rather than waiting two more days to planetfall."

Chapter 9

Year 8068, summer

The scout craft looked tiny nosed up against *Kirov's* forward docking station. On *Kirov's* command deck, Ivan held his impatience in check while the docking tunnel extended and locked in place. He swung around and strode towards his quarters, head high and hands clasped behind his back. Crew members scurried out of his way and bowed their heads as he passed.

Ivan waited in his main stateroom, where a breathless Bernie Fischer appeared a few minutes later. As soon as the door shut behind him, Bernie heaved an exaggerated sigh, stretched out his arms, and twirled a full three-sixty. "My, my, how the other half live!"

The corner of Ivan's mouth twitched. His quarters hardly represented luxury. Clean and comfortable, and with enough clear deck to pace without risking scraped shins, but *Kirov* was still a fully functional warship. All things were relative. "A scout was the fastest ship available. The only vessel faster would be a *Sword*, and even I can't persuade the Admiralty to part with one of those. How was your journey?"

"Short on space. Shorter on privacy. On the glass-half-full side, I enjoyed the privacy of a small store room, which was soundproof enough. And of course the comms encryption on a scout is second to none."

"So you were able to keep track of my affairs?"

"Well enough. But the crick in my neck tells me you have something both important and sensitive to discuss."

Straight to business, which is why Ivan tolerated Bernie's irreverent manner.

In terse sentences, Ivan recounted his meeting with Scipio Firenzi.

"How in all of Space could this have slipped by us?" Bernie growled. His usually relentless good cheer evaporated.

"Obviously we don't have spies everywhere we need them. Paul has hidden behind smokescreens before. While he's been visibly busy securing the networks he knows we know about, maybe he's managed to set up a parallel organization."

"Well, we'll just have to see about *that*." Bernie frowned. "Hang about. There's another much simpler possibility that fits the known facts. How sure are we that this Conclave is real?"

"We aren't," Ivan said, drily. "It's possible Scipio is plotting to implicate me in a conspiracy to commit treason."

"You mean, if you take tangible and provable steps to work against the Emperor ..."

"Even if the target of those steps is a fiction ..."

"It's still a conspiracy. Huh. Damn."

"The problem is, well two problems. First I don't see how Scipio gains from that."

"Number two?"

Ivan hesitated, analyzing the source of his intuition. "I found I believed him."

"Three problems, actually," Bernie mused. "Scipio's contacts with you can hardly be secret. How does he stop himself getting dragged into any conspiracy witch hunt? You said you had information to sink him."

"Mutually assured destruction," Ivan murmured. "A saying from pre-history, but apt in this case. For better or worse, we're tied at the hip now."

"So, knowing your twisted mind, you've already got ideas for how to field this thermal grenade milord Scipio's lobbed at us."

"Two objectives come to mind." Ivan held up a finger. "One. Before anything else, we need to check out Scipio's claims."

Bernie's eyes glazed over. Ivan was used to this expression. Nothing of the darker aspects of Ivan's business were ever committed to even

a secured and encrypted device. Everything resided in Bernie's spec-
tacularly tortuous mind. "For now, let's ignore the Emperor's shadow
organization that we know nothing about. I'm willing to bet not all
the Families have gone to such lengths, and they must all be involved
by now. Someone out there might let slip something that friendly ears
might pick up. I'll start with the Wala, and Dom Calvino. They are
smaller and usually looser on matters of security."

Ivan nodded agreement. "And the second objective, assuming the
rumors prove true ..."

"I take it you would not be in favor of this Conclave going ahead?"

Ivan professed to look shocked. "Whatever made you think I'd consider interfering with the Emperor's plans?"

"Sixteen days in a scout ship. I'd bloody well hope only high treason
would warrant such secrecy that encrypted communications can't be
trusted."

"Fair enough. So, what do you think?"

"Getting five other Families, with centuries-old feuds and grievances
to settle, to even breathe the same planetary air let alone sit around a
table together?" Bernie pursed his lips. "Not a task I'd like to tackle. I'm
kinda glad you lean the other way. It won't take much prodding to upset
things."

"In her prime," Ivan mused, "my mother made an art form of goading one Family or another into an argument."

"We start by sowing a teensy bit of discord between Habradim and
Dom Calvino. There's already a trade dispute simmering there. If we
flood the Habradim market with cheap metals under the Dom Calvino
stamp—"

"And you can make that convincing?"

"Natch. Besides, the deception won't have to stand scrutiny for long.
Once the fuze is lit, the damage will be done."

Ivan nodded. "And I believe the Wala still regard Scorflac as dis-
puted territory. A raid to knock out their planetary defenses would have
the Firenzi up in arms."

"And then when the Wala see Firenzi forces massing on their near
border, they in turn will assume the worst." Bernie hesitated, then a wolfish grin spread across his face. "Ivan, can I suggest a fallback scenario?"

Ivan cocked an eyebrow.

"If this turns out to be some kind of elaborate hoax on Scipio's part—"

"I deem that unlikely."

"Okay, but if ... then you give me leave to nail the little shit."

"You're talking about assassinating a member of another Family's nobility?" Ivan's tone was deceptively mild. He tried to keep his amusement from showing.

"Come on." Bernie pouted. "I've got to have something to look forward to on my long and lonesome confinement in a three-crew ship."

Ivan wondered what Bernie might come up with. He wouldn't like to be in Scipio's shoes if this turned out to be some kind of hoax.

"Oh. While I'm here. Interesting morsel of information that I'm not quite sure what to make of."

Ivan frowned. It was unusual for Bernie to be at a loss for connections and avenues to pursue.

"That pet project that PDC was so keen to complete. The battle system. Obviously the Admiralty has sealed the whole project under a cloak of secrecy, but I understand the fleet has returned to normal circulation and the battle system is essentially complete."

"But effectively mothballed, I hear," Ivan said, "until such time as it can be distributed and commissioned as a *fait accompli*."

"So PDC get paid and they're happy. But it sounds like someone in the fleet weren't so keen."

Ivan's frown deepened.

"The fleet stayed out of reach to keep the testing alive before they could be officially told to stand down."

"This I already know," Ivan growled.

"When the regular messenger ship failed to check in, Admiralty sent a corvette to the test site. It found an automated buoy with a message file."

"Someone left breadcrumbs?"

"Trying to alert the Emperor and get the fleet intercepted before trials could be finished."

Ivan squinted at Bernie. "Surely the message file was encrypted."

"Naturally."

"You broke the encryption?"

"Didn't need to. The corvette's captain was one of ours. She brought the message back to us, we let it get picked up by its intended recipient." Bernie inspected his fingernails. "People are so much easier to break than electronics."

Chalwen secured the door to her office in the guard house. These few square feet hardly deserved to be called an office, she'd seen bigger prison cells, but it *did* offer privacy. Far beyond any standard arrangements.

Non-standard arrangements, installed by trusted members of the Bureau of Counterintelligence, included surveillance countermeasures and complete soundproofing. Most of the time, hidden microphones transmitted sound back and forth preserving the illusion of an ordinary wooden door. A coded instruction on her notepad, and the usual hubbub of working life in the nerve center of the imperial bodyguard faded to silence.

Once Chalwen was connected and her identity verified by a deep inspection of her surgically-implanted passkey, more layers of encryption and misdirection were applied from the other end of the link by more sophisticated comms than she had access to. The connection was as unbreakable and its path untraceable as it was possible to achieve.

Across the palace, the planet, and many other worlds of the Imperium, hundreds, maybe thousands, of individuals were going through similarly secretive measures.

Chalwen had no idea how big this group was. She doubted anyone did, other than the Emperor himself. It had grown since its early days under Empress Florence, and maintained its secrecy. Even though they were now working directly for the Emperor rather than against the old Empress, the empire they inhabited was no less hostile to their views.

A faint melody in the background confirmed that the link was active. Chalwen curbed her impatience as she waited. A tray of food cooled, untouched, to one side. Her mind raced at the possibilities. The summons she and Henri had received went far beyond the usual covert interactions of their local cell.

At last, the music faded to an expectant hush.

"Welcome, members of The Hidden Light, and thank you for your patience." Emperor Paul's voice rolled through the office. "It takes a lot to bring so many of you together, but extraordinary times merit extraordinary measures. This is as close to a full meeting of our membership as it is possible to arrange. Today I have some new developments to bring to you."

Chalwen's chest tightened. This had to be something big to warrant assembling the whole group like this. It was risky. So many people across the empire closeting themselves away simultaneously, so many connections hitting the network, there was always a chance someone would notice something odd.

"You all know how divided the empire is, factions with their own ideals and self-interest. Trying to steer such a ship is nigh impossible. Push in one direction and half the empire scatters to the four winds just on a matter of principle. The official hierarchy is at once all-powerful, yet curiously powerless to effect any real change. I issue edicts, the Assembly passes legislation, and most of the time, the planetary governments and interplanetary conglomerates simply shrug and carry on as before."

An electronically disguised voice broke in, "Is that the reason for the new Bill with the Assembly?"

The Emperor laughed. "It's true the Members' Interests Bill catches the public's eye, but the real work I want to talk to you about is far less visible. At least, in its early stages. If this work succeeds, it will create a drive in the right direction that will weaken a lot of the opposition we face."

A murmur of muted conversation rose then quickly fell as the comms system sifted out what was clearly incidental noise, not intended to address the group. Chalwen herself fought to hold her tongue, to still the questions she and everyone else in the meeting were dying to ask. The Emperor would announce his plans soon enough, but only when the background noise subsided.

Quiet descended. Everyone else seemed to have come to the same realization. Finally, the Emperor said, "I plan to hold a Conclave of the Families, to discuss common ground that might lead to lasting peace on our borders."

This time, the noise didn't abate, and the communications board on Chalwen's desktop lit up with status lights showing people wanting to speak. The comms techs moderating the meeting suppressed the chatter and recognized the first speaker.

The desktop showed a codename, Blue Sky. "Do you really think you can bring all six Family heads into the same room at the same time?"

"Yes, I believe so," the Emperor said. "It won't be easy. Nothing like this has happened in the last three hundred years. Even raising the suggestion in the wrong quarters at the wrong time would fan the flames of jealous mistrust."

"The Empress's approach to diplomacy didn't help," Blue Sky grumbled.

"Not just on the military front either," another voice cut in. "Her spies did a fine job of pitting one Family against another."

Paul said, "On the other hand, I've made the most of my early years showing a break with the past. I've been able to build enough bridges to at least broach the subject without getting laughed out of the room."

Chalwen struggled to process what the Emperor was saying. His announcement had come out of the blue. There must have been months, maybe years, of work behind the scenes to reach this point but the finely-tuned palace grapevine hadn't picked up a sniff of it. What kind of network did Paul have working for him to keep it so secret?

"Today we are honored to be joined by Shadowland, who has been the principal architect of this initiative."

Shadowland? Chalwen's heart thudded and her head swam. So the rumors were true! Lorenzo Skamensis, elder brother to Ivan and Paul, was still active in this group. The Emperor had hinted from time to time of help from beyond the borders of Skamensis space, but Chalwen had had no contact with or direct word of the exiled Lorenzo in many years. It seemed he'd simply dropped from sight.

Now here he was, in essence if not in body.

And that answered her own question. Lorenzo had a vast network of contacts spread not only through his own Family's space, but throughout the known worlds.

"Our Families have been in a state of conflict for millennia," Lorenzo's voice, like a ghost from years past, raised goosebumps across

Chalwen's scalp, "with allies today becoming enemies tomorrow, then friends again to turn against a common adversary."

That voice brought back so many memories of those fraught and terrifying days. The early days of Paul and Lorenzo's secret defiance. Covert operations, intelligence gathering, midnight raids, blackmail, even torture. Some of the acts she'd committed sickened her even now, but it was all with the goal of curbing Empress Florence's worst excesses.

"It's a delicate balance," Lorenzo continued, "negotiating here, pleading elsewhere, calling favors, and brokering promises."

Chalwen's face cracked in a broad grin. That was still the old Lorenzo.

"Each Family brings a long list of grudges that they insist get tabled for discussion, and opposing Families equally insistent that they'll refuse to attend if the topic is even mentioned. It's been a long road, started the day after Paul's coronation in fact. We are gradually aligning the Families into agreement on at least the principle of a meeting."

"How far have you got?" an anonymous voice asked. Chalwen couldn't make out the coded designation on the side of the comms display. Her vision was blurring while her mind raced.

"The Families di Brugui and Wala have agreed, but only if all six Families are at the table. Habradim and dom Calvino have yet to commit. It all hinges on the Firenzi. If they commit now, the others will fall into line."

Something was bothering Chalwen, though. In the sudden lull in the speech, she pressed the "talk" button and asked, "Given that this is such a delicate negotiation, why are you bringing this whole group into your confidence? The wrong word to the wrong person could sink this endeavor."

In the long silence that followed, Chalwen blushed unseen and anonymous behind her code name, but still uncomfortable. She felt foolish. How could she think to question the Emperor's judgment like this? And yet, it was an important question. She clung to that thought.

"A fair question," Lorenzo said at last. "Up to now we've relied on secrecy and a very small group of people to lay the foundations. This initiative is not yet public knowledge, obviously, and it won't be for some time. But too many people have been involved now for the confidentiality to hold. We'd be foolish to expect that. Word will leak out. Rumors will circulate. We don't know when, but it will happen most likely sooner than later." He paused. "I think I'll allow my brother to fill in the rest."

"I'll start by acknowledging the importance of the question that Tungsten asked."

Chalwen squirmed as the Emperor spoke—he'd spotted her code name, and though it would be meaningless to most of the group, he knew exactly who'd spoken—but she also felt a glimmer of relief at his words.

"I intended to touch on this anyway. First, there is a matter of trust. You are my champions, occupying positions at all levels across my administration. You all know a handful of your colleagues, people you can trust and turn to in times of need, so you know you are not alone. You hold the seeds of change. You are the sinews of resilience. That is why you were chosen to join this group. If I can't trust you, every one of you, then who?"

This was all familiar pep talk. Nothing new.

"But now it is a matter of practicality and timing. As Lorenzo ... Shadowland ... says, these talks of a Conclave have involved too many people on too many worlds for the walls of silence to hold. So you now have a vital part to play in keeping this ship on course. The moment this news reaches certain ears, there will be opposition. There will be people trying to sink us. You are my eyes and ears, alert to what's going on in the empire. Now that you know what's happening, you can help steer opinion, quell rumors, advise us of trouble brewing."

The Emperor paused to let his words sink in.

"Make no mistake, this will turn into a bloody battle."

Chapter 10

Gregor Pavlenko stared at the closet in the telemetry cabling room that one of his brightest and most reliable maintenance engineers had opened up. Dry heat crinkled the skin on his forehead in the cramped compartment and a tarry odor hung heavy in the back of his mouth.

Thick sheaves of multicolored wires twined up the center of the closet and branched out to connection points. Everything was neatly labeled, and matched the pages of schematics on the engineer's notepad. "So," Gregor said, rubbing his eyes and glancing over his shoulder at Una, "everything is as it should be?"

The young engineer cocked her head and flicked her eyes from notepad to closet and back again. "From a random audit of about three hundred sub-circuits, I'd say so. Everything I've seen so far is in order. The PDC contractors trained us on the new systems, and it all looks exactly as they said it would."

"Okay, what did you want to show us?"

"The trouble is things like this." The woman traced cables and components with her fingers. "This is part of the original feedstock flow monitor. Here it joins onto a new circuit, part of Maestro's system health monitor. Back to original wiring. New again. Original." Her fingers skipped from one section of the cabinet to the next.

"It's all interwoven," muttered Una. Her breath rasped hot in Gregor's ear.

Gregor huffed. "This means you can't treat Maestro like a bolted-on sub-system that you can simply unbolt again. It's so deeply-rooted, it's now an integral part of Violet."

"And," Una added, "the same goes for the system's programming."

"So, it would be a big job," Gregor mused.

"It's beyond big." The engineer shook her head. "I've studied the schematics for months now, and I wouldn't know where to begin unpicking something like this. Usually, with any system like a weapon or power plant, there's an obvious order to assemble it in, and a procedure to safely disassemble it again. But this thing's so riddled with feedback loops, start in one place and you'll fry equipment elsewhere, but start there and you risk a power surge here."

Gregor's shoulders slumped. "If I've got this right, you can maintain it, you can repair it when it breaks, but you can't remove it."

"That's about the size of it."

"That's bloody ridiculous," Una blurted out. "Can't we just disconnect the power first then pick it apart?"

"You'd think so, wouldn't you?" the engineer said. "But Violet has emergency internal power sources. Always has had. And those now suffer the same problem of interconnectedness as everything else." She glanced over her shoulder at the open hatch and lowered her voice. "Bigger problem is in the main power couplings themselves. Next compartment along, which is why I brought you here in the first place."

Gregor and Una exchanged worried glances as the engineer led them through double doors displaying electrical hazard warning signs.

Behind the armored internal walls of the compartment, the background noise of the warship faded, but the long and narrow space hummed with an energy of its own. The short stubble covering Gregor's scalp stood erect, each hair trying to distance itself from its neighbor. Next to him, Una's short hair framed her face in a shimmering dark halo.

With the practiced care of long familiarity, the engineer stepped over a fluorescent hazard line on the floor and stood perilously close to a set of cables and jointing boxes held away from the far wall by heavy-duty insulators.

"One of the main power couplings into plasma feed three." She pointed out a cluster of components crusting the nearest joint. "With the usual load of telemetry, of course, but here's what I can't fathom." She pulled out her notepad and shuffled through pages of schematics. "Readings are going into the main battle decision system, which I guess you'd expect. But everything in there's a black box. Vendor proprietary. I can't access it so I don't know how the information is used, but there are controls back out to systems I don't like the look of."

"Such as?" A queasy sensation crawled around Gregor's stomach.

"Blast doors and air evac in this room, for one."

Una frowned. "Most of the electrical and engineering compartments have evac systems. Part of fire suppression."

The engineer gestured to a set of sensors above the door behind Una. "Like that. Those systems are self-contained and locally managed. This new circuit is part of a network tapped into ship's environmentals." The woman gave them a puzzled look. "The *whole* ship. Why would Maestro need access to that?"

After Gregor thanked the engineer for her research, he and Una huddled together across a mess table. He toyed with his food half-heartedly. "It makes sense, in a warped kind of way, when you think about it."

Una screwed her face up. "How do you figure that out?"

"Well, a big part of the purpose of the battle system is to carry out the mission regardless of the crew. Admiralty might issue orders that people on board might object to."

"Okay, so?"

"So," he whispered, "what if the designers went further? Not just making the system autonomous, so it can complete orders without humans in the loop, but giving it the ability to defend itself from active interference?"

"You mean if the crew mutinied, and tried to sabotage the weapon—"

"The most obvious way being to cut off its power."

"It can retaliate against the crew?" Una gaped, then hastily looked around for any nearby eavesdroppers in the sprawling mess. "Seriously?" she hissed.

Gregor kept his voice low. He'd chosen a crowded section of the mess for this talk. The babble of voices should drown out their words. He was more worried about electronic eavesdropping than being overheard by a random diner. "First, look at what we know. What we've seen. It's as if someone deliberately designed the system to be unstoppable."

Una chewed her lip. "The way it's been built and threaded into the existing structure sure makes no sense to me. I mean, nobody builds systems like that. Nobody."

"So, either the designers were unbelievably incompetent ..."

"Or the integration was deliberate."

"And that opens up the whole question of motivation, because this is now more than a simple weapons project. Why would they do that? What was the goal? And"—Gregor stabbed the table with a forefinger—"given that mindset, what else did they sneak in along the way?"

"Okay, I see how you got there. It's downright sinister."

Gregor sighed and gazed down at his neglected supper. He stabbed a chunk of curried lamb and forced himself to savor it while he thought. "So, you can see what's got me worried. I would dearly love to be proved wrong."

Una scowled. "The last part, the self-defense bit, is pure conjecture. But even setting that aside, I can't imagine an innocent explanation for how thoroughly PDC locked us into their product. What's worse, how was this even allowed to happen?"

"We had no oversight on this project. The Admiralty gave the contractors free access."

"Do you think the captain has any inkling of this?"

"There's a good question, and I don't think I can just walk up to her and ask. One thing I am sure of. Whether or not the captain knows what's happening, or anyone high up in the Admiralty for that matter, the Emperor wouldn't have ordered this."

Una fixed him with a calculating look. "Not sure I'd pretend to know what's on the Emperor's mind. Surely *that* must be light years above even *your* pay grade."

Gregor squirmed in his seat. He longed to share his burden. Secrecy, playing a double life, had felt glamorous at first but now he just felt alone, and all too often these days this ship felt like hostile territory. But The Hidden Light took the 'Hidden' part of its name very seriously.

More seriously, Gregor hadn't truly known until now how dangerous this double life might become. He thought back to the spyware someone had dropped on his notepad. Whoever it was not only had resources, they wouldn't be playing games. He'd wondered, in the last few weeks, if the local ImpSec offices maybe suspected him of treason against the Emperor. If they knew he was part of a group that the Emperor trusted above all others, they'd back off. He'd be safe. But all parts of the imperial administration had factions whose interests only tangentially aligned with any one emperor's. If he crossed the wrong faction, he'd just become another accident statistic.

He had no choice. He had to find a way to pass on this new information.

He glanced at Una. From her concerned expression, his inner turmoil must be showing. He forced a smile. "Let's just say, I have contacts close to the Mosaic Palace. Don't ask me how I know, but I'm sure the Emperor wouldn't approve of what we've uncovered."

———◆◆———

"Magister, I have a direct hail from an unidentified craft shadowing our course."

Ivan looked up, startled, from the reports littering his desktop. Goosebumps prickled his skin. Nobody should be able to contact them directly without access to *Kirov's* comms signature, a highly classified piece of information.

"Elaborate," Ivan rasped, his mouth suddenly dry, "on exactly what you mean by 'shadowing'."

"They're paralleling our course," the captain reported from the command deck, "including a series of evasive maneuvers when they first made contact."

Ivan's thoughts raced. In the million cubic light years between Devonia and Magentis, finding them, let alone following them, should have been impossible. Hopping beyond light speed, both craft should have been invisible to each other. "How do you know they're shadowing us?"

"They're transmitting their location in real time."

"And how close are they?"

"Our primary fields are almost touching."

The goosebumps grew goosebumps. "That's not recommended practice, is it?" Ivan's voice was soft.

"Look on the bright side. If the fields interfered, we'd never know about it."

Small mercies, Ivan thought. He could picture only one person who might have this kind of technical capability. The bitch was showing off.

"Drop us out into realspace. I will be paying our shadow a visit."

What in Space did Honorina want this time? This had been quite a year for unasked-for contact. It couldn't be the Maestro project—that was all wrapped up as far as PDC was concerned—but the prickling unease remained. Something monumental must have riled the obese merchant, and thinking back to his conversation with Scipio Firenzi, Ivan suspected he knew the answer. He strode from his suite and arrived at *Kirov's* command deck just as the tactical plot and external visuals lit up with a close contact.

The captain swore, and the lieutenant at the weapons station tensed over her controls.

Ivan and the captain exchanged glances.

"Stay calm, everyone," the captain said. "Grand Duke, do you know these people?"

"I do."

"Friendly?"

"Hardly." Ivan couldn't keep the venom out of his voice. "But on this occasion we're in no imminent danger."

Deep in interstellar space, there was no ambient light to give them a good look at the intruding ship. Instead, imaging radar painted a ghostly rendering on the screen.

"That has to be as big as an *Enforcer*," the captain whispered.

It certainly matched the veteran Firenzi battleships in size, but there all resemblance ended. It was unlike any class of ship Ivan recognized.

"Look at the size of those tracking arrays." The chief engineer's eyes bugged at the screen. "I'm guessing that fucker can outrun a *Sword*. And those discharge vents ... they're packing serious power in that hull."

The comms tech called out, "Unnamed ship requesting the Grand Duke's presence via forward dock."

"Requesting!" the captain ground out. "Does there appear to be an option?"

"I suggest we acquiesce," Ivan said mildly, though his heart hammered. "I will board. Alone."

Docking tubes always made Ivan queasy. Within the confines of a ship, artificial gravity fields kept to a strict orientation. Here in the fifty yards of flexible tunnel, the vivid turquoise floor of the tube was still 'down', but the floor in this case curved up and twisted slightly to the right. The evidence of the eyes conflicted with the pull of gravity.

Ivan gritted his teeth and paced the length of the tube, emerging in a gleaming white airlock.

Beyond the airlock, he could hardly believe he was still on a ship. Ivan was well used to naval architecture, usually traveling either on board a warship or his own *Kirov*, which itself had been converted from a fast attack cruiser. His suite on *Kirov* was spacious and comfortable, but still largely bowed to the practicalities of warship design, with machinery intruding in odd corners and exposed ducts and wiring trunks festooning the ceiling. Ivan had never seen the point in concealing something that didn't get in his way, nor in pretending his quarters were something they weren't.

But the hallway that opened up in front of him wouldn't have looked out of place in an imperial palace. The first impression was of extravagant space. The hall was maybe thirty feet wide and at least as tall, and curved gently out of sight a hundred yards away. His feet were cushioned on a luxurious bottle green carpet. Tall bronze and crystal uplighters every few yards cast a soothing glow on sculpted ceiling panels. Even the air felt clean like a mountain meadow, with no stale flatness of endless recycling.

Despite its power and warlike capabilities evident on the outside, this craft had been built from the keel up to pamper its owner.

Ivan registered all this in a couple of seconds as he paused at the end of the hall waiting for an invitation to proceed.

A solitary figure, pale-faced and androgynous in white tunic and form-fitting boots and leggings, stood to one side. A servant? His guide? The expressionless person gestured down the hall, a disturbingly mechanical movement, and set off in that direction. Ivan shrugged and followed.

He couldn't decide whether his feelings at such shows of extrava-
gance were of envy or contempt. Regardless, it was all in keeping with
the owner.

As they walked, Ivan noted subtle details that betrayed the true
nature of their surroundings. In between doors, mirrors, and wall
hangings the occasional comms panel was recessed discreetly into the
mock-marble walls. At intervals, barely-visible joints in floor, walls, and
ceiling showed where foot-wide strips were designed to recess and allow
blast doors to slide across and seal off the corridor. This may look like a
palace, but there was serious function beneath the gloss.

At last, his silent guide led him into an antechamber. Wordlessly, the
creature signaled Ivan to wait, then disappeared through the far door.
Moments later, Ivan was ushered into a larger chamber and the door
closed behind him. Ivan felt ice between his shoulderblades, though
he carefully set aside questions of whether it was wise to allow such a
machinelike being behind his back. The greater threat, in all its fleshy
abundance, clearly lay ahead.

"Honorina Philip. Your surprise audiences are always a pleasure. I'm
just never sure for whom."

Honorina didn't bother to haul herself upright and there was
nowhere for Ivan to sit. No matter. He found it easier to think on his
feet.

It was impossible to tell the true extent of the room. Striped
awnings hid the ceiling, richly-colored rugs covered the floor, and hangings enclosed the space, swaying gently in artificial breezes. The whole
gave the appearance of a large tent, but there was no telling who or
what lay beyond the drapes. Honorina reclined on a carved couch, with
a camp table beside her. Lamps on poles lit the room, and a pierced brass
incense burner in the far corner filled the air with a cloying perfume.

The weapons dealer glowered at Ivan. "Your presence was necessary.
I don't often allow visitors on board *Bringer of Tears*, but I happened to
be in the neighborhood at an opportune moment."

"You do realize you only have to ask and I'll be happy to schedule
a meeting. Rather less melodramatic than deep space games of chase."

"As I said. Opportune."

"And you risked your neck pulling so close in to a hopping ship."

Honorina snorted. "Of course we didn't. We just made you think we were. Added incentive for you to stop of your own accord rather than us having to stop you." Ivan carefully managed his expression to avoid revealing shock at the power this implied, but she dismissed the feat with an irritated wave of her hand. "You have a problem."

Where do I start, Ivan wondered. But he simply eyed Honorina coldly.

"Your brother."

"*Your* Emperor, you mean?" Ivan had the satisfaction of seeing a flicker of annoyance cross Honorina's face.

"He is trying to rally the Families."

"I believe the civilized worlds call it a Conclave." Now *that* caught her by surprise. It was rare indeed for anyone to be even half a step ahead of Honorina Philip. "I know."

"Stop him."

Ivan inspected his fingernails. The first objective he'd recently discussed with Bernie Fischer had already been met. Honorina may not know everything that happened in all corners of space, but Ivan could be certain that any information she chose to act on would have been vetted to a hairs-breadth of certainty. And she wouldn't have risked intercepting him and bringing him on board her personal craft unless she was deadly serious. In fact—the sudden realization shocked him so deeply he had to clamp his teeth together to keep his disquiet from showing—in doing so she'd revealed a great deal about her ship's capabilities. Not something she would do lightly.

He was acutely aware that he couldn't afford any hint of weakness in front of this woman. She had her business empire to defend, and this Conclave—the prospect of widespread peace—represented an unacceptable threat. More to the point, she seemed to think she could order Ivan around like some lap dog.

Time to probe for more information. "Do you really imagine Emperor Paul has any chance of succeeding?"

"The fact that he's made so much progress without any part of it becoming known until now is telling. That's not a chance I'm prepared to take."

So, she regarded the threat as credible. It gave Ivan little satisfaction to learn that Paul's network had eluded Honorina's spies as well as Bernie's.

"I don't need to remind you that I don't take orders from anyone but our lawful emperor. Though you are welcome to suggest mutually beneficial courses of action." Ivan forestalled the expected eruption with an upraised finger. "I say this only so you know that events you will see unfolding stem from decisions already made, not from any sense of obedience. Suffice to say, preventative measures are in hand."

Honorina grunted. "And I shouldn't need to remind you that I will take matters into my own hands if your efforts fail to meet my approval."

Ivan gave a tight smile. "I think we understand each other."

Chapter 11

Year 8068, autumn

G regor scowled at his notepad. Traitorous piece of equipment. The intrusive routines were still there, watching his every electronic move, and probably listening too. Through his notepad, he could be sure his movements, purchases, and other interactions would be tracked.

Getting a message out. Easy.

Without being detected. No chance.

He turned his attention back to a detailed report on Maestro the maintenance engineer had prepared for him. The findings were brutal but factual, just as Gregor had asked. He added his own analysis of the threat to the battleship's operability. He had no illusions that the report would ever be read by anyone in authority, other than by the spies peering over his shoulder.

No mention, obviously, of the Emperor's order to cease work on Maestro. He couldn't risk revealing his knowledge of *that* order. Who knew which side his unwanted chaperones might support?

About that ... he thought hard. He could easily justify the work on this report, it was part of his job, but there was a risk of appearing disloyal no matter how objectively-written. Each side had its own perspective on what facts were acceptable. In the wrong hands this could be damaging to him, potentially fatal.

Gregor chewed the inside of his cheek and slapped a big "Draft" stamp on the front page. He added a page of brief annotations in flaring red: *Conclusions? Recommendations? Confer with Admiralty? Were the risks anticipated? Interested stakeholders? Clear further action with captain.* Random thoughts, questions, prompts, together they screamed *unfinished business*, uncertainty, and hints of career-preserving ass-covering. To be dealt with later.

The report held all the information he wanted to convey, but he had no way to send it anywhere. Any attempt to transmit it or copy it off the network would be seen and probably blocked. Maybe he didn't need to. He couldn't *send* it, but he could leave it for others to find. With suitable prompting.

Setting aside the report, Gregor pulled up *Wrath's* itinerary and his personal address book. He was due some leave, he just needed to find the right person to spend it with. Gregor wracked his memory as he scanned the list of names, trying to recall where his colleagues might be stationed now and matching them up to upcoming ports of call.

His face split in a broad grin as his finger hovered over one name in particular. An old comrade-in-arms from their distant cadet days. The grin softened as memories surfaced of the catalogue of pranks they'd cooked up between them, and misdemeanors committed while thumbing their noses at the authoritarian regime. They'd been lucky to not be caught at anything too career-limiting.

Perfect. And Lieutenant-Colonel Larry Marco was still stationed groundside, a regular day job in the dockyards. Regular hours. No family commitments, as far as Gregor knew. Gregor composed and sent a brief message. "Docking in Cendithor next month. Lining up a few days outdoor R&R and a bucketload of beer. You free?"

The hook suitably baited, Gregor filed the draft report in a corner of his workspace where it would quickly be backed up for safekeeping. Within minutes, copies would be distributed to various corners of the navy network. Because it hadn't yet been formally submitted to any authority, it hadn't yet received a security classification so still lay outside the more secure zones.

Within reach of people on the outside with suitable tools and access. Once they knew where to look.

The Clerk of the Floor intoned names and votes, starting with the poorest and most remote worlds and working up to the richer worlds. The votes from the districts of Magentis were traditionally announced last.

Chalwen squirmed with impatience. This archaic practice seemed to have no purpose. The votes had already been cast and registered with the Clerk's office and would be a matter of public record as soon as this interminable process was done. Why prolong the suspense?

Not that there was much suspense here. The vote on the Emperor's transparency bill was going as expected, with fewer than one in ten Members calling in favor. During the lengthy and acrimonious debates over the past weeks, all manner of reasons had come out in opposition. No one, of course, admitted to having anything to actually hide.

She looked away from the sparsely-populated Assembly Room floor—most Members, it seemed, preferred not to show their faces today and voted from the comfort and obscurity of their offices—and the growing tally of opposition displayed on screens around the chamber. Henri, at her side, appeared entirely absorbed in the ritual, looking down now and then to make notes on his notepad.

Unlike the chamber floor, the viewing galleries around them were packed. In the rows nearby, filled with palace functionaries, officials and business people, expressions mostly showed satisfaction or disinterest. People didn't like the thought of more work to do or more scrutiny of their affairs. But as she craned her neck and took in the sweep of the upper galleries the frustration and anger was tangible. That explained why most Assembly Members chose to be absent. This bill was popular among ordinary folk, fed up with entrenched corruption in the ruling elite. While she had sympathies for both groups, Chalwen felt sick at heart for Paul, also notably absent from the chamber today.

At last it was done. Forty-one in favor, three hundred and eighty-three against with five abstentions. A massive and embarrassing 'fuck you' to the Emperor.

Silently, they filed out with the crowd streaming towards the Great Vestibule. Henri tugged Chalwen's arm and they cut through a quieter corridor past the state rooms and banquet hall. They skirted the

Fountain Court and emerged into sunlight at the back of the concert hall.

"I don't know about you, but all this legislative palaver is thirsty work." Henri grinned and steered them into the shade of a portico where a servery dispensed refreshments to palace staff.

"The vote was a disaster! Why are you looking so happy?"

Henri smirked at Chalwen as he ordered two minted ice teas. "What did you imagine just happened back there?"

Chalwen slumped into a chair at a vacant table. "The Emperor just got his ass handed to him by his elected advisers."

She scowled at a group of clerks at the next table who turned with startled and disapproving expressions. Where does *your* allegiance lie, she wondered. She shook herself. She had to stop this paranoia. These days the palace felt like a foreign land with hidden threats around every corner.

"That's one way of looking at it." Henri placed drinks on the table and sat. "You do realize that passing the Bill never was the point?"

Chalwen squinted at Henri over the top of her glass. "The Emperor called in a lot of favors to get that Bill presented. He even, somehow, persuaded Ivan it was a good idea." She screwed up her face and took a swig. "At least, not a *bad* idea. Point is, he wouldn't have done that if he didn't want it to pass."

"Yes, it would have been a powerful tool in shutting off the flow of dirty money, but we were far more interested in the debate than the outcome."

Light dawned. "Rattle the cage and see who squawks?"

Henri grinned, a wolfish expression.

"I always find that dynamiting fish makes it hard to tell which are safe to eat, and which were already dead."

"Ah, yes. Not everyone opposing the Bill necessarily has something to hide."

"And you've taken that into account." Chalwen knew Henri's thoroughness well enough that this was a statement, not a question.

"Some opposed the Bill on a variety of idealogical grounds. Either they think that they can vote more freely without people checking where their money is coming from." Henri checked off the points with his fingers. "Or they think this is simply the start of a move to regulate the Assembly more strictly, a small step to further tyranny. And some just believe in privacy as a matter of principle. Those people are of no interest to us."

"Sounds like you already knew more than enough about Assembly Members' motivations."

"Up to a point. This confirmed a lot of what we already knew. But we were closely watching the ones we didn't know about. See which way they ran. See who they spoke to, and who spoke to them, in the lead-up to the vote. Even without knowing the exact content, the surreptitious in-person meetings and encrypted comms chatter threw up some most interesting patterns."

Chalwen glanced at the nearby tables for signs of anyone showing an unhealthy interest in them. She leaned closer. She suspected Henri had already said more than he strictly should, and there was more to come. She had no qualms about the glaring breach in security. This was not idle gossip, but two members of The Hidden Light sharing information in pursuit of the Emperor's business.

"There are nearly fifty targeted investigations launching right now." Henri's voice was little more than a whisper. "We've always known there was a shedload of dirty money washing through the system, but it's always been a needle in a haystack. Now we know where to shine the spotlights."

"So, your fishing expedition proved fruitful." She cradled her glass, feeling droplets of condensation trickle over her fingers.

"It threw up one set of connections that we always suspected but never realized ran this deep." Henri's tone had lost all trace of levity now. "Several arms consortiums hold far greater influence than we ever realized."

Chalwen sipped her drink to wet a sudden dryness in her mouth. "Most politicians don't want to be seen openly warmongering. In public they all claim to want lasting peace and prosperity."

"But their real fortunes are tied to ongoing conflict."

Another connection clicked into place. Struggling past a lump in her throat, Chalwen whispered, "They'd also have a vested interest in this Conclave failing."

"Worse, they'll want to ensure it never even starts."

Ivan lounged at the back of *Kirov's* command deck, watching the crescent of Magentis grow. The menacing ring of orbiting battle stations lay behind them, heavy artillery stood down by the Grand Duke's personal identity codes.

The remainder of the journey had given him time to think, and he was impatient to be back in the capital and at the heart of affairs. To be able to talk to his contacts in person, without committing words to the heavily-watched interstellar network.

His five months away, coincidentally missing the worst of the Prandis summer, were a necessary duty. The Grand Duke had to spend time in his fiefdom, to see and be seen, but they'd taken him away just as trouble was brewing. That was an unfortunate quirk of fate. Everything had seemed so calm and under control when he'd left Magentis. Ivan curved his mouth in a wry smile. Fate was teaching him the evils of complacency.

"We'll touch down in thirty minutes," the captain announced.

That, Ivan thought, was one of the benefits of commandeering and converting a small warship for a personal yacht. A fast attack cruiser was one of the largest vessels with landing capability, and it saved him the inconvenience of transferring to a ground-to-orbit shuttle. They'd land on the outskirts of the capital and he'd be in his office within the hour.

None too soon. There was a lot to catch up on, especially Bernie Fischer's progress with his sly sabotage.

Ivan shivered. He'd opposed Paul often enough, but all within the realms of normal political maneuvering. And he'd done a lot in his lifetime that would be a death sentence for anyone subject to the usual laws of the land. As a high member of nobility he was largely immune from such concerns, but this time he'd taken a step into new territory. Not even his rank would protect him from a direct act of treason.

In joining forces with Scipio, he'd committed himself fully to taking the throne or die trying.

Paul's approach to ruling was too weak. Popularity with the masses didn't count. The Emperor didn't seem to realize the anger he was riling up among the rich and powerful, the people who really counted. Without someone strong at the helm, it wouldn't be long before the empire tore itself apart and the Family Skamensis would be nothing more than a passing dynasty in the history books. Ivan would not let that happen.

Honorina Philip's threat of action had to be a last resort. The Philip Drayson Coolidge Defense Conglomerate, and other similar organizations, were powerful, but they also walked a tightrope. Families, freeworlds and many of the richer outworlds, dealt both openly and covertly with the arms suppliers. But competition between them was stiff. Contracts could easily change vendors and sources of revenue dry up if the buyers thought that a dealer was starting to play politics rather than pure business.

The Conglomerate's future depended on them remaining scrupulously neutral in their dealings. If it ever became known that PDC had made a direct move against a Family head, they'd be dumped in a matter of days.

The fact that Honorina even considered it showed how serious she was.

Yes, Paul had no inkling of the shock waves his ill-considered actions were raising.

Chapter 12

A shadow crossed Chalwen's peripheral vision. She tensed, and slowly lowered the dumbbells to either side of the bench she lay on, ready to drop them and roll into a fighting crouch at the first sign of trouble. She usually saw the gymnasium complex as neutral ground, unlike the canteen where brawls and hazing sometimes took place. All the same, she didn't like being approached while lying on her back, bench-pressing with a weight in each hand. She was vulnerable.

"I thought I'd find you in here."

Chalwen relaxed at the sound of Henri's voice. She lowered the weights all the way down, then swiveled herself to a sitting position. The weights room, a long and narrow space cluttered with benches and racks and free-standing machinery, echoed with the sounds of grunts and creaks and the swish of ventilation that couldn't quite wash away the sweat and armpit odor.

She glowered at Henri. "You should know better than to sneak up on me like that."

"Why? Here you're unarmed." He gave her an innocent look.

Chalwen huffed. He had her there. She'd never managed to best him in hand-to-hand bouts. Put a knife in her hand and she might have a chance. She'd opt for a beam pistol from a safe distance to be sure.

"Thought you might like a run to wind down."

It came as no surprise that Henri Chargon, spook extraordinaire, would have known exactly where to find her and how far through her routine she was. She'd planned on a few more sets with the weights yet, but in the mirrored wall she spotted Lieutenant Shan Bresk swaggering into the gym with his crony, Arnie Stokes, padding along behind like an obedient dog. A few laps of the parade ground suddenly seemed a more enticing prospect, even in the afternoon heat.

While she wiped down the bench with a towel, she murmured, "I guess this isn't a purely social call."

Henri jogged on the spot. "I needed the exercise—"

"Like a puppy needs a second tail."

"And I have news to impart. Some Light business." Nobody who didn't know about The Hidden Light would have made anything of the slight emphasis in the otherwise innocuous phrase.

Chalwen placed her weights back on the rack. Across the room, Lieutenant Bresk scowled at Henri. As a rule, guards didn't mingle with others from ImpSec, even though the imperial bodyguard technically came under ImpSec's banner as a branch of Internal Affairs.

Silently, she begged the surly lieutenant to say something, anything, that would give Henri an excuse to call him out. But Henri had a dangerous reputation and Bresk was too smart to try his luck.

Henri simply jogged on the spot, gaze fixed on Bresk, and with a faint smile curving his lips. She wondered what was running through Bresk's mind. Nobody here had ever beaten Henri Chargon in a fair fight, and as for the last person to try his luck at an *unfair* fight, well, after his unexplained disappearance the rumors had flown fast and furious. Rumors that Henri had neither encouraged nor denied.

"Let's go," she said.

Henri nodded and loped through the far door and up the stairs. Chalwen gave one last look at Bresk and Stokes, heads together and whispering furiously, before she followed and hastened to catch up.

Out the doors and onto the parade ground, summer had yet to fully relinquish its hold on the desert city. Chalwen's shirt was drenched by the time she slowed to Henri's easy pace. They jogged shoulder to shoulder for two laps of the ground until their breathing had steadied. Henri had judged well. They had the ground to themselves at this time of day.

At last Henri broke the silence. "Sea Breeze had his skills of diplomacy tested this week."

Chalwen glanced sidelong at Henri. Except when off duty, her place was with Julian. She had few opportunities to hear first hand what was going on in the Office of Deliberation unless the Emperor asked Julian to be there. Although these days he took the Crown Prince more and more into his meetings, he'd been preoccupied behind closed doors all week.

Of course Henri had more extensive sources of information.

"The Habradim accused Dom Calvino of dumping raw products and crippling a fragile local industry."

"They're always crying foul about something," Chalwen said. "Any substance to the talk? Either way, Dom Calvino wouldn't take accusations kindly." She chuckled. "Was it swords or pistols at dawn?"

"There was no talk of a military response, but you know how touchy the Dom Calvino get about their honor."

Chalwen shuddered. "There's a feud for life. At best, they wouldn't be speaking to each other for the next century."

"Exactly." Henri's expression was grim. "This wasn't your usual trade spat. It was a set-up."

Chalwen stumbled and caught herself, taking a few paces to settle back into her stride. She held her patience as they rounded the corner and jogged the long length towards the barracks, with its rows of windows and any number of hidden onlookers. Only when they again faced away from prying eyes did Henri continue.

"We tracked a shipment coming into Calvino space labeled as finished machine parts, part of a legitimate quota, then shipped on as bulk grain."

"Let me guess. It wasn't grain when it landed."

"Nor was it ever machine parts. It was raw copper all the time. Container labeling altered en route. Then when it arrived there was a discrepancy between labeling and manifests which Habradim customs officials spotted, and cried foul. It looked like Calvino was trying to sneak metals through."

Chalwen whistled.

"Thankfully, we were already on to them. They made the mistake of sourcing the copper from a Skamensis world, and it tripped some alarms. We advised both Families."

"So that was the end of it?" Somehow this didn't seem like something to keep the Emperor up at night.

"Hell, no. Both Families were already flinging accusations and counter-charges through diplomatic channels. It was ready to spiral out of control."

"Clearly it didn't."

"Paul mediated a peace. Showed them they were being set up, and bought back the consignment at top price, made reparations to both sides. Throw in a couple of minor trade contracts to show how beneficial peace and harmony can be, and they're more behind the Conclave than ever."

They jogged on in silence back towards the barracks.

"The real sweetener though, is this. A few corrupt officials on each side of the border were collared and handed over to the other Family to deal with."

Chalwen spluttered at that. "So, rather than being dealt with in the local courts, likely nothing more than a misdemeanor ..."

"They face a hostile court system and get hung out to dry."

"And both Families can wreak a bit of satisfying vengeance." She chuckled.

"Point is, this is what Paul and Lorenzo talked about. Someone is trying to spike any chance of getting the Families around the table. The battle has started."

———— ·•·•·· ————

Sun peeped above the roofs of the Mosaic Palace and lit the far boundary wall of the riding ring. The stables still lay in the shadow of the family quarters when Julian led Coal out onto the path.

Chalwen nodded to the guard escort fanning out at a discreet distance and clearing the way down to the river. Julian mounted and set off at an amble, while Chalwen jogged alongside.

Grand Duke Ivan waited for them on the bank. His own bodyguard led their mounts onto a flat-bottomed river boat. Chalwen was thankful to see no sign of Shan Bresk today. She found most of Ivan's squad easy enough to deal with when he wasn't there to stir up trouble.

She'd already conferred with the opposite squad leader and agreed for her team to manage the near side of the Meadow on foot while Ivan's mounted guard kept watch on the two riders. Most of her own team crossed the hundred yards of sluggish waters in a fast launch while Julian and Ivan exchanged greetings and boarded a more ornate barge. Chalwen followed with the last two of her squad, and took up station in the stern as the pilot cast off.

Chalwen glanced up and down the river, unable to shake off a sense of unreality. The tranquil scene contrasted so sharply with a profound sense of falling off the edge of a cliff.

Since her last talk with Henri, Emperor Paul had included Julian in more of his affairs so Chalwen had enjoyed more insight into events across the empire, if 'enjoyed' was the right word. Border skirmishes, populist movements stirring uprisings on remote worlds, prominent politicians and public servants ousted from office enmeshed in scandals, ill-timed leaks of sensitive and damning communications … the list was endless. Taken individually, there seemed nothing remarkable, this kind of thing happened all the time. But collectively, patterns emerged showing a hidden cohesion at work. Random events should work as often in Paul's favor as against, but the growing catalogue of seemingly unrelated irritants all worked to push in one single direction. An unseen hand was orchestrating a campaign to wreck any chance of the Families coming together.

Of course, Imperial Security monitored events and used their usual covert channels to head off anything that looked like it might lead to outright war, but their goals and their reach didn't go far enough to bring about the radical breakthrough that the Emperor was angling for.

The Hidden Light, and Lorenzo's extensive networks beyond that trusted group, was more active. At least, those members who were in a position to help. Henri, she knew, was neck-deep in collating intelligence and advising operatives across known space to defuse tensions. Chalwen herself felt frustratingly on the edge of affairs. Her one job was to keep the Crown Prince from harm, and that role afforded her no chance to make a real difference to the underground war of nerves that played out across the six Families.

IAN S. BOTT

From her post in the stern of the barge, Chalwen eyed the Grand Duke with distaste. He made no secret of his stance on Paul's policies. Given the chance, he'd take Family Skamensis back to the draconian days of the old Empress, and yet around Julian he came across as nothing more sinister than a doting uncle.

What was his game?

One thing Chalwen could see, Julian enjoyed his uncle's company. And Ivan had promised more regular outings like this one. Time alone with the Crown Prince. Her stomach knotted. Now *there* was an unhealthy influence if ever she saw one. At least Julian would soon be away for a few weeks, taking a trip to one of the border worlds to see some of the empire's trade connections first hand. All too brief an interlude. Chalwen glared once more at Ivan's back as the barge nosed against the jetty and Grand Duke and Crown Prince led their horses ashore.

If there was one glimmer of hope to lift Chalwen's dark mood, it was that—so far—the Emperor had succeeded in defusing the multitude of political and diplomatic upsets. It even seemed that the underhand opposition might eventually work in his favor. The other Family heads were starting to see the groundswell of events for what they were, and were growing wary of yet another obstacle in the peace process. And with wariness came a growing anger that someone was trying to manipulate them.

There were even signs that Josef Firenzi might throw his weight openly behind the Emperor. If they could achieve that, the rest of the Families would surely follow suit rather than risk being left out in the cold facing an alliance of the most powerful forces in known space.

Chapter 13

Miles of landing fields, docks, and machine shops carpeted Cendithor's landscape to the horizon as Gregor's shuttle made its final approach. A world of contrasts, a small civilian population scratched a living from the land on the far side of the globe but this continent was unreservedly navy.

Gregor strode down the shuttle's ramp, with industrial smog catching in the back of his throat. A ground car screeched to a halt a few yards away, and a short round man rolled out of the driver's seat. "Pavlenko, you fucking ship rat!" White teeth flashed through a thick growth of greying beard.

"Larry Marco, ground hog hop jockey!" The two friends met in a bear hug. Gregor glanced over Larry's shoulder into the car. "You brought company?" He should have expected it, but this complicated matters slightly.

Larry waved at the vehicle as his companions opened their doors. "Lieutenants bin Moser and Hofmeister. That's Josie and Garand, seeing as we're off the clock. Part of my maintenance crew. Pissheads both, and up for some outdoor stuff."

"What you have in mind?" Josie shouted above the roar of a departing shuttle.

"Who the fuck cares?" Garand answered. "Long as there's beer involved."

"Booked a bunkroom at White Sands," Gregor said. He threw his travel bag into the back of the car and shrugged. "Four won't be a problem. Not that we'll be there much."

They piled back into the ground car and Larry took off in a shower of spitting gravel. "White Sands. Three hour drive. See if we can make it in two." He grinned.

The road arrowed straight as a ruler across an industrial plain, past towering hangars and warehouses, low-lying offices and dormitories. Landing fields buzzed with shuttles and heavy transports. Squat bunkers of beam batteries protected ground-capable warships landed for maintenance.

"So," Josie said, "what's the plan?"

"Forgive her," said Garand. "Obsessive planner. Needs to learn to relax."

Gregor grinned. "The plan is there is no plan. There's plenty to do. Mind you ..." He paused in thought. "If we can rustle up a couple of spare grunts on resort there's a stuntag tourney tomorrow. Teams of six."

"Stuntag?" Garand piped up from the back. "What parameters?"

"Ten acres outdoors," Gregor answered, studying his notepad. "Woodland and semi-urban ruins."

"He wants the stun settings," Josie said, with a knowing leer.

"The tourney is professional level rules, so a few minutes' paralysis and the stun rounds will *hurt*."

"Yessss! Let's kick some ship rat ass."

"Hey!" Gregor yelled. "Senior ship rat here."

"Honorary ground hog." Larry laughed. "For the duration."

Gregor winced inwardly at this open acceptance and his own dishonesty. He had an ulterior motive for this whole escapade, as Larry would realize soon enough. He swallowed his guilt. Hell. It was still an outing. He might even have fun.

The navy yards ended with an imposing perimeter of heavy ground defenses, and the road rolled on through hills giving way to rugged mountains in the distance. Talk turned to mundane topics for the next hour, catching up on each other's news in the year or more since they last met. The road turned a corner giving a sudden and panoramic view across a glittering lake. The air tasted clean after the dust and chemical taint of the yards.

Larry broke the appreciative silence. "What do you make of the Emperor's peace talks?"

Gregor caught the edge in Larry's voice. He paused for thought. "Ambitious, trying to get five other Heads around a table together. Why? You worried about your job if the Families suddenly get along together?"

Behind him, Garand snorted. "If we're heading for peace, why's every warship within two hundred light years suddenly getting their drives and weapons tuned up? We've never been busier."

"True." Jovial Larry seemed subdued. "Hope for peace, prepare for war. Best make the most of this leave. There's storm clouds gathering. I can feel it."

Further talk gave way to mounting excitement as an overhead sign marked the gates to White Sands resort. A hundred square miles of rugged pursuits to burn off excess testosterone.

Larry parked outside the main resort office and Gregor signed for their bunkroom. "You two." He pointed to the two junior officers standing idle by the car. "Stow our kit in the bunkroom. Meet us back here in fifteen."

Gregor and Larry strolled through the foyer towards the booking office at the back of a gift shop. It was time to get to the point of this excursion. Gregor took a deep breath, and brought Larry to a halt with a hand on his shoulder.

"Remember the young training officer you fancied back in cadet school?"

Gregor pointed to the tablet clipped to his belt, and tugged his earlobe.

Larry stared blankly for a moment, then understanding dawned. "Those were interesting times, weren't they?"

"The drill sergeants had eyes everywhere." Gregor chuckled but the look he gave Larry said he was deadly serious. "I took big risks helping you two meet up without getting caught." He pointed discreetly to a rack of message capsules in a display alongside the door, and held out two fingers. "This outing is for old time's sake."

Larry nodded. He remembered the times Gregor had passed messages for him in those heady and dangerous days.

Weak with relief, Gregor said, "I thought we'd take trail bikes out to Slugg's Canyon this afternoon. Burn up some back country trails. Hope the swimming is still good out there. Then get wasted around a campfire and sleep it off under the stars." He was speaking for the benefit of any hidden eavesdroppers and Larry knew it.

"Sounds good." Larry grunted. "Fuck! It's been a while, hasn't it?"

Gregor stared. "Larry! Seriously? You live dirtside, you could be out here every weekend if you wanted."

Larry shrugged. "You know what it's like on base. You never think of being a tourist in your own backyard."

Gregor slapped him on the back. "You sort out the rentals and other shit, I'll pick up beer and something to soak it up with."

Half an hour later, with gear and provisions strapped to the back of rugged bikes, they sped through the resort complex and into the semi-tamed wilderness beyond. They picked a spot overlooking a sheltered lake, dropped off kit bags and cool boxes, then spent the rest of the afternoon biking and swimming.

Hours later, with a campfire crackling, and a supply of firewood stacked up for the evening, Gregor caught Larry's eye.

Larry gave a tiny nod. To the group at large he said, "Anyone up for a last dunk while we still got the light?"

Gregor opened a beer and settled himself on the worn trunk of a fallen tree. "I'll mind the fire. Got a report to finish off."

"Even on leave?"

"Even so." Gregor grimaced. "Privilege of rank."

Larry nodded and dropped his pack by the log. He winked at Gregor and tapped one of the outer pockets.

As soon as the others were out of sight, Gregor reached into the side of Larry's pack and retrieved a pair of tiny message cylinders.

Silently, he opened out the metallic film of the first cylinder and pulled out a stylus. Referring to his notepad, he transcribed the header details of his draft report onto the message sheet. A cryptic series of words and numbers, which he double- and triple-checked, it would mean nothing to most people. A navy officer would recognize the general format and realize it pointed to somewhere in a navy personal workspace, but they'd also realize they had no way to access it through network security.

The message appeared useless, but Gregor wasn't asking anyone to break into his workspace. On the second message capsule he wrote out details of the document's backup schedule. The vast, multiply-replicated archives were a much easier target for an outside hacker. Here lay an unacknowledged weak point in the system, never felt worth fixing because finding anything in the archives without knowing the header key of your target was like finding the right grain of sand on a beach.

Taken together, the two messages provided a suitably talented hacker with a relatively soft target for a virtual shopping expedition. Better still, even if the report itself got moved or trashed, its ghost would live on for months yet in the archives. Gregor added his Hidden Light codename to both messages and addressed them to an anonymous drop box used by the Light. He returned the capsules to the pack's pocket and put away his notepad. Larry, not under ImpSec surveillance, would drop off the capsules when they returned to base.

It was done. All Gregor had to do now was enjoy the rest of his shore leave, and pray to Unity his messages both found their way to someone who'd know how to read them.

Chalwen's head spun with the effort of tracking movements of people through the trade convention's cavernous main hall. Another field trip for Julian, off-planet this time to the border world of Stour, and the region's largest trade fair. Long avenues of stalls criss-crossed the stadium-sized hall, representing merchants from all six Families as well as many freeworlds and outworlds.

The palaces and city streets of Magentis had always presented a security challenge but they at least were familiar. Chalwen knew the ebb and flow of life on the imperial capital, and could spot undercurrents and anomalies in her sleep. This was a whole new level of complexity.

Doctor Vicky stayed close by Julian's side, quizzing him relentlessly on the history and importance of various foodstuffs and textiles, electronics and machinery, and the strengths and influence of the regions represented in the aisles they browsed.

Chalwen hung back, innocuous in civilian clothing. All eyes were on the Crown Prince and his uniformed escort, leaving Chalwen better able to survey the surroundings as a whole, alert to threats.

Julian paused to talk to a gruff sounding character, dark-haired and pale skinned. The banner over the stall identified him as a Firenzi trader.

Common enough, this close to Firenzi space. Two women at the back of the stall stood and bowed at Julian's approach, before sitting and resuming their own private conversation, poring over their tablets and ignoring the royal party. It took effort on Chalwen's part not to say anything at this glaring breach of etiquette. It would be interesting to see if Julian noticed the show of disrespect, but he seemed more interested in talking to the front man.

With a mental shrug, Chalwen resumed her scan of their surroundings, noting with approval the cordons her squads maintained around Julian. An obvious presence of uniforms kept the crowds at a manageable distance, while plainclothes guards mingled and stood ready to deal with trouble.

"If I understand you correctly," Julian said, "you don't have your own goods to sell. You're selling a service."

"Indeed, Sire. We manage a trusted infrastructure ..." The merchant coughed gently. "That is, warehouses and reliable transportation routes that other traders can use to move their goods to market."

The merchants' talk seemed courteous enough, but a glint in the man's eye raised Chalwen's hackles. She watched him surreptitiously from the edge of the crowd, senses alert to anything out of place.

Tara, the squad lead on duty this afternoon sidled over. "Something's bugging you."

"Can't pinpoint it," Chalwen muttered. "Something about this guy's manner. Take the lead when Chickadee moves on. I'll hang around a bit, see if they're up to something."

"Got it," Tara said. "And I can see these crowds are troubling you. Don't worry, we've got this covered."

The merchant, Callum Steinway according to his name badge, turned away as Julian, Doctor Vicky, and his guard escort moved on down the row. Chalwen spotted a roll of the eyes at Callum's colleagues and a rueful shake of his head. His manner no longer looked threatening, but Chalwen's curiosity wouldn't lay quiet.

She ducked behind a screen and found herself in a curtained-off backstage area running behind the stalls. A murmur of conversation filtered through the curtains. Callum and one of the women seated behind a desk at the back of the stand spoke in low voices in a Firenzi dialect. Chalwen strained to make out the conversation, close enough to Ploorbellin standard to be comprehensible.

"Spare me the airs and graces of the bloody imperials," the woman growled.

"Aah, the lad sounds harmless enough," Callum answered. "And he's too young to know any better."

The knot between Chalwen's shoulder blades unwound. The hidden animosity she'd sensed was nothing more than peer envy.

"The father's the one to watch," the woman continued. "He makes fine speeches too, but I wouldn't trust him far as I can spit."

The crawling under Chalwen's scalp returned full force. This was Paul they were talking about.

The voices lowered to a whisper. Chalwen crept closer, but could only make out the odd word. The unfamiliar dialect didn't help, but was that weapons and security they were talking about?

Footsteps sounded nearby on the other side of the curtain. Chalwen retreated hastily and slipped through an opening back into the main concourse. She caught up with Tara and confirmed the squad leader had matters in hand, then she found a quiet corner to open a line to the local ImpSec field office. A whispered series of codes into Chalwen's comms unit, and she had a secure connection to Magentis, and to Henri Chargon.

"Henri, I have an interest in a member of the Firenzi trade group here on Stour. Can you find out where they're staying?"

She gave him the merchant's name. While she waited, Chalwen said, "And one more favor, given your impressive skillset, can you dummy me up a business card? Just needs to stand civilian scrutiny, nothing too deep."

A faint chuckle sounded in Chalwen's ear. "Just like old times."

"Just like old times," she agreed quietly.

———•+•———

In the warm glow of a dimmed candelabra, Ivan folded his arms across his chest and relaxed into the embrace of a reclining chair. In his private suite at the Acacia Club, he felt more at home even than his quarters or formal office in the Mosaic Palace.

He closed his eyes, but not in repose. Against the red of his eye-lids he replayed his line of logic, plots and instruction held only in his mind, not recorded and not yet even spoken. The pieces fit together well. Bernie Fischer would be able to add polish and finesse, but the outline was sound.

A gentle tap at the door roused Ivan from his introspection. At Ivan's acknowledgment, a club steward ushered Scipio Firenzi into the room.

"Scipio. I was glad to hear you were here on Magentis." Ivan unfolded himself from the chair and gestured the younger man to a pair of antique couches facing each other across a crystal-topped coffee table. A second steward had already set out a tray with refreshments.

"You didn't think I came all the way into Skamensis space just to visit you at Greyspire?"

"Not at all. But a thousand light years is a lot of space to cover. No guarantee you'd be anywhere nearby."

Ivan would never describe himself as superstitious, but he couldn't help seeing Scipio's presence here and now as a good omen.

"Brother Josef wants a deeper trade presence in the heart of other Families' territories, not just on the border worlds." Scipio sniffed. "I'm his messenger boy."

"A role that allows you to go places and see people without arousing suspicion."

Scipio seemed to ponder this viewpoint. He shrugged. "Good for us, I suppose. Is there any risk in me being here?"

Ivan sneered. "Of course ImpSec will be aware that we're meeting, but no matter. We each have an army of business and political connec-tions to maintain. The odd fortuitous meeting will be lost in a schedule of legitimate appointments. Let them think what they want."

"All the same, you must have a damned good reason for inviting me here."

Blunt as ever.

Ivan studied Scipio pouring a horse-killing shot of Torremis Dark Roast into a standard teacup, which looked fragile in his meaty paws. Wordlessly, Ivan selected a demitasse for himself. Such unlikely partners, he mused. They had much in common, and yet were worlds apart in so much else. He steered his thoughts back to the matter at hand, sensing a growing impatience in Scipio.

"We've both fanned the flames of discontent across the Families, but my dear brother is proving too good at stamping them out."

"Then we need to up our game," Scipio growled. "You have thoughts?"

"Direct action to upset the Conclave is being thwarted, but I believe we can set up a killer blow indirectly." Ivan smiled. "It will take some delicacy."

"I can do delicate ... when I need to."

"It occurs to me there are still many people openly suspicious of the Emperor's motives. Lasting peace is a tantalizing carrot to dangle, but what if it turns out to be the bait to a trap?"

"But there *is* no trap, no ulterior motive," Scipio protested. "Is there?"

"Of course not, but all we have to show is the *appearance* of a trap."

"Very well." Scipio slurped from his cup and set it back on the table. "You've obviously got something in mind to spook the Families with."

"Think back to our talk at Greyspire. How did you feel when I told you how far our new advanced battle system had progressed?"

Scipio frowned in thought. Then he sat back and nodded.

Good. Ivan wondered sometimes at the younger man's intellect, but when it came to underhand dealings the Firenzi heir caught on quickly.

"It was a shock," Scipio muttered. "And it could easily be seen as a betrayal."

"That was my thinking. Imagine being approached by someone offering friendship, and then spotting an unsheathed dagger hidden behind their back. Imagine the cries of hypocrisy—the Emperor preaching peace while secretly arming himself for war."

"Hmm." Scipio frowned. "This battle system. I understand it's smart, but not a full AI?"

"Correct."

A sly smile spread across Scipio's face. "But we only have the Emperor's word for that, don't we? A word that's already tainted?"

"That's one hell of a specter to raise." Ivan chortled. "We can make use of that."

Scipio pulled a scroll from the inside pocket of his jacket and unrolled it on the table. He made some notes on the surface and studied the information flowing past his eyes. Eventually he grunted in satisfaction. "It's hard to find a single cause or an affront that would unite enough people together, but if we can sell this as Imperial treachery, that might just do it." He rubbed his hands. "The Humanity League will have a field day, and they enjoy huge support among a load of anti-science fringe groups. Then there's the Association of Masterful Healers."

"The medical researchers?" Ivan raised an eyebrow. He'd expected the medical community to be behind the peace process.

"You wouldn't believe the politics those scientists get up to. But one thing they have in common, they're paranoid about outsiders trying to steal their secrets. And they're vain enough to believe *any* conspiracy is all about them."

Ivan absorbed this while he sipped from his cup. "You've already figured out the kinds of groups we're after. Strong beliefs in meeting aggression with aggression, and powerful enough to force Josef's hand given the right provocation. The ground will need to be prepared carefully. Sow suspicions. Seed rumors. Prime people to be on guard for treachery. We want them deeply suspicious of the Conclave without openly opposing it ... yet."

"But when those suspicions get confirmed ..."

"You get the idea. I'll be ready with a media firestorm I can trigger at the right moment."

"We need them to react with anger, though, not fear," Scipio said. "They should believe this secretive research is a sign of desperate weakness on Paul's part, and that Skamensis is ripe to be taken."

"But it won't be enough to just rile up the Firenzi. Do you have enough reach within the other Families to bring them all around against Skamensis?"

Scipio's eyes widened, then he gave Ivan a calculating look. "You're after more than scuppering the Conclave."

Ivan hesitated. How much should he let Scipio into his confidence? Then he realized Scipio had already spotted the issue. Firenzi antagonism alone would bury the Conclave without directly involving other Families.

"My ambition does go further," Ivan admitted. "A *widespread* uprising on top of the scandal of secret and illegal weapons development will be enough to sink the Emperor for good. A motion of competence would pass easily in that climate, and Julian is not ready to take the throne. The Assembly will appoint me."

Scipio scowled. "I see *you* stand to benefit. What do *I* get out of this scheme?"

"Surely that's obvious?" Ivan's surprise was genuine. "Those same parties you mobilized against Skamensis, would they approve of their Family Head being taken for such a fool?"

The younger man pondered. "Deposing the Emperor will be easy for you with the Assembly running scared and howling for blood. It won't be the same easy task for me, but I can see some groups maybe stooping to more drastic measures. With the right helping hand ..."

Ivan laughed. "That part I leave to you. In fact, I have to leave much of this in your hands. Any hint of my involvement, and people will be suspicious of *my* motives in undermining Paul."

———•◦•———

From a seat in one corner of the lobby, Chalwen pretended to read from her tablet while actually studying the flow of people crossing the carpeted expanse into the Red Star.

Henri's research furnished her with Callum's accommodation and his regular out-of-hours habits. She was in luck. After a half-hour stakeout, her target emerged from the depths of the hotel and headed towards the bar across from her vantage point.

She gave the merchant a minute, then followed. He was easy to spot, propping up the bar and swirling clear liquid in a small glass. The first of many, according to Henri's prying into his spending record.

Trying not to appear too obvious, Chalwen strode up to the bar a few feet along from Callum, and caught the eye of one of the bar staff. "Vermandsee wheat beer, if you have it."

The barman nodded and reached for a glass from under the counter.

"Wait, do you have the dark on tap?"

Of course, Chalwen knew exactly what they had available, courtesy of Henri.

While the barman scurried off, the merchant gave Chalwen an appraising stare. "Bit of an acquired taste. But you don't sound like a local."

"A rare treat," Chalwen answered. "Can't get this stuff back home."

"Hmm." The merchant tossed back the glass he held, and signaled to the barman. To Chalwen he said, "You've tempted me. Just a shame they don't bring in a decent Vermandsee stout to add to the range. I might have a word with one of my colleagues about that."

"Let me get this," Chalwen said. "I'm glad to meet another aficionado." She paused, and feigned a casual tone she didn't feel. "Does that mean you're in the import business?"

Before long, she'd got the merchant talking freely about his business this side of the Skamensis/Firenzi border.

Of course, she then had to sell her own fictitious story in return. Her scalp prickled with the sense she was straying deep behind foreign enemy lines. "I have an established network across the heart of Skamensis space," she said, "with onward supply chains to Dom Calvino and Habradim.

"What lines do you deal in?" His eyes took on a wistful glaze. "The high end market must be strong in the capital region, with all that nobility kicking around."

With a sigh Chalwen said, "People are blinded by the glamor of luxury lines—fine textiles, artworks, exotic foods—but demand is fickle."

Callum gave a commiserating shake of his head. His interest was clear, but tempered by a wariness at the rich prize they were discussing.

"The way I see it," she continued, "there's always a market for everyday items. Food, medicines, machinery. But you need to transport and warehouse stock in bulk. Exactly the kind of operation you already have on the border worlds, but running right through the heart of our space in main centers of population."

Dammit! It looked like he knew all this already, but wasn't being drawn. How far could she afford to push? She tried a different tack.

"Of course, there's plenty of shippers selling transport and storage, if you like paying snooty imperials a premium for second-rate service." She scowled. "The closer you get to Magentis, the more fucked up the attitude. I'd rather deal with folks who know what it means to earn an honest franc, but nobody seems interested."

Callum grunted and swigged his drink. "I am looking for a couple of secondary sites to expand my infrastructure into, especially further rimward towards di Brugui. There's a lot of planetary representatives at the convention who know the security and real estate situation."

At last! There was the opening Chalwen needed. "Sounds like you're sticking to the borders. With all the markets in the heartland, what's stopping people like you extending your networks deeper in?"

A nervous glance over his shoulder, then Callum leaned in and whispered, "You didn't hear this from me, okay?" Chalwen nodded, wondering at his earnest plea. "I'd be risking my shipping license if this gets back to Imperial Security. They're twitchy and vindictive fuckers."

It was all Chalwen could do to stop from protesting. After all the years under Florence, ImpSec had earned a brutal reputation and deep distrust that would take decades to shake.

"I stick close to the borders so I can defend my assets if things get sticky."

"Defend?" Chalwen whispered back. "Who from?"

"Officially we're friends with the Emperor, but how long will that last? First sign of aggression and who gets caught in the middle?"

"Foreign nationals." Chalwen nodded. "I can see how that would make you nervous."

"I've lived on Stour for twenty years. This is my home now, and I'll fight before I let myself get rounded up into some detention camp."

"You really think that could happen?"

"It's happened before. People imprisoned. Assets seized. We are but chaff before the winds of war."

Chalwen drained her glass and signaled for a refill. Her mind raced. Her initial worries about this man had proved unfounded. He wasn't hostile, just scared. But the kind of mistrust she'd heard here raised a whole new set of worries. A sample size of one was hardly proof of a trend, but if others shared his views it didn't look good for the peace process. Politicians and the higher-ups could talk all they liked, but grassroots sentiment could easily undermine them.

Callum's expression brightened at the sight of a full glass. "At least here, Firenzi forces might have a chance of helping us, or I might be able to make a run for it if things got really bad."

"Listen, I have connections." Chalwen opened her notepad and pulled up the fake business card Henri had sent her. With a flick of her stylus she sent it to Callum's device. "If you hear anything more than idle rumors, let me know. And if things settle down and you're ever out Magentis way, look me up and we'll share a beer."

Year 8069, winter

Chalwen ignored rivulets of sweat trickling down her back as she strode to one side of, and one pace behind, Prince Julian. Prandis winters were barely cooler than summers, and muggy as hell. Doctor Vicky kept pace at Julian's other shoulder. Palace buildings loomed high around them as staff went about their morning duties.

The unexpected summons, interrupting Julian's morning lessons, unnerved Chalwen even more than the endless litany of civil unrest of the past few weeks. What could the Emperor want with Julian at such short notice?

A ring of regular palace guards kept the bustling crowds at bay in the courtyards. Chalwen's own staff were less obtrusive. Stationed on rooftops, at intersections, and mingling with the crowd, they formed a discreet and alert perimeter.

Past the concert hall, they entered the refined hush and soft air of the family office building. Julian's own suite lay here, but today they hurried down the length of the building and into the Emperor's adjacent offices. A liveried sergeant ushered them into a dim-lit side chamber, where a wall screen gave them a view into the Office of Deliberation.

Julian glanced, puzzled, at Doctor Vicky, who shrugged. "The Emperor asked you here for a reason. My guess is that today you're to be a silent observer." Julian frowned and settled on a couch where he had an unobstructed view of the wall. Chalwen was equally puzzled. If they were to observe a meeting through a comms screen, they could have done so from anywhere in the palace. Regardless, however strange the instructions might appear, you didn't question an urgent summons from the Emperor.

Chalwen scanned the room, hardly noticing the bodyguard taking up positions. Even here in the heart of the palace, they went through the same procedures as if they were entering an enemy stronghold. It was automatic. Chalwen would have noticed in an instant if they *hadn't* observed the protocols.

More noticeable was a young woman standing near the back of the room in nondescript civilian clothing. She had a stillness about her that would invite most people to treat her as part of the furniture, utterly innocuous. Even her pale skin and freckles, a rarity in Prandis, did little to make her stand out. Chalwen was not most people, and the woman's evident practice at blending in shrieked alarm bells in her mind. Spy or assassin. Likely one of Henri's secretive colleagues.

Chalwen eased herself towards the back of the room, where she could watch both Julian and the mystery woman. Her movements weren't stealthy enough. The woman glanced Chalwen's way and for a moment a pair of piercing hazel eyes made Chalwen feel utterly exposed.

The woman gave a faint smile and the tiniest nod. *I see you.*

Chalwen scowled back and, ignoring her own sudden self-consciousness, finished moving herself into position. The stranger knew what had been running through Chalwen's mind, but Chalwen still had a job to do.

From her new vantage point, she noticed that the nearby office wasn't empty. Apart from the usual ring of guards in ceremonial dress, Grand Admiral Gabriel bin Jovin stood in uncomfortable isolation in the center of the room. Chalwen felt a tug of sympathy. The rotund and florid head of the Admiralty had always seemed a decent enough, if rather dour, commander. Being made to wait on the Emperor's pleasure was never a good sign.

She glanced sidelong at the silent woman with renewed interest. Why would the murkier branches of ImpSec be interested in the Grand Admiral?

A flurry of movement on the screen. Emperor Paul Skamensis strode from a side door and sat behind his desk. The admiral bowed his head.

"Grand Admiral, do you recall a project the Admiralty was working on a year ago?"

No small talk, Chalwen noted. The admiral was in deep trouble in some way, and his barely-concealed flinch at the Emperor's words betrayed his anxiety.

"I'm sorry, Sire, could you be more specific? The Admiralty pursues thousands of projects in any given year."

Hah! Chalwen was no interrogator, but even she could tell the admiral already knew exactly what Paul was referring to.

"An automated battle system to be installed in the *Swords*." Somehow the Emperor kept his tone casual, as if reminiscing on last year's choice of menu for the midwinter festival. "A system that would be able to conduct a set of orders fully autonomously, taking decisions out of the hands of frail and fallible people. Something stepping dangerously close to the realms of generalized artificial intelligence."

The admiral paled. Chalwen felt her jaw hanging open. For all the sophistication of specialized electronics the empire possessed, true artificial intelligence was strictly off-limits to research.

"I gave the order last winter to terminate the project. So, Grand Admiral, imagine my surprise to learn that the project was, in fact, completed. Six months ago."

"Sire, the squadron conducted tests hundreds of light years—"

"I'm well aware of the fleet's disposition at the time," Paul thundered.

Chalwen blinked. She'd never before heard the Emperor raise his voice in anger. The Grand Admiral also looked stunned at the sudden fury, and staggered half a step backwards before bringing himself back to attention.

"Also," Paul continued, "that there were regular messenger craft relaying between the fleet and the nearest comms point. Any order, *given due attention*, should have taken a matter of weeks to be actioned, not months and too late."

The admiral started to stutter a response, trailing off into abject silence when the Emperor raised his hand.

"I can only conclude that my order was *not* given due attention. I await your explanation with deep curiosity, after you've given the question your deepest attention. If I don't see some courts martial in the coming weeks, of people who clearly acted covertly and outside their authority, I'll have to assume that you take personal responsibility."

The Emperor skewered the admiral with an icy glare. "Dismissed."

Grand Admiral Gabriel bin Jovin swallowed, bowed, and turned to leave.

What now? Chalwen wondered. The Emperor sat at his desk, hands clasped in front of him, lost in thought. She exchanged worried looks with Doctor Vicky, who was probably also wondering why they'd been brought here so urgently to witness this particular interview.

Paul didn't appear to move or give a signal. Maybe he'd previously given instructions, because he still looked lost in thought when the door opened and the sergeant entered and bowed to Julian. "The Emperor will see you now, Magister."

They trooped through to the Office of Deliberation. Chalwen acknowledged the squad leader of the Emperor's own bodyguard and stood to one side. Here was the one situation where she willingly deferred to another guard. She'd learned her lesson on boundaries back in Cravel Braz, but there were still some immutable pecking orders to observe. The Emperor outranked a Crown Prince, and so did their respective guards.

Paul stood and waved Julian and his tutor to a circle of chairs set around a coffee table.

They sat and waited expectantly. The strange woman had accompanied them, and stood to one side, seeming to blend into the background of fleur-de-lis wallpaper and Chensing pottery planters.

At last, Paul came out of his reverie. "Julian, what would you do if someone you trusted, someone you'd appointed to an important position close to you, betrayed your trust and went against your express wishes?"

Okay, so this was a lesson after all, and today it seemed was a day for getting straight to the point. No pleasantries. If Julian needed coaching, that was Doctor Vicky's domain. Paul was clearly referring to the Grand Admiral, but the question had been couched in more general terms. Chalwen relaxed and considered the question herself. What had the Admiralty, collectively, been thinking? How had they managed to defy the Emperor like that? They must have been under pressure from someone almost as influential.

Julian scowled in thought. "It would depend on how bad this betrayal was."

"Fair enough." Paul smiled. "Always the analytical one. Always looking for more information. Let's say it's bad. Something that could be argued to be treasonous. What then?"

"Then it's clear. They'd need to be punished. And I wouldn't want them anywhere near me again."

"So, should I have let the Grand Admiral walk out of here just now? Shouldn't I have had the guard take him away in manacles to be tried and executed?"

Julian stayed silent, sensing the test in the question. He grimaced. "Did he give the orders himself? And anyway, who else was involved? In fact, you said it was a navy project. There must have been others involved, maybe hundreds?"

Paul nodded. "Thousands, in fact. Though most would be unlikely to know of my orders in the matter."

"But how does it help to let him go? Couldn't you just hand him over to ImpSec to interrogate?"

Paul inclined his head towards the strange woman. "That's where Lady Laskenza comes in. Rather than question the Grand Admiral directly, we'll see who he talks to, who helps him spin a credible explanation, and what records he or others try to destroy."

"You'd risk them destroying evidence of treason?" Chalwen was so aghast, she blurted the words before remembering her place here.

The Emperor raised an eyebrow.

The quiet woman, Lady Laskenza, smiled across the room. "They'll even think they've succeeded. But there really is no risk involved. For us, anyway."

"Back to my earlier question." Paul turned to Julian. "You're right, of course, betrayal like that needs to be dealt with. But it's just as important to make sure you're punishing the right people. I leave it to my most trusted specialists in Imperial Security to get to the bottom of that mess."

Chalwen wondered if the enigmatic Lady Laskenza was a member of The Hidden Light.

"But looking to the present and the future," Paul continued, "this revelation presents a big problem for the Conclave."

"Is that why you were so angry?" Julian asked quietly.

The corner of Paul's mouth quirked. "Maybe, in part. I don't appreciate being undermined. What will the other Family heads think when they learn of this new capability? How can I stand in front of them preaching peace when my own military is arming itself for automated warfare?"

"Sire, if I may ..." Chalwen ventured.

Paul glanced at her, frowning at the breach of protocol, then nodded. Their old friendship and her membership of The Hidden Light allowed her some latitude.

"This capability exists. It's clearly the fruit of years of development, from long before you started talks of a Conclave, and who's to say how long it might have been lying dormant and confidential?"

Paul grunted. "You think I can claim plausible deniability? I don't think that will wash with already-suspicious Families."

"Maybe not, but it does give you a point of leverage. We can dismantle this battle system if all parties come to the table, and ensure the research never sees the light of day."

"But I *want* it dismantled. Not much of a bargaining chip."

"But nobody outside this room needs to know that."

The Emperor stood and paced the width of the office, deep in thought. "My views were already known outside this room, but you may have a point. Like it or not, we have a capability that the other Families would wish to see disarmed. Thank you, Lieutenant. You've provided much food for thought."

The formal address, so different from their talks behind closed doors as members of The Hidden Light, reminded Chalwen that she had to be careful. Too much familiarity with the Emperor would arouse suspicions. Paul had elegantly brought the discussion to a close.

The barge glided across the River Vishira bordering the southern side of the Mosaic Palace. Technically, mused Ivan, it wasn't a barge at all but a heavily-disguised air cruiser. Although it sat a few inches down in the water, it didn't truly float. Some past emperor in a fit of whimsy, and maybe suffering badly from seasickness, had commissioned this one-off craft to carry him in more comfort while maintaining the illusion of sailing.

Probably better for the horses, too. Ivan's own grey stood patiently beside Coal, Julian's gift from Crode, as the barge nosed into the meadowside dock and locked itself firmly in place.

Ivan and Julian mounted up.

Behind them, across a hundred yards of water, the teeming sprawl of the palace already seemed a distant world. Ahead lay three square miles of semi-tamed grassland. Millenia ago, this was an oasis in the middle of desert, around which the original town of Prandis grew. Now it was the Emperor's back yard, walled off from the rest of the city. Those walls were lost in the distance behind contours and stands of trees.

With an un-princely whoop, Julian kicked Coal into a gallop. Ivan gave a rare smile and followed more sedately. Julian was good on a horse, and the miniature Arabian had a forgiving temperament. The sun had risen high enough to light the terrain safely. As for other threats, squads of guards had already dispersed discreetly to provide a security cordon.

Julian was already out of sight around a bend in the trail leading up the bank. One of these days Ivan would treat him to a ride in proper wilderness, where you could roam for tens of miles without seeing evidence of humanity. But for now he contented himself with these increasingly regular early morning jaunts.

At least Julian seemed happy, and didn't chafe at the limitations of this park in the middle of the city.

Ivan nurtured these times alone with his nephew, the intelligent and *impressionable* Crown Prince. Away from the influence of his tutors, and especially his father, Ivan used these outings to gently nudge Julian's thinking into admiration rather than revulsion for the Skamensis heritage.

Of course, as the official heir Julian would stand in Ivan's way to the throne, but he didn't see that as an insurmountable obstacle. Ivan's vision reached further than temporary rivalries. Paul was the serious obstacle, but the job of emperor was dangerous and Ivan had the patience of a hunter. Once he'd set the empire back on its rightful course as unquestioned leader among the Families, with obeisance enforced by strength rather than flimsy treaties, he'd need an heir himself to take up the reins.

When Ivan caught up, Julian had stopped at the top of a bluff over-looking a green valley. An octagonal pavilion stood at the far end, three hundred yards away. Ponds dotted the valley floor, with paved paths skirting the banks leading to hides and jetties set on stilts over the water.

"It's so peaceful up here, this time of day."

There was an odd touch of melancholy in the young prince's voice today.

"Uncle Ivan, I've heard some people say we're close to war."

Ivan looked around, startled. "Where did you hear that kind of talk?"

"Just talk." Julian looked embarrassed. Had he been eavesdropping on unguarded discussion in his father's meetings, or listening to servants' gossip? "But it makes sense. Father is bringing the Family heads together to talk peace." Julian scrunched his face up in puzzlement. "Why would he do that if there was no danger of war?"

Ivan stared out across the acres of private parkland. Here and there on the horizon, the boundary wall was visible as a smudge of beige between trees. Beyond, glimpses of rooftops revealed the sprawl of the city surrounding them. He looked at Julian, boyish features patient and inquisitive with a maturity beyond his years.

"Your trainer has you practice set poses, and taught you to tune yourself in to what's going on inside you. You must be aware of how your body works just to stand still. Muscles in constant tension."

Julian nodded.

"What would happen if every muscle in your body suddenly relaxed?"

"I'd fall down."

"Just so. Muscles are working against each other to keep you upright, but you wouldn't say they're at war, would you?"

Julian laughed. "That would be silly!"

"Exactly so. There is tension ... *necessary* tension ... but that doesn't mean conflict."

"I see."

"The empire is like a person balancing, striving to reach ever higher. People are the empire's muscles, constantly in tension with one another."

"But not necessarily at war." Julian's tone was thoughtful.

"The Emperor is trying to bring about a more formal agreement between the Families, to reduce the tension."

"And you think this is a bad idea."

Again, Ivan was impressed by the insightful intelligence on show. He gazed back at the horizon. "Yes, I rather fear it is."

———— ·•·• ————

It was only a small strip of land nestled between a retaining wall on one side, that separated it from a little-used pathway down to the river, and the back of one of the blocks of staff quarters. Gates at either end hung on corroded hinges that nobody bothered to clean because nobody ever came this way.

It was a secluded but neglected corner of the palace grounds that Chalwen had come to regard as her own. Somehow it had been overlooked by the regular army of gardeners and cleaners, omitted from the detailed inventory of cross-indexed and code-numbered spaces that identified the ponds and courtyards, beds and boxes of foliage under their regimented care.

Rather than point out the obvious clerical error, Chalwen had assumed her civic duty to care for this forgotten patch. Her private retreat from the backstabbing intrigues of palace life. Over the last two years she'd cleared the unruly undergrowth choking the enclosed space. She'd tamed the creepers cloaking the wall of the staff quarters, though she left a good thickness higher up to obscure the view from the few windows on that face of the building.

Clearing the debris without being seen had posed a puzzle at first, until she settled on creating a heap at either end of the enclosure just in front of the gates. Anyone passing by would see nothing but an overgrown and seemingly impassable tangle. You had to squeeze through the gate and a few feet down the wall to find your way in. Then suddenly you were in another world, with paths of beaten soil meandering through neatly-tended beds.

Chalwen teased the tendrils of a miniature vine from the stem of a fragrant quince and followed it back to the root. With careful, almost regretful movements, she dug down to make sure she left nothing of the invasive pest in the ground.

"It's the eternal paradox of the gardener."

Although absorbed in her work, Chalwen had heard Henri's stealthy entrance past the screen of debris so his voice didn't startle her. She finished uprooting another vine and threw it in the bucket by her side.

"You have a passion for bringing forth life, but spend most of your energy killing things."

She glanced over her shoulder and got up from her knees. "Seems to ring true for both our day jobs too."

"I bring beer by way of compensation." He waved a small cool bag which gave a muffled clink.

Chalwen dusted off her pants and dragged over a pair of packing crates to sit on. "You don't touch this stuff often. What's the occasion?"

For the first time, she noticed his appearance properly. His normally clear skin looked baggy under his eyes, and his cheeks sagged, dragging down the corners of his mouth. Shoulder length black hair hung lank and lifeless. To cap it all, he slouched in crumpled civvies, a sweat-stained tunic and loose pants.

"I guess the beer is more for your benefit than mine. At least you haven't resorted to drinking alone."

"Yet." He sighed and twisted the top off a bottle. Chalwen reached uninvited into the cool bag and retrieved a bottle for herself, now genuinely worried.

At last, she broke the silence. "Did you sleep in those clothes?"

Henri swigged and nodded. "All of two hours. Sorry. I just needed a breather and some sane company for half an hour."

Chalwen barked a laugh.

"ImpSec's being swamped with all these investigations going on. Right now I'm running on empty, and so are most of the department. We do whatever we need to keep ourselves running."

"Sanity's not my strong suit, but you know where to find me if you need to unload."

"Appreciate it. The fallout from the transparency bill gave us more than enough to dig into, but at least that's regular work and being shared across the division, all above board. But we've now got a highly sensitive internal op going on too."

"The Grand Admiral?"

Henri nodded. "There had to be a lot of direct and indirect collusion within the service. That's always trickier to approach. So the load is falling to a very small team."

"There was someone I didn't recognize at that meeting who screamed covert ops. Do you know her?"

"Distantly. She's a specialist. Data mining and electronic countermeasures." Henri took a long swallow. "And if that wasn't enough, there's more Light business to attend to."

"The Conclave. More orchestrated sabotage?"

"Not this time. Or rather, yes that's all still happening but it's under control. It's making people nervous, though, and Sea Breeze is hoping to clear the logjam once and for all."

Chalwen gave Henri a quizzical look.

"He's bringing Josef Firenzi here for a face-to-face."

"To Prandis?" Chalwen almost dropped her bottle in shock.

"The whole effort is highly secret and venue still under wraps. I reckon Henriss. But definitely here on Magentis. Expect to hear something through channels soon, and I think he'll want Chikadee present, so you'll likely be in the thick of it at last."

Chapter 15

A rare rain shower the day before left grass vibrant and trees glistening. Damp earth scented the air, but even the fresh dawn today failed to lift Ivan's despondency. The best efforts of Bernie and whoever Scipio Firenzi was working with on his side of the border had failed to ruffle the Emperor. It seemed like Paul had an unparalleled diplomatic machine smoothing over disagreements and wooing fractious Family heads with his dangerous pipe dream.

And now, ominously, Scipio had been cut out of some secretive arrangements his half-brother was cooking up. Thankfully, the arrangements between Scipio and Ivan still proceeded to plan.

Scarcely a ripple marred the surface of the river, mirroring the ultramarine arch of a cloudless sky. The empty pit in Ivan's stomach told him it was the calm before the mother of all storms. He prayed he could ride out the whirlwind he and Scipio were preparing to unleash.

"No running today," Ivan called, as he led his horse onto the river bank. "Today we take a gentler tour of some of the less traveled paths in this park."

Julian gave him a puzzled frown, but something of Ivan's mood must have crept into his voice because the young prince stifled the expected protest. He meekly circled and came alongside as Ivan led them onto one of the labyrinth of minor trails twisting through thickets of ancient Veshi oaks, a rarity this close to the equator.

They paused in a sun-dappled clearing and Ivan checked that the bodyguard had stopped out of earshot. "Julian, remember the talk we had a few weeks ago, about the prospects of war?"

Here in this secluded glade, the thought felt like an obscene intrusion. But the timeless solidity of the centuries-old trees reminded Ivan of human frailty and impermanence. Barring some catastrophe, these slow-living plants would outlast dynasties.

"I did my best to reassure you that war is a long way off. But, I realized afterwards that there is always the threat of danger. There's no immediate need for fear, but it's best to prepare." As he spoke, Ivan wondered what intuition prompted him to share the secrets he was about to divulge. Was his bleak mood a result of facing the reality of his decision, or did the decision stem from his sense of impending catastrophe? Which was cause, and which effect?

"I know your bodyguards train you to look after yourself, and they have procedures and resources that you won't even be aware of."

"I feel safe with Chalwen looking after me."

That startled Ivan. "The lieutenant?" That was the one his own bodyguard lieutenant held in such contempt. As far as Ivan could tell, she was passably competent but nothing more. Certainly nothing to engender such trust. "Regardless, there are some secrets that remain private to the Family. Your father would likely say it's too soon, but you're getting close to your eleventh anniversary. I'd be remiss if I didn't give you another means to protect yourself, to stay safe if all else fails."

Ivan studied the youngster at his side. He must be burning with curiosity, and yet he held himself with remarkable control, regarding Ivan with an unnerving maturity and intensity. Did he pay such careful attention to all his lessons?

"What I'm about to show you is known to very few people. Not even your personal bodyguard. Do you understand?"

Julian nodded.

"I know the palace should be safe, and there are endless bolt holes and ways out. But if ever you find yourself alone and not knowing who to trust, trust no one."

They left the horses and proceeded on foot. Ivan pointed to a waist-high rock by the side of the path. "Pay close attention now. Ask no questions, just watch and remember."

As they passed, he rapped the rock twice on top and pushed into the brush beside the trail. Another rock. Three taps. A few feet farther and they were hidden from view, squeezed between thornbush and a sheer rock face ten feet high. A final tap on the cliff, and Julian gasped. An opening had silently appeared. He'd have to duck to pass through, but it was wide enough to admit a grown man.

Ivan reached inside and touched a panel, hastily withdrawing his hand as the entrance sealed again. "I've shown you enough. Do you remember that sequence? The taps in the right spots prime and activate the opening mechanism. Anything out of place, and nothing will happen."

Mute, eyes wide, Julian nodded.

"Come. We need to be back in sight before the guards get twitchy. I've two more to show you elsewhere in the park."

As they rode, Ivan said, "All you need to know is how to find and enter the hideouts. Once you're inside, everything you need to know will be obvious. There are standard control panels to close and open from within, monitors tied to external spycams, provisions for weeks if need be, and tunnels to hidden exits that can only be opened from inside."

"Why is this so far away across the river? This wouldn't be much use against an assassin. I'd never reach it."

Of course! Ivan remembered his own childhood. Training in personal security always dwelt on the up-close attacks. "It's still inside the walls, but if the palace itself is ever attacked with overwhelming force, safe hides like this should survive."

"You're talking about an aerial bombardment." Julian looked sick. "Surely our battle stations can deal with invading fleets?"

"War is unpredictable. Nothing is certain." Ivan understood the source of his dark mood. He was doing his best to scupper the prospect of a Conclave. That game was dangerous. He believed he could keep the Families off balance, just enough to humiliate and unseat the Emperor, without descending into all-out war, but nothing was certain. In the chaos of a direct assault on the planet, there was no knowing who would survive. Ivan was determined to be in a position to seize the throne, but what if he himself died? Whatever happened, there must be a Skamensis still to take the throne.

"Study your surroundings like you've never done before."

Julian stared at his suddenly earnest tone.

"Don't depend on your bodyguard to keep you safe. I'm sure you've slipped away and explored on your own sometimes?"

Julian's shy grin answered him.

"Good. This is no longer a game. Develop your self-reliance. Whatever you learn that others don't know could make all the difference one day."

"My treat this time." Chalwen pointed to one of a pair of insulated boxes on the ground alongside the customary packing crates. The makeshift seating was joined this evening by a round wrought aluminum table over which Chalwen draped a linen cloth.

"High dining this evening? Just as well I dressed up for it." Henri gestured to his slightly creased uniform, then reached into the cooler for a bottle.

At least you've gone to the trouble of finding a uniform, Chalwen thought. She took that as a good sign, and was relieved also to see a healthy touch of color in Henri's cheeks. She kept her thoughts to herself, and opened up the second box. "When did you last sit down for a proper meal?"

"Do such things still exist?"

Chalwen pulled steaming dishes from the hot box, and Henri let out a low groan as cinnamon, cumin, and aromatic vegetables permeated the early spring air.

He glanced at the distinctive logo embossed on one corner of the box's lid. "Sellick? I had no idea they did a full meal package like this to take out."

Chalwen chuckled. "You're too used to catering over on the west side, near ImpSec. Half the guard house uses Sellick when they get tired of mess hall food. But you need to be in her good books to get service like this." She produced a pair of sturdy enameled plates and steel forks, and began unclipping lids from the dishes.

The high retaining wall that bounded one side of the disused plot cast shade on the unofficial garden, and brought a welcome cool to the evening. A few brief cloudbursts in recent weeks ensured the plants would survive for a while yet, but they'd been badly neglected as Julian's schedule grew ever more intense, and the demands on the bodyguard increased in response.

While Henri loaded his plate, Chalwen studied his face. The last few months had taken its toll. She was reluctant to spoil the moment with talk of work, but time was short and they had pressing matters to discuss. "What news of the Emperor's investigation into the Admiralty?"

Henri took a few mouthfuls and a swig of beer before answering. "One thing's for sure, this was no spur-of-the-moment act of defiance. Once that project was under way, it was virtually impossible to stop. Most of the Admiralty administrators and contract lawyers that the Emperor accused of dragging their feet aren't to blame. They were handed an impossible task."

Chalwen gazed at Henri in shock, her serving spoon hovered over her plate for a few seconds before she resumed helping herself. "That makes no sense. Nobody, but *nobody*, gets the best out of an imperial contract."

"Well, the PDC contract pretty much had us over a barrel."

"How did that happen? Where were the Admiralty lawyers through all that?"

Henri leveled his gaze at Chalwen. "Where indeed? Some of them were undoubtably actively complicit. But tracking them down and proving it will be a game and a half."

"That suggests collusion right through the military." Chalwen's stomach lurched. Suddenly, the thought of food didn't appeal. This was too much like her suspicions of entrenched treachery within the palace grounds. Space! Was this part of some bigger conspiracy?

Henri's earlier words suddenly struck home. "Wait, we had a major new contract with PDC? I thought they were out in the cold after allegations of bribery a few years back?"

"Odd, isn't it? And remember all those other investigations we launched into Assembly Members' connections?" Chalwen felt cold at Henri's fierce and predatory grin. "Let's say, PDC has developed an extraordinarily long reach."

"People with those kinds of resources will be hard to nail." Chalwen speared a piece of curried lamb with ferocity to emphasize her words.

"We're peeling back the layers. Or rather, Simone is." Henri noticed Chalwen's puzzled glance. "That's the data forensics expert you met when Paul confronted the Grand Admiral. She's amazing to watch. All those records they thought they'd erased along the way? Brought out in all their damning glory."

"Is she part of the Light?"

"Don't think so. At least, she didn't respond when I dropped a recognition phrase into the conversation one lunchtime."

"She sounds useful."

"She wields her search tools like an assassin wields a blade. Grand Admiral bin Jovin is finished," Henri whispered. "There's no evidence he did anything overtly criminal, but he clearly turned a blind eye to a whole host of contractual terms that don't follow normal protocols."

"What would prompt him to do that?"

"I suspect he was bowing to pressure from a higher power. Not the Emperor, but someone higher than Grand Admiral all the same."

"That rather limits the possibilities," Chalwen said sourly. "But I bet there'll be no provable connection."

Henri grunted and shoveled another forkful of food.

"Surely now it's out in the open, Paul can simply dismantle the system? Write off his losses?"

"Even that's not as easy as you'd think. Right now we have an exclusivity clause. PDC won't sell the technology to anyone else. But if we disarm the battle system they're free to sell to the next bidder ... and that's not something the Emperor wants to see happen."

Chalwen chewed and nodded. "Paul could probably enact some decree or other to get around that, but even the Emperor is wise to work within the boundaries of the law."

"Truth deeper than most people realize." Henri ripped a flatbread into neat quarters and mopped up some sauce. "Few people appreciate just how little real power an emperor holds when he's swimming against the tide. Florence could dictate terms on a whim because she had the military, Imperial Security, half the Assembly, and most of the big interstellar combines behind her. That's a lot of inertia and active opposition."

Chalwen shivered. Just how far did those tentacles reach? "So Paul's got a real problem here, hasn't he?"

"What's worse, a team of weapons specialists has been looking at the installation."

Something in Henri's tone made Chalwen perk up and pay even closer attention.

"They report that the system is technically impossible to dismantle."

"That's not possible!" Chalwen snorted.

"Okay. Maybe not strictly true, but they were very clear that it would be easier to pull out the entire weapon system and install a new one."

Chalwen stared at him, aghast. "I won't even ask what kind of incompetents ... wait ..." Her mind whirled. "That was deliberate too. Part of a pattern. They sewed this up contractually *and* technically."

"It speaks to an uncommon level of dedication. They have a lot at stake, and won't sit still for any threats to their profits."

Chapter 16

Year 8069, spring

Surprised and groggy, Chalwen tumbled out of bed and groped for her notepad to silence its nagging beeping. It was the Firenzi shipper, Callum Steinway. As she accepted the call, Chalwen wrestled her mind into the persona of a Magentis trader still looking for business partners.

Her heart thudded as she realized she hadn't thought through what might happen if Callum ever *did* call her back. She honestly didn't expect to hear from him again, yet here he was. She glanced around her cramped room to make sure nothing was visible to show her ImpSec connections. Thankfully she wasn't in uniform. That could have been awkward. She sat up and positioned the tablet so her head was framed by the darkened window behind her.

"Oh, blast!" Callum said when he saw her. "I thought I'd got the time difference right."

It took Chalwen a moment to realize what he meant. She laughed when she remembered the fictitious business card Henri had made for her showed her home location in Henriss Garden, the other side of the planet. "You did," she said. "I happen to be in Prandis right now."

"Sorry to wake you. I just wondered how much news you get from the border worlds."

"Only what's in the public channels. How are things looking on Stour?"

"A lot of us are hunkering down, keeping a low profile." His voice lowered to a conspiratorial whisper, as if that would shield him from any eavesdroppers on the deep space network. "I'm fortifying my compounds. If things go sour and some local authority tries to confiscate my stock, they'll have to fight for it."

"What? You can't honestly fight off the government."

"Wow." It was Callum's turn to laugh. "You really do lead a sheltered life on the capital world. I'm not worried about planetary government. I can't beat them anyway and they mostly play by the book. It's the small fry and local thugs. They see an opportunity to muscle in and clean out a defenseless foreigner while the provincial garda look the other way."

"Sorry to hear that. I've heard nothing about this. Is there anything I can do to help?"

Callum shook his head. "Traders across space are looking out for each other. I remembered you said you had networks, so I called to warn you, if you have interests outside Skamensis space I suggest you do what we're all doing. Prepare for trouble. Things are going to get ugly."

"Is it really that bad?"

"I guess you'd see it differently from where you're sitting, but things out here are tense. Lot of speculation. The Emperor's trying to bring the Families together, but some say it's a trap. I honestly can't say one way or another. Here's the thing, though. I keep hearing the same warning: watch for the two-edged sword."

Chalwen sniffed. "A common enough phrase, surely? Double-edged sword, means something that presents dangers as well as advantages."

"No! This is maybe not best in translation. This particular wording is from stories long ago, and warns of treachery. Not an everyday phrasing, yet I hear it whispered again and again. And then I hear the same thing from some Wala colleagues. Exact same. Can't be coincidence," he hissed. "These rumors all come from the same source."

Chalwen's mouth hung open. She hastily closed it and grimaced as Callum's meaning became clear. "Someone is poisoning the well."

"And you can be sure we'll get drowned in the middle of it."

As she ended her call with Callum, a new thought hit Chalwen with such blinding force she almost fell off her bed. It took three tries before she could calm the trembling in her hands enough to call Henri. Cold sweat formed on her scalp and her mind raced while she waited for Henri to answer. All thoughts of sleep vanished.

Come on! It wasn't like Henri to take this long. The guy seemed to hardly know the meaning of sleep!

Again and again, the Emperor's interview with the Grand Admiral echoed in her thoughts.

At last Henri answered. His mussed hair and bleary look told her he really did sleep. Sometimes.

"Paul has to scrap Maestro, properly, before word of it gets beyond a few select groups in the Admiralty." Hastily Chalwen recounted her talks with Callum Steinway. "So, imagine you're one of the Family heads thinking about joining the Conclave, surrounded by suspicious nobles and politicians warning you to watch for treachery. You hear about this secret program right when the Emperor is trying to persuade you to lay down your arms, make yourself vulnerable ..."

Henri ran his fingers through his hair. "Space alive!"

"We need to alert Paul. Keeping Maestro a secret is going to blow back in our faces big time. We have to find a way to defuse that quark bomb."

"It's not that simple though, is it? It will take years to unpick the system. Either that or a complete rebuild. And then PDC will declare the contract voided and will sell Maestro to the next bidder."

"Damned PDC," Chalwen spat. "That fucking system is more a liability than anything."

"What?" Henri's eyes narrowed. He leaned forward, suddenly intense. "You can reach Paul, can't you? I know you can set up a private meeting without anyone knowing about it."

Chalwen nodded. This time of night it would be tricky and it had damned well better be worth it.

But the eagerness of Henri's mood infected her. He grinned. "I think there's a way out."

———— • ————

Morning sun slanted in through the windows of Ivan's sitting room, and lit the distant dome of the Green Throne Room in a blaze of glory. Breakfast waited on the cherrywood dining table.

Ivan seated himself, glad of the morning quiet, and poured a cup of tea. The peaceful scene matched his mood. Recent reports from Bernie confirmed that Scipio's rumor mill had taken root among the more suspicious and hostile factions both in the Firenzi and di Brugui camps. The other Families would soon follow. The powder keg was primed and ready to explode.

While sipping his tea, he opened his tablet out on the tabletop and perused the morning's briefings. All mundane, until a priority flag flashed in the corner of the tablet. Ivan frowned. Fresh reports from his spy network. Emperor Paul had issued a communique to all the Family heads through their diplomatic channels. Secure and private, not yet public knowledge, but that surely was only a matter of time.

As he read, Ivan's eyes widened in disbelief and mounting horror. Paul had officially revealed Maestro to the Families. A risky move, but how would the Families see it? A move like this, showing such vulnerability, was unprecedented.

"In the interests of full disclosure, and in a show of good faith," the communique announced. Paul described Maestro not as a fearsome weapon, but as an obstacle standing in the way of peace, a problem for all the Family heads to solve. A project started under Florence and concluded in secret, that Paul wanted no part of.

He'd placed control of the battle system under Imperial Seal, so no one but the Emperor himself could give it orders. Ivan snorted. That wouldn't reassure anyone. But there was more. He'd openly invited observers from each Family to inspect the installation in the *Swords*. Dammit! He'd positioned the fearsome battle system as an unwanted liability, talking up how badly it compromised the warships' general readiness and how difficult it would be to dismantle safely.

The blood drained from Ivan's face. He felt dizzy. Honorina Philip would be furious with this accusation. PDC weren't specifically mentioned in the communique, but their reputation was on the line nonetheless.

There was worse to come. Paul promised the Conclave would discuss adding this kind of automated technology to the prohibited list, too close to a general AI for comfort. If he succeeded, he'd neatly sidestep the contractual ramifications of removing it from use and prevent it from being sold elsewhere.

Ivan revised his assessment of Honorina's reaction. Furious didn't come close.

Worst of all, Paul had pre-empted and defanged Ivan's carefully-staged media onslaught.

With a roar, Ivan swept the tabletop clear. Porcelain shattered. Tea splashed. Food littered the priceless Monsk rug.

———•◆•———

Ivan drew heavy drapes across the windows of his private office, blocking out the view across the Fountain Court and the floodlit Legislative Assembly Room beyond.

Acoustic fibers woven into the plush fabric deadened any sound from inside the room, augmenting the layers of sound-dampening polymer in the windows themselves. Eavesdropping devices could pick up vibrations from reflective surfaces hundreds of yards away, but not when you knew how to foil such intrusions.

Electronic spycams and microphones were another matter. These suites of offices, reserved for the most senior members of the imperial household, were covered by state-of-the-art spy jammers provided by Imperial Security as a matter of routine. Equally routinely, Ivan knew, Imperial Security themselves felt entitled to bypass their own jamming service whenever they deemed fit. So Ivan deployed his own range of detectors and countermeasures. He scowled as he found and neutralized a new audio pickup that hadn't been there yesterday.

Private Secretary Bernie Fischer lounged across the desk from Ivan, casting an eye over his own electronic arsenal. "We're clean," he announced.

"So," Ivan said, "highest privacy, extreme sensitivity. Those were the codes in your message. We have maybe fifteen minutes guaranteed before ImpSec cuts through the noise."

"I've had reports of a credible threat against the Family." Bernie didn't mince words. "There's a lot of people out there who want to see you on the throne. The arms lobby in particular has grown impatient with Paul's pacifist leanings." Bernie's tone turned ominous. "The prospect of a Conclave reaching even the foundations for a peaceful settlement is a step too far."

"We already know that." Ivan's eyes narrowed. "And Paul's revelations about the battle system will have crossed a line for them. Do you really believe they're about to take matters into their own hands?"

"With extreme prejudice. They aim to remove Paul and all immediate heirs."

"Removing Paul is a necessary evil." Icy cold formed a knot in Ivan's stomach. "The rest of the family is off-limits." The ice turned to white heat of anger. Anyone who truly stood for him should *know* that. But then, he reminded himself, these factions only stood for him to the extent that he helped their own bottom line. Mercenaries all. No principles.

"Still a family man at heart, then?" Bernie's eyes twinkled. "You should have married. But that's why I thought you might want to intervene rather than simply let the plot run its course."

Ivan poured himself a cup of tea and sipped while he collected his thoughts. With a jolt, he thought back to his ride with Julian, barely three weeks ago, where he'd talked about personal safety and developing his own self-reliance. What prescience had prompted him to do that?

Mental gears, briefly stunned into inaction, started turning again. Something here didn't feel right. He teased out the anomaly. "Setting up an assassination is no small undertaking, and any of the consortiums would surely be taking an unacceptable risk. It would only need the smallest suspicion that they'd meddled in Family affairs and they're history. Besides, we still have ample opportunity to simply derail the Conclave."

"I wondered about that, too. But Paul is dodging all our attempts to disrupt his plans. And even if we stymie this one and what will Paul try next?"

Ivan nodded, thinking back to his conversations with Honorina Philip. "He's made his position unquestioningly clear. He'll always be a threat to their bottom line." And that is something Honorina Philip and her partners would not tolerate.

"Exactly so. And I think the affected business interests have been rather rattled by just how far he's progressed in such short time. He's not only serious, he actually has a realistic shot at success."

"I can see them being concerned enough to take dramatic measures. I trust you've unpacked the mechanics of this plot. Structure. Weaknesses. Options for us?"

"My information says there's only a small team involved here in the palace. PDC only has time to activate one sleeper cell. There'll be little in the way of backup support."

Ivan glanced at the time display on the desk. "Our countermeasures will be under threat," he muttered. "We'd better conclude this discussion."

"A word in the right place would stop it in its tracks. You could turn this information over to Imperial Security."

"And explain how far my network reaches?" Ivan shook his head. He had a fleeting sensation of hurtling off a cliff. Events moved too fast and too far outside his control. This was his *brother* they were discussing. Paul. Maddening, stubborn, misguided, but still his brother.

His brother, whose weakness threatened the foundations of everything Ivan lived for. He had no choice. "This threat could be the best opportunity I'm likely to see in a decade. If it really is a small team with little local backup, we can swallow their plot in one of our own."

"So, let someone else do the heavy lifting while you steer the ship?"

"As long as the ship is worth commandeering. Your assessment of their likelihood of success?"

"High." Bernie grinned. "I was going to say, frighteningly high, but I sense that is now a *good* thing?"

Ivan allowed himself a grim smile. "Indeed. It's hardly worth subverting a lost cause."

Chapter 17

Year 8069, summer

Wind keening across the coast at Cravel Braz had lost its winter bite, and early summer sun glinted on a far-off flawless sea.

"Josef Firenzi? Here? On Magentis?" Ivan suddenly felt foolish repeating the obvious, however impossible it sounded, but his agitation was very real. His horse skittered, sensing his mood.

Ivan calmed his own mount then reached across to help Bernie who was clinging to his saddle horn with a wild gleam in his eyes. Ivan had been expecting a more routine update on the plot against the Emperor, and Bernie's plans to turn it to their advantage. A cynical and vindictive thought crossed Ivan's mind that Bernie deserved the discomfort for springing this bombshell on him, but his official private secretary and secretly efficient fixer had many useful talents that excused his lack of equestrian skills.

The moors overlooking the town restored a sense of perspective. Ivan's bodyguard kept watch on the trail and surroundings from a respectful distance, ignoring Ivan's unusual outburst. They were well used to the lengths and subterfuges the Grand Duke went to when he needed privacy. Occasional cross-country rides with a man who detested the smell and sweat of horses was nothing unusual.

As they resumed a stately amble, side by side, Bernie gritted his teeth. "In two days' time. A Firenzi squadron is already standing by in a deep orbit, awaiting clearance to approach."

"And we're only just hearing about it? This must have taken a massive amount of organization."

"I believe the visit itself is low-key, and off the record. No announcement, and no official engagements."

"Even so, the security must be extensive. Surely something must have reached the ears of one of your spies."

"The preparations looked like just another drill, until the last minute."

"Yes," Ivan mused. "A security force kept in a constant state of readiness is expensive, but the benefits go beyond simple practice."

Josef Firenzi, meeting in person with the Emperor. Whatever Bernie said, the two Family heads must have been planning this visit for a long time. Many months at least. Is this, rather than Paul's moves against Maestro, what finally goaded Honorina into such risky measures as plotting an assassination? That was true desperation, but with Firenzi backing, the Conclave was assured to go ahead. The wavering Families looked to Josef for guidance.

A sudden insight struck Ivan. "You said the meeting is to take place at Henriss? The Emperor will be flying out there with his family. An outing they'd already planned, but they're hitching a bit of covert diplomacy under cover of that same trip. That's the point of attack. Honorina must have had some intelligence about this visit from the outset."

"It's possible," Bernie conceded. "Their plot is solid, but it did have the feel of something put together in haste."

"And our countermeasures are in place?"

Bernie smiled. "We have half the palace administration in our grasp. They're surrounded and they don't even know it."

Marcus Tyee flapped his hands, fussing like a mother hen over the gaggle of servants pulling clothes from closets and dressers. "Sire, please pay attention. The climate in Henriss is several degrees hotter than Prandis. You must be properly equipped as well as dressed for formal introductions."

"What's Josef Firenzi like?" Julian ignored Marcus and addressed the question to Chalwen. "This will be my first meeting with a proper Family head."

Chalwen suppressed a smile and took pity on Marcus. "That is why it's important to make a good impression, as Master Tyee is trying to help you do." She caught Julian's eye and pointed towards Marcus. "I'll answer your questions as best I can, but you must also attend to your packing."

Julian glanced at the row of servants, and pointed to each in turn. "Yes. Yes. No! Marcus, you know I hate that peacock design, it's too young for me now. And what happened to the space black tunic with the imperial acacia? The one I got on my anniversary? Add a sash and it will be perfect for the main formal reception. Oh"—he pointed again—"and three of those traveling cloaks. Now, Chalwen, tell me about Josef."

Chapter 18

Ivan Skamensis and Bernie Fischer strolled along the courtyard that ran beneath the walls of the main imperial family quarters. A courtyard was perhaps too tidy a name for the irregular open space, now teeming with guards and officials and administrators. The wall that surrounded the emperor's private garden towered to Ivan's left, offering a sliver of welcome shade from the early afternoon sun. People sat on benches idling their time in games and chatter.

Ivan made his leisurely way in the full glare of the sun. The heat didn't trouble him, and he wanted to be seen. He knew better than to ask Bernie any questions. Despite his heightened state of nerves and the enormity of what was about to happen, he had to trust that everything was exactly where it should be at this critical moment. He took a deep breath to calm mounting anxiety, and reminded himself there was no stopping the events now in motion.

Behind him loomed the round bulk of the emperor's personal hangar, while windows of the administration offices looked down on him to his right. A waft of spices hung in the air cutting through the heavy scent of baked earth. A steady stream of people drifted to and from the main kitchen block that peeped around the far corner of the administration center.

A sharp metallic bang broke through the lunchtime babble from somewhere beyond the imperial quarters. People stopped and turned towards the noise. Guards rushed through the stunned crowd.

Bernie looked thoughtful. "That sounded remarkably like a beam rifle's power pack malfunctioning in the confines of a troop carrier." He sucked his teeth. "Hope no one was hurt."

Ivan signaled to one of the guards who'd been shadowing him and Bernie. "Confirm the source of that noise, then reassure the Emperor and his family that there is no cause for alarm. Everything is under control. However, respectfully ask that he and the family wait in their quarters until I come for them."

As he watched the guard hurry away, under his breath he muttered to Bernie, "I hope no one *was* hurt."

Bernie whistled innocently and gazed off into the distance. "No one of consequence."

———•—•———

Marcus Tyee wrung his hands together imploringly. "Magister, it's time. You need to rejoin your family and be ready to leave."

Out in the middle of the riding ring, Julian kicked Coal into a canter.

Chalwen grinned to herself as she turned in a slow circle, scanning the surrounding skyline. She was often the one chivying Julian along to his next engagement, but today he was entirely in Marcus's hands. She and her team could concentrate on guarding, rather than timekeeping and nursemaiding.

Sun blazed off the sidings of the stable block and the imposing walls of the imperial family quarters beyond. To the north, the palace infirmary cast shadows their way. North and west, yellow walls, weathered and ancient and half smothered in vines, hid the on-site power and sanitation plants. A welcome breeze drifted from the river and square miles of green meadows behind her.

Julian turned towards the small group of onlookers and heaved a visible sigh. "I know. I'm coming. It's just that it'll be *weeks* before I see Coal again."

Chalwen's grin widened. In the last year, Julian and Coal, his gift from the Supreme Judge, had become inseparable. She still felt queasy at the time Julian spent in his uncle's company on their morning rides, but there was no denying the bond they shared.

A loud bang split the air from some distance off.

Chalwen whirled towards the noise, drawing her pistol. It seemed to have come from the far end of the imperial quarters, out of sight beyond the infirmary block. In less than a heartbeat she decided there was no nearby threat, but a cry behind her turned her attention back to the riding arena.

Julian writhed on the ground, screaming in pain and scrambling away from Coal's flashing hooves. Chalwen cursed. A stable hand raced forward to take the spooked horse in tow.

"Chikadee down. Medic to riding ring." The words into her transmitter came automatically through a dizzying rush of adrenaline. No drill this time. There may be no assassin nearby, but the Crown Prince was hurt and who knew what dangers might lurk under cover of the disturbance? And what the heck *was* that explosion?

A glance to either side confirmed the bodyguards taking up protective stations around their charge. Javarro, the squad leader, snapped crisp orders.

One of Javarro's squad knelt alongside Julian and started a field assessment. "Injuries, likely fractures left arm and lower leg, no immediate sign of head or body injury."

"I knew to tuck and roll," Julian gasped, sounding more offended than hurt.

"Patient is conscious and too damned responsive for his own good," the guard growled good-naturedly.

Chalwen felt a rush of relief that Julian was fighting back. "Glad your training kicked in, but we'll need to work on your technique once you're mended." Keep it light. Keep his spirits up. The pain and shock will knock him sideways all too soon. Chalwen managed a smile, despite the cold hollow she felt inside at seeing the Crown Prince, heir to a galactic empire, sprawled in the dust at her feet. No matter that it had happened so fast she couldn't have prevented it, she felt responsible.

Julian rolled his eyes then grimaced in pain when the guard adjusted his position and balled a rolled-up jacket under his head. "Father's going to be pissed, isn't he?"

"Let me worry about him. He'll be too relieved that it wasn't worse to be really angry."

A two-wheeled gyro-balanced stretcher carrier and a team of paramedics kicked up dust as they drew near. It was only a hundred yards to the infirmary, thank Space.

A few minutes later, the medical team transferred Julian to a bed in a private room, while a posse of doctors fussed with charts and equipment.

Turning her back on the quiet chaos, Chalwen led Marcus Tyee to one side. His plump face and soft skin led people to misjudge him. His face screwed up, seemingly close to tears, but the hard glint in his eyes almost hidden by soft cheeks said otherwise. He was looking for someone to kill, but lacked a target for his frustration. It was an accident. A simple, damnable accident. He needed to feel useful.

"Fetch a change of clothes from the Crown Prince's quarters. I'm sure he'll want to be on his way as soon as he's patched up."

Marcus blinked, then nodded and scurried away.

Somewhere outside, the sounds of vehicles and shouted orders drifted through the open window, bringing Chalwen's thoughts back to the cause of the accident in the first place. An explosion, somewhere near the senior family offices if she'd judged the direction correctly. There would be more injured coming in. Things must be under control otherwise the whole palace would be ringing with the sound of alarms by now, but she quietly tagged one of the guards to find out what had happened.

The palace's senior medical officer caught Chalwen's eye. Her fair skin and blue eyes made her stand out among the largely Prandiski staff even without her shock of bright yellow hair. "It is as the paramedic first stated." If the doctor's outward appearance suggested brash self-confidence, her manner was the polar opposite. Her tone was nervous and hesitant. Beyond that initial eye contact, her gaze flitted from notepad to patient to window, and back to her notes, all without looking at Chalwen.

Chalwen leaned closer to follow the details, shrouded in a strong Firenzi accent, as the doctor delivered her report. Foreigners, but they produced first class medics.

"Thank you, Doctor." Chalwen took a deep breath, wishing the the next conversation would be as easy, and thumbed her communicator to life. "Secure channel to Sea Breeze." She issued a code to confirm her authority.

The Emperor answered immediately, as if he'd been waiting for a call.

"Magister Summis, I have news to report. The Crown Prince has been injured and is being cared for." Her formal wording was chosen from a pre-arranged set of stock phrases, instantly conveying the situation—serious but not life-threatening, and under control.

The Emperor huffed. "Cut the formality, Chalwen, it's just the two of us in this conversation. Truthfully, how is he?"

So, Paul already knew something had happened. Not surprising that he'd have a few of his own lines of communication within the palace. No 'what happened?', it was straight to 'how is he?'

"They're setting his arm as we speak. Ankle is sprained but unbroken. Negative on concussion or internal injury. He's cheerful and enjoying the attention, like any eleven-year-old would."

"I suppose the medics want to keep him in their eager clutches?"

"Doctor Bertolli advised against travel until they've observed him overnight."

Paul swore under his breath. "I can't delay our flight. Miriam and I need to be in Henriss this evening."

"I understand. I'll explain the situation to him."

"You can escort him there when he's fit to travel."

"The Crown Prince will be disappointed. You know how much he looks forward to travel time with his family."

A long pause. "I know. But this is something I've been putting off all year. I think it's time the Crown Prince and I stopped traveling on the same flight."

"Understood." Chalwen heaved a mental sigh of relief. This was something she'd been badgering Colonel bin Merrin to broach with the Emperor. "I think it would best come from you that this is a permanent arrangement. That is a talk between father and son."

"Agreed." A hint of laughter crept into the Emperor's voice. "And to make up for his disappointment this time, just this once you have my permission to take him up in a two-seat fighter instead of a regular cruiser."

A smile creased Chalwen's face. What young boy could resist a flight in one of those sleek and deadly craft?

———— • • ————

Ivan paused on the balcony overlooking the emperor's personal hangar floor. The hangar lay open to the sky. Dark specks against dazzling blue showed the fighter escort forming up to accompany the Emperor's cruiser.

A quick glance around the perimeter satisfied Ivan that the few guards at their posts were all clandestine followers, thanks to a handful of surreptitious shift changes in the preceding week. Most of the normal guard complement had been drawn away by Bernie's diversion.

Bernie Fischer met Ivan at the bottom of the stairs, and led him across to the cruiser's open hatch. "We're all set, but I knew you'd want to review preparations in person."

A fair comment, but Bernie's anticipation felt too close to mind reading for Ivan's comfort. On the one hand, it was good to have some-one competent at the helm of Ivan's network, but on the other someone with such intimate knowledge of Ivan's plans and aspirations was always going to be a weakness or a threat ... sooner or later.

Up the ramp and to the right, the cockpit lay empty.

Bernie noted Ivan's gaze. "The reserve flight crew has been sum-moned. The pilot suffered a sudden onset of illness, and the co-pilot has taken herself off the roster as a precaution." He pursed his lips and nodded. "Very diligent pair, I must say. They completed the cabin checks and passenger manifest before they signed off, so there's nothing back there for the relief crew to check on. They should be commended for their dedication."

"Shame they'll be the obvious suspects for sabotage and treason." Ivan turned his back on the cockpit.

Bernie tutted. "Well obviously *someone* on the inside must have had access to the craft to slip a device past security."

Down a short passageway, the door to the main cabin stood open. Ivan glanced inside. Convincing body doubles of the imperial family, and the very real members of the Emperor's bodyguard were strapped into their seats.

Ivan could detect no whiff of the airborne drug that had killed the guards in the middle of their security inspection. He stepped inside and entered the code on the comms panel that would show the Emperor was on board and not to be disturbed.

As he pulled the door closed, hearing it lock behind him, he felt a twinge of regret at the loyal guards who'd just given their lives in the service of their Emperor. Their *current* Emperor, for a short while longer.

He nodded to Bernie. "There'll be no possibility of tissue identification, of course." It was a statement.

"Please!" Bernie looked offended. "These Firenzi incendiaries are in a class of their own. They won't even be able to conduct a body count, let alone identification, when this little baby goes off."

And that very fact will cast suspicion on the Family Firenzi. "Now, we must not be seen here when the reserve flight crew arrives."

Without a backward glance, Bernie slipped down the ramp and melted into the shadows at the edge of the hangar. Ivan hurried back up to the balcony and through the double set of armored doors leading out of the hangar. He strode past a lone guard—another of his loyal crew—and out onto the bridge linking the hangar to the Emperor's personal quarters. The hangar and quarters towered above the bridge, while the sprawl of other palace buildings spread out on either side.

As he entered the residence and climbed the time-worn staircase to the Emperor's quarters, Ivan had no need to fake his agitation. The plot was in motion and he was fully committed, for better or for worse.

His heart pounded when he reached the top of the stairs and saw the Emperor striding towards him. Dammit! Why can't emperors just follow instructions? With barely a nod of deference, he headed Paul off on the broad landing. "Sire, this is not safe."

Paul looked startled, then his face turned grim as Ivan steered him into an alcove, out of hearing of the guard stationed in the stairwell. "Brotherly familiarity has its limits. There had better be a good explanation for this."

"There is." Ivan glanced over his shoulder. "We have credible intelligence of a threat on your life. Your bodyguard is checking over the cruiser. Until they give the all-clear you need to stay put."

"Is this related to the earlier disturbance?"

"Too soon to say, but I don't believe in coincidence."

Paul stared at Ivan. His eyes narrowed. Footsteps clomped up the stairs several floors below, a small squad of guards approaching quick time. A faint whine from outside cut through the clatter. Paul gaped and hurried to the window at the end of the landing. "That's my cruiser," he gasped.

Ivan's hands snaked around the Emperor, one to remove his side-arm while the other ripped the communicator from his lapel.

Paul whirled around, realization dawning as he saw his own weapon aimed at him.

"Just a precaution." Ivan held up the communicator. "There's a localized blanket anyway while we secure the premises. Co-operate, and the family will not be harmed. You have my word on this."

"Your word," Paul spat. He glanced towards the guard, then caught Ivan's grim and determined expression. His shoulders slumped. "No. Ambitious yes, and jealous, always scheming ... but always a man of your word."

Ivan nodded as the squad of troops rounded the last flight of stairs. Two stationed themselves on either side of the Emperor. The rest waited by the curtains screening the main hall of the residence.

Without a backward glance as the guards escorted Paul away, Ivan hurried down the hall. He took a moment to calm himself. He pushed to the back of his mind the enormity of his actions. It was necessary. The empire would fall apart under weak leadership. He would mourn Paul as a brother, but the needs of the empire didn't allow him any latitude there. But he would not see the rest of the family harmed. They would live out a comfortable life in exile. That was his focus now.

He pushed open the door and saw Lady Miriam playing cards with Josephine and Florence. She looked up, her mouth twisted in distaste but no obvious suspicion.

"There's been a change of plans. You'll have heard of the distur-bance outside the concert hall a little while ago. These guards will escort you to a place of safety." Ivan scanned the room. "Where is the Crown Prince?"

Lady Miriam stood. "Julian is indisposed. And why are you bringing us this news? Where is Colonel bin Mellin?"

"The Colonel is busy, making arrangements for your safety." Ivan took a deep breath and moderated his tone. "This building has been compromised. It was the Emperor's wish that you accompany me without delay. Please, where is Julian. He needs to join you."

"You will not judge what is best for my son." The air between them turned frosty. "He is in the infirmary and will remain there until the medics release him."

Ivan ground his teeth but somehow managed to keep his displeasure from showing. They were running short on time. "As you wish, My Lady. But your own safety depends on haste." He released a pent-up breath when Lady Miriam finally nodded and beckoned the four children to follow.

Ivan excused himself as the guards ushered the family away, and turned to find Bernie Fischer at his elbow. Barely controlling his anxiety, Ivan pulled Bernie by the elbow further down the hall. "The Crown Prince is not with the rest of the family!" he hissed.

Bernie huffed, his lips pursed in a brief pout. "Well, I must say, that is inconvenient."

"Incon—" Ivan lowered his voice to a hoarse whisper. "Inconvenient? It's disastrous. He was injured at the last minute and taken to the infirmary instead of the family quarters."

"It's a complication, nothing more. I'll arrange for a discreet extraction and clean-up. Records will show that he was discharged in time to join the Emperor."

Chapter 19

Something from the corner of her eye bothered Chalwen. She looked towards the door, where light from the hallway beyond shone a warm yellow through translucent panels. Frustrated, she turned her gaze back to the room where Julian hauled himself gingerly upright in bed. The two members of the bodyguard also in the room remained alert but untroubled. Her attention wasn't on them, it was on her peripheral vision, trying to pinpoint what was nagging at her.

She had it. Not a presence, but an absence. A cold, clammy sensation crept over her. She inched towards the door and eased it open. There should have been a pair of palace guards outside, casting shadows on the panels, but the hallway was empty.

Completely empty.

Nobody sat at the nurses' station at the far end of the hall. No voices or clattering carts echoed from further away. The whole wing seemed deserted.

Waves of hot and cold now washed over Chalwen as she battled with indecision. There had been an explosion, something to do with a troop transport near the concert hall. Fatalities. People would naturally be busy, there was nothing to worry about. And yet, the guards posted here—household guards, she remembered, not from her own squad—should have still been at their posts. Could this be yet another drill cooked up by the colonel? No. They were here by accident so he couldn't have planned this, and the similarities to the eerie absence of security at Cravel a year and a half ago haunted her. She gritted her teeth and pushed her doubts aside.

Keeping the door fractionally ajar so she could watch the corridor, Chalwen thumbed her lapel transmitter and murmured a clearance code, listened, then softly spoke another series of codes. The general palace comms net was constantly monitored. The first code switched her over to a more secure line, from where she could more safely switch again to a private and encrypted channel before anyone listening could follow her. Even this was risky. Eavesdropping devices nearby could home in on her conversation, and encryption could be broken.

The wall at her side supported Chalwen when her legs weakened in relief at Henri's soft voice in her ear. A connection to the known world in the surreal hush. In those few seconds her imagination had run riot, picturing the whole palace complex mysteriously vacated. She swallowed hard before daring to speak, afraid that maybe she was already too late. "Henri, something's up. I think Chickadee is in danger. I need eyes on the infirmary block, and a safe route out of here."

The pause was longer than Chalwen would have liked. When he finally answered, Henri's voice revealed his worry. Chalwen's palms suddenly slicked with sweat. Henri was *never* worried.

"Things are definitely not right. Most of the surveillance in your area and around the imperial quarters is disabled."

"Someone doesn't want to be seen." And that someone clearly had friends in low places.

"I can't spot incomers for you, but safe to say your position is compromised. On the other hand, you're also invisible to them."

Chalwen signaled to the bodyguards. "We have to move," she murmured. "This place just became a kill box." She looked over to where Julian sat on the bed, staring at her with wide eyes. The bodyguards' expressions hardened. Chalwen breathed silent thanks that she'd assembled such a competent team. They'd already accepted the situation and were ready for action, no questions, no confusion.

"Can we defend this position?" Javarro muttered, straight to business.

Chalwen gave the room a cursory once-over but she'd already reached a conclusion. She shook her head. "We need an extraction, but I don't know who to trust."

"We're on our own then."

"Agreed. Henri, any movement in the service levels?"

"Quiet so far, and cameras still operating, which tells me they're not coming in from there."

Mind made up, Chalwen threw a cloak at Julian. "Not a drill." He swallowed and nodded.

Javarro helped him on with the cloak while Tara, the other body-guard on duty, kept watch.

"You and Tara will be our diversion." Chalwen pointed at another of the Crown Prince's cloaks draped over the back of a chair, thanking their luck that wiry Javarro was a similar build to Julian. "Act hurt. Take the outside stairs at the far end and make for the hangar. There should be a fighter escort left behind that I was going to take the Crown Prince in. If you get that far, take the escort and high-tail it out of here. If you get a chance, alert the rest of the squad, but trust no one outside of our unit."

Senses straining, they slipped through the door. All quiet so far. Javarro and Tara hurried in one direction while Chalwen led Julian the other way. A few yards down the hall, a door opened into a service closet. Chalwen ushered Julian in and eased the door closed. As she stealthily released the handle she heard several pairs of muffled footsteps pass by in the hall outside. Maybe they'd spotted the decoys, maybe not. Either way they wouldn't be looking this way. Yet. Chalwen was under no illusions that their hiding place would save them, but it wasn't an obvious escape route, especially not with an invalid.

At the back of the closet, a hatch opened into a cramped shaft and an iron ladder descending into darkness. Julian blanched, and glanced at his splinted arm and strapped leg.

"It's okay, I missed my morning workout. Please excuse the familiarity." The last was little more than an afterthought as Chalwen slung the Crown Prince across her shoulders in a fireman's lift. Without giving him time to react, she swung out onto the ladder and pulled the hatch closed.

She started down the ladder, counting rungs as she descended. Things went easily at first. Julian's weight seemed little more than a combat backpack. Chalwen pushed aside the fact that she wasn't carrying a backpack, but the heir to the empire, with a hundred foot drop beneath them. And her hands were getting slippery on the iron rungs.

At the first catwalk below ground level, Chalwen stepped off the ladder for a moment to wipe her palms on her pants and readjust Julian's weight on her shoulders. "Not far now," she murmured. No sounds from above. How long could their luck hold? She gritted her teeth and resumed their painful descent.

"Henri?"

"Still here. I've shut off cameras in service levels for the entire zone, but I doubt it will last for long. Tried to make it look like their own sabotage got carried away. Hopefully the fact that it's a whole zone won't give any clues to where you're heading." A pause. "Where *are* you heading?"

Chalwen swung onto another catwalk and into a service tunnel. She carefully lowered Julian to his feet. Yellow lights at intervals cast a sickly glow into the distance. A whiff of rotting grass filtered from gratings running along the tunnel roof.

"We need to get off the palace grounds. I'm going to try the river." Every sound whispered back at her in the dank air.

"Hiding out underground would be easier," Henri said, "until we can find a way to extract you, but you'd have to go deep to stay out of sight."

Chalwen chewed her lip and glanced at Julian. On her own, or with a fully able companion, she'd take that suggestion and chance the maze of ladders, catwalks, machinery and service sub-basements beneath the palace. But Henri would need to disable more of the surveillance network that infested all indoor spaces. And their opponents had at least one agent inside the security service. Someone would notice sooner or later, and figure out which direction they were going.

No. Her original thought offered the best hope. Above ground, cameras were fewer and easier to avoid. That just left human observers to worry about.

Then, they still had the problem of how to leave the walled grounds. Chalwen parked that problem for the moment. They had to put some distance between them and the infirmary.

A brashly-lit white-painted corridor lined with pipes, then a catwalk circling a dizzying drop into the depths. More corridors and ladders.

Chalwen supported Julian as best she could, and he bore the pain of his ankle with little more than the occasional grimace.

At last they emerged onto a catwalk running down one wall of a wide tunnel. Rushing water sounded through a series of pipes below them. They were getting close.

"Henri, I'm at the main fresh water inlet. How far does your blanket extend?"

"All the way to the river. No alarms sounded, yet."

The chill between Chalwen's shoulder blades deepened. In a normal situation, the Crown Prince missing from the infirmary would have the palace on high alert by now. The silence spoke volumes.

Several flights of stairs wound upwards. At least Julian could manage those without being carried.

As they neared ground level, Chalwen drew her beam pistol. "Wait here," she whispered.

The top of the stairs emerged at the back of a small workshop. A pair of metal hatches in the floor, each wider than a truck, covered an access shaft back down to the machinery spaces below. Workbenches lined the walls with tools stacked in racks above them. Windows along one side, and in the double doors at the far end, admitted shafts of sunlight.

The workshop was clean and well-kept, but a thin layer of dust and a faint smell of damp concrete gave a sense of abandonment. It must have been weeks since anyone last visited.

Chalwen's gaze roved over the eaves and door lintels, looking for signs of active electronics. All routes to and from palace grounds clocked visitors' passkeys. If anyone in the security office was looking for them, the electronic signature would leap out like a beacon. There were very few control points within the grounds, other than a few sensitive areas, but you never could be sure.

She returned to the stairs and signaled Julian to join her.

They crept out a side door into a narrow alley alongside the workshop. A road ran in front of the workshop, along the river bank.

Julian tugged on Chalwen's sleeve and pointed. "If we can cross to the Meadow, I know of a hideout we can use."

Chalwen frowned. A hundred yards to their left, a wooden pier jutted out into the flow with a pair of small launches tied up alongside.

She squinted that way and soon spotted the guards she was sure would be there.

"It's too open," she muttered. "We'll never cross the river unseen."

Worse, figures moved in the distance on the far bank. Beyond lay the royal meadows, thousands of acres of green oasis in the heart of the desert-bound city. Julian was right. If they could cross the river they could hide out indefinitely, but it seemed out of reach.

"Those are palace guards," Julian whispered.

Chalwen nodded.

"They'd let us across. Aren't they supposed to be on our side?"

Chalwen mulled over the question, a perfectly natural question to someone brought up in the cloistered life of a royal. "*Supposed* to be. And the likelihood is that they are on our side. But until we know for sure, we take no chances."

Julian looked disappointed, but not yet alarmed.

The grounds were eerily quiet. It was a surreal setting, outwardly peaceful in the afternoon sun. The scent of mint and lemongrass hung heavy in the air. Insects buzzed and rippled the sluggish flow of the river.

Still no alarms sounded. A trail of sweat trickled down Chalwen's spine. Could she possibly have misjudged? Maybe imagined the danger? Spooked by paranoia? She'd be humiliated and busted to latrine duty if so. But if she was right and she didn't act, the consequences were too dire to think about. She had no choice. Safety first.

"Chalwen."

She started at Henri's unexpected call.

"I'm picking up some chatter. Direct lines only, not the general net. Sounds like a covert pursuit going on around the north end of the quarters."

"Tara and Javarro," she muttered. "I hope they don't get themselves killed."

"You sent them out as a decoy? Smart. Looks like it might be helping."

She squinted out from cover again. The guards she'd seen by the jetty were gone, but there was still movement on the far bank.

"At least this side's quieter, but we still can't cross." She slumped back against the wall and screwed her eyes shut in frustration, trying to think.

"There's a way through the wall."

"What?"

Julian pointed in the other direction, where the boundary wall met the river bank. At Chalwen's sharp glance, Julian looked sheepish. "I used to go exploring on my own. Whenever I could slip away."

Chalwen grunted. "This I have to see." She signaled him to follow her behind a row of boathouses. A retaining wall on the palace side of the narrow road provided some shelter from prying eyes, and the road and boathouses soon gave way to trees and bushes right down to the water's edge.

Julian left the road and squeezed through a stand of bushes. They emerged into a natural clearing, blue sky above, but seemingly cut off from the rest of the world. Several natural tracks led off into deep gloom and overhanging branches. The ground beneath their feet grew soggy. Soon they found themselves in the shadow of the outer wall.

"There's some flood drains running through the wall," Julian whispered.

Chalwen gazed up at the wall, and along to where it jutted out into the river. "Makes sense. If the river runs high, you'd want to stop it getting backed up behind the wall. But they'll all be sealed off with gratings."

Julian gave her a sly look, and pointed to the nearest opening. "You'll probably want to have a word with the Grounds department after this."

There was indeed a grille barring the way, but the masonry on the near side had crumbled away leaving a gap just wide enough to wriggle through.

They stumbled in darkness through calf-deep water, Chalwen supporting Julian and keeping him from pitching headlong on the treacherous footing.

At the far end of the tunnel, the grille had been buckled inward. A decaying tree trunk almost blocked the way. "Must have been swept down years ago," Chalwen muttered. "I think I *will* need to speak to Maintenance when we get out of this mess."

They squeezed through the gap and into another thicket. Reeds swayed above head height, and Chalwen's boot squelched in deep mud.

Behind them, the palace wall stretched north away from the river, then angled around to the west before turning the corner that marked the far end of the grounds.

"Henri, we're out."

A low whistle sounded in Chalwen's ear. "And not a blip on any perimeter alarms. There's a loophole we'll have to look into."

"I need to get Julian to a place of safety until we know who we can trust. Somewhere no one will find him."

"Hmm." Henri hummed softly to himself. "Palace comms chatter is ramping up. No general alarm raised as yet, but people definitely know something's up. Questions are being asked. Only a matter of time—"

"Before the whole city is crawling with search parties," Chalwen muttered. "And it's a lottery whether we get found by friendlies or hostiles. We need to go to ground now!"

"No, we need to take control of the situation."

"How?"

"They took care to clear the site and suppress surveillance. Whatever they're doing—"

"Whoever 'they' are ..."

Henri ignored the interruption. "It was meant to be done by stealth. No witnesses. I don't think they'll risk a move out in the open."

"So we need to come out into the open." Chalwen's stomach churned at the thought. What if Henri was wrong? "Should I have just gone to the palace gates after all, and turned ourselves over to the guard?"

"Not visible enough. There's only a handful of guards actually at the gate. Surveillance compromised, and they could probably arrange for a whole guard unit on their side ... or a few unwanted witnesses to silence after the fact. No. You did the right thing. I've got something in mind that's harder to brush away. You need to make your way to ImpSec."

"Imperial Security? The main center? How does that help? We'd run the same risk at the lobby there as at the palace gates. We already know they've got help inside the building."

"For one, surveillance here is intact, so there'll be a record of your arrival."

"Unless someone can get at the logs."

"Agreed, but it's better than nothing. And second, I think I can arrange a large enough audience that there'll be no chance of covering it up."

"You going to send a mob to the front door?"

Henri chuckled. "That's not a bad idea. I'll see what I can come up with. Actually that might help draw some hostiles out of the way. They'll be motivated to intercept you before you reach the lobby, but that's only a diversion. You'll be coming in through a side entrance off The Shambles."

"I don't have clearance to get through those doors."

"I'm sending someone to meet you. Codename Bluebell."

"Bluebell will have a bit of a wait. We've got to cross half a mile of Riversedge before we get there."

"Keep the Crown Prince's identity concealed. What's he wearing?"

Chalwen groaned to herself. Julian's cloak screamed royalty. She motioned him over. "Sorry about this, Sire."

She whisked the cloak off his shoulders and inspected the inner lining. "Too clean," she muttered. She stooped and rubbed the lining in the mud. She brushed the worst off and inspected the result, then draped it back over his shoulders inside out.

"Won't pass a close inspection, but I doubt people will get too close. A guard escorting a vagrant into custody?" She gave a humorless smile. "Keep it tight around yourself, so the imperial colors don't show, and keep that hood pulled over your head."

They edged along the base of the wall, partly to stay under cover, and partly because the acres of land bordering the river here were a reed marsh. Eventually they came to the corner of the wall, and drier ground, and the edge of the city's sprawl of poor housing. Chalwen helped Julian haul himself up a steep bank and into a dark alley between the first rows of houses. The stench of urine and rotting vegetation was overpowering, but at least they were finally out of sight of the palace walls.

The air was still and oppressive in the narrow streets. In this labyrinthine slum few people were out, thankfully, and those that were took one look at Chalwen's uniform and gave them a wide berth.

All the same, Chalwen's scalp prickled. She could sense shadows flitting from doorway to doorway, never too close, but never far enough away. She checked the fastening on her holster and helped Julian as best she could while giving herself room to draw her weapon if needed. She tried to reassure herself that there was unlikely to be any danger of assault. The locals would simply want them gone, and attacking a palace guard would bring down unwanted attention.

After the first few alleyways, the squalor of the riverside slums gave way to larger buildings and cleaner streets. This was still a poor quarter, but better kept, and there were stores and inns here and there on street corners. And more chance of meeting a patrol.

Julian limped more slowly, leaning heavily on Chalwen for support. He hadn't complained, but his face was etched in pain. They still had nearly half a mile to go.

"This isn't going to work. If we're stopped by a patrol I need to keep up the pretense of escorting you to the nearest hostel. You can't be seen leaning on me like this. It'll look suspicious."

She cast around for a hiding place, and eventually settled on a small fenced yard off a side street, where a gate hung ajar. "Wait here and stay out of sight. I'll be quick."

Chalwen hurried until she found a tiny hardware store, and returned a few minutes later with a broom and a roll of industrial tape. She flattened the bristles and wound the tape around the broom head to form a padded rest.

Julian took the makeshift crutch and tested his weight on it. He nodded. "Let's move."

Fifteen minutes later, Chalwen peered around a corner to survey the windowless facade of the Imperial Security building.

The streets were busier here. Well-heeled citizens hurried past, casting disapproving stares at Chalwen's mud-splattered uniform and the vagrant wretch she had in tow. She put on her best air of authority and glared down anyone who looked too closely. But this was no good. They were attracting far too much attention, and the moment she stepped out from cover they'd be on camera, visible to any of the duty watch who cared to look.

Nothing for it, they had to trust that Henri had managed to arrange a safe entrance. There, a hundred yards away, a narrow portico sheltered a forbidding armored door. She tugged on Julian's arm and strode purposefully across and along the street.

At the door, she stood for a moment at a loss. "Henri?" she whispered.

The door swung open, whether in response to her plea or because someone was watching from inside, she couldn't be sure.

A florid face peered around the half-open door. "Bluebell," the man muttered.

"Chickadee," Chalwen replied.

The man grunted and beckoned them to follow. They slipped inside and down a flight of stairs. Julian gasped and stumbled near the bottom. Chalwen caught him and checked him over. His face was grey and beaded with sweat. Crap! This was no way to treat the heir to the throne. Fucking fine job of bodyguarding she'd done. If they got out of this alive, the colonel would have her hide.

"Not far," their guide whispered. They were in a long empty hall, green carpet, whitewashed walls. Steel grey doors lined the walls, unmarked except for cryptic room numbers. "Quickly now, we're on camera. There'll be people here any moment." He led them a few yards down the hall and into a wider cross corridor. A guard stood silently beside the single polished door in this hallway. Chalwen's heart thumped in her chest and she started to reach for her pistol.

"My colleague. It's all right."

Footsteps clattered from a stairwell further along. He gave a worried glance that way as he pushed open the door and shoved them through.

Chalwen started to protest, then gazed dumbstruck as a hundred pairs of eyes turned her way. The noise of conversation that had washed over them as they entered slowly died to an expectant silence.

They stood at the front of what looked like a theater or lecture room. Tiers of desks and chairs rose towards the back of the room.

"Holy shit, Henri," Chalwen whispered. "What have you done?" This was a place she'd read about endlessly but never expected to see for herself. This was the fabled operations room, nerve center of Imperial Security for the whole of Skamensis space.

The silence lengthened. Somewhere in the far corner, someone coughed.

Julian pushed back his hood.

The nearest officer gasped and stood, then bowed low. A rumble swept across the room in a widening circle as chairs were hastily pushed backwards and the rest of the security personnel, the security of the realm momentarily forgotten, did likewise.

Chapter 20

"The Crown Prince has been seen and identified, by a whole roomful of credible witnesses." Ivan's tone was grim and his mood even grimmer as he paced the deeply-carpeted expanse of his office.

"That's a bummer." Bernie's relentlessly cheerful manner grated more than usual. He caught Ivan's eye and seemed to finally catch his mood. He shrugged. "I guess we fall back to a defensible position."

"Thankfully, I believe in defense in depth. I trust there's nothing to link us to the arrangements we layered onto the original plot?"

"I'm confident we're clean. The Emperor and the family are safely hidden."

"Have you ..." Ivan struggled to phrase the question.

"Not yet, but Paul will be dealt with soon. You needn't know the when or the how. The rest of the family won't be harmed. Any minute now, all eyes will be on events a thousand miles away, then we'll move them off palace grounds as planned."

"And the original sponsors of this plot suspect nothing?"

"As far as they are concerned, everything went to plan other than the Crown Prince missing the flight." Bernie tapped his chin thoughtfully. "Well, almost everything. They did lose a couple of operatives in the line of duty. Tragic accident."

Ivan cocked an eyebrow at him.

"Once they'd planted the bomb, they were in the way of the team doing the body swap. I needed a diversion and I needed them gone." He held up one hand then then other. "Birds … stone."

"So, what about those last minute arrangements?"

"The impromptu extraction team was discreet. There are few traces to deal with. Shame the Crown Prince is so visibly alive and well."

"I'd hazard a guess the sponsors will take steps to tidy up that loose end."

"Very likely. I take it this time we sit back and let them proceed."

Ivan's gut lurched, but at this stage it was necessary collateral. His mouth twisted and he didn't trust himself to speak. He just gave a curt nod.

"You're genuinely fond of the boy, aren't you?" Bernie pursed his lips. "ImpSec will suspect foul play within the palace. They'll realize the cruiser was sabotaged here so that's what they'll investigate. They may even follow the trail back to PDC but that's not our problem. Meanwhile there will be heightened security, and Julian may yet live. What then?"

"In that unlikely event, we move to a new plan."

———— • • ————

The colonel's office appeared disturbingly ordinary after the bizarre events this afternoon. Chalwen squinted against harsh reflections from the windows of the senior staff quarters opposite. Outside, palace life continued as normal. "My first duty is to protect Chickadee. When I judged the location to be compromised and untenable, I chose to evac."

"You judged?" Colonel bin Merrin stared across his desk at Chalwen as she stood at rigid attention. "On what basis?"

"Things clearly weren't right. Palace guards and medical staff had left their posts." Put like that, it sounded incredibly feeble. No wonder the colonel looked fit to blow a gasket.

He waved his hand irritably. "With that explosion in the troop carrier there was a lot of confusion and a gap in co-ordination. Not something to be excused, but it happened. We're looking into it."

And I'll wager the trail will be just as confused, Chalwen thought sourly, with a lot of hasty well-meaning decisions that just happened to leave a gaping blind spot centered on the Crown Prince. But she bit her tongue. That line of thinking smacked of desperation.

"I've no doubt we'll uncover complacency or actions worth a reprimand. I'll have to tighten the training."

It seemed bizarrely amusing that the colonel so neatly mirrored Chalwen's own thoughts, just from a glass-half-full perspective.

"But *you*, Lieutenant ap Gwynodd, you are in a league of your own! This is an incredible breach of protocol," Colonel bin Mellin barked. "Can you imagine the uproar when the Crown Prince was found to be missing?"

"That is exactly the question." Chalwen's emotions cycled between relief, blazing anger, and bedwetting terror at the furore she'd incited. "We've been missing for over two hours."

The colonel squinted at her. "That's not possible."

"Exactly," she yelled, anger momentarily in the ascendance. "The alarm should have been raised within minutes. Why wasn't it?"

Chalwen had the satisfaction of seeing the colonel hesitate, uncertainty clouding his expression for the first time. She pressed her advantage. "More worrying, if you check with your colleagues in the palace guard house you'll find large gaps in surveillance records around the family residence." Chalwen suppressed a momentary pang and hoped Henri had managed to cover his own tracks well enough.

"Do you understand what it would mean if that turned out to be true?"

"That there was a conspiracy within the palace to abduct the Crown Prince." The words came out quiet and matter of fact, but the room seemed to darken as if a shade had been drawn over the sun. Blue sky still blazed beyond the windows, but the shadows seemed darker and more unreal.

Chalwen shivered. The colonel sat back, momentarily stunned at the blunt statement. It was the incomprehensible conclusion they'd both been skirting around, unwilling to put it into words. But now it was out there, the reality hung there between them, invisible but unavoidable.

"How deep would such a conspiracy have to run?"

Chalwen couldn't tell if the colonel was asking a serious question, or simply baiting a trap to convince her how ridiculous her paranoia was. She settled on a straight answer. "It wouldn't have to involve many people, but it would need collaboration in the right places, and a meticulous degree of co-ordination."

Colonel bin Merrin shook his head, exasperated. "I can't begin to tell you the implications if such a conspiracy existed. I don't see how I can even begin an investigation without looking like an idiot."

"Are you really suggesting we ignore the possibility?" Chalwen was aghast. She so badly wanted to be wrong, but too many things said otherwise.

"There is no 'we' here, Lieutenant!" He squeezed his eyes shut and rubbed them with a long sigh. "Oh, I'll do some digging, starting with those surveillance records, but it will need to be off the books. I'll have to call in some favors to do this discreetly. Needless to say, when it all proves pointless I'll bust you down to Private. And you're suspended from duty until further notice."

He glanced up and saw Chalwen's dumbstruck expression. "You can't be surprised. I've done my best to stand up for you over the years, but far too many people in the ImpSec hierarchy see you as a lost cause. Most of the time you come across as a moderately competent bodyguard, but you lace that with moments of sheer stupidity or clumsiness." He shook his head. "This really outdoes everything that's gone before. I'll do my best to explain this farce as another drill, or something, but popping up in the heart of the operations center like that isn't something that can be ignored."

The silence stretched out. Chalwen struggled to process what she was hearing.

A commotion outside broke the hush. An orderly, red-faced and breathless, burst through the door with nothing more than a perfunctory knock. Chalwen gaped and the Colonel looked like he was about to burst. The orderly took a couple of heaving breaths, holding his hand up to stem the tirade he knew was brewing, then blurted, "The Emperor ... cruiser ... gone down."

Colonel bin Merrin leapt to his feet. Chalwen followed him to the outer office where simmering bedlam reigned.

A comms tech, a young woman in her twenties, beckoned the colonel over. Her face was pale, and her voice was strained but steady. "Reports from the fighter escort all agree. Crossing the eastern coast of Traplinki, *Nightwish* blew up."

Chalwen felt faint. The colonel looked like he might be sick, but the enormity of the woman's words felt unreal. There had to be a mistake.

"Repeat and confirm report," the colonel said. How did he manage to sound so calm? "Positive identification? That really was *Nightwish* they saw?"

The tech talked to the distant escort, and glanced at her neighbor's console. "Confirmed. We've lost *Nightwish* from the plot. No transponder."

"Visual report?" Chalwen asked. "Who had eyeballs on them?" The colonel shot her a sidelong look, seeming to realize for the first time that she'd followed him out of his office.

The tech consulted her notes. "One of the escort reported a high intensity flare. Rescue teams are converging on the crash site, still half an hour out, but ..." She stifled a catch in her voice. "Escort already carried out low level passes and report little wreckage. The craft was incinerated."

The sense of unreality deepened. "That's not an engine explosion or regular on-board malfunction." She caught Colonel bin Merrin's eye and whispered, "That's a military grade device."

He turned back to the tech. "Any missile trail? Anything unusual on the plot prior to the explosion?"

"Negative, sir."

Under her breath, Chalwen murmured, "Had to be planted before take-off. Colonel, we *have* been compromised."

Jaw clenched, he took her elbow and steered her away from the line of desks. "I will remind you, Lieutenant, that my earlier instruction stands. You are suspended from duty."

Chalwen stared at him. *Seriously?*

"I imagine being relieved of duty will leave you with time on your hands. I expect you to use it wisely." His tone held a ferocious intensity. "In particular, I do *not* expect you to go poking your nose into irregular happenings here in the palace. The whole of ImpSec will be stirred up like a nest of fire ants, and I am duty bound not to question the integrity of their investigations. Not at a time like this. I will be too busy here to keep a close watch on you, so I trust you *not* to go around asking questions of your own. Do you understand?"

Chalwen narrowed her eyes at him. His lips formed a thin line and he gave a brief nod.

"Understood. I'll keep out of your way." She saluted, then said, "Just find out what happened to the Emperor."

Chapter 21

Sweat streamed down Gregor Pavlenko's face and saturated his shirt. He readied himself to serve again. His opponent, navigation officer Jerve van Verden danced on the balls of his feet. Gregor glanced over his shoulder at the older man, noting how he'd positioned himself on the court. He was expecting a standard serve off the front wall dropping into the far corner. With a flick of his wrist, Gregor instead sent the ball off the front and side walls to drop on the center line and behind him.

Jerve grunted and leaped across the court to meet it. He recovered well and sent the ball neatly skimming the side wall, so close Gregor had trouble scooping it out of the rear corner and returning the shot.

Mid rally, the ship's intercom burst into life with a piercing alarm tone. Both men stopped in their tracks and raced to the door at the rear of the enclosed court. It took a split second for Gregor's mind to over-rule the instinctive reaction. Belatedly he realized this was not a call to general quarters, but it did signal an urgent announcement.

Jerve had also come to the same realization, and stood, panting, facing Gregor with a worried look.

"Attention, ship, this is Captain Ivanka Borodina."

Gregor wondered at the uncharacteristic catch in her voice.

"I have received an encrypted transmission from Magentis, which the communications and security teams on board have spent the last half an hour verifying. The message is authentic."

Jerve and Gregor exchanged looks of alarm. "War?" Jerve mouthed silently. Gregor frowned and shrugged.

"It is with a heavy heart that I have to report that the Emperor and many members of the imperial family have been killed."

There was a long silence. Jerve's blank look must have mirrored Gregor's own expression. Coming out of the blue like that, it was too much to take in.

The captain resumed, her voice harsh and commanding. "Details are sketchy still and I have very little to share. We are still receiving reports which will take time to decrypt and verify. You'll understand that with such grave news, everything is being triple-checked for authenticity. I ask each of you to continue in your duties, as I know you will. I have one further thing to ask, which I know will be harder for you, that you refrain from pointless speculation and rumors. An investigation is under way, and facts will emerge over time. We don't know what the immediate future will bring, but as of this moment we are moving to a state of high readiness, repeat, high readiness until further notice."

***

Early morning in Prandis Braz, the sun rising above the palace rooftops hit Chalwen like an oven. A typical summer day in the capital. People went about their business, but the atmosphere was anything but typical. A few gave Chalwen curious glances as she passed, news of her escapade in the security offices had leaked out but that was eclipsed by the tragedy that had hit the Family. Most faces wore blank expressions of shock. Too soon for grief.

An accident. That was how the imperial propaganda machine was spinning it, but that fooled no one. The Emperor's craft was too well cared for, and the pilots too well trained, to allow for accidents. People were looking for a villain here.

The copper and glass frontage of the palace infirmary loomed ahead. With no official duties, Chalwen felt that a visit to the Crown Prince in a personal capacity wouldn't raise too many eyebrows. After yesterday's ordeal, he'd been moved back to the infirmary. Chalwen's scalp prickled at the thought, after this place had so nearly become a trap, but she was in no position to object.

Besides, if this place couldn't be secured then where else in the palace would be safe?

Up stairs to the wing where the private rooms lay, Chalwen was relieved to see a full bodyguard squad on duty with Javarro in charge, plus a squad of the regular palace guard.

Javarro headed her off as she approached. "You had us all worried yesterday, but it's a bit harsh of the colonel to pull you off duty." He walked Chalwen a few yards away from the door where Julian was being held.

"I think I failed another test," Chalwen said glumly. Space, but this was hard. When she'd caught the colonel's meaning, she hadn't realized it would involve deceiving her own staff. However, her distressed tone wasn't entirely an act. Something else she hadn't banked on was the vicious palace rumor mill working overtime. Even her own guard squads were unsure what had happened, and seriously wondered if she really had been jumping at shadows.

And she was unable to set them right.

It was enough to make her question her own judgment. But she *knew* she hadn't imagined things. Just because the enemy hadn't shown their hand didn't mean they hadn't tried. As soon as Julian was known to be safe, they'd simply backed off and cleared up all trace of their activities.

"You saw how quiet the infirmary was yesterday." She hadn't seen Javarro since then. She decided it would only be natural to chew things over, even if she had to keep up her pretense of ignorance. "There's no way everyone would have been pulled away from this wing with the Crown Prince here. That's totally against protocol. Don't you think that was suspicious?"

That's right, make it look like she was seeking reassurance. Chalwen needed to know what the palace grapevine was saying. Someone might have let slip something they shouldn't.

"I don't know what to think." Javarro looked distressed. "Me and Tara made it to the hangar okay. No one tried to intercept us, but the palace guards wouldn't let us in the hangar. Heightened security, they said, after the accident in the troop carrier. Everyone was twitchy, that's all."

"But of course, there was dirty business going on after all, wasn't there?" Chalwen didn't mention the running feet in the hallway after she and Julian had hidden, or the sabotaged surveillance across large quarters of the palace. Javarro knew nothing about that.

"The word in the barracks is someone sabotaged the Emperor's cruiser," Javarro muttered under his breath. "But what does that have to do with the Crown Prince?"

What indeed? Everyone seemed to think the Emperor was the target, the rest of the family happened to be in the way, so why come after Julian? Loose ends. He was supposed to be on that same cruiser. She kept that thought to herself and instead nodded towards the closed door. "How is he? He's just lost his whole family. How the heck do you tell a young boy something like that?"

Javarro shrugged. "Thankfully that duty fell to others." His mouth worked, deep emotions clouded his eyes, then he regained control. "I don't think any of us truly believe it yet."

"Can I see him?"

"I'm sorry, Chalwen, you wasted your time coming over. Chickadee has been sedated. Nobody is allowed in except his bodyguard and medical staff that we've cleared."

And Chalwen was officially off the bodyguard. Javarro didn't need to explain. Her shoulders slumped and she nodded.

"He's in good hands. We'll make sure nothing happens to him."

"Of course he's in the best hands. Who the fuck picked you all?" A wry smile took the bitterness from the words. She slapped Javarro on the shoulder and pushed him towards the rest of his squad.

Turning in the other direction, Chalwen double-checked the duty roster on her notepad and strolled over to the desk at the end of the hall.

Thankfully, despite the tragedy yesterday that had stunned the whole of civilized space, discipline and routine still ruled here within the palace walls. The well-oiled administration machine ticked on, oblivious to the trauma and roiling emotions that beset its human components.

The nurse, a man in his fifties with thinning hair turning to grey, looked up as she approached. He regarded her blearily through red-rimmed eyes. Chalwen was sure she looked no better.

"Lieutenant?"

"I understand you were on duty yesterday afternoon, yes?"

The nurse sighed. "I don't know what this is about, but I really don't have the time to talk." He slumped in his chair and half-heartedly shuffled documents about on his desktop. "Patients to attend to. Please excuse me."

Chalwen glanced up and down the hallway, noting the absence of anyone in obvious medical distress. "Look, I'm sorry to have to trouble you like this, but Security believes the Emperor's assassination may have begun here in the palace. We're following up anything out of the ordinary in case someone saw something that might lead us to the traitors."

He squinted at her. "I don't know what I could have seen from here."

"We're covering all angles."

The nurse straightened in his seat. "You really think this might help catch the killers?"

"Maybe, maybe not. I won't know unless you answer a few questions. Me? I want to see the bastards burn."

His eyes glinted. "Count me in," he said grimly. "Yes, I was on duty in the afternoon."

"Were you at this station the whole time?"

"Except for when I was called away. I was messaged to say all spare staff were needed near the concert hall. That explosion, you know? Hell of a mess."

Chalwen raised her eyebrows. "And you left your post with the Crown Prince in your care?"

"Of course not!" His eyes widened in horror. "I'd only just come on duty, and the Crown Prince was already discharged. I say, did that explosion have anything to do with the Emperor's death?"

Chalwen stifled a squawk of disbelief. Keeping her tone as conversational as she could manage, she asked, "How do you know the Crown Prince was gone?"

"There would have been guards posted down there"—he gestured down the hall, where Chalwen's colleagues prowled restlessly—"but there was no one there. And I checked the admissions log here."

"Would you mind showing me?" Chalwen's heart thudded and she fought to appear calm and casual.

The nurse tapped on the desktop, hesitated, then scanned the document up and down. "That's weird," he muttered. More searching while Chalwen quelled the urge to fidget in frustration, then the color drained from his face. "This can't be right. This is the correct entry but yesterday's admission is showing an 'incomplete' status now. When I checked yesterday it said 'discharged'. I'm sure of it." He gazed up at Chalwen, pleading in his eyes. "It's rare to have a Royal in here and I take it very seriously when we do. I know what I saw."

"So," Chalwen said, as gently as possible, "just to be clear, you didn't go to the room itself to confirm it was clear?"

The nurse shook his head.

"And I'm going to guess that the message was flagged 'urgent'?"

"Of course. And I knew we'd already taken in casualties, so I figured it was a big job. As soon as I checked there was no one on this wing who needed me, I grabbed my medical bag and ran."

This was worth following up. Henri would have some digging to do. Firstly, where had that message come from? And secondly, if someone had altered the infirmary records they may have left some trace behind. "Thanks, you've been very helpful."

As she turned to leave, the nurse said, "The oddest thing though. Turned out I wasn't really needed after all. By the time I got down there the paramedics had pretty much cleaned up. Well, I wish you luck in your hunting."

⎯⎯⎯ ⎯ ◆ ⎯ ⎯⎯⎯

Along with all the senior officers on board, Gregor crammed into the large operations briefing room next to the command deck.

The Emperor, dead. The thought rang through his mind with a sense of unreality. The empire had lost its head, and so had The Hidden Light. The lights of the briefing room and chatter of his colleagues felt remote.

With its rows of seating facing the front, this was the only room in the warship's command complex large enough to take the hundred or so officers from lieutenant up. Normal briefings never took all senior officers away from their duties, and happened in one of the more comfortable conference rooms nearby, but these were not normal circumstances. Even so, Gregor thought wryly, the imperial navy had a procedure to handle even these most extraordinary of times. Watches had been temporarily handed over to warrant officers, with standing orders to maintain the ship's status and heading for an hour.

The doors at each end of the room sighed shut and an abnormal hush fell. Thick armor and soundproofing blocked most of the normal sounds of the ship. Only a muffled shuffle of feet and a nervous cough broke the silence as everyone waited for Captain Borodina to speak.

She seemed in no hurry, gazing at a scroll on a lectern as if she was oblivious to the attention now focused on her.

At last she looked up. "Some of what you're about to hear is classified. I need strict confidentiality around parts of this briefing. If you hear a whisper of this among the crew you will quell the rumor and remind people of the need to wait for confirmed facts. However you will report any such talk to the local ImpSec office for discreet follow-up."

Someone at the back of the room snorted. Gregor suppressed a shiver down his spine. In ImpSec terms, discreet did not necessarily mean gentle.

"Publicly-available facts first," the captain continued. "The Emperor is dead, along with the Lady Miriam, and Josephine, Florence, Matthew and Jonathan. A number of members of the imperial bodyguard also perished. The cause was a mid-air explosion. Crown Prince Julian and Grand Duke Ivan were not on board, and are accounted for and safe in the Magentis capital."

The mood in the room lightened noticeably. Gregor still sensed a deep and raw anger at the blow to imperial dignity, but beneath that, unbelievably, he sensed a surge of relief. Officers muttered to neighbors. Gregor caught fragments about the Grand Duke.

He still felt too numb to process emotions, but he wanted to scream at the obscene sentiments around him. The Emperor was dead, but most of the company was relieved that the Grand Duke still lived. Someone on the far side spoke the thought ... the *hope* ... that was on their minds. "Does this mean Ivan will be emperor? Surely Julian's too young."

Captain Borodina gave a bleak smile. "I won't bow to speculation. That question is in the hands of the lawyers and the Assembly. As far as I'm concerned, anything is possible, but that is not our concern right now."

Gregor rested his elbows on his knees and steepled his fingers in front of his face to hide the disgust he knew he must be showing. He felt sick at the thought. Paul dead, bad enough. But Ivan as emperor? He shuddered.

Wrath of Empire was a deeply traditional ship, steeped in the ways of Empress Florence and her forebears. Not for the first time, Gregor thought about requesting a transfer elsewhere. He'd always managed to keep his own views to himself, and in this charged atmosphere his life probably depended on it. But his value to The Hidden Light lay in his position at the heart of a crew so clearly on Ivan's side. He was a spy in enemy territory, now more than ever.

"Now, the parts that are not in the public domain," the captain continued, once the muttering subsided. "Ninety-nine percent certainty that this was no accident."

"An assassination?" someone called out.

"Likely. And the signatures from the wreck strongly suggest a weapon of Firenzi origin."

"Everyone in known space has access to those weapons," Gregor blurted out.

"True enough." Captain Borodina surveyed the room. "I can't impress on you enough the need for cool heads. Some of this is still speculation, but that won't stop people from acting if they're angry enough. The last thing we need right now is a ship to turn renegade and set out on a revenge mission."

The captain gestured to Commander Anya Schevchenko, who headed the local office of Imperial Security on board *Wrath*. Anya was small in stature but big in personality, with an overwhelming cheerfulness that lulled people into forgetting the ruthless and sometimes barbaric demands of her job.

Anya stood and faced the room. "ImpSec HQ is following several lines of inquiry, and you can be damned sure heads will roll. The only question is whose."

"Make sure they burn first," someone called out to scattered applause.

For once, the bloodthirsty outburst didn't bring a smile to Anya's lips. "I can't emphasize enough the sensitivity of this situation. Family Firenzi may not have been formal allies, but their interests have aligned with the Emperor's often enough in recent years. Rumors about their possible involvement have been spreading fast. Suspiciously fast."

"You mean an organized campaign to cast blame?"

"Looks like it, so we can't play into their hands. This is the kind of rumor that you need to be alert to, and you need to stamp it out."

Captain Borodina gave Anya a brief nod of thanks. The ImpSec officer sat. "I know you all have questions," the captain said, "but I have no answers at this time. You'll receive information as more comes in. We will remain at high readiness, but we will not be running silent yet. We need to stay on grid to receive updates and orders." She paused and swallowed hard, visibly struggling to control herself. "One thing I can promise you. If the evidence confirms a Firenzi assault then there will be retribution. What form that takes will be up to the new emperor to decide, not us."

Chapter 22

Grand Duke Ivan Skamensis sat and placed his palms on the wide desk in the emperor's Office of Deliberation.

"Suits you, Sire." Bernie Fischer nodded approvingly. Across the expanse of the office, the squad leader of his bodyguard grinned.

Ivan gave an irritated shake of his head. His mind had been far away. He hadn't meant to look like he was striking a pose. Royalty didn't preen themselves with the trappings of power, they simply stepped into what was rightfully theirs.

He gazed around. This place felt far too open, with its sweep of windows looking out onto the Fountain Court. It would take some getting used to. Paul must have had his own security against surveillance to rival the measures Ivan had installed in his office in the building next door. But that security didn't belong to Ivan. Not yet.

He'd already received Bernie's report in suitable privacy. The remainder of the Family had been successfully evacuated from palace grounds and would soon be on their way off-planet. They would lead a comfortable, if isolated and anonymous, exile on a world near the outer fringes of Skamensis space.

That just left Julian.

An unwanted loose end, but not one that Ivan could afford to tie off. Bernie had strict instructions to leave Julian alone. Maybe Honorina Philip's remaining network of assassins would remove the problem now he was out of the infirmary, in which case Ivan had to be visibly unin-volved. Another death right now would turn the full glare of ImpSec's trigger-happy suspicions onto Ivan, as the most obvious beneficiary. He had to make sure those suspicions were diverted in the right direction.

Right, meaning desirable, not necessarily correct.

And if Julian survived, Ivan was working on more layers of fallback plans to keep him off the throne.

A disturbance at the door interrupted his musings. Ivan recognized members of Julian's bodyguard pushing past the household guards at the door that led from the senior family members' suites of offices. It was a sign of the tensions in the palace right now that the two squads had almost come to a confrontation. Normally, the various contingents of guards going about their business were no more noticeable than the surrounding air.

Julian entered the room and gazed around. His arm was strapped across his chest, and he limped only slightly on his damaged leg. A light-weight but sturdy protective cast peeped out beneath loose-fitting pants. He made an unhurried circuit past the informal couches and low tables where Paul used to entertain privileged visitors.

"I was told I'd find you here. That is the emperor's desk."

How could a child's accusing glare unsettle him so? Ivan felt unac-countably embarrassed at being caught behind the desk. He shouldn't be, but his position and claim to the throne was still fragile and this stern-faced youngster was standing in his way.

He sighed. "I need no reminding of that fact."

"You are not the emperor." The tone was calm and matter-of-fact. A flat and undeniable statement.

Ivan was also uncomfortably aware that this encounter would be the stuff of palace gossip within the hour. His bodyguard would be dis-creet, for the most part, but Julian's squads were stoutly loyal to Julian. The best of Bernie's efforts had failed to turn a single one of them.

In her heyday, his mother would have simply executed anyone who displeased her like this. How times had changed. He needed to talk to Bresk about guarding his privacy from chance encounters like this.

"Of course not." Ivan fought to keep his tone soothing. His presence here must have touched a raw nerve, and although Julian was just a youngster he could wield formidable power if he ever realized it. "But someone with experience needs to keep the machinery of empire running while we go through the formalities of succession."

"And we all have lavish offices and access to imperial records." Another undeniable fact.

"True enough. But I find that the right setting gives a useful perspective. The world hasn't stopped turning. There are many matters that need my—our—attention while the line of succession goes through the legal process. More than ever, the empire needs some measure of constancy, so I try to imagine what my brother would be thinking, how he would act."

"And you find that sitting in his chair helps you with that?" Julian shrugged.

Ivan considered a reply, then realized that line of conversation had been effectively ended, with Julian having the last word. Was that the result of boyish directness, or something more calculated? For the first time, Ivan saw the potential here for a serious challenger. Someone must have been coaching Julian in how to conduct himself, boosting his self-confidence, readying him to take his role as imperial heir seriously.

For a fleeting moment, Ivan calculated the odds of disposing of Julian and his bodyguard right here in the heart of the palace. Across the room, Bernie narrowed his eyes, clearly also running the math. He gave a microscopic shake of his head, visible only to Ivan. If only life were so simple.

Ivan would just have to play this game out more carefully. He lounged back in the chair like he belonged there. Julian walked stiffly across the office and past the desk, to stand gazing through the windows at the expanse of rose beds and dancing fountains. His movement appeared casual, but Ivan decided it had to be deliberate. Only the emperor ever advanced to this end of the room.

He'd half expected Julian to demand he vacate the desk, a demand which he'd have no practical way to enforce. Depending on Julian's tone and mood, Ivan would have had a choice of responses. He could simply ignore Julian or openly refuse and force a climb down, or he could acquiesce gracefully as one would humor a child. He could choose a path that retained the high ground and made Julian appear weak, foolish, or petulant.

But with this simple act, Julian had neatly turned the tables. He'd staked his own claim in this office just as Ivan had done, and dared Ivan to object. And, of course, Ivan couldn't say anything without drawing more attention to his own violation of protocol.

He decided to change tack. "While you were indisposed, I took the liberty of declaring a month of official mourning across the empire. That is standard protocol. And, I hesitate to mention it, but when you're ready we'll need to discuss how best to lay our family to rest."

He couldn't see Julian's expression, with his back to the room, but his shoulders hunched slightly. He stood for a few more moments, then turned. His face was unreadable. "I expect to be fully involved in the funeral arrangements."

Ivan nodded and controlled his own expression to conceal his surprise. Maybe Julian was keeping his feelings under tight control, but the self-assured youngster in front of him seemed to have aged far beyond his eleven years.

"Naturally. In fact I feel it only right that you should take a leading part in the arrangements. Paul was my brother, and I feel the pain of loss too deeply to express—" Ivan had no need to fake the sudden rush of emotion. Ordering his brother's death had been necessary, but doing what was necessary for the future of the empire had come at a crippling personal cost. He brought himself back under control. "But you, Julian, I can't begin to imagine your loss."

Besides, Ivan thought, keeping you busy will keep you away from the real levers of power.

Secure in her office, Chalwen pored over schematics, reports, and duty rosters. She massaged her eyelids with her fingertips and slumped in her seat. Three days. Blind alleys everywhere.

"Whoever tampered with the records and the surveillance covered their tracks well." Henri repeated the same thing he'd been saying for these past three days. Chalwen peered from between her fingers at his image on the desktop comms pane. Bags under his eyes, and unkempt hair showed his fatigue, and his tone betrayed deep frustration. "If I could bring in a proper investigation team ..." But he didn't need to finish the thought.

"The colonel was clear on that point. Our offices have been compromised. We don't know who may be involved, and we don't want to tip them off that we know."

"I suspect they already know. I have a strong sense that someone is still running interference. Every time I follow up a line of inquiry, the evidence either gets muddied or simply evaporates before I can dig deeper."

"And many of the trails you were able to follow lead mysteriously back to one or other of the dead guards."

"Yeah. That's so obviously untrue. How can someone who died in the troop carrier order a change of guard on the Crown Prince and summon unneeded medical help an hour later?"

"It's as if someone was toying with us."

Silence fell as the two of them pondered, each sunk in their own dark thoughts. Between them, they'd untangled the mess of communications that day, the tapestry of superbly-timed orders that had cleared the way for intruders to approach Julian's infirmary room unseen and unchallenged. Henri had traced those orders back to sources that made no sense: people who were already dead, people who Chalwen had interviewed and who she was sure couldn't have done what the records suggested they did, and a handful of people who'd simply vanished in the meantime.

"Henri, is this a real time picture?" Chalwen pointed to the schematic in front of her showing internal surveillance coverage. "I thought the whole network was back online."

"Yes, and no. That's the current picture, and the techs in ImpSec are still fighting glitches."

At Chalwen's astounded expression he added, "Someone planted a replicating logic bomb in the network, that's still causing rolling outages. The techs are getting good at spotting and squashing glitches when they appear."

"Hasn't anyone in the hierarchy joined the dots yet and figured that this shows there was a conspiracy inside the palace?"

Henri sighed. "As far as the hierarchy goes, your 'conspiracy' remains unproven and a likely product of a keen but deranged imagination. This is officially viewed as unrelated."

It was Chalwen's turn to sigh. The colonel was convinced, she knew. The patterns they'd uncovered were too calculated and too widespread to be accidental, but until they pointed to a meaningful target that the higher-ups could act on, the colonel was keeping this investigation off the record. "Are they saying the outages are random, then, and not part of a deliberate concealment?"

"That's the official line."

A thought struck Chalwen. "Do you have archived snapshots of this outage picture?"

Henri nodded and worked the desktop at his end.

"If you can, try playing it forward like a video from the time the explosion happened in the troop carrier."

After a few minutes' trial and error, Henri pieced together the view Chalwen wanted. They watched the timeline. Chalwen gasped. "Most of the outages do look random, but look here, for two days there was *always* a blind spot *here*, and then suddenly a stable corridor joining that to the service gate behind the barracks."

"This shows purpose," Henri agreed grimly. "Someone was hiding something deep down in the basement levels. All hidden behind a smokescreen."

"That complex is down beneath the State Apartments." Chalwen studied the map, memorizing the location and the route there through the underground labyrinth. "Stay in touch, Henri, I'm going to take a look."

Beneath the guard house, a sub-basement access led deeper into the network of service corridors beneath the palace grounds. Each of the hundreds of buildings had its own power and air conditioning, plumbing and sanitation, all of varying stages of antiquity and in varying states of repair.

Chalwen threaded her way through a honeycomb of redoubts and safe rooms installed by a paranoid emperor a thousand years ago, and past bottomless shafts circulating air from the cool depths. Occasionally she crossed paths with teams of maintenance engineers and solitary inspectors roaming the depths. After a quarter mile of meandering, she entered an echoing derelict machinery space, a long-decommissioned and abandoned power plant that once drove the palace's magnetic shields. Decaying hulks cast bizarre shadows in the dancing light of a glowtube. The air was cold and dry, and smelled of old plaster dust.

"Henri," she whispered, "I'm getting close, but it's a large space. Can you narrow it down a bit?"

"Not from the pattern of blind spots. The zones are too broad. I can see you, though, so whatever they were up to, they're finished."

"Wonder how well they cleaned up, then. This place is well out of the way. I don't think there'd be any reason for someone to come by here accidentally."

Chalwen's scalp crawled and she couldn't shake the feeling of being watched. She drew her beam pistol and shone her light in a slow three-sixty.

Dust lay thick on the floor, undisturbed for decades. Or was it? Treading carefully to avoid raising a choking cloud, Chalwen approached a side door leading back out to the service corridor. She knelt and held the glowtube low so its light shone across the floor. Patterns showed in sharp relief. Someone had been here and covered their tracks.

Sweeping the light from side to side, Chalwen saw the trail of disturbed dust led past the casing of a derelict heat exchanger and into a side room.

"Someone's been here," she muttered for Henri's benefit.

The side room looked like it had once been a control room. Empty racks would have held consoles. A closed door to her left caught her attention. Scuff marks on the floor looked fresh.

Heart thudding and pistol at the ready, Chalwen eased the door open.

"Bingo!" At a glance Chalwen noted the clean floor and a row of camp cots along the far wall. They looked new. More puzzling, so did the lock on the door.

She quickly cleared the room and the handful of doors at the far end. Store rooms, a tiny galley kitchen stripped of equipment, and a bathroom that still looked functional. This suite would once have been a ready room for shift engineers.

But they'd been gone from here hundreds of years since. People had lived here only days ago. A few crumpled wrappers lay in a corner. A half-eaten ration bar still looked fresh. Is this where the saboteurs hid while they planned and executed their killing and Julian's aborted abduction?

"Chalwen."

Henri's voice in her ear startled her. She'd instinctively drawn her weapon again and was quartering the control room looking for threats.

"You'll have to come back to this inspection. The surveillance black-outs were supposed to be fixed, but right now, there's a blank spot right underneath the imperial quarters."

Chalwen froze. "A random blackout?" she stuttered.

"Looking too stable. I've been watching it for a few minutes while keeping a lookout for you, and I'm starting to think it's significant."

Even while Henri was speaking, Chalwen sprinted through the machinery space. She wracked her brain for the fastest route there. Three flights up a stairwell and she burst into a well-lit corridor, startling a couple of servants wheeling a food cart.

"Sound a general alarm, Henri. Get some guards over to that zone and start a search." To cover her bases, she placed a call to the colonel. In between heaving gasps of breath as she ran, she outlined the situation.

She slowed as she neared the edge of the blacked-out zone. Where should she start? The zone covered about three acres of service sub-basements and who knew how many levels down. She curbed her rising impatience and decided a systematic approach was needed. She headed for a major stairwell near the center of the zone, and worked her way around the exits on her level.

Nothing amiss. But up or down from here? Down, Chalwen decided. If an intruder was trying to access the rooms above, she had to trust that the bodyguard would be able to deal with the threat. But all the plant machinery would be found down below.

Level after level she descended, working through the surrounding corridors and plant rooms for signs of intrusion.

Then she came to a door that seemed to be propped shut. Chalwen put her shoulder to it and heaved the door open. A body slumped against it blocked the way. She squeezed through the gap and checked for a pulse, but the gaping throat and pool of blood told her the automatic gesture was wasted.

The body also told her she was on the right track.

"Henri," she whispered. "Level seven, southern quarter. Maintenance worker down, professional execution. What's in this direction?"

A few seconds' pause. "Main ventilation trunk."

"For the residence?"

"Including the imperial quarters."

"Shut it down," Chalwen hissed. She felt weak.

"Already working on it, and backup is on its way, ninety seconds out."

"Too long." Chalwen edged down the hall and peered over the railing of the catwalk at the end. "See if you can get cameras back online. Going silent now."

A machine whine grew louder as she edged along the catwalk. Ducts four feet across plunged into the depths and rose above her head. An opening to her right led into an anteroom. The sound of machinery grew louder, masking any noise Chalwen might make, but also masking any sounds from an intruder.

She peered around the next doorway. A large and bright-lit room stretched into the distance. A maze of pipes and ducts twisted across the ceiling, and rows of green-painted panels with lit displays stood like sentries along both walls.

A figure hunched over an open panel.

Chalwen raised her beam pistol.

The intruder must have had supernatural hearing or a sixth sense.

And lightning reactions.

Chalwen ducked back as a bolt sizzled off the doorframe beside her. She loosed off a blast of her own, aiming purely by reflex.

A scream told her she'd managed a lucky hit.

A barrage blistered the wall opposite her, but Chalwen was oblivious to the electrical fury. Her mind had just caught up with the brief glimpse of the intruder, and she reeled from the shock of recognition. "Sergeant van Buren," she called. "We have this zone surrounded. There's no way out. Drop your weapon and we can sort something out." That was a lie. Chalwen knew it and so would the sergeant, but it was worth a try while she wracked her brain for other options.

Another discharge crackled the air, but it didn't go anywhere near Chalwen. The sergeant lay down covering fire, pinning her down, buying time.

There was only one possibility. "Henri! Evacuate the residence. Poison in the ventilation."

Even as she spoke, the overpowering white noise of banks of fans whirred down to silence. But was it already too late?

A final shot and a thud, then silence. Chalwen peered around the door, ready to snatch herself back, but she needn't have bothered. As soon as the machinery shut down, the sergeant knew she'd lost. A beam pistol shot at close quarters up through the angle of the jaw didn't leave much room for error. And no opportunity for questioning.

Hands shaking, Chalwen holstered her pistol and hurried over to the panel van Buren had been working on. Inside the exposed space, a bank of evaporators injected moisture into the main duct. The canister taped to one of the ducts looked out of place, and it was still hissing through a nozzle into a crudely-drilled hole in the duct casing.

And the system was shut down. No circulation to carry the airborne poison up into the building. That was a good thing for the people up there.

Not so good for Chalwen.

She turned and ran, feeling her legs weaken and her vision dim as she slammed into the doorframe.

The anteroom seemed to stretch in front of her, defying all laws of geometry.

The floor tilted and swayed like a heaving sea.

Darkness.

Chapter 23

Chalwen woke to dazzling sunlight streaming through an open window, a thumping headache, and a taste in her mouth like something had died in there. Months ago.

She squinted against the light, and realized she was in a small ward in the infirmary.

"Best not to try moving just yet." A young male nurse appeared in the edge of Chalwen's vision. "We're still flushing the crap out of your system, and there'll be some residual paralysis for a while."

Another face swam into view.

"Henri?" Chalwen croaked.

"In the flesh." He gave a crooked grin. "They let me out of my crypt for special occasions."

Memory flooded back. Chalwen lurched half-way upright then sagged back. Every muscle in her body ached. "Crown Prince?" she mumbled.

"Safe. We were lucky."

The nurse leaned over and adjusted a thicket of tubes strapped to Chalwen's left arm. "Told you to stay still. Are you going to be a problem patient?"

Chalwen struggled to recall his name. The face was vaguely familiar, but she couldn't place it. That bothered her. She shook her head, and then wished she hadn't.

"For what it's worth," the nurse said, "two servants downstairs passed out, and we treated another three for low level exposure. Of all the casualties, you're in the worst shape."

"Chickadee and the bodyguard have been evacuated while we clean the residence," Henri added. "The Grand Duke wasn't in. Everyone else is accounted for."

The door slammed back on its hinges. "Lieutenant ap Gwynodd. What kind of mess have you got yourself into this time?"

Chalwen groaned to herself at the sound of Colonel bin Merrin's voice, but even in her fuddled state she was finely attuned to the colonel's moods. She realized this was a bantering tone, not a chewing-out. "Trying my hand at human canary, Colonel. Felt like I was due for a career change."

The colonel joined Henri at her bedside. A brief smile was replaced by a grim expression. "Leave the poison detection to real canaries, Lieutenant. You're back on guard duty as soon as the medics clear you."

"What about my investigation?"

The colonel hissed and looked pointedly at Henri.

It took a moment for Chalwen to catch on, then she barked a short laugh. "No secrets here, Colonel. This is Second Lieutenant Henri Chargon, ImpSec Intelligence."

The colonel squinted at Henri. "Is this an official visit? I can vouch that Lieutenant ap Gwynodd was acting fully within my purview."

"I know. I'm fully aware of Chalwen's recent activities and my presence here is out of personal concern."

"Friends in Intelligence, hmm? So, you're my lieutenant's secret weapon. Did you have anything to do with her grand entrance in Central Ops?"

Henri leveled a cool gaze at the colonel. "You should know better than to ask *anything* about what I do in the line of duty."

On the surface his tone was cordial, but an undercurrent of liquid nitrogen stopped the colonel in his tracks. He started mumbling an apology then coughed and straightened. "Of course. You're quite correct."

Yay, Henri! Chalwen had never seen the colonel at a loss for words before, but she also noted his rapid and gracious recovery. To cover the awkward silence, she said, "Can anyone fill me in on what actually happened?"

Henri nodded to the nurse. "If the patient is stable, we need a few minutes' privacy."

The nurse shrugged and left the room, closing the door behind him.

Colonel bin Merrin came straight to the point. "You guessed right. This was poison, targeting the Crown Prince. We've analyzed the poison. Slow Sleep."

Chalwen gagged. Her limbs suddenly felt impossibly heavy. "How much did I breathe in?" she whispered.

"The fact that you're awake and talking now should tell you the answer."

"Was this a suicide mission?" Chalwen thought back to the poorly sealed nozzle. She couldn't remember whether or not van Buren had been carrying a mask.

"Sergeant van Buren probably had an exit strategy, possibly involving accomplices within the palace. She would have known there was a high risk of capture, but even handling something this deadly, I don't think she planned on dying in that room. You simply interrupted her before she could seal the intake hole properly. From that point on, the plan changed. She hit the release and just aimed to hold you off for the few seconds it would take to empty the canister into the duct."

Chalwen glanced at Henri. "Lucky you were already arranging to shut down the plant." She shuddered. "How can someone have got so close? Anyone tampering with the ventilation plant should trip any number of alarms."

Henri grimaced. "We already know this was an inside operation. Nothing in van Buren's records suggested a security risk. If she didn't get flagged in regular screening we have to assume others slipped the net too."

"Slow Sleep needs time to act." Chalwen was thinking out loud. "It dulls the wits before paralysis sets in, so the victim doesn't realize what's happening. But someone in the room keeling over could give the game away."

The colonel said, "She struck when the guards in the Crown Prince's suite had finished a round of inspection, turned in a report to the guard house, and would be settled for a while."

Chalwen frowned. "They've been trained not to do their rounds in any predictable pattern."

"Nevertheless, van Buren knew all our movements down to the minute."

"She didn't take me into account."

"You weren't on the duty roster."

A queasy feeling churned Chalwen's stomach. "So it was only by chance that the Crown Prince is still alive?" The colonel nodded. Another thought struck her. "That means they have people spying on us. Either inside the guard house, or with access to sealed records. She did have accomplices, who are still out there somewhere."

"It gets worse," Henri said. "That poison is rare and fiendishly difficult to get hold of. It's one of the Firenzi specialities."

Chalwen screwed up her face. "Doesn't say much. All the Families and the big corps have assassins, and most of their drugs and poisons come originally from the Firenzi laboratories."

"On its own, I agree, but I've seen preliminary reports from the Emperor's cruiser."

The colonel gave a strangled squawk. "How ..." He trailed off into silence under Henri's level gaze.

"Only the Firenzi make the kind of high grade incendiary that took out the cruiser."

The queasiness increased. "And Josef Firenzi and his entourage ..."

"Are currently enjoying our protective hospitality," the colonel finished the thought for her, "at the Palace of Butterflies in Henriss Garden."

"They're being held on the planet?" Chalwen was aghast.

"The Grand Duke felt that was the best place to secure their safety. They're in an outer wing of the Palace of Butterflies."

"Why the Grand Duke?" Chalwen wondered. "What did the Crown Prince have to say about it?"

The colonel looked troubled. "He stays in his office. He seems to have zoned out. This has been harder on him than any of us could imagine."

"So we have Ivan at the helm?"

"Seems like it. Unless Julian asserts himself, the Assembly will need to meet and pass some kind of bill of succession to install a leader."

Chalwen's head swam. "That's dangerous enough, and probably what everyone's concerned about right now, but having another Family head on the planet while we're leaderless is like sitting on a quark bomb."

"Two questions seem most salient." Henri's voice was calm and quiet, but charged with anxiety that seemed to electrify the room. "First, who knows there's a Firenzi delegation groundside? Second, who knows of the circumstantial evidence linking the assassination to the Firenzi?"

Chalwen's stomach surged. She lurched to one side and retched over the side of the bed. The nurse rushed in. "Dammitall, ap Gwynnod, what in Space are you doing?" He kicked a bucket into position under Chalwen's face. Luckily there was nothing more than a thin stream of clear fluid. She retched again, then flopped weakly back onto her pillow.

While the nurse fetched a damp wipe and cleaned Chalwen's face he glared furiously at Henri and the colonel. "She's in a fragile state. She'll be dizzy and nauseous for days yet. Sudden excitement to be avoided, do you understand?" Without waiting for an answer, he said to Chalwen, "Good job we emptied your stomach when you came in. Intravenous nourishment only since then."

"Hah! So that's why I feel like I could eat a horse?"

"Funny." He grimaced. "Just try eating solid food and see how funny you think it is on the way back up. As for you two, out! Now!"

"No," Chalwen croaked. "I appreciate the concern—"

"Professional responsibility," the nurse growled. "And I'm not impressed by rank or position, so don't even try pulling that crap on me."

"Regardless," said Chalwen, finding her voice strengthening despite the acid burn still in the back of her throat. "You want to keep me quiet. If we don't finish this conversation I'll tear this room apart in frustration. You haven't seen me agitated yet, and you don't want to."

The nurse stared in disbelief. "You have to realize you'll slow your recovery and do yourself harm if you raise your blood pressure like this."

"That's a risk I need to take, and believe me the risk is greatly lessened if you let us get on with it."

"What's so important that you're prepared to defy common sense?"

"Imperial affairs of state," the colonel said, solemnly.

Henri added, with a perfectly straight face, "And matters of imperial security, which I'm afraid you don't have clearance to hear."

The nurse huffed. "I can smell bullshit a mile deep, but okay. Ten minutes, and then I expect you two gone and you"—he prodded Chalwen's shoulder—"will be a model patient in return."

"Deal." She hesitated. "And none of that was bullshit."

The nurse met her gaze for a few seconds before he averted his eyes, nodded, and left.

"So," Chalwen said, "back to Henri's two questions."

Colonel bin Merrin frowned in thought. "The Firenzi visit was arranged under strict secrecy. Trouble is, the logistics involved are daunting. We kept it to a minimum but there must be hundreds of people in the know. Only trusted members of the imperial administration, of course."

"Trusted." A cold pit opened in Chalwen's stomach. "Like Sergeant van Buren? Like whoever in the palace sabotaged *Nightwish?*"

The colonel grimaced and nodded. "Exactly so. And as for the second question ... the forensic results I'm confident are secure." He eyed Henri. "I'll have to assume you obtained access through approved channels, otherwise we have a serious problem. The problem here is that there were eyewitnesses to the explosion, military eyewitnesses who know the visible signatures of various kinds of ordnance. It won't be long before someone draws their own conclusions and says something unguarded."

Chalwen sat up straighter, with a helping hand from Henri. "One question I think we need to bring out in the open, strictly between us." Her mouth twisted as she tried to find a way to phrase the question properly. "Do either of you hold any real suspicions of the Firenzi in this?"

Colonel bin Merrin chewed his lip. "I know the evidence points that way, although every piece of it has other possible explanations. I can't discount it."

"Maybe I asked the wrong question." Chalwen felt foolish. What drugs had the medics been feeding her? "Do you think Josef himself would have anything to do with this?"

The colonel's mouth opened in an 'Aah' of silent understanding. He shook his head. "I can't believe it. There are many factions in the household, and especially in the Special Service, that I would happily place at the heart of any dirty plot. But it makes no sense for Josef Firenzi to back an assassination just when he's paying a clandestine visit."

Henri added, "Josef is ambitious, and hardened. You can't stay head of a Family without that. But I've never once heard anyone accuse him of being dishonorable."

"More than that, Emperor Paul trusted Josef. I know that's hardly conclusive, but Paul had a nose for deceit and this is out of character for Josef."

For a moment, Chalwen saw indecision in Henri's face. He shook himself. "Chalwen's right. We need absolute certainty among the three of us, at least. One thing I can let you know, Colonel, just within this room. I know you had suspicions that you weren't in a position to act on officially. Chalwen and I made inquiries ... off the books, as it were."

"We got nowhere." Chalwen couldn't hide the bitterness in her voice.

"But," Henri continued, "the patterns of clues we followed don't fit any of the networks of Family spies we know about. This plot went too deep. This entrenched collusion right through our own organization is unlikely to be the network of an outside party. It points rather closer to home."

The colonel stepped back, looking stunned.

"Come on, Colonel," Chalwen whispered. "This is where you thought the trail might lead."

"So, not the Firenzi, then? Certainly not Josef. And if the enemy is inside, where do we start looking?"

"We don't," Henri said quietly. "We don't need to. With the assassination plot against the Crown Prince, the whole might of ImpSec is focused on this problem now. No more room for amateur sleuths."

"Fair enough," the colonel said. "I'd prefer to get back to simple bodyguarding."

A profound weariness swept like a wave over Chalwen. Relief? Or disappointment? She couldn't tell. As her eyes closed, she said, "Colonel, whatever we may believe, Josef Firenzi won't be safe on Magentis. The Grand Duke must get him off planet without delay."

Chapter 24

Chalwen cursed again and again as she made her painful way from the infirmary to the guard house. Her walking cane clacked on the flagstones, the only concession she would make to the bossy nurse when she overruled his objections and discharged herself.

Residual paralysis, the medics told her. The pain should ease with time, drugs, and careful treatment, but she may never regain full mobility. That didn't bear thinking about. Emperor Paul had placed his trust in her to look after Julian. How could she do that now? The mental anguish eclipsed the physical pain. Damn that assassin. Damn whoever lurked behind this whole fucking mess. She growled in the back of her throat. Her days as an imperial family bodyguard were likely numbered, but she shoved that thought aside. Until she was ordered to stand down, she'd resume her duties. The colonel had said something about the medics clearing her first, and that hadn't happened yet, but she had no qualms about capitalizing on her recent foiling of an assassination. Just let them try to sideline her.

A medical orderly kept pace with her halting progress so she kept her curses under her breath, but each step plumbed her subvocalized vocabulary to new depths.

The orderly made notes on his notepad. "I know it's pointless asking you to take it easy. This bag contains a small stock of medipens to help manage the pain. I've requisitioned stronger ones you can pick up at the infirmary if you need them. I suspect you will."

Chalwen gave him a sharp glance, then gasped as a stumble jolted electricity up her leg. "Thanks," she muttered.

"I've seen your type before. Driven. You won't ease up, so the best we can do is help you survive your own stubbornness." He made more notes. "The other medipens will help you keep solid food down, in small quantities. I'll have a stock of liquid nutrients sent up to your office. They'll stay down, but they taste like urine."

The heat of morning was building up, and the long courtyard between the kitchens and the palace offices bustled with soldiers and household staff going about their business. Chalwen gritted her teeth and plodded on. She'd been going mad in the infirmary, starved of information. There was trouble in the realm and she had work to do. All very well the colonel saying leave it to the professional investigators, but she still had a Crown Prince to protect. She'd be guilty of professional negligence if she failed to guard against the unseen threats.

In her mind, she sifted through the leads she and Henri had followed. There had to be a pattern there, some common element, something that would give them a new line of attack.

They were at the bottom of steps leading up into the guard house when a low moan shook the air, rising in tone to a shriek. Again and again.

The palace was under attack.

The alarm jolted Chalwen out of her thoughts and she stumbled on the bottom step. This time the curse came out full volume, and a stream of invective followed her as she raced up the stairs on legs of fire.

Inside, past a reception counter, Chalwen pushed open the inner door, thankful that her passkey and security clearance were still active.

"I'll just leave this here, then," the orderly called out, handing her medications to the duty officer behind the desk.

The main office was a controlled seethe of activity and tension, but Chalwen could read the mood in an instant. The alarms outside were a call to action, but the tone and pattern of orders and questions in the room told her that the situation was under control. She studied the nearest status screen and a collage of monitors covering the far wall. Some of the tension eased from her shoulders, and she found a nearby desk to lean against. Views from the main gates showed a large crowd covering half the plaza outside. Waving banners, placards and fists said this was not business as usual.

She leaned forward and tapped one of the comms techs on the shoulder. "What happened?"

The elderly man glanced over his shoulder. "A semi-organized protest formed in the Vestibule. Then a group tried to march on the Assembly Room. While the guards were distracted, a smaller group broke through to the Green Throne Room."

"Protest against what?" Chalwen asked, but a pit formed in her stomach.

"The Firenzi murdered the Emperor. People are demanding action. Revenge." His tone was flat. "Anyway, the palace guard rounded them up quick enough. Reckon we're looking at an all-night sit-in out there, though." He gave the impression he would happily join the protests outside if he could.

"Do you really believe that? That the Firenzi were behind it?"

He shrugged. "ImpSec's sitting on a ton of evidence, apparently."

"Your job is to stick with known facts," Chalwen growled. "Don't get caught up in rumor."

She spotted the colonel on the far side of the room. He caught her eye and waved her over. Chalwen limped across the room, cane clacking angrily on the floor. Twenty pairs of eyes followed her in sudden silence as she followed the colonel into his office.

"How did this get out?" Her voice was more resigned than angry.

"ImpSec is chasing its tail trying to pinpoint the leak, but that's moot now. All the news and chat channels are carrying it, and the speculation is snowballing."

"Finding the source is hardly moot if someone is orchestrating this," Chalwen hissed. "Was this put out there deliberately by someone here? To what end? And what more damage might they do?"

The colonel grunted. "You and I know that, but we've been chasing these shadows for some time now. Not everyone has the benefit of seeing all the threads laid out together."

"You think these are the same shadows?" Chalwen felt behind her and propped herself up on a low cabinet standing by the door. "The

Emperor's cruiser, the attempts to take and then to kill Julian, and now this?"

"It sounds a random collection, doesn't it?" The colonel waved Chalwen to close the office door and to sit. He fumbled in his breast pocket for a nicodyne spray. He gazed at the cylinder in his palm for a few seconds, then directed a shot into the back of his mouth. "As you said, to what end?"

Chalwen shook her head when the colonel offered her the spray. "The cruiser and the attacks on the Crown Prince make sense together, when you remember that Julian should have been on that flight and lost as well. But to seed unrest, whispering to the media, what does that achieve?"

"There have been riots and protests outside government offices in all planetary capitals. Firenzi-linked businesses torched. People want blood."

"I don't believe it," Chalwen muttered. "I'm gone two bloody days and the whole empire goes to pot." She looked up sharply. "I've been out of touch for two days, imprisoned in that damned infirmary with Doctor Doom gloating over me. I assume the Firenzi entourage is safely on their way out of Skamensis space by now?"

The colonel wouldn't meet her eyes. He had taken a sudden keen interest in news feeds scrolling across the desk surface.

"What?" Chalwen thundered. "What is the Grand Duke thinking?"

"Who knows?" The colonel looked up. The nicodyne had done nothing to ease the depths of weariness in the back of his eyes. "All I can say is, it would be too risky to move them now. The kind of escort that goes with a Head of Family can't be arranged without people knowing about it. Seems we can't trust our own security and guard services. Why imagine the military is clean? Think of all the naval units up there. A ground-to-orbit shuttle is small and vulnerable. All it takes is one pro-active captain to see an opportunity to settle a score."

They sat in silence for a few minutes. Chalwen massaged her legs until a chilling thought wormed its way past the haze of pain. "All it needs now is for someone to let slip that the Firenzi Head of Family is here on Magentis," she whispered. "That can't be allowed to get out."

Colonel bin Merrin glanced down at his desktop. His face turned grey. "Too late."

Chalwen set the defenses in her office, relieved she hadn't been moved while officially suspended from duty. Emperor Paul would have ensured that nothing untoward happened to members of his covert organization, but Emperor Paul was dead. Chalwen wondered who now would be in a position to pull strings and make things happen. If she was ousted from this office, could she set up comparable privacy measures anywhere else? And, this thought chilled her more, would another occupant discover the extraordinary measures secreted here? That would set alarm bells ringing, and the wrong people could easily draw the wrong conclusions.

She shivered, feeling more vulnerable than she'd ever felt. Without their main sponsor, they'd all entered unknown and dangerous territory. If ever members of The Hidden Light felt moved to jump ship, this was it.

Dammit! Chalwen recognized avoidance when she saw it, even in herself. Now wasn't the time for emotions, she had work to do, but she couldn't keep damming up her feelings. She circled a pit of raw pain, a whirlpool sucking her in. She needed a release. She checked the sound-proofing measures protecting the office, then gripped the head of her walking cane till her knuckles whitened and gave vent to a scream of anguish. As she forced the last dregs of air from her lungs, the scream tailed off to a growl of fury.

That brief expression of grief would have to do, for now. Paul was gone. Julian still lived and, in that, Chalwen took some measure of satisfaction, but right now even bigger dangers threatened. Time to see what remained of the Light.

With a trembling hand, Chalwen leaned her cane against the desk and eased her legs into a more comfortable position.

She activated the comms screen and provided the codes to summon whatever members of the secretive organization would respond. She gave an hour's grace, the shortest notice she could reasonably provide for people in positions high and low across the empire to receive the message and to find a place of privacy to join in the call.

Even that brief delay chafed at her. Time was slipping away. She brought up news feeds and transferred them to the wall across from her desk.

A knock at the door. Chalwen let in a medical orderly, a young woman carrying a heavy-looking carryall over her shoulder and a mess tray balanced in one hand. Chalwen recognized her. They'd never exchanged words and if Chalwen had ever known her name it was lost in a medical haze, but this one had often been in the background smiling quiet approval whenever Chalwen found the strength to argue with the nurse.

She recognized an ally, and managed to turn a grimace of pain into some semblance of a smile as she turned and settled back into her chair.

"Nutrient packs, and stronger medications." The orderly placed the mess tray down in front of Chalwen and slipped the bag from her shoulder. "Just break the seal and drink from the spout. But I stopped by the mess and picked up a chicken and lentil broth. Something more filling that you should be able to keep down."

Chalwen's nose twitched at the aroma wafting around the room. She had time to kill and welcomed the distraction.

"Those bastards are *here?*"

Startled, Chalwen looked up to find the orderly staring at the wall. The collage of feeds multiplied, focused on one subject. For a few moments, Chalwen's mind blanked in horror. She'd set search filters to scour the ocean of feeds and chats for credible mentions of the Firenzi family, knowing it was only a matter of time before the obscure reference Colonel bin Merrin had spotted hit the mainstream. But the speed with which the rumors spread shocked her, and the sorted catalogue of results exploded into the thousands, then the millions.

"How can they be on Magentis, and still be alive?"

Chalwen glanced sidelong and her horror deepened. The shy and friendly face of the orderly was fixed in a poisonous scowl. If anyone bearing the Firenzi name had walked into the office at that moment, Chalwen could easily picture this youngster tearing them apart bare-handed.

"Is that how they managed it? Sabotaged the Emperor's craft? They were here the whole time?"

"Listen, Missy, I don't know what garbage newsrooms you listen to, but Josef Firenzi is not your enemy."

"But Security proved they—"

"Take a look around you," Chalwen barked, drawing a wide-eyed stare from the orderly. "Where are you standing? This is the *heart* of Security, charged with keeping the imperial family safe."

She took a breath, realizing how contradictory that sounded with most of the Family dead. She also recognized the insurmountable task ahead combating juicy falsehoods. This girl was intelligent, but her training was in medicine. What would she know about plotting assassinations? So what nonsense could a skilled propagandist spin that she'd accept, wide-eyed and credulous?

"We failed dismally. We let the Emperor down, and the whole of Magentis with him, and for that I can't apologize enough." Chalwen struggled to her feet and tottered there without her cane to give her support. She reached and took the orderly's hands in hers. "We failed *you*. And that makes me sad beyond measure, but it also makes me angry."

The girl nodded.

"I've spent the last days more furious than I've ever felt," Chalwen continued. "You stand there spitting feathers at a newscast, but you can't begin to imagine what I'd do to the perpetrators if they ever crossed my path." She let go a hand and gestured towards the floor. "Down in the basements here we still have rooms filled with devices that people thought civilization had left behind a century ago. I would joyfully use those rooms' full potential with anyone even remotely connected to this plot."

"Lieutenant, I work in the infirmary. I try to save lives, but in this case I'd probably join you."

"And if I thought you might be persuaded to violate your professional code of ethics, I'd invite you to patch them up so I could do it all again."

A flicker of uncertainty crossed the girl's face.

Chalwen clutched her hands fiercely. "If anyone is motivated to nail the murderers, it's us, here in the guard house. Do you think I'd let someone walk out of here if I thought for a moment they might be guilty?"

The orderly shook her head.

"So if I tell you I *know* it wasn't Josef Firenzi, you'd better listen."

———•─•———

The aromatic broth sat heavy in Chalwen's stomach as the hour ticked by and she engaged the security protocols once more. The medications seemed to be having an effect, though. Her queasiness was down to nerves, and the nagging pain had dimmed to manageable levels.

It was with jittery anxiety that she reconnected her comms screen.

She breathed a deep sigh of relief to see over ninety connections listed on the desktop, and more were signing in as the seconds ticked by. It was surely only a fraction of the full reform group, but what could she expect at such short notice? It was a blessing that a few dozen people found her pleas worth responding to. And she was thankful to see Henri's code name among them.

That, she suddenly realized, had been the easy part. How quickly would she lose them if she wasn't convincing?

She took a deep breath. "Greetings. Any one of us can call on the Light to respond to a critical threat to the empire. That last resort has been exercised only a handful of times to my knowledge. This isn't something I do lightly, and if I've misjudged the situation then I'll gladly accept whatever censure this group sees fit." With formal niceties out of the way, she paused to marshal her thoughts. "I called this meeting because I believe we do face such a crisis. Without clear leadership to turn to, we may not survive the unrest about to swamp us."

The silence unsettled her. That's the trouble with meetings behind blank screens, she had no way to read people's reactions. Were they with her? Skeptical? Even listening?

"I'm sure by now you've seen the gutter feeds, and the story is making its way into mainstream channels. Reports of Firenzi involvement in Emperor Paul's death, and now reports that the Head of Family is our guest on Magentis."

That got a reaction. Brief snatches of sound, intakes of breath, growls of anger, before the comms system filtered out background noise that clearly wasn't someone trying to speak.

"I can assert that one report is false, the other is true." Even as she spoke, Chalwen realized she was moving too fast. Sweat streamed off her face. The relative cool of the office, insulated from the worst of the Prandis daytime heat, felt airless. Her throat tightened as snatches of anger and disbelief made it past the comms filters.

But at least nobody was openly contradicting her ... yet.

"Let's look at the true part first." She needed to lead them to their own conclusions. Being so close to events in the palace, she had knowledge that probably none of them had other than Henri. Convincing them of what she knew would be an uphill slog. "My question, to the collected wisdom present, is this: why is Josef Firenzi still on Magentis?"

There was a long pause before one of the members broke the silence. "The official stance is that it's too risky to move them."

"Not what I heard," another one said. "My sources say they are being held in connection to the Emperor's death."

A third joined in. "Or as hostages."

"So, the official position is that there is no official position. At least they're safe behind the palace walls."

"It's a palace, not a fortress. Put a big enough and angry enough mob outside the gates and there's no guarantee they'll be kept out."

Faceless names swirled in front of Chalwen as each person spoke.

"And that's without some kind of co-operation from inside."

That last comment silenced the meeting. Chalwen was thankful that someone else had reached the same conclusion. Into the shocked hush, she said, "Too many things have happened recently that could only be done with inside help. To me, this looks like a set-up."

"I think you'd better explain."

Crowsfoot? thought Chalwen. Who the heck comes up with these names? Aloud, she said, "Someone has killed the Emperor. What if that same someone is trying to remove the next most powerful Family head as well?"

"Why?"

"Think about this. What does it look like from the outside?"

"If you believe the media hype, it looks like a simple slugging match between Skamensis and Firenzi. Assassination followed by revenge."

"Followed by a crippling war between the two Families, that would bring them both to their knees—"

"To be mopped up by whoever's next in the pecking order?"

"Or some coalition, maybe." Chalwen paused to rein in her racing thoughts. "But, yes, that kind of weakening would leave a huge gap to be filled. This is why I believe we face a crisis. It's not fully out in the open yet, but it is coming with all the force of an avalanche."

"So, Tungsten ..."

The breath hitched in Chalwen's throat when she saw the code sign. *Shadowland*. Lorenzo himself was in the meeting.

"What do you propose we do?"

Lorenzo's presence weighed her down. Here was someone who could easily fill Paul's shoes ... if only it were that easy. Chalwen was doing her best to guide and educate the Crown Prince, but she would never have presumed to advise Paul. He'd always thought at least three steps beyond anything Chalwen could imagine, and Lorenzo's mind was at least as capable. Maybe more so. That had made him more dangerous, and earned him exile under Empress Florence while Paul remained.

Nevertheless, she steeled herself. What she was proposing wasn't politics or statecraft. It was simple humanity.

"The Firenzi contingent is not safe in Henriss. No matter what you believe of their guilt or innocence they can't be lynched by a Magentis mob, and the media is being manipulated to make that happen. If Grand Duke Ivan won't move them, we need to do it ourselves."

She winced at the expected protests. One in particular touched a nerve. "That's crazy! This group was formed by Paul, before he was emperor, to help him fight Empress Florence. We have no business help-ing a Firenzi noble."

Chalwen stifled a howl of frustration. "We were formed to fight for a principle, not a person. With Paul gone, how long before the next Florence rises up? We should be organizing to stop such a setback, not fight it after the fact."

An awkward silence, then someone spoke up hesitantly. "I'm not seeing the connection."

"Think of it this way. If Josef Firenzi is killed, on Magentis, what happens? You already said it. A crippling war. It's inevitable. And what kind of ruler thrives in times like that? Ivan would be in his element. It's inevitable. The Assembly would never agree to Julian's succession if we were pitched into open conflict. They'd have a Declaration of Competence voted on before you could draw breath. Even if you don't agree on higher principles, pure self-interest says this is a calamity we must prevent."

Come on, Lorenzo! Say something!

"If we agree you're right, what can we do?" The code word Starburst slid to the forefront of Chalwen's desktop. "We're just a bunch of anonymous voices behind a screen."

"Is that what you think?" Chalwen's voice rose. "Are you freakin' kidding me? We may be anonymous to each other, but think about it." She took a deep breath. "I am an officer in the imperial bodyguard." She imagined she could hear the massed intake of breath on the other side of a hundred comms screens. "I know another member in real life, who is high up in ImpSec."

That was too much for someone. "Lorenzo ... Shadowland, I mean ... stop this madness. This is a crass breach of security. We stay anonymous for our own security."

Lorenzo remained silent. It seemed this was the time to ask forgiveness rather than permission. She plunged on. "This hiding behind code words has to end. It served to protect us from betrayal from within, back in the early days, but with Paul gone it's getting in the way. We need to come together as a body now, to work together, not in isolation. To use each other's position and skills properly."

"That's something that we already do from the center, to good effect." Behind the masking distortion, Lorenzo's voice sounded amused.

"And that center now has one critical weakness," Chalwen said. "You. We've lost Paul. If anything happened to you, we'd be sunk, unable to meet at all. The Hidden Light will fail."

"You make a good argument. As it happens, it's something I've given thought to before. You're asking that we unmask ourselves to each other. That's a decision that will need to be left up to each of you individually, but I agree, the time has come to work differently. We need to decentralize to some extent. Those of you who fear exposure can keep your privacy, but those who choose to do so can make themselves open to the group. It won't be a free-for-all, we need some fences between us, but I'll set up a group of technicians to form a clearing-house of contacts."

"Thank you, Shadowland."

"And I've had time to think about why you brought us here."

"Mount some kind of madcap jailbreak, you mean?" Chalwen missed the coded identity behind the sarcastic tone. Her vision blurred in sudden weariness at this endless carping.

"Even so." Lorenzo's voice was even and unfazed. "Some of you were here in the early years, in Florence's time. That was before Paul was emperor, of course. And we must remember what we used to do then. We took it on ourselves to curb excesses. To intervene where we could, to set events on better courses. It was never about serving Paul, or me for that matter. It was always about averting disasters where we could make a difference."

Lorenzo paused, a long dramatic moment. Chalwen had forgotten about that trait, ever the showman. It brought memories back of times long past. Memories she'd rather stayed buried.

"I thank Tungsten for reminding us of that heritage. Josef Firenzi is in harm's way. Maybe not by the hand of a tyrant, maybe only through leaderless inaction, but that doesn't matter. That harm would definitely bring disaster to a big slice of humanity. It seems to me this is in perfect keeping with our original purpose."

The silence lengthened. It seemed Lorenzo was stepping back. This was Chalwen's meeting, after all. She chewed her knuckles hard, the pain bringing fresh determination and focus. "We need to act fast, so above all I need people here on Magentis who can help physically. Who knows who each of you are? I can't begin to guess. But one thing I'm sure of, every one of you is a force to be reckoned with individually. Just think what we can do together."

An anonymous voice asked, "What do you have in mind? I'm ready to help if I can."

"We need assets on the ground. Military, security, communications, logistics, household staff, especially at Henriss. You all have skills to offer, but we likely need more than that. Some of you will have to reach into your own networks, recruit people you trust.

"Nobody is keeping you here. If you want to help, stay on the call, otherwise feel free to leave, but only stay if you are one-hundred percent committed. Some of us have a jailbreak to plan."

Chapter 25

Bucket seats of a troop carrier were never designed for comfort. The six most trusted members of Chalwen's squad in the back of the bulky vehicle didn't seem bothered, judging by the quiet banter between them, but Chalwen struggled to ease the electric jolts stabbing up her shins. She'd eased back on pain meds today, needing to keep her wits sharp.

She'd rather be in the driving seat but had reluctantly surrendered that to Skinner, one of her bodyguard squad leaders. Instead, she resigned herself to navigating their route through the outskirts of Henriss Garden, with Henri's help from distant Prandis.

"I don't have much surveillance in the suburbs," Henri murmured in her earpiece, "but from what I can see, your path looks clear. The city center is a gong show but the outlying districts are quiet."

"You're telling me," Chalwen muttered. The residential district they were passing through was a ghost town. To Skinner she said, "Left at the next plaza, then right three blocks down."

She checked in with Eve, one of Skinner's squad members, up in the observation cupola overlooking the cab.

"Relax, Lieutenant," Eve said. "Eyes peeled and sensors hot, scanning sides, back, and skyline all around."

The windows of the troop carrier were both armored and tinted. Nobody could see into the cab, but there was nobody around to try.

Even the market plazas, that should be bustling with early evening trade, were deserted.

"Have you ever seen anything like it?" someone whispered from the body of the vehicle behind Chalwen. "Gives me the shivers."

"Look on it as a blessing. With the landing field by the palace blocked off, and having to drive from the commercial field on the other side of the city, I'm all for quiet roads."

"All the same ..."

The squaddie—that sounded like Wilder whispering back there—had a point. There were no signs of calamity or forced evacuation, but it was as if the entire population had been spirited away.

They approached a half-mile-long bridge linking the city's peninsula to the island where the Palace of Butterflies sat. Skinner slowed as they neared the corner of the last building before the waterfront esplanade.

"Hold here," Chalwen ordered. She was gratified that Eve took the hint without needing an order, and turned her instruments towards the path ahead.

"Bridge itself is quiet. Ditto near bank to the west. Have to move out of cover to see anything eastwards."

"And the far end?"

"Scanning at magnification and in IR. Crowd gathered eastwards, a mile away. No activity on the bridge. No evidence of roadblocks. I don't think anyone's paying any attention this way."

Chalwen chewed her lip. "Henri, we're going to pass through a bottleneck on the seafront, and join with the bridge from Via Magentis. We have crowds on foot nearby. What's it like further along?"

"Bad," Henri said. "That's where all the population's gone. People still moving across the main bridge to your south to join the protest outside the palace gates. Stay away from the main road. I'm highlighting a military route through Regent's Park on your notepad. Gated, so no civilian vehicles, and not many people are wandering that way on foot."

"And the gates?"

"Sending you the codes now."

"Wonder what that crowd will do when they see us?" Skinner said. "We'll be exposed on that bridge."

The dilemma. Take it at speed, knowing the noise would attract attention the moment they opened up, or try to sneak across quietly? It all hinged on the mood of the crowd. Chalwen reached a decision. "We cross at a normal cruising speed. Try not to look threatening, or like we're in any kind of hurry. There's been no reports of violence so far. Don't want to spook them."

The troop carrier slid out from cover and onto the bridge. Chalwen's eyes were on the milling crowd in the distance. As they reached the half-way point, it seemed a few people had turned to watch them, but thankfully there was no rush to head off the intruding vehicle.

Up in the cupola, Eve called out, "Lieutenant, we've got movement on the far bank. Road still looks clear, but pedestrians coming out from cover."

Chalwen squinted ahead to where stands of trees fringed the wall of the park. Small knots of people emerged and drifted towards the bridge. Some, though, headed back into the trees while others joined the slow movement in the direction of the Palace of Butterflies, still five miles away. There didn't appear to be any organization, any leadership or obvious motivation. It was just a sparse collection of individuals, not yet gelled into a mob.

Before they reached the nearest group, Skinner slowed to walking pace. "Keep it steady," Chalwen said, even though every nerve screamed at her to tell Skinner to gun the throttle and barge through the crowd.

"They look more curious than hostile," muttered Eve.

By now, they were committed. People closed in behind them, but parted in front.

"Take us west, away from the palace."

Skinner turned. The crowd thinned. Chalwen jumped at a hollow clang from the sides of the carrier. More bangs echoed through the armor.

"Dammit," Eve shouted. "The dumb fucks are chucking *rocks* at us."

"Screw this," Chalwen growled. She reached for a panel in front of her and hit a button. A piercing siren wail hurt her ears even inside the protection of the cab. Outside, people clapped hands to ears and staggered away.

As soon as they were clear of the pedestrians, Skinner took them back up to cruising speed. To their left, the park wall came into view. When they came to a gate, Chalwen transmitted the access code. The knot between her shoulder blades didn't ease until the gate had clanged shut behind them.

At this point, the park was little more than a narrow strip half a mile wide forming a secure zone at the back of the seaward defenses. Another gate in a steel fence let them onto a smooth paved road.

"Now we must hurry."

Skinner responded by opening up the throttle. The troop carrier lunged forward with a throaty bellow. To their right, a wall broken by occasional beam emplacements protected the southwestern shore of the island. To the left, beyond the roadside fence, tree-studded parkland rolled into the distance.

Some protesters, maybe looking for a way into the palace complex, had scaled the park walls. The sound of the vehicle brought them running but the smooth uprights of the fence made climbing difficult. The carrier roared past, eating up the last few miles to the palace.

In only a few minutes, the outer perimeter of the palace loomed above them. Squat and windowless buildings hundreds of yards across jutted out from the circular boundary wall. Half a mile away, the top of the park wall was tinged with orange from bonfires dotted around the palace landing field. Showers of sparks leaped into the gathering dusk.

The road led them to a side gate set in the wall like a beach cave in gleaming masonry cliffs. The outer gate opened, and banged ominously shut behind them, leaving them in a tunnel sealed at both ends.

A sergeant strode out from a guard office set into the side of the tunnel. Chalwen opened her door and stepped down to meet him. Even at a distance, she could see he was furious.

"What in the name of Unity are you damnable idiots doing ..." He trailed off as he caught sight of Chalwen's lieutenant insignia, and the Mosaic Palace designation on her lapel.

"Advance squad, imperial bodyguard," Chalwen announced. "The Crown Prince is expecting to visit as soon as the hubbub dies down, and we need to carry out a security inspection."

"You picked a right barmpot time to plan a royal visit. Can't it wait?"

Chalwen gave the sergeant an icy stare. "Will you be the one to inform the Crown Prince that his wishes are *inconvenient* to you?" For once, she was glad of the imperial bodyguard's reputation for elitist arrogance. The bizarre timing *should* make the sergeant suspicious, but the bodyguard's well-known disdain for the concerns of lesser mortals made the lie credible. "We managed to get here despite the five-mile no-fly zone around the palace. You don't think a few protestors are going to sidetrack Family Skamensis, do you?"

The sergeant mumbled a denial.

"One more thing. This vehicle will be returning to the landing field shortly. You will make sure it passes back through this gate without hindrance."

As they nosed through the inner gate and into the palace grounds, Chalwen called Henri. "We're in. Hope you've got our help lined up inside."

"Affirmative. You've got the schematics. Straight three hundred yards, then left past the stable block. Sussex House is up on the left."

Skinner grunted in response. Chalwen opened her window to get a better feel for their surroundings. The troop carrier seemed brutally out of place in the elegant avenue surrounded by tended gardens and white-washed buildings. Other than the rumble of the vehicle, everything seemed tranquil in this quarter of the grounds. The massive ziggurat of the Hall of Music loomed above graceful colonnaded terraces, mirrored by the Temple of Reflection further away. She craned her neck to take in the palace's central tower that soared, floodlit, half a mile into the sky.

A sound drifted over the rooftops, an exultant outcry from ten thousand throats, distant yet chilling.

The troop carrier turned off the avenue and onto a narrower road leading to an imposing frontage. From the corner of her eye, Chalwen glimpsed a squad in full armor in the distance double-timing in the direction of the main gates. She shuddered and studied schematics on her notepad to confirm the ornate edifice two hundred yards ahead was their destination. She checked her own equipment, knowing the rest of the extraction team behind her was doing likewise.

The center of the building frontage was dominated by a portico. The road ran right through the building and into the next quarter, where the main palace gates lay.

Dark figures lurked in the shadows of the near archway. Chalwen tensed, then relaxed when she saw these were neither vigilantes nor regular guards. Skinner halted the carrier just inside the archway.

A wide-eyed skinny girl, barely into her twenties, hurried around the front of the vehicle.

Chalwen eyed her dark civilian dress. Unremarkable, anonymous. Probably as good as anything for a covert operation. She murmured, "Tungsten."

"Ensign Gemma Merkel. Signals." The girl climbed the running board and whispered in Chalwen's ear, "You'd know me as Crowsfoot." She must have caught Chalwen's glance at her five companions lurking in the shadows. "They know what they're getting into, and I trust them."

"Do they?" Chalwen hissed earnestly. "To outside appearances, we're about to abduct a Head of Family currently enjoying imperial hospitality."

A distant roar echoed through the tunnel. Gemma shrugged. "Think they'll continue enjoying the hospitality when that crowd breaks in?"

Chalwen pursed her lips. "Your crew knows to stay back? We'll do the dirty work, dealing with the guards. Your job is to cart them off to a place of safety once we've knocked them out. We'll do our best to leave no lasting damage." But, she thought, even the best-laid plans never survived first contact with the enemy.

"Okay," Chalwen called over her shoulder, "let's do this." She climbed stiffly down to the ground while her own squad emerged from the back of the troop carrier.

Skinner eased the vehicle down the tunnel and disappeared through an arched opening half-way down. Chalwen marveled at how quietly the massive vehicle could move when it wasn't in a hurry.

"Watch the perimeter, Henri, we're in position."

"Acknowledged." Even suave Henri's voice sounded tense. "Sending you the latest guard positions inside as of thirty seconds ago. Surveillance in the building is now off, so I'm as blind in there as the palace security crew. You'll have to be quick. Most of the attention is on the protests outside, but it won't be long before someone notices."

They were committed.

Gemma eased open a side door and led them into a servants' corridor running along the ground floor of the building.

The grip of the needle gun felt utterly wrong in Chalwen's hand. She was used to beam pistols and rifles, both military and civilian grade, as well as knives and nightsticks and all manner of improvised close-quarter weapons. Everything she'd handled and trained with felt reassuringly substantial. The unfamiliar needle gun—little more than a hand grip with an insignificant barrel mounted on top—felt like a toy in comparison, but they wanted to minimize casualties. Besides, a beam discharge would trigger alarms that even Henri couldn't suppress.

That wasn't all that was wrong. Chalwen glanced again at her notepad and had a queasy feeling she'd seen this before. An unnatural absence of guards at posts. The same playbook she'd seen at Cravel and Prandis. Her scalp crawled. Other than a token presence—accomplices or unfortunate collateral?—someone had cleared the way to the Firenzi delegation, and she was sure it wasn't for *her* team's benefit.

They sidled along the hall, and Gemma pointed at a door. Chalwen nodded, and checked her notepad again before slipping it into a pocket. She wiped sweat from her forehead, but couldn't do anything about the uncomfortable trickle down her spine. The day's tropical heat had turned the corridor into an oven. She wiped her palm and checked her grip on the unfamiliar weapon. As long as they hadn't moved, there were guards posted beyond the door on either side. This had to be done quietly. There would be more posted in an atrium just a hundred feet away.

Chalwen exchanged a glance with Tara, her second-in-command on this part of the mission. Also, the best shot. A brief exchange of hand signals and the whole squad knew what to expect.

They palmed their needle guns. Chalwen took a deep breath, opened the door, and strode through like she belonged there.

Tara followed.

The expected challenge came immediately. "Hey! This is a restricted area. State your business and authority."

"Imperial bodyguard. Here's my authority." Chalwen raised her hand as if offering some ID. At this range, the weapon hardly needed aiming.

The guard looked startled, then slumped to the ground. Chalwen lurched forward to break his fall and deaden the sound. A grunt behind her told Chalwen that Tara had nailed and caught the other guard.

The door opened. Two of Gemma's companions dragged the unconscious guards out of sight. They'd stash them in a nearby storeroom and administer a short-term memory blocker. When they recovered from the drugs, the guards would have no recollection of anything from the past hour.

The rest of Chalwen's and Gemma's squads joined Chalwen and Tara in the hallway, then Tara and Wilder, another of her squad, turned and started towards the atrium. They had a long hallway to traverse and Chalwen cursed not being able to move like she should. Enviously, she watched Tara and Wilder glide silently, followed at a safe distance by Gemma's clean-up squad. Chalwen winced at every clack and scrape of boots on stone. At least the walls were plush with sound-deadening hangings.

A whisper in her ear took Chalwen's mind off the hot needles stabbing up her calves. "The main gate has been breached. Civilians are inside the grounds, mostly milling around, but there seems to be a more focused group heading your way."

A cold shiver wracked Chalwen. Ferociously she pushed the pain aside and made as much haste as she could. By the time she'd limped to join the vanguard, the fight was over. Two guards lay comatose nearby, and Skinner and Eve had dealt with two more on the far side of the atrium where they'd parked the troop carrier.

She brought them together and said, "Looks like we'll get company within the next few minutes."

"And," added Skinner, "if someone managed to engineer this whole protest to cover a hit squad, you can be sure they'll be professionals."

"You and Eve, cover our backs. Tara and Wilder, lead the way."

Another pain-wracked hallway, Chalwen did her best to keep up, but all thoughts of stealth were now off the table. Tara rushed up to the double doors at the end and tried the handle. "I don't suppose, before we carted those guards off, anyone thought to search them for keys?"

Without a word or the slightest hesitation, Wilder stepped up and kicked the door in. "Keys are so last year." He grinned.

The grin vanished when a uniformed arm swung a club from behind the wrecked door. Wilder deflected the worst of the blow, then turned to deal with a second attack from the other side. Tara stepped in to grapple with the first assailant, and the rest of Chalwen's guards threw themselves into the melee.

Chalwen took a moment to assess the scene. She counted four Firenzi guards near the door, quickly subdued by her own squad. Several more guards formed a cordon around a makeshift barrier of overturned tables across one corner of the room. Some of them brandished clubs that Chalwen realized were broken-off table legs. Behind the tables huddled a frightened group of civilians.

The remaining Firenzi guards outnumbered Chalwen's small group, most of whom were busy restraining the four on the floor. It seemed the Firenzi contingent had also done the math. They advanced.

The crackle of beam discharges split the evening sky beyond the windows lining the far side of the room. Ah, fuck it! Chalwen drew her own beam pistol and fired three shots into the ceiling. "Stand down," she yelled into the sudden shocked silence. She pointed to her official insignia. "Imperial bodyguard. I can see you're expecting trouble." She gestured to the windows. "Trouble is on its way. That mob has breached the main gates. We're here to get you out, but we must hurry."

The head of Josef's bodyguard, a slight woman with a face like curdled cream stepped forward. She wore a breast flash showing the rank of major in the Firenzi military. "What's going on out there? We've had access to news reports and reckoned we should prepare for the worst." She glanced out the window where more flashes lit the darkness. "But we were told this site would be secure."

"Whoever thought *that* didn't reckon on someone stirring up a mob. And I don't think they got past the gates without inside help."

The major looked shocked, then she drew a deep breath. "I've seen you before. You used to accompany Emperor Paul, didn't you?"

"Years ago," Chalwen acknowledged.

Outside, raucous shouts grew louder. Movement caught Chalwen's eye. Across the floodlit courtyard beyond the window, people surged around the far corner a hundred yards away.

The major glanced at Josef Firenzi, who nodded.

Chalwen turned to Josef. "I have transport to get you, Lady Margerite, and a small guard squad off the planet. We can hide the rest of your party in a secure bunker until the fuss dies down."

"Is there anywhere safe in the palace?"

"The mob wants *you*. When it's known you're no longer in reach, they'll have no interest in anyone else. Now we must move!"

As if to punctuate her words, glass exploded into the room. Needing no more urging, the group hurried down the hall and into the deserted atrium. Eve waved them across to the far hallway, where Skinner and the rest of the squad stood guard.

Chalwen gathered Josef's entourage together and pointed to Eve. "The corporal here will lead you to a more secure place to wait." To Eve, she said, "Stay in the upper service levels. Avoid the surface. You have the codes to pass through security doors."

Eve huffed. "I've got this. You get the VIPs out safely." She opened a service door at the end of the hall, and gestured to the Firenzi staff to follow.

With the Firenzi nobles and the bodyguard, Chalwen limped in the other direction. They skirted a courtyard where the troop carrier could be seen past the columns of a covered walkway.

"This is where we part ways," Skinner announced.

"Wait," Josef said. "Aren't we leaving in that?"

Chalwen grinned. "We are not. That's a distraction. Good luck, Skinner."

That brought a sly smile from the sour-faced Firenzi major.

With the remaining squad members, Chalwen headed through another wing of the building and down stairs. Pain stabbed up her legs now with every step, but she gritted her teeth and plowed on. They had a lot of steps yet to descend. This was madness! Why did she insist on leading the mission herself? She fumbled in her pocket for a medipen and surreptitiously lifted the corner of her tunic to apply it. She had to hold it together for a while longer.

Their route took them through service tunnels, then back out into the muggy twilight. With nerves stretched to the limit, they crossed the southwestern gardens to the base of the outer wall, where Chalwen keyed the codes to pass them through a deserted guard room and small gate house. Outside the palace walls, they found themselves at the top of a cliff that plunged two hundred feet to the beach. A path zig-zagged back and forth below.

For Chalwen, the climb down was an eternity of both physical and mental pain. At any moment, she expected the shouts of exultant discovery and the dazzling beams of spotlights pinning them to the crumbling cliff face. And yet the night remained supernaturally quiet. From the heights of the palace walls, there was neither sign nor sound of the tumult within.

She didn't even have the comfort of Henri's voice in her ear, advising of events within the walls. He was busy for now with his own tasks. She had to trust that he'd managed to disable the sensors that would warn the main gate house of movement on this path.

At last they reached the beach. Surf grumbled a few feet away.

A shallow boat sped in from the night and grounded its prow on the sand. The guards helped Josef and Margerite aboard, then hauled a protesting Chalwen unceremoniously over the bow. She made one last grumble, then slumped thankfully to the deck and massaged her calves.

With a grating hiss, the boat pulled free and surged parallel to the shore.

The boat showed no running lights and the helmsman wore night optics. In the near-darkness Chalwen was dimly aware of cliffs hemming them in on both sides. The rush of their passage echoed from both sides as the channel narrowed. After a few minutes, open sea beckoned. The boat bounced in the chop and surged over a ponderous swell.

Space alive, that was stupid of her. She'd insisted she had her injuries under control, but her pig-headedness had endangered the mission. She wasn't fit for this. She squeezed her eyes shut to block the flow of angry tears. If not this, then what in Space *was* she fit for?

No! she'd beat that fucking poison. Training, therapy, determination, she wouldn't give in. And she still had a job to do.

While Chalwen grimaced at the pounding under her thighs, Henri rejoined her comms. "Half an hour to the rendezvous. The air cruiser will meet you on the headland across from the city, well outside the no-fly zone. All quiet."

Henri paused. "Too quiet in some parts. I've heard nothing recently from Daffodil."

A chill washed over Chalwen. Daffodil, their member on the inside providing them safe passage past the orbiting security around Magentis, was missing.

"You realize this is only rated for suborbital flight?" the pilot murmured.

Chalwen glanced out the cockpit as deep blue gave way to star-speckled black. "It's airtight, isn't it?"

The pilot grunted.

"And you can fly it as long as we're within the planet's gravity well?"

The pilot rolled his eyes. "I said 'rated'. Some kind of liability thing, I think."

"Exactly. It was less obvious getting hold of a suborbital craft than a full spacegoing cruiser." Chalwen stared down at the growing crescent of the planet below them. "With any luck they're scouring Traplinki for possible landing sites, deciding how to head us off."

Spaceworthiness was the least of her worries, they still had a screen of battle stations to get past. But they had no choice but to stick with the plan and hope Daffodil had made the necessary arrangements. Chalwen studied the comms screen. One downside to not having a space-rated craft, planet-hoppers lacked anything but the most rudimentary sensor equipment. She just had to trust the Firenzi forces were out there, some-where, and would find them.

Tiny blips on the screen showed orbiting battle stations. The one patrolling *Sword* was on the far side of the planet. There were no truly weak areas in the planet's defenses, but the skies above them were as clear as they could be. "Take us up."

It didn't take long for the security cordon to respond. The comms hissed to life. "Unmarked cruiser, this is battle station *Hyperion*. You are entering controlled orbital space. Identify yourself and return to subor-bital flight immediately."

Chalwen leaned over and thumbed the comms to transmit. Trying not to let the pounding in her chest affect her voice, she reeled off the authentication code the Hidden Light member had provided.

A long pause, then, "Unmarked cruiser, drop to low orbit and await further instructions."

"Negative, *Hyperion*. This craft is flying under the Firenzi diplomatic flag, returning Josef Firenzi to his fleet." While the crew of the looming battle station digested this claim, Chalwen muttered to the pilot, "Any sight of the Firenzi battleships? We could use a bit of backup here."

The pilot shook his head. "With this equipment? We don't have the range. Last I heard, the fleet was being held in far orbit."

The comms crackled to life again. "That's impossible. Josef Firenzi and his entourage are being held at Henriss Garden for their own safety."

"Henriss Garden is anything but safe for the Firenzi family. Put me through to the watch officer immediately so I can explain the situation."

"A few protestors?" the anonymous traffic controller scoffed. "The palace guard will keep them under control."

Chalwen snapped, "Bullshit, *Hyperion*. Check your latest feeds from the Palace of Butterflies, and tell me *that* is under control."

"*Hyperion* is warming up one of their main batteries," the pilot muttered. "Everything's aimed away from the planet, but the moment we pass their orbit we'll be lit up like midsummer."

"Unmarked craft, why is your identity not transmitting? I instruct you to hold and prepare for boarding."

This was, Chalwen ruefully acknowledged, another problem with choosing a regular air cruiser. Unlike a registered spacegoing craft, cruisers like this were unnamed and carried only a local government ID. "Battle station *Hyperion*, this is an air cruiser registered to the imperial bodyguard at the Mosaic Palace. Sending you registration details now. We are here on official security business, escorting Josef Firenzi to a place of safety."

"My turn to call bullshit," the controller sneered. "What in Space would you be doing up here in a standard air cruiser? Only smugglers try to sneak past with their ID silenced."

"Check the registration I sent you. We extracted Josef Frenzi from imminent harm in Henriss, intending to land him elsewhere. But if secure lodging in an imperial palace isn't safe, then I'm not risking my charge anywhere on Magentis. I am returning him to his fleet."

"They're not buying it." The pilot's voice was calm, but his knuckles were white on the cruiser's controls. "Coming into range in ten seconds, and that nearest battery is hot and ready."

"Dammit, *Hyperion*, do you want to be responsible for starting a war between two Families?"

The Firenzi major elbowed Chalwen aside. "Hello battle station *Hyperion*, this is Major Damra Chort, Firenzi Bodyguard. I'm transmitting authorization from the late Emperor Paul Skamensis granting Family Firenzi safe passage through Magentis space." She clicked the comms off and said to Chalwen, "I assume credentials like that will bypass the petty bureaucrats and catch the eye of a senior officer?"

Chalwen eyed the grim-face major. "Why didn't you tell me earlier you had one of those?"

The faintest smile creased the major's face. "Wanted to see if reason would prevail first."

Chalwen breathed a sigh of relief when they finally cleared the orbiting cordon after delivering Josef and company to the waiting fleet, leaving just her and the pilot to return home. There were tense moments again while they identified themselves to an incredulous traffic controller on battle station *Crius*, who couldn't believe a regular air cruiser would be approaching Magentis from space-side. Fortunately, this time a senior officer appeared on the comms within moments and cleared them to pass.

Chalwen thought she could see the invisible hand of ImpSec pulling strings, a view confirmed when Henri hailed them a few minutes later. "You're instructed to land at the secure field by the courthouse in Prandis," he said. "You'll be debriefed on landing. No further communications until then."

The pilot exchanged worried glances with Chalwen. She glanced down at the navigation screen which now showed a flight path bypassing the commercial landing field and guiding them along a narrow safe corridor into the heart of the city. She shrugged. "Our objective was met the moment we handed Josef over unharmed. There was little chance of us coming out of this unscathed."

"I guess I hadn't thought about what happens after."

"Sorry. I never got around to planning an exit strategy."

The comms embargo tormented Chalwen on their descent. She desperately wanted to ask about the rest of her squad and their helpers. And was the rest of the Firenzi contingent safe in Henriss? But Henri's instruction had been clear enough, and these were not things to discuss on open comms. Chalwen and the pilot were exposed and in for a world of hurt when they landed, but there was no need for their accomplices to be identified and dragged through the muck.

At last, the late afternoon panorama of Prandis Braz spread before them, and a few minutes later the air cruiser settled on its landing struts in an enclosed and empty landing field.

A grim-faced lieutenant climbed through the hatch the moment the craft landed, and handed Chalwen and the pilot each a hood. Chalwen glanced out the hatch to glimpse a squad of guards lined up with weapons drawn. She nodded to the pilot and pulled her hood on. Rough hands helped her down to the ground and hustled her across the landing field. She did her best to walk steadily, despite the stabs of pain shooting up her legs. Being marched blindfolded into the unknown was unnerving. Sun warmed the back of her head, giving at least some sense of direction. What now, she thought, are we going to simply disappear? She quelled a moment of panic. The instructions had come from Henri, and she trusted him utterly. The question was, who was in charge down here? Was Henri calling the shots or just acting on instructions?

She stumbled on an unseen patch of unevenness and caught her balance. A hand on her arm halted her, then guided her up a few steps. Sudden cool and footsteps echoing told her they were indoors. A few turns, and doors slammed shut behind. Through the musty hood, the air had an oily industrial scent. They must be in some kind of service corridor.

Without warning, Chalwen's hood was whipped off her head and she blinked in the sudden glare of stark overhead lights. The pilot was still with her, and the surly lieutenant, but the rest of their escort had disappeared. They were in a narrow room mostly filled with large pipes and sheaves of wiring.

The lieutenant reached behind a metal junction box and pulled out a backpack. "Change of clothes," he growled.

"What ..." the pilot started speaking, then stopped himself.

"I'm the only one who's seen your faces. The only one who could identify you. As far as the guards back there are concerned you're now in ImpSec hands, and nobody will be surprised if you're never seen again."

Chalwen allowed herself a glimmer of optimism. He wouldn't go to such lengths to hide the identity of someone who'd never be seen again. Without hesitation she tipped the backpack's contents onto the floor and chose a nondescript pair of leggings, tunic, and lightweight cloak.

"Hurry now," the lieutenant hissed to the pilot. Chalwen had already stripped off her uniform, which the lieutenant bundled into the backpack along with their hoods.

When they were both changed, he led them to the far end of the plant room and paused at a door, listening intently to his earpiece. Finally he nodded and muttered, "Confirmed."

The door opened into a blue-tiled corridor. The lieutenant gestured to the left. "Here we part ways. Go to the end and through that door, and wait." Without another word he hurried in the other direction.

Chalwen hastened to the door, with the pilot following. In the small anteroom beyond, they didn't have to wait. Henri beckoned urgently from another door to one side. With a sigh of relief, Chalwen followed him down a flight of stairs. She had completely lost any sense of direction. She assumed they were somewhere underneath the imposing courthouse that dominated one side of the city's main plaza.

"Just act normal now," Henri said. "We'll be on camera and the place will start to get busy. Nobody knows of your involvement with the episode at Henriss, and it's best things stay that way."

Chalwen was glad of the warning. They stepped out into a broad hallway with tall windows either side above head height, that washed the space with evening sun. The place teemed with people hurrying about their business. Chalwen finally recognized the link corridor between the courthouse and the adjacent Imperial Security building. Nobody paid them any attention.

An alert young corporal in spotless dress uniform admitted them through a security barrier at the far end of the hall. Despite Henri's company, a sharp prickle of unease ran down Chalwen's spine. So many people entered this building and never again saw the light of day. But Henri cheerfully guided them down a side corridor and into an empty and windowless meeting room.

"Room is secured," he said. "We can talk freely here. I need to warn you both not to mention this outside. This mission created quite a stir, once it got out that the Firenzi head had escaped. A lot of people on the ground are furious, and the media are whipping them up still."

The pilot collapsed into a chair, relief and weariness clouding his face. "So that's why you went out of your way to hide us on the way in."

Henri nodded.

One thing puzzled Chalwen. "I'm grateful, but I don't understand the point of all these moves to cover our tracks. All our passkeys will have been clocked at the Palace of Butterflies."

Henri gave her an innocent look. "No such records exist. We believe a number of data stores were erased by the conspirators who opened the palace gates, to hide their tracks."

"What's happened to the rest of the team?"

"Eve and the Firenzi entourage are still holed up in Henriss. The palace guard have restored order after a night of chaos, and we're making arrangements to repatriate them. Most of your squad have returned to their duties. They'd have liked to be here to greet you, but they need to keep up the pretense that they were here the whole time."

"How are we going to get the rest of the Firenzis off-planet? If the public is so worked up, they might settle for any Firenzi blood they can spill."

"We managed to give the impression the entire contingent was rescued at once. I reckon there's some head-scratching going on trying to figure out how that was achieved. Your actual escape route is still a secret. It makes it look like the lot of them simply vanished. There'll be a lot of troop and security movements in and out of the Palace of Butterflies in the coming week, so an extra secured flight will be easy to hide."

"And Skinner?" Chalwen was painfully aware that he'd had probably the most dangerous assignment after they'd freed Josef.

"Also good, but he had to go to ground in Regents Park for a while. He got through the gates without trouble, and left the vehicle as soon as he was out of sight. I took it from there under remote control as planned. This is what I wanted to show you." Henri activated a wall screen and brought up a set of visuals from the empty troop carrier. Chalwen recognized the fenced road leading past the edge of the park. "If anyone inside the palace leaked our movements, the hope was for all attention to be on this vehicle, and not looking for people making an escape on foot."

"You used your troop carrier as a diversion?" The pilot barked a laugh. "Sorry, I wasn't privy to all the details of the rescue, just the rendezvous points."

"How far did the vehicle get?" Chalwen asked.

"Two miles into the park, then there was a roadblock. They had shaped charges and cutting torches. Anyone inside wouldn't have stood a chance." Henri grimaced. "You were right. Someone inside the palace was informing the mob."

They watched the attack play out in silence. A handful of masked attackers worked with military precision, disabling the troop carrier's drive and blowing open the cab. "That was no mob," Chalwen whispered. "It was an organized execution party."

Once again, she studied the visual feeds sent from the decoy vehicle. "Hold there," she called sharply. "That side view. Back up, and magnify the left middle distance." She squinted in frustration. "See those boxes under the trees? Magnify and enhance."

Henri let out a low whistle. It took all Chalwen's strength to not be sick as the image sharpened and the motif stenciled on the boxes became recognizable.

"Swiftsures," the pilot muttered. "Short range missiles, but they could easily pick off anyone trying to take off from within the palace grounds. None of our combat training ever gave us a viable defense against those fuckers. They were expecting an escape attempt by air."

"Or just hedging their bets," said Henri. "Who's to say they were expecting an escape at all?"

Chalwen's gaze was still fixed on those innocuous-looking grey boxes. "More to the point, how in all of Unity did they manage to smuggle those into the city, let alone so close to the palace?"

"More inside help?"

"Exactly. The more I see, the more it seems the whole administration is riddled with traitors."

"I don't think the answer is that simple." Henri frowned in thought. "Paul represented a radical departure from centuries of Skamensis norms.

What we're seeing could be a groundswell of resistance. People who want to return to how things were before Paul took the throne."

"People working against their lawful emperor? Traitors!"

"Like The Hidden Light working against Florence?"

Chalwen opened her mouth, but no words came. Henri had a point.

"Technically," he said, "they're loyal to Family Skamensis and would see themselves as patriots, not traitors. They just want a different Skamensis on the throne."

"A return to Florence's glory days?" The sick feeling overwhelmed Chalwen. "They want Ivan!"

The following morning, Chalwen limped through the reception room and into the cool depths of the Crown Prince's office. With first the one then the other of them holed up in the infirmary, she'd seen nothing of Julian since the assassination, but she was troubled by what she'd heard.

From the reports of Julian withdrawing from palace life, she'd expected to find him lurking alone in either his quarters or his office, but she had to force her way through a crush of people at the door to the inner office, helped by Javarro clearing a way from the other side. Her eyes widened as she took in the line of people leading from the door to the front of Julian's desk.

Julian looked up and she was even more shocked at his empty eyes and haggard expression. Despite his evident fatigue, his face lit up as he saw her. He waved away the nearest visitor and stood, plodding stiffly around the desk to meet her. He looked at Chalwen's walking cane and grinned. "Aren't we a pair now?"

"Glad to see you on your feet. That broom didn't really suit the heir to the throne."

Julian's grin faded. "You've paid a price for looking after me. Again."

Chalwen was thankful he didn't ask about her recovery. She'd insisted this morning on speaking with the senior medic in person. Helena Bertolli had tried to be upbeat, but her careful hedging spoke volumes. The poison that Chalwen had inhaled was a treacherous nerve agent. The few people who survived a Slow Sleep attack rarely went completely unscathed.

She hastily changed the subject. "Who are all these people?" She gestured to the waiting crowd.

Julian pointed to the nearest, a portly man already balding despite his youthful face. "Representative of the Prandis Musician's Guild." Julian waved his hand down the line. "Clerk of the Imperial Wardrobe at Henriss, fireworks display organizer, ummm ..."

"Purveyor of fine wines," announced the woman next in line.

"Event catering."

"Henriss office of highways."

"Enough!" Chalwen closed her eyes and counted slowly to calm the fury welling inside her. "Preparations for the Royal Family's funeral are important, both to the empire and to you personally. I get that. But there are other matters equally pressing."

"But I *want* to be involved. I insisted."

"Involved, yes. Buried, no." Chalwen turned to the Musician's Guild representative. "Who sent you to this office?"

"The guard at the gate directed me here, but I was contacted by the office of the Grand Duke."

Chalwen raised an eyebrow at the next in line.

"Likewise."

Others down the line nodded agreement.

"Ivan," Chalwen muttered. "What's he up to?" To Javarro she said, "Clear these people out of here. They can leave their details at the gate and they'll be contacted again in due course. But first, call a ground car to be at the door in two minutes. Neither of us are in a fit state to make haste on foot."

The few hundred yards weaving through lunchtime crowds felt like an eternity to Chalwen. She needed to make inquiries to unearth whatever game Ivan was playing with Julian, but first she had to open the Crown Prince's eyes to his naivete.

It was probably as well Javarro was driving. Chalwen would have mowed down a dozen people by now in her impatience. He called ahead and had a small squad meet them at their destination.

Chalwen refused to answer Julian's questions about where they were going. "Not far," was all she said. "Meanwhile, reflect on the role of an emperor. How often do you remember your father putting up with an office full of people laying claim to his time?"

Julian looked thoughtful. "He was always busy."

"With ambassadors and heads of state, and within the palace, heads of department."

"And all on his own terms," Julian said. His voice was grim. One lesson learned.

The car glided to a halt. "Welcome to the household administration offices," Chalwen clambered down to the ground then helped Julian out.

Julian gazed up at the rows of windows overlooking the courtyard. "I've seen this building often enough on the way to our hangar, but never been inside."

"Then it's about time. Think of it as an impromptu field trip, and one you'll do well to remember in future. This is an important place to get to know." She grinned. "Almost as important as the palace kitchens."

They let themselves in at a side door and up a wide staircase, one painful step at a time. Across a long hallway, Chalwen pushed open a large door. "Anna!" she called out.

An elderly, white-haired Wala woman rose from behind a desk. "Lieutenant ap Gwynodd. How dare you leave it so long between visits?"

"Things to do, Princes to save."

Anna grinned then noticed Julian limping behind Chalwen. "Magister! I beg pardon. We are hardly in a fit state to greet royalty."

"Please," Julian said. "No formality. This is an unannounced visit. In fact, I'm not sure what we're doing here." He cocked his head expectantly at Chalwen.

"You'll see. Anna, is Jemima in?"

While Anna spoke into a comms screen on her desk, Chalwen turned to face Julian. "Sire, you have an entire office here whose job it is to deal with all those merchants, bureaucrats, and trades people."

"What is this place?"

"This is the office of the Master of Circuses."

"I've heard of it, but never paid much attention. We don't have many circuses in Prandis."

Behind Chalwen, Anna snorted. "You haven't hung around the Assembly enough, then. Jemima will be here shortly."

Julian gave that quizzical look again.

"Jemima specializes in planning events," Chalwen said.

Julian sighed, realization dawning. "Such as funerals?"

"Including funerals, yes," said Anna, walking over to join them. "This department handled arrangements for Empress Florence. It will be a sad duty but also an honor to look after Emperor Paul."

"But there are thousands of decisions to make," Julian protested.

"We know." Anna's eyes twinkled. "We have books of protocol going back thousands of years covering eventualities like this. There are set forms for most of what we need to do."

"This office will deal with most of the details," Chalwen added. "Most especially, they'll have all the direct dealings with those long lines of merchants who were pestering you."

Anna leaned in with a conspiratorial air. "I'll warn you, Jemima can appear very abrupt, but she knows what she's doing. She'll consult you on important details, but once she understands what you have in mind we'll make it happen. Our office is good at that. Dare I say, the best in the empire?"

Julian looked puzzled. "Then why did Uncle Ivan not send me here in the first place?"

"Why indeed." Chalwen's voice was grim. She did her best to hide a deeper concern.

"He wanted to keep me busy, didn't he?" Julian whispered.

"And I don't think it was for your mental welfare. Don't worry, Sire, I intend to get to the bottom of that mystery. But while we're here, have you ever met Artur Stiles?"

"The Master of Circuses? I know of him but Father never got around to introducing me."

"Sorry, Chalwen," Anna said. "You're out of luck right now. He's over at the Assembly Rooms doing final checks on all the draperies and floral arrangements for a time of mourning."

"Why would the Assembly Rooms need to be dressed? They're not sitting during the time of mourning."

"The Grand Duke called a special sitting, this morning." Anna glanced at a collection of displays on the wall behind her desk. "I expect they're getting ready to start the session about now."

Suddenly Chalwen felt like she was standing on quicksand. "Javarro," she yelled to the bodyguard waiting just outside the door. "Get back to the car. We need to get over to the Assembly Room. Now."

The usher looked up, startled, as Julian and his entourage approached the double doors leading from the imperial dressing room into the Assembly Room. He recovered his composure quickly. "Magister Summis." He bowed. "I'll have the Sergeant at Arms announce you."

"No," said Chalwen. "We don't want to interrupt proceedings ... yet."

The usher looked flustered and started to protest.

"It's okay," Julian reassured him.

Chalwen cracked open the door.

"And you say the Crown Prince is unable to be here in person?" The speaker was somewhere off to one side out of Chalwen's line of sight.

"Sadly true." That was Ivan. "I fear he's overwhelmed by grief. Perfectly understandable for a youngster who's just lost his parents and siblings."

"Where is he?" Chalwen recognized Abraham Crode's voice. "If the Assembly is to determine a motion of fitness, he should be here, or someone to speak on his behalf."

"He is occupied making preparations for the funerals. As far as I know, he hasn't stepped outside his office in the last six days except to sleep."

"Despite an assassination attempt, right here in the palace?" That was one of the Assembly Members speaking from the back. Chalwen tried to place the accent. Tinturn, maybe?

"Even so. His obsession is single-minded."

"Are you claiming he's incapable of taking on the throne?" Same speaker.

"I would presume no such thing. That is for this Assembly to determine. However, as a doting uncle, I would be loath to burden him so soon after such a devastating loss."

"I've heard enough," Julian said. He pushed open the door and limped out onto the dais. Chalwen and the rest of his bodyguard followed.

Chalwen was thankful to see that Ivan at least hadn't taken the emperor's seat. He stood on the next step down and to one side, facing the floor of the Assembly. A scattering of Members in their seats gaped at the Crown Prince's unexpected appearance. As Chalwen expected, there were few present in person for an emergency session called at short notice. Indicators on the table in the center of the floor showed more were attending by remote comms.

"Fitness is not yours to presume, as you so rightly said, and neither is my willingness to take on burdens." Despite his evident anger, Julian managed to keep his voice calm but firm.

Ivan turned, startled. "Crown Prince! I am happy to see you've emerged to take an interest in imperial affairs once more."

Julian turned a frosty glare on Ivan. "Funeral arrangements are in good hands, Uncle. It seems to have slipped your mind that we have offices of expert staff to handle such things."

Hah! Chalwen thought. He learns fast.

"Meanwhile, I believe this extraordinary sitting was convened for a purpose. Maybe the Clerk of the Floor could move the proceedings along?"

The Clerk glanced at Ivan then nodded at Julian. "As you wish, Sire." She turned to the floor. "I see tabled a Declaration of Competence."

Chalwen's jaw dropped. She wondered if Ivan might have proposed a Regency Act to allow him to rule on Julian's behalf, but he'd gone straight for an outright declaration to rule Julian out of the picture.

"Is there a Member willing to bring this Declaration to the floor of the Assembly?"

There was a long silence. Julian stood alongside Ivan, feet planted firmly and arms folded in front of him. As he stared across the floor, Members avoided his gaze. A few shuffled in their seats.

"Final call for a proposer."

The silence stretched out five more heartbeats.

"I find the Declaration unsupported. It is removed from the table."

Chapter 27

A warship never slept, but the small hours of the ship's night saw a natural lull in activity. Gregor was off duty, but sleep eluded him. Tensions on board grew as the Emperor's funeral drew near. That was only to be expected. They'd been in a state of high readiness for the last ten days, only a step down from general quarters, and frustrated in having no enemy to turn their anger on.

And so *Wrath of Empire* simmered with emotion at the unavenged insult.

Laying the imperial family to rest would bring no relief, just a sharpened awareness of the lack of retribution. That, Gregor was well aware of. He'd been keeping his crew busy with a rotating schedule of overhauls to keep their weaponry at peak readiness. Crews coming off shift should be too tired to make trouble, and yet there'd been a distinct undercurrent of violence this afternoon that he'd spent all evening trying to pinpoint.

All evening, and long into the night.

Restless and still at a loss, Gregor drifted ghost-like through the combat operations room, nodding greetings to the alert shift crew. Nothing triggered his senses. This wasn't the seat of the malaise.

He circled the power connection rooms feeding into the zero-gravity weapons chamber that ran the height of the ship to protrude from her belly. Nothing amiss.

On a hunch, he took a transit pod up to the main hangar deck that shared the the battleship's bloated mushroom cap with the weaponry of the battle platform.

He roamed between dormant freighters and gunships, and climbed a companionway to a catwalk with a panoramic view across the hangar. To his left, vast sets of doors led into three ship-sized airlocks from which *Wrath* could launch a fair-sized invasion fleet. To his right, the hangar space wrapped around the armored walls surrounding the head of the main plasma cannon.

A kit room across from his vantage point led through an airlock and into the weapon bay, one of the secure access points into Gregor's demesne. A handful of maintenance engineers milled around, fastening protective gear and safety harnesses ready to begin the next shift's overhaul duties.

Gregor peered closer. One of the group looked shifty. Hanson, a deck hand. The man was trouble and always looked shifty, so there was nothing new there. He'd be cleaning up after the engineers, except, Gregor checked on his notepad, Hanson wasn't due on duty for another three hours.

Sure enough, he left the group, but instead of heading for the transit hatch he slunk in the direction of one of the hangar workshops.

Gregor backtracked down the companionway and approached the workshop area under cover of the parked craft. He moved quietly while scanning the way ahead for signs of Hanson.

As he went, it occurred to Gregor that he had no idea what he might be getting into. The unspoken anger and suppressed savagery he'd sensed all day preyed on him. Shipboard security might not get here in time to avert a tragedy.

He thumbed a transmitter on his collar and called the watch officer down in the combat operations room. "Valen? Pavlenko," he whispered. "I have a small problem on hangar deck main I need help with. I saw Wallace and Lievars just going on-shift into the feed complex. Raise them for me and send them out to ..." Gregor heard voices from a hatch up ahead that stood ajar. "The electrical engineering repair shop. And if I don't report back in five minutes, send a security squad and medics."

Out here, the hangar appeared empty. Catwalks overhead could have hidden lookouts, but they'd have no way to communicate from up there without using traceable comms. He was as close to the workshop as he could get, leaving thirty feet of open deck to cross. Anyone behind that door would have a clear view. Gregor left the cover of a stripped-down troop carrier and sprinted for the hatch. As he shoved it open, he dodged a fist flying his way. He caught the forearm attached to the fist and helped it to connect with the bulkhead alongside him.

His assailant, a kitchen hand by the insignia on her lapel, grunted and turned to run.

"Oh no you don't." Gregor grabbed her collar and twisted the fabric savagely, choking off her warning cry.

He jumped at movement in the corner of his eye, then relaxed when he realized he'd been joined already by Wallace and Lievars, two old hands he could trust to back him up.

"Take this one," Gregor said. "Hold back and keep her quiet, but be ready in case I need an assist."

Kit lockers lined the compartment. Another door at the far end stood ajar, through which angry voices echoed.

Gregor sidled up to the door and assessed the scene in a few moments.

The workshop was lined with tool racks and workbenches, with clear deck space down the middle for winching in large drive and shield assemblies. That space had become an impromptu fighting ring.

Two muscle-bound grunts supported a third man between them. At a glance, Gregor saw that, although he strained to free himself, he was unhurt so far. He faced off against a tough-looking woman whose face twisted in a snarl.

Gregor also took in the fifty or so surrounding onlookers. Most were eager for the fight to come, but a small group held apart by a cordon of guards looked anxious and sullen.

At a guess, the man being held was here to be taught a lesson by the dominant parties, with a small group of colleagues either for support or to bear witness to what happened when people backed the wrong side.

Gregor breathed a small sigh of relief. This was a grudge match, not a lynching. Each side backed their own champions. Even though it looked like one group was a more willing participant than the other, there would be rules and codes of honor here. As long as some rudimentary discipline held sway, he had a chance to defuse this.

Small mercies. But still dangerous.

Gregor flung the door open with a resounding clang, and strode into the stunned silence. He was careful not to acknowledge Hanson, who was seated on a makeshift throne to adjudicate the fight. Gregor stationed himself directly in front of Hanson, with his feet planted shoulder width apart and his back to the troublemaker in an unmistakable show of contempt. This was the most dangerous moment. Gregor strained for any sound from behind.

When none came, he nodded to the two thugs, who released their captive. The man was pale but defiant. The woman opposite looked thunderstruck.

"Names," he snapped.

The man started, then saluted. "Corporal ap Nicel, Sir. Fitter, first class."

"Corporal Denziel, Sir," the woman announced. "Electrician's mate."

Gregor clasped his hands behind his back and surveyed the room before bringing his focus back to the two in front of him. "I will hear your dispute."

Again, he listened for sounds behind him. He'd openly usurped Hanson's purpose here, but he was now sure the man wouldn't try to wrest control from a senior officer. If the audience had been whipped into an unthinking mob it would be a different matter. Co-conspirators and incidental accessories to a crime could be persuaded to stay quiet, and there were endless ways to dispose of a body on a warship the size of a *Sword*. But naval discipline was too deeply entrenched to be broken now the heat of the moment had passed.

He stared at Denziel. "Looks to me like you're the plaintiff here. Speak."

Denziel gulped. Her aggressive manner had evaporated in the face of cold authority. Nevertheless, she straightened and pointed to ap Nicel. "This one's been sticking up for the Firenzi bastards who killed the Emperor. That's treason in my books."

Ap Nicel swore. "Firenzi had nothing to do with it. That's not how they work."

"Yeah? Their weapons. Had their grubby pawprints all over it."

"The Firenzi head was on Magentis. Supposed to meet with the Emperor. If he'd had anything to do with it he'd have made damned sure to be light years away."

"That's got to be horseshit." Denziel's voice oozed contempt. She seemed to have momentarily forgotten Gregor was there. "Did anyone actually see him there?"

"There was trouble in Henriss. Half a million people broke into the palace to find him."

"Half a million?" someone called out from the other side of the workshop. "How big's the fucking palace?"

"Okay, not everyone got inside. But that's the numbers they gave protesting in the park outside the gates. Point is, they knew something. My uncle lives in Henriss. They heard the Firenzi were there."

"So," Gregor cut in with a sneer, "they're stupid enough to stage an assassination right when their Head of Family is our guest on Magentis? And whatever you may think of the Firenzi, they've never been know for assassinating children in cold blood."

That last statement shut them up. After a few seconds, muttering started at the back of the room. Gregor could only make out a phrase here and there, but the tone was grudging acceptance rather than threatening.

"Besides," Gregor resumed in a voice sharp enough to cut through the rising babble, "our job is to follow orders from the Admiralty and leave the investigating to people better placed to investigate. If the Firenzi *were* behind the plot, we'd now be at war." He glared at Denziel. "Of course, if you profess to know more than our colleagues in ImpSec, I'm sure I can arrange a private interview."

Denziel blanched at the implied threat. A quick gaze around the room confirmed the audience, earlier baying for blood, now looked sheepish. None met Gregor's eyes.

"Ap Nicel and Denziel," Gregor barked. "Report to Captain's Rounds on the first day watch. The charge is brawling."

"But ..." the woman whined.

"The brawl never started, you're going to say," Gregor growled. "A technicality. It was about to." He glared Denziel down to silence.

Ap Nicel grimaced but nodded. Technically, he was the injured party, but he must have come up here of his own volition even if he'd been given no real choice. He must also have realized this minor discipline was the best outcome he could have hoped for. Gregor had to be seen to be even-handed to have any chance of healing the still-simmering resentment.

Finally he turned to face Hanson. Unsurprisingly, the deck hand had tried to slip away while Gregor's back was to him, but he hadn't counted on Gregor having backup. Wallace and Lievars dragged him through the hatch back into the main workshop.

"Hanson." Gregor's voice was as cold as interstellar space. "The captain will deal with you separately."

⎯⎯⎯•◆•⎯⎯⎯

In the privacy of her office, Chalwen set a covered mess tray on one side of her desk. She activated the comms screen and provided the codes to join the meeting called by Lorenzo.

She toyed with her food. The medical orderly hadn't been exaggerating. The nutrient pouches sent over from the infirmary sustained her but tasted like piss. She fought back nausea by sheer force of will, and swallowed a few mouthfuls while members of The Hidden Light trickled into the meeting.

At last, Lorenzo opened proceedings with a recap of the successful mission to rescue the Firenzi contingent from their captivity in Henriss.

"For the last few years," he concluded, "this group has been more about talk and influence, diplomacy and pressure. I'm glad to see we can still organize ourselves to direct action when the need arises. I have a feeling we'll need more of it in the times to come."

At Lorenzo's invitation, Chalwen then summarized the Grand Duke's attempt the previous day to sideline Julian.

"I'd heard reports," someone said, "but they didn't make it sound too serious. Hearing a first-hand account, this behavior is troubling."

"If he's become this brazen," added another voice, "who's to say he won't make an even more drastic move?"

Lorenzo cut in, "That is why we must be careful. I want to know why we didn't get a sense of his intentions until it was almost too late, and then only by immense good luck."

"Our attention was on the plight of the Firenzi family, and before that, the foiled assassination attempt."

At my insistence, Chalwen thought glumly. She should have seen that Ivan would seize the opportunity to usurp the line of succession. She wondered what other legal tricks he still had to play with. Could he even challenge Florence's original decision to appoint Paul rather than Ivan as her heir? What a can of worms *that* would open up.

"How do we know the Grand Duke wasn't behind the poisoning attempt?"

That brought a few moments of silence. Chalwen offered her own opinion. "From what little evidence we've seen so far, that looks like an outside operation. The same actor that we've implicated in the Emperor's death."

"Regardless," said Lorenzo, "I think we can all agree that Julian must be declared emperor. Ivan's coronation would bring us right back to the worst days of the old Empress."

One of the anonymous members asked, "The question is, would Julian follow the absent father or the very present and domineering uncle?"

Chalwen said, "His path isn't set. He has a good heart, so as far as I can see, it's our job now to keep Ivan as much as possible at arm's length."

Someone else on the conference said, "Julian has always been close to Ivan. I understand that he spent more time in Ivan's company than his own father's."

Chalwen had to remind herself that she was still just an anonymous code name to most of the people in this meeting. "I am in a position to work closely with Julian. What you say is true, but I still believe his heart lies more with Paul's. To me, the real question is whether or not we take him into our confidence."

A long silence followed.

At last, Lorenzo said, "At this stage, I think it best that we don't. We don't know how he might react, and revealing a hidden family member just when he thought he'd lost everyone would be traumatic. We stay in the shadows, and guide him as best we can."

" I understand this must have been a trying few days for you. It doesn't show."

Ivan grunted and let fly. The arrow thunked into the center of the target fifty yards away. On the surface, Supreme Judge Abraham Crode would have to be talking about the recent disappointment in the Assembly, but Ivan was also reeling from the escape of Josef Firenzi.

"All things need to be put into perspective, Abraham. I find archery to be a marvelous form of meditation."

He wondered if the judge had any inkling of Ivan's maneuverings to bring the two Families to the brink of war. The Assembly would have wanted an experienced military man on the throne, not an untested youngster. That would have made a permanent takeover so much easier. And with Scipio working behind the scenes in the opposite camp, they'd have brought the Families back from the brink, but not before a few fat contracts had changed hands to keep Honorina Philip at arm's length.

Ivan's next arrow grazed the ring next to the center.

A muted gasp sounded behind him from the small gathering of onlookers the other side of a protective screen. "A rare slip," the judge commiserated.

Dammit! Any approach to meditation was a long way off right now. Rather than the serenity of meditation, Ivan channeled his anger. Whoever had masterminded the Firenzis' escape would pay. He pictured the silhouette of a face in the distant target, and placed his third shaft dead center. He took a moment to relax the savage stretch of lips across teeth, and turned to acknowledge a polite patter of applause. In the last year, Ivan had cultivated a close working relationship with the Supreme Judge. You couldn't call it friendship, but there was a certain accord around the benefit of traditional values. It helped that they shared a keen interest in competitive archery, and their frequent contests on the range in the basement of the Acacia Club always drew a sycophantic audience.

While Crode sighted his first shot, Ivan wondered again about that impossible escape. It was early days yet, but so far Bernie Fischer had made no progress identifying the culprits. The rescue mission had appeared out of thin air, and the perpetrators had vanished again just as quickly, along with any records of their activity. It was as if Bernie himself had planned it.

"Good shot, Abraham." This was going to be a tough match. Ivan would need his full focus to beat the judge, but that was why he relished these meetings.

"Your problem is you only follow the money."

Ivan gave the judge a startled look at this seeming non-sequitur. Crode calmly placed his second shaft alongside the first.

"You were relying on Assembly Members looking after their own financial interests. You forget they have other pressures to bow to."

"Everything comes down to money at the end of it," Ivan growled.

"You hunt, don't you? In the wild?"

Another non-sequitur. Was the wily judge deliberately trying to rattle him?

"I could claim that everything comes down to the kill shot at the end of it," Crode continued, "but in order to make that shot you have to pay attention to the landscape, the sun, the wind."

Ivan pondered the analogy. He had a feeling he knew what the judge was saying. "Wealth is the goal, but the landscape, positioning yourself to make wealth, contains many factors not immediately financial in nature."

Crode's third shot put him ahead of Ivan in the scoring.

A buzzer sounded a long note to signal the end of the round, and an attendant scurried over to retrieve their arrows.

"Emperor Paul was *popular*, Ivan. Not always with the people you talk to, but with the masses, the people ... the *voters*."

"And Assembly Members need to pay attention to the masses in order to stay in power. There is nothing new or remarkable there, Abraham."

"Maybe not, but all the same you misread the landscape. The wind changed while you were stalking your prey. As long as you could paint young Julian as a weakling, hiding from the world, unfit to take office, you had a good chance. It was a reasonable gamble. But the moment Julian made that timely and impressive entrance, that gamble was lost. Standing on the stage in front of the Assembly, in that moment he was his father's son. Any Member who supported a motion so openly in violation of the evidence would face some career-limiting questions back home."

The attendant hurried up and placed their arrows in quivers standing by their sides. Ivan cast a glance back over the onlookers. There were a few Assembly Members in the audience, people Ivan had counted on to start the ball rolling. They all averted their gaze when he looked their way.

He should feel irritation, anger, betrayal, but a glacial calm descended on him. The emotions washed through him without taking hold, leaving a cold calculating machine in their wake.

He drew, and released. The arrow slammed home into the center of the target.

"Just to confirm, there is no legal avenue by which you could declare someone other than the Crown Prince the right person to take the throne." One of the duties of the Supreme Judge was to rule on questions of succession, but Ivan already knew Crode's answer.

"The line of succession is clear. Without compelling grounds, such as a ruling from the Assembly, if I'm asked to make a judgment on who should succeed Paul my hands are tied. As things stand, there is no legal argument against Julian taking the throne. You have no standing. Let's be clear. I am not your ally, any more than I am your enemy in this matter."

Thunk! A second arrow quivered within a hair's breadth of the first.

"I wouldn't ask you to do anything but your duty under the law."

Thunk! Ivan's third shaft joined its brethren.

"But," Crode mused, "a young emperor will need some well-chosen advisors. During his formative years, those advisors will hold as much power as if they sat on the throne themselves. Good shooting, by the way."

While Crode placed his own three arrows firmly in the bullseye, Ivan came to a grudging acceptance that the throne itself was out of his reach, for now. The law and the Assembly were against him, and beneath it all he felt an unseen tide of resistance. Julian should have died by the hand of Honorina Philip's assassin. Failing that, the Assembly should have moved to declare him unfit to rule. And Josef Firenzi should have died at the hands of the mob. Through unforeseen interventions none of those things had happened. That couldn't be coincidence.

"It seems you are in mind of the hunt, Abraham. What say you we switch to moving targets?"

Without waiting for an answer, Ivan signaled to the range marshal. The static targets were wheeled off to one side, and targets resembling game animals both small and large began to slide into view.

Well, Ivan would have to stalk his prey more carefully. He grinned as he nailed a target through the heart. The hunt was on.

———◆·◆———

A sense of unease crept over Chalwen as she crossed the outer office of the guard room. Her scalp crawled. There was something off in the air, and she felt people's eyes on her as she turned down the hallway leading to her office. The unease deepened when she noticed her door standing ajar. She never left her office open like that.

Unease turned to shock when she found her office, her few square yards of privacy, unrecognizable.

The chair behind her desk had been replaced by an ancient commode. Alongside the desk stood a walking frame. Someone had taped a makeshift dial to the front of the frame with a large knurled knob and a pointer. The settings on the dial read 'Slow crawl', 'Hobble', up to 'Emergency stagger'. A large red button on the desk was labeled 'Medic alert'.

There was a bedpan under the desk. Yes, it was full.

Most of the pranks were childish, but one feature gave her the chills. On the wall opposite her desk, someone had crudely scrawled the words 'Ghost Lover' in white paint. Ghost. An offensive nickname for Firenzi natives, based on their typically pale skins. This had to be a reference to her involvement in Josef's rescue.

Somehow, she'd been identified.

—————•-••——————

Ivan gazed across the Fountain Court at the tall windows of the Office of Deliberation. One day, he thought. One day.

He turned as Bernie Fischer slumped into a cushioned chair across from the desk. His private secretary hadn't fully recovered his pervasive cheerfulness. He was still adjusting to Ivan's change of course. They'd stretched for the finish line, then found they still had a marathon to run. Too many setbacks, in too short a space of time. They were all feeling the disappointment, none more so than Ivan, but if *he* could soldier on, they all could.

"Bresk, you had a possible lead on the crew who delivered Josef Firenzi back to his people."

Lieutenant Bresk stepped forward. "An acquaintance of mine in the household guard was on duty when the cruiser landed. Two people were escorted off and into ImpSec. Faces and insignia covered, nothing to allow for identification. Not seen again since."

"Nothing new there," Bernie said. "But we've still not been able to identify either of them. Somebody buried in ImpSec must have been covering tracks."

"My acquaintance was part of the escort before handing them over. Reported one of them showed signs of a limp. Assumed it was the result of an injury during the mission, but we do know one person not walking properly. Suffering what I hope is permanent damage."

Ivan exchanged glances with Bernie, who looked equally puzzled.

"Maybe not someone you'd normally pay any attention to."

The venom in Bresk's voice lit a glimmer of recognition in the back of Ivan's mind. "The Crown Prince's head of bodyguard? Your counter-part?" Ivan pictured the woman. Plain. Unremarkable. By all accounts barely competent. He found it hard to believe she'd be behind his frustrations. All the same, she had been in the wrong place at the wrong time twice now, in her defense of the Crown Prince. A third time would be beyond coincidence.

"I understand that particular officer is no longer fit for duty," Bernie sneered.

"A message has been sent. She won't be there long." Bresk's mouth twisted in disgust.

Curious. He'd usually relish the opportunity to belittle a rival. Maybe the message hadn't had the desired effect. Regardless, Ivan felt it of little consequence. Let Bresk deal with his own problems. Ivan turned to Bernie. "When the Crown Prince takes the throne, he'll need all the expert guidance he can get."

"He's holding out on making any appointments." Bernie shrugged. "Refuses to discuss it. I think he's still in denial."

"Nevertheless, there will come a time. Who do you think might he appoint?"

Bernie chewed his lip. "He needs a full council at his side. Not something the boy is used to. The logical place to start would be with the advisors already appointed by Paul."

"I'm thinking specifically of a political or diplomatic advisor."

A hint of a grin touched Bernie's lips. "And of course those happen to be areas where you have an acknowledged expertise. Let's see, that would be Holland Bearnice and Ivana bin Durin respectively."

"I hear Ivana's health isn't too good."

"There's a good chance she might find herself unable to continue in her role." Bernie's voice and expression were a picture of innocence. "Although more untimely deaths might attract attention."

"Holland, on the other hand, is still going strong," Ivan mused. "If ever there was a picture of rude health, that man is it."

"Rude being the operative word. I don't know how Paul put up with him."

Bresk coughed. "I hear Holland's wife has been seeing a member of the Imperial Color Guard in between more official engagements."

"And is Holland aware of this?" Ivan raised his eyebrows in genuine amazement. He quickly revised his assessment of the abrasive councilor's wife.

"No, Sire, and his wife would be very keen for matters to stay that way."

"Keen enough, do you think, to persuade her husband it's time to take a well-earned retirement?"

———•———

Chalwen stood to attention in front of Colonel bin Merrin's desk, trying not to show the pains stabbing up both legs.

The colonel looked troubled. "I understand there's been some bother in the guard house."

"It's nothing, Sir. It's been dealt with."

Javarro had surreptitiously pulled in a few members of his squad and helped her clean up the mess. Overruling his outrage, Chalwen had been emphatic that there would be no retaliation. The palace couldn't afford an open feud between factions within the imperial bodyguard.

The colonel's voice was quiet. "You know you'd be within your rights to file a complaint. We'd be required to investigate."

Chalwen tried not to grimace. That wasn't how disputes got settled in the guard. "I don't believe you'd find anything to act on."

That much was likely true. Bresk and crew would have covered their tracks, and intimidated anyone who'd seen anything into silence.

"And you know I won't stand for you taking matters into your own hands."

"Completely understood, Sir. The thought hadn't crossed my mind."

Not quite true. The one token act of revenge she'd sanctioned involved returning the bedpan, contents and all, to its rightful owner. Henri and Simone between them unearthed the code to Lieutenant Bresk's gym locker and arranged for a surveillance glitch at the right moment.

"This incident does unfortunately highlight something I can't ignore."

Chalwen's palms at her sides turned clammy.

"What's the outlook for a full return to health?"

This was the question Chalwen was dreading, one thing she couldn't bluff her way out of. "The medics can't say." She struggled past a tightness in her throat. "I'm working through a stiff program of therapy, and they're measuring some progress against the nerve damage."

"Which, I believe, is slower than you'd like."

Chalwen pressed her lips together, not daring to speak, and nodded.

"You'll continue in your official post pending a fitness review. You realize, of course, that you need peak fitness to manage full duties as a bodyguard."

"How much time have I got?"

"Your next assessment is in two weeks. At that point, I need a lieutenant in charge of the Crown Prince's bodyguard fully fit for duty ahead of the state funeral."

Chalwen felt faint.

The colonel didn't seem to notice her distress. He turned to his desk. "Dismissed, Lieutenant."

Chapter 29

"Sire, you can't keep putting this off. You must appoint a political advisor." Doctor Vicky's voice was as close to despair as Chalwen had ever known.

At her shoulder, Marcus Tyee wrung his hands in silent pleading.

Afternoon sun slanted across the Fountain Court throwing shafts of brilliance onto the floor of the Crown Prince's office. A small group of scribes and assistants clung to the shadows of the far wall, trying to blend in with its marquetry panelling. Chalwen couldn't blame them. There was no more of the distracting busywork Ivan had tried to swamp Julian with, but the realities of ruling a vast empire were taking their toll.

"Enough," Julian yelled. "Why am I surrounded by people telling me what I *must* do?" He whirled and strode out of his office and down the hall, trailing a retinue of bewildered attendants in his wake. The office door had been standing open and his tirade must have carried the length of the building.

Chalwen signaled to Skinner to carry on and supervise the bodyguard squad as normal. She limped behind as best she could, swallowing her own frustration and despair. Every passing day reminded her of the looming fitness assessment, and her obvious inadequacy. By the time she let herself through a side gate into the walled garden of the imperial family quarters, the Crown Prince was disappearing into the west wing, a hundred yards away, where his own suite lay.

She climbed the stairs. More raised voices drifted towards her, becoming clearer as she reached the next landing.

"I already have too damned many people 'advising' me. I always thought the idea of advice was that the decision was up to me! Yet everyone's advice feels more like orders these days."

Chalwen gritted her teeth and hastened on. She had to intervene before the young prince said something that couldn't be undone.

"Approve the household budget. Meet ambassadors. Appoint advisors. Next you'll be telling me when to eat my meals and when to go to bed. Oh, wait, you already do!"

Chalwen arrived to find Julian with his back to the room staring out the window, hands clenched at his side. His personal aide and tutor looked helpless and shell-shocked, and his bodyguards looked uncomfortable at their posts, but at least nobody seemed yet to be mortally offended and ready to walk off the job. Or worse.

"Everybody out." Chalwen's voice was quiet but firm. Doctor Vicky gave a hopeless shrug and Marcus Tyee gave one last beseeching look at Julian's back before complying.

"You too," Chalwen whispered to Skinner. He glanced at Wilder, who'd completed his routine scan of the suite, and nodded.

"So, Lieutenant," Julian said stiffly over his shoulder. "Are *you* going to lecture me on what I need to do?"

Chalwen shook her head. "Only as it pertains to your personal safety. But I am going to beg your leave to sit. Your ankle has healed well, as you showed us on the way here. I may never be so lucky."

"Space alive! You don't have to ask. Not in private."

"It's hard to show vulnerability when you feel your position is precarious." Chalwen reached behind her for the arm of a chair and carefully lowered herself down with a grimace. "I'm grateful for your patience, but I wonder how much longer you can put up with a crippled bodyguard."

Julian gaped. "Chalwen, I'd never get rid of you! Surely you know that?"

"But I'm hardly fit to discharge my duties." She eased her legs into a more comfortable position. "Forgive me, Sire, if I don't feel as secure in my position as you'd have me believe. We can't have freeloaders on the staff, so I carry out my therapy, take my meds, and try to hide my discomfort so as not to appear weak."

"I ... I didn't realize. You hide it too well."

"It's dangerous to admit our weakness with predators circling, sharpening their claws," Chalwen continued as if Julian hadn't spoken. She gazed down, massaging her right calf. "I think you know what I mean."

From the corner of her eye, she saw Julian whirl back to the window. The room was quiet. After a few moments she looked more closely and saw his shoulders shaking. Chalwen heaved herself upright and hobbled over. She rested her hands on his shoulders. He stiffened, then slumped back into her arms.

"It's okay." She fought to keep the catch out of her voice. "I miss them too. All of them."

The sobs came now, fast and furious and harrowing. This was new ground for Chalwen. She'd never before had to deal with a grieving child.

"You've hidden it well, too. But you can't keep it bottled up. What you're showing is humanity, not weakness."

"Bu—but I can't," Julian stammered between sobs. "I'm sup—upposed to be strong. Be the Emperor."

"To the Assembly, yes. To the admirals and the judges and the merchants. But you need to unload somewhere or you'll kill yourself. Your father knew that."

"My father." Julian pulled away. He wiped his eyes on his sleeve and stumbled away a few paces. His aimless movements turned into restless pacing back and forth across the room. His face worked in indecision. At last he turned toward Chalwen, but his eyes remained downcast. "If I take the throne, it feels like I'm abandoning Father. Like I've cast him aside." The words came out as little more than a whisper.

"And appointing an advisor is one step down that road."

Julian nodded miserably.

"In fact, you've taken no steps, really, to establish yourself as Emperor, to gather around you the people and the knowledge you'll need. You're still surrounded by the same retinue you've always had as Crown Prince."

"I can't possibly replace him," Julian wailed. "What do people expect of me?"

"Nobody expects you to be another Paul. You need to figure out who Emperor Julian is. But you're young yet. There's time. Besides, think about the alternative. It would be more of an abandonment if you *didn't* take the throne and carry on where your father left off. Your grandmother chose Paul over Ivan for a reason."

"Uncle Ivan wants it, though, doesn't he?"

Chalwen gritted her teeth. "More than you can possibly imagine."

"Sometimes I think it would be easier just to let him have it, if this is how the rest of my life is going to be."

"There used to be a saying," Chalwen paused to recall the wording, "that those who most desire to rule are exactly those who shouldn't be allowed to."

Julian stared, then laughed. "I can see something in that, but can you imagine sitting someone on the throne who *didn't* want it? They wouldn't last the week." The moment of laughter evaporated. "Is Doctor Vicky right? Do I need a political advisor?"

"I know she's brilliant in her own right, as is Marcus, and everyone else you have around you. You have a good team, for a Crown Prince."

"But ...?"

"But there are things, many things, none of us can advise you on. We're just not knowledgeable enough. Politics is one of those areas. Military matters, too. Economics. Law."

Julian puzzled. "Surely that one's settled, though? Crode is the Supreme Judge. Who better to advise on the law?"

Chalwen snorted. "He'll pass judgment on cases brought before him, but he doesn't make the arguments. He can't be a judge *and* be your legal counsel at the same time. It's a conflict of interest. You need someone who'll look for ways through the maze of the law to achieve your goals. Someone who'll do their utmost to *persuade* the judge to rule in your favor."

"I can still keep you, though? You, Marcus, Doctor Vicky?"

"For as long as we can be of service."

Julian drifted back to the window and stared out. "I've grown up with you all. I know I can trust you. I ... I don't want some complete strangers sharing in our secrets. I guess I need more people around me, but I wish I didn't."

"Oh, we'd do our best, if you insisted, but the Imperium needs something better than fumbling amateurs. If you're to honor your father's memory, you need help in many areas that we can't do justice to."

"I've been in meetings with Father and his advisors." Julian's voice quavered. "They all look down on me. I know I'm young, but they treat me like a child."

Chalwen's voice hardened. "Anyone does that, they'll have me to reckon with."

Chapter 30

Chalwen leaned heavily on her cane as she hobbled through the east gate behind the barracks and into the teeming streets of the city. This was her first real break since the assassination, and her mind was fried. Where had the time gone? She and Henri and a trusted army of sleuths pored over logs and reports, tracked down witnesses, banged their heads sore against one dead end after another. As an added difficulty, they had to keep out of sight of the official investigation, which Chalwen was convinced would yield scapegoats but no real culprits.

The sabotage of the Emperor's cruiser had been covered up with the same befuddling efficiency as Julian's attempted abduction. The only people they could definitely link to those events were dead.

Sergeant van Buren seemed to be at the center of events. Those bodies in the wrecked troop carrier had been identified, and she'd been known to be associated with them. More suspicious still, not that the official investigation seemed to care, the victims of the troop carrier blast were not all guards as you'd expect. They included a groundsman and a flight maintenance engineer. People who had no business in a troop carrier. The only conclusion Chalwen could draw was that someone had been clearing up loose ends.

But the trail stopped at van Buren. If she was the linchpin, she had to be receiving instructions and equipment from outside somehow. That link was still a mystery.

The state funeral was almost upon them, preparations made, though thankfully Chalwen had nothing to do with the logistics. She was just trying to hang onto some relevance as the head of Julian's bodyguard while her tortured legs showed up her inadequacy at every turn.

The city blocks here catered for working people, many steps up from the warrens of Riversedge the other side of the palace, but still a long way from the high end districts north and east from here. Squat stone buildings with deep shaded colonnades shielded people from the desert sun. A few more ostentatious piles of steel and thermal polymer broke the skyline. Burnt flint battled with evening aromas of cooking.

City guards loitered on street corners. From the corner of her eye, Chalwen caught pointing fingers and heads bent in whispered gossip. She groaned inwardly. Her exploits with the Crown Prince had stripped her anonymity, and somehow rumors of the Firenzi escape had started to leak out. Nothing to directly associate her, but suspicions abounded.

She found herself outside Sellick's restaurant, almost on autopilot. She decided to treat herself to a meal and sit by the river.

"Lieutenant!" Esme Sellick herself bustled out from behind the counter when Chalwen limped through the open door. She eyed Chalwen's cane. "You should stick to standing guard, hmm? Leave running around rescuing people to others, no?"

Chalwen's heart stuttered, then she reminded herself that everyone here would know about her brush with poison. "Saving royalty *is* my job, Esme. I just need a full meal for one, with all the trimmings. What's good tonight?"

"We have a fine chicken pilaf. Heart warming. Flatbread and tasty relishes." Esme wore a mourning armband of twisted red and white ribbon, though her face creased in elderly good cheer. She had reason to be cheerful. The establishment was busy as usual, including a group of household guards in one corner. Chalwen hadn't been exaggerating to Henri when she said this was a regular haunt. "Look like you need a lift, yes?" She spooned food from the hot counter into reusable containers while she spoke.

"You have a carry bag? I need one hand to help me get around."

"Be sure to bring it back!" Esme cackled and packed the dishes into an insulated bag with a shoulder strap.

Chalwen stared at the bag with its recognizable logo on top, struck with a sudden sense of recognition. She'd seen this emblem recently, but out of place. She was sure of it. She wracked her memory trying to place the image. Something she'd not paid attention to at the time, somewhere in the background. Where was it?

"Lieutenant! You okay?"

Chalwen started. Esme was trying to hand her the bag. Chalwen muttered an apology and paid, then hurried back out into the street. The river would have to wait. She had security footage to search.

Three hours later, food long since forgotten on one side of her desk, Chalwen had it. She stared in disbelief at the images glowing on the desk surface.

She thought long and hard about what to do next. She had to be sure. She called up one of the covert investigation team, a weapons specialist that both Henri and Colonel bin Merrin had vouched for and taken into their confidence. The petite woman turned up, slightly out of breath, fifteen minutes later.

"Sorry to drag you over in person, Sabina." Chalwen engaged her office's privacy measures. "It's hard staying out of ImpSec's sight when they're so twitchy."

Sabina flopped into a seat and propped her feet up on the side of Chalwen's desk. "No biggie. I was only in the middle of repairing a beam rifle. Left the rest to my gopher and hoofed it over. How can I help?"

Chalwen noted the young tech's eagerness. The palace may be riddled with people dissatisfied with Paul's ways, but there were also people keen to solve the riddle of his death. "You've studied the recordings of *Nightwish*, the explosion's blast characteristics. Walk me through it again. I want to understand what kind of device could cause that."

The weapons tech answered without hesitation. "It had to be a really specialized incendiary. Not your common warhead. Fast flash, high temperature. I think it had to have an additional oxidant in the mix. Once the burn started, anything in range, even the hull of the craft, simply became more fuel."

"You've been trying to pinpoint the supplier?"

"Only the Firenzi have the materials tech to design a substance like that, but there's no telling who manufactured it. Any one of the big defense corps would have the capability."

"You say it's specialized, but if it's that effective why isn't it in widespread use?"

"It burns incredibly hot, but it's not actually an explosive. No significant blast radius."

"So, not typically used as a warhead. I get it." Chalwen chewed her cheek. "Do you have enough data to figure out how big a device it was?"

For the first time, Sabina hesitated. "Now we're getting more into guesswork. If we had better telemetry in those escort craft I'd be able to estimate temperature and combustion radius better, but it vaporized nearly half the cruiser, so ..."

"All I need is a rough size. Grenade? Backpack? Suitcase? Bigger?"

"I'd say between backpack and suitcase."

Chalwen's shoulders sagged. She gazed at the carry bag neglected on the corner of her desk. Another dead end.

"That includes the booster oxidant, of course."

"Wait. Would all that have to be one package?"

Sabina laughed. "As long as the oxidant was nearby, no. In fact, it would work better spread out over a few yards. Just that's not how you'd assemble it into a warhead."

Chalwen's heart thumped. "So how big would each piece need to be?"

Sabina held her hands a foot apart. "The device itself would likely be about yay big. And a few similar sized packs of booster."

"Would each piece fit in one of those?" She pointed to the food bag.

Sabina studied it. "I reckon that would do it. Wait. You haven't ..."

"No. It's food. You hungry?"

Sabina unfastened the bag, and the smell of cooking filled the room. All of a sudden Chalwen's appetite returned. Esme was usually generous with her portions. There'd be enough to share.

Feigning a casual tone that she didn't feel, Chalwen asked, "For the kind of blast you saw, how many packets do you think they'd need?"

"Real guesswork, but I'd say between three and maybe six blocks of oxidant."

"So, add in the device itself and you're looking at between four and seven bags like this?" Chalwen pointed to the image on her desktop, taken from inside the imperial family hangar while the cruiser was being readied for flight. In the background, a low wagon held an assortment of trunks and cases, and a row of six distinctive insulated food bags identical to the one on Chalwen's desk.

"That would do it. But how did they slip it past security? They screen for explosives and common poisons on the way into the hangar."

"But you said this isn't a true explosive. And the detectors are tuned to ignore signatures of fuel and lubricant or they'd be tripping all the time. Plus"—she pointed to the bag—"notice how we only smelled the contents when we opened it up. These bags have exceptional lid seals. There'd be very little leakage for the detectors to pick up."

A few more calls, and Henri and Simone, the ImpSec data forensics expert, joined Chalwen and Sabina.

Chalwen quickly outlined what they'd uncovered. "I knew something was bugging me," she concluded. "And I've checked while you were on your way over, there was no outside catering on the manifest."

"There wouldn't be," Simone said. "Imperial family flights are always provisioned from the palace kitchens."

"All the more reason to think that's how the device was moved aboard. In front of everyone's noses."

Sabina grimaced. "Surely one of the guards would have spotted something."

Chalwen pointed to the guard nearest the wagon. "That one died in the troop carrier shortly after. Either he *did* see something he shouldn't have, or he was part of the conspiracy."

"Just not senior enough to survive," Henri said. "But anyone could have got hold of some of those bags. It doesn't mean Esme was actually involved."

Chalwen rubbed her eyes. "Okay, you have a point. But then think about it. She's outside the palace, and there must be dozens of those bags going backwards and forwards daily. I bet the guards at the gate never give them a second thought. And nobody thinks twice about a member of palace staff popping out to Sellicks for a quick bite. What better way to set up a conduit into the palace?"

"I've been recreating van Buren's movements." Simone consulted a scroll in her lap. "She used to be a frequent patron of Sellick's. Not enough to trigger a suspicion, but this information puts it in a new light."

"Besides," Sabina added, "Everyone knows how protective Esme is of those carryalls. If you borrow one, don't dare forget to return it. A half dozen gone missing like that? It would be a crime of the highest order ... unless she already knew where they'd gone."

Henri exchanged glances with Simone. "We need to bring her in for questioning."

Chapter 31

"I'm not moving far." Chalwen gazed around the tiny room that had been her home for the last six years. She tried to strike an upbeat tone, even though her heart felt empty.

Javarro sat on the corner of the solitary packing box next to the bed. "From a garret in the eaves of the guard house, to the main staff quarters? All of a hundred yards."

"I think you've actually traded up," Skinner added. He nudged the packing box with his toe. "Is this it?"

Chalwen nodded sadly. "A porter will be up soon to take it away."

After she'd laundered and returned her guard uniforms and equipment, there had been remarkably little left. And now she thought about it, this bare room could hardly be called a home. It had been somewhere to hang her uniforms and to sleep, maybe one night in three, when she wasn't crashed at her desk or napping in the ready room in the family quarters while waiting for her stint on watch.

The room itself was no loss, and as Skinner said, her new home a short distance away was an improvement. But surrendering her place in the guard house was symbolic of a deeper loss. She'd come out of basic training and into the specialized regimen for VIP protection, where her attention to detail and a nose for trouble landed her a coveted place in the imperial family bodyguard. All that training, what use was it now?

She'd been part of the Crown Prince's guard for half the youngster's life, and protecting members of the imperial family was *her* life.

"You'll be reporting direct to Major Carter now," Chalwen said. Anything to divert talk from her own situation. "She's good. You'll learn a lot from her."

"She's too much by-the-book." Skinner scowled. "I can't imagine *her* organizing a raid to rescue a foreign Head of Family."

"Nobody here did, either," Chalwen cautioned. "Remember that."

"So," said Javarro hesitantly, "what will you be doing now?"

"Classified," Chalwen muttered. She'd been told she wouldn't be able to reveal anything about her new line of work, and she finally began to appreciate the fine line Henri must have been treading all these years. But the truth was, she herself had no idea what she was supposed to be doing. Something in Intelligence, Colonel bin Merrin had said. "All I can say is that the colonel thought my talents—those that don't involve physical movement—would be suited to a role in Imperial Security. A desk job." She sniffed. "All I'm good for now." She'd said it. Voiced her deepest dread. Out of the field and into a windowless office somewhere to wither away.

"You have friends there, too, don't you?" Javarro asked. His forced cheerfulness fooled no one.

"One or two."

A knock at the door, and a pair of porters entered. Javarro hastily stood and squeezed himself into the far corner to give them room in the suddenly cramped space. Without a word, they took a handle each and lugged the box away.

One last glance around for anything left behind. Chalwen picked up her cane leaning against the end of the bed. "And that's it. To be honest, it's probably for the best. With so many of the Family gone now, the colonel's reorganizing the guard details. We have too many lieutenants, and I'm sure I was for the chop anyway."

———— ·◆· ————

Gregor Pavlenko hung back as a noisy crowd three hundred strong bustled down the ramp of the ground-to-orbit shuttle. When crew disembarked on shore leave, rank offered no protection against rough shoulders and sharp elbows.

He nodded to a sergeant at the foot of the ramp checking off names on a notepad, and wondered how many of the main company disappearing through the far doors would need picking up from gutters or emergency rooms later.

Thankfully that was someone else's problem.

In the sudden hush he glanced around at his remaining companions, a small group of seven officers, mostly lieutenants and lieutenant-commanders. "We have to keep it civilized tonight. The grunts have two days. We're back in four hours."

Not so thankfully, he was the senior officer in this group, and so the responsible adult in the room.

Una Spelze nudged Gregor towards a row of ground cars lined up outside the hangar, and signaled to the rest to follow. "Most of that lot will be heading to the strip behind the port admin building. Bars, brothels, casinos ... they know how to part francs from fools without it feeling too painful."

Gregor grimaced, and looked up at the night as they emerged into fresh air. A heady fragrance of blossoms and unfamiliar foods mingled with the steam of a passing shower on hot stone. After months cloistered in shipboard sights, sounds, and smells, planetfall overwhelmed the senses.

To Una he said, "You know this city. I think we're in your hands."

"I already figured that." Una grinned over her shoulder. "And right now I'm sick of imperial food. There's a gorgeous little bistro a couple miles over, past the warehouse district."

"Bistro?" someone muttered. "Sounds poncy."

"As long as they have beer," another said. "They do have beer, don't they?"

"And food," Una confirmed. "Trattoria Torremis."

"Torremis?"

"Foreign, Jimi. From Eloon."

"Eloon? What's that like?" Gregor asked. They'd been on high readiness ever since the assassination. Everyone was ready for a break, even if only a brief one.

"Exotic." Una grinned. "But subtly so. Aromatic. I think you'll like it."

"Swanky, if they're true to tradition. I read about Eloon cuisine once."

"Firenzi," growled one of the lieutenants.

Una snorted. "They're as Firenzi as I am. Fourth generation Stour as far as I know, but Stour is on a crossroads and as cosmopolitan as they come. Lots of traditions mixing in here. Get used to it."

They piled into a couple of cars, and Gregor used his notepad to pay while Una tapped in a destination address. A few minutes later, they'd left behind the sprawl of warehouses and workshops surrounding the port, and pulled up on a quiet street.

The neighborhood looked like a mix of business and residential. Nearby storefronts were lit with displays but looked closed for the night. The only signs of life came from a coffee house three doors down, where a few patrons lounged under spreading parasols braving the occasional brief shower, and from a tavern on the corner. A glance at the gaudy faux-old-world exterior told Gregor that was a place best avoided. A heavy bass beat and drunken laughter echoed along the street from open windows.

"Looks deserted," Gregor muttered, turning his attention to the darkened windows of Trattoria Torremis. "Are you sure they're still in business?"

"I checked their directory entry this morning." Una hurried over and tried the door. "Odd. It's not like we're that late this evening, either."

A woman's face appeared in the window and glanced up and down the street. Una waved. The face disappeared and the door opened. The owner gave the group a nervous smile. "Are you here to eat?" Although the woman had the pale complexion of someone from outside Skamensis space, she spoke with a broad Stour accent.

"That was the plan." Una gave Gregor a worried glance and turned back to the woman. "Are you open?"

"We are." The owner opened the door wider and gestured for them to enter. "We're just keeping a low profile right now."

"Trouble?" Gregor asked as he passed.

"Threats of," she answered. "All talk, nothing more, but life's been hard since the Emperor ... well ..." She closed and locked the door behind them. "Friends I grew up with suddenly don't want to know me. I've had supply contracts cancelled for no reason. It's not a good time to look different."

Gregor's scalp prickled. He glanced through the glass, but the street outside still looked quiet.

Inside, a scattering of dim table lamps revealed half a dozen patrons regarding the newcomers curiously.

The eight ship's officers crowded around two tables pushed together, and ordered drinks.

Gregor scanned the menu. "I don't recognize anything here." He looked around the table and saw most of the others were as much at a loss. "What do you recommend?"

Una sighed. "You provincial stay-at-homes need to get out more. Leave it to me." She turned to the waiter, who looked like the owner's son, and conferred in low tones.

While they talked, Gregor scanned the room more carefully, alert to the subtle tension. The owner had retreated to behind a counter, and kept eyeing the door nervously. The few other customers talked quietly, but their voices were anxious rather than intimate. Whatever it was, the navy visitors weren't the cause of their nervousness.

Drinks arrived. The mood relaxed.

Running feet outside snapped Gregor back to full alertness. There was something off about the shuffling gait. He stood and turned in time to see the window explode towards him. He stumbled and barely stopped himself tripping over a metal trash can rolling across the floor.

More missiles crashed through the window. Gregor felt his forehead and picked out a shard of glass. He kicked his chair out the way and headed to the door, the rest of his crew at his heels. "Raise the watch officer," he hissed to Una. "Give them our location and request backup."

To the rest of the officers he shouted, "No weapons. I won't have the navy firing on our own people." He didn't have time to complete the obvious thought: unless they fire first.

They piled out into the street to find a mob of maybe twenty people milling outside. Someone threw a punch at Gregor, a wild haymaker which he dodged easily. Without hesitation he sank a balled fist into the assailant's gut, then ducked as another attacker swung a length of pipe at him. He found himself at close quarters with the pipe-wielder. A sharp elbow jab distracted the man while Gregor relieved him of his makeshift club.

Now armed with something less lethal than a military-grade beam pistol, Gregor whirled around and took stock. His companions had already formed a cordon around the shattered bistro frontage. A quick head count confirmed the officers were all standing. At least six groaning heaps, shadows on the street, showed the attackers' casualties. The rest, still outnumbering Gregor's side two to one, surrounded them.

Gregor kept a sharp watch for his two most prominent fears—weapons more sophisticated than clubs and knives, and any signs the crowd intended to torch the place. The latter seemed unlikely, though. This was a targeted attack, and fire was too indiscriminate.

He singled out a lanky man in the center of the crowd who everyone else seemed to be deferring to. Gregor could spot a mile off a group of grunts looking to their commanding officer for direction.

The man wouldn't meet Gregor's eyes, and seemed to be fixated on a point on his head. Gregor was suddenly aware of a wet trickle down his cheek, and wondered what he must look like. "I've been in space for the last six months," he bellowed, "defending *your* borders. This is my first landfall in that time, and you have the fucking temerity to chuck a *trash can* at me?"

The man finally found his voice. "We got no beef with you. It's those Firenzi traitors we want."

Still glaring at the ringleader, Gregor called out, "Lieutenant Spelze. I'm notoriously bad at reading memos, so please remind me, are we in a state of war with Family Firenzi?"

"As at nineteen hundred hours, we were not, Sir. Otherwise we'd be at our stations instead of trying to enjoy some well-earned R&R."

The man glanced left and right at his colleagues. "I'm not talking about war. I'm talking about the Emperor and his kids. Their lot are all in it together."

"Space alive," Una burst out. "Can you even hear yourself?"

"Who exactly is 'their lot'?" Gregor sneered. Then his manner changed. He didn't try to hide his raw emotion. "Show me the evidence and I'll be first in line to tie them to a burning pole." The leader took half a step back at his vehemence. "But that's been shown to be bullcrap, so back the fuck off. These are imperial citizens and they are under my protection."

A warning shout behind Gregor came too late. Pain split his skull, and he collapsed to his knees. He struggled to stay awake and upright.

Three blinding flashes splintered the night through Gregor's fluttering eyelids.

Shit, his last thought came as awareness faded. They do have firearms.

———•—•———

With more than a little trepidation, Chalwen left the Mosaic Palace through the main portico and stepped into the full glare of morning sun slanting across the mile-wide plaza fronting the palace. It was early yet, but the transition from the shaded interior of the palace was harsh and she immediately broke out in a sweat in the midsummer heat.

Great, she thought, as her civilian tunic dampened under her armpits. Way to make a good first impression. She knew the Imperial Security headquarters and adjacent court house were linked into the subterranean network of corridors that descended hundreds of feet beneath the palace, but that section was unfamiliar territory to her, and there was no guarantee that her clearance would pass her through the necessary gates. Besides, she had instructions to announce herself at the main entrance and ask for directions.

Ahead of her, bottle green glass and textured sandstone of the ImpSec building looked demure and understated next to the dazzling steel geometry of the court house. But then, ImpSec didn't like to draw attention to itself.

She climbed the steps, leaning heavily on her cane, and entered the building. A polymer barrier bearing the imperial crest slid aside as she approached. So, her passkey was recognized and her access clearance updated already. Imperial bureaucracy could be highly efficient when it wanted to be.

A fresh-faced youngster looked up from a reception desk to one side and waved her over. "Lieutenant ap Gwynodd? Commander Stanhope is expecting you. There's an elevator—"

"Stairs don't frighten me," Chalwen growled. The receptionist looked startled. Chalwen calmed her tone. "The exercise is good therapy."

"Of course," he said. "Carry on down the hall. Take a right about fifty yards along and you'll come to a stairwell. Up to level four and follow the signs for the Intelligence main reception."

As she walked the hallway, leaning on her cane but doing her best to hide her limp, Chalwen took in her surroundings. Not so much the details, as the *feel* of the place.

Beyond the public chambers and state rooms, many buildings of the Mosaic Palace oozed antiquity. Everywhere was clean, but worn, and old-fashioned beyond belief. Many of the offices in the guard house sported paneled wainscots in real wood, edges worn silky smooth by feather dusters shooing the grime of a hundred generations.

In contrast, Imperial Security headquarters was clean and comfortable, and hummed with a fresh energy that surprised her. This building evoked an almost universal dread that was hard to dispel. An invitation to appear here rarely boded well, and too many such invitations were issued at gunpoint. But the building's grim reputation was at odds with the airy interior. Only the workers thronging the hall, going about their business with guarded focus, hinted at hidden tensions in the air. This place teemed with secrets.

Nobody gave Chalwen a second glance as she found the stairwell and heaved herself up flight after flight.

On the fourth floor, signs guided her around the corner and through a clear door into a wide reception room cluttered with tables and circles of chairs. There were maybe twenty people standing, sitting, talking or studying notepads. An elderly woman hurried towards Chalwen as she stepped into the room. "You should have taken the elevator. You're late." Her tone seemed to hold more amusement than animosity, but Chalwen had the uncomfortable feeling she'd been under surveillance from the moment she'd entered the building.

The woman pointed Chalwen through an outer office and through another door.

"Lieutenant ap Gwynodd," she announced.

"Of course!" An angular man unfolded himself from a chair and hurried around his desk. "Boris Stanhope. So you're the one who foiled an assassination in the palace. Good work. Came at a cost, though." He glanced at the cane in Chalwen's hand. "You stuck with that for good?"

Chalwen's gut twisted. "Hope not, but the medics reckon there's permanent damage. I'll never be as active as I once was."

"You caused a bit of a stir down in the operations room, too. Did you do the right thing?"

Chalwen considered, startled by the unexpected question. "Something wasn't right. I acted on the basis of information I had at the time." She felt this wasn't the time to mention her ongoing concerns about traitors in the palace. She also had no idea how much the Chief of Intelligence knew about the help she'd had from within his own organization. He seemed to be waiting for her to say more, but she needed a better sense of the man before revealing too much.

Boris Stanhope let the silence draw out a few more seconds before he grunted. Somehow, Chalwen had the feeling she'd just passed an invisible test.

"Colonel bin Merrin speaks well of you. Unorthodox way of thinking." He narrowed his eyes at Chalwen. "You'll need that."

"I appreciate the chance to continue serving Imperial Security. Can you give me an idea what I'll actually be doing?"

"Obviously you won't be out in the field. I'm putting you in Civil Watch, back office."

Chalwen struggled to place the name from her brief study of the bewildering hierarchy, and quickly gave up. She felt lost.

The Intelligence chief gave no obvious signal, but the door behind Chalwen opened. A short man bustled in, eyes bulging from a comically round face. "You're the ex-bodyguard?"

Chalwen swallowed a burst of anger, and simply nodded.

"Well, come along then!"

Commander Stanhope didn't appear to notice the man's manner. He said, "I'll leave you with Taraq Marand. He heads the unit where you'll be stationed."

Taraq strode off down the hall. Chalwen followed as fast as she could, but couldn't keep up. She wondered what was the point of that meeting with the Intelligence chief. Surely he didn't greet all newcomers in person like that? Maybe it was a courtesy to the colonel, who'd arranged her transfer.

Taraq turned and scowled. "Hope your mind's quicker than your legs." He looked her up and down, and sniffed. "We usually take on *trainees* in their early twenties."

"Trainee?" Chalwen spluttered before she could stop herself.

"Forget anything you think you know. The Intelligence world is a deeply technical field. You're going back to school. You'd better be sharp." He turned and carried on down the hall. "And don't imagine being on first name terms with the Crown Prince will cut you any slack here, either."

They took the elevator down to level two, with Taraq muttering something about not having all day to wait for a cripple, and through a maze of corridors and some more open spaces lined with doors. It looked like most business here went on behind closed doors, because they passed very few people on the way.

"This is you," Taraq said at last, pointing to a door that stood ajar. "You'll find a workspace opened up on your notepad with orientation material and a training schedule. Read carefully. Follow instructions. Be on time."

Chalwen opened her mouth to ask what this department did, and who she'd be working with.

Taraq shushed her impatiently. "Everything you need is in the workspace. If you need a nursemaid, you're in the wrong office." He turned to leave, then said, "One more thing. It shouldn't need saying but I suppose I must. You don't discuss your work with anyone outside your unit. You'll be assigned investigation files. You report your findings direct to me, no one else."

He turned towards the door then turned back. "Oh, one last thing. Of course you'll need to turn in your notepad and be issued with a clean device. Who knows what crap you've got loaded onto that thing." He gave Chalwen's notepad a look normally reserved for something organic and several months dead, then he was gone.

Still reeling from shock, Chalwen stared at the tiny cubby hole. After the worn but homely walls and furniture in the guard house, this place felt cold and clinical. She shivered. It occurred to her that she had no idea even where to find washrooms, or a canteen. Somewhere on the way up to Commander Stanhope's office she was sure she'd smelled cooking so there had to be facilities to serve this huge building. In fact, she wasn't even sure she could find her way out to the street again without wandering around at random, and ... she stuck her head out the door and glanced up and down the hall ... there was no one around to ask.

With a sigh, she brushed away a hint of damp at the corner of one eye, set her notepad on the desk, and settled down to read.

Gregor's pain was still there, but manageable. The street swam into not-quite-focus. In the blurred shadows, he made out the reflective stripes of a field medic's tunic.

"Welcome back." Alongside him, Una feigned cheerfulness. "One of the assholes we downed was only winded. Lying low, waiting for a chance to break through the cordon and run."

"I saw weapons' flashes."

"That was Jimi. Discharged his sidearm into the ground as a warning. As soon as they saw we were armed and serious they fucked off."

Gregor groaned. He'd said no firearms, but things were about to get out of control. Heck, he'd never really been *in* control. Just blustering and hoping that would be enough to make them back down. Jimi had made the right call under the circumstances, but Gregor had wanted to take at least some of them in for questioning. He squinted up and down the street. The casualties were gone. Escaped? Or taken in? "Were these locals, do you think?"

"Harian—the owner—ID'd some of them."

"So, they probably grew up around here, at least some of them, and know the family." Gregor winced as the medic applied something cold to the back of his skull. "What would make you turn on people who've been a part of the community your whole life?"

"Something stirred them up. The local ImpSec office is treating this seriously. Seems like there've been threats made to other families too, but up to now it's been just talk."

"This didn't look like talk to me. So, this lot have Firenzi ancestry and run a place that does some high-end cuisine." He couldn't think straight. Everything was too fuzzy.

"Was popular, too. Right until a couple of weeks ago. Seems right now any Firenzi connection's enough to paint a target on your back."

"That must be one helluva problem living so close to the Firenzi border," Gregor growled in frustration. He thought back to the fight he'd averted in the hangar. "Are people really buying that assassination bull?"

Una gave him a weary smile. "Us officer types are trained to think for ourselves. Most people have outsourced that capacity."

News broadcasts covered the solemn state funeral of Emperor Paul Skamensis. Chalwen hunched over her desk and sourly swept the live streams to one side. She should have been *there*, alongside the Crown Prince. So many nobles gathered in one place openly invited an assassination or act of terrorism.

Normally, the Emperor's passing alone would be marked with such ceremony. There were precedents for dealing with close family members who died at the same time—assassinations were not uncommon in the eight thousand years of the modern age, and they were not always without collateral damage—and lesser individuals were mourned separately.

Normally, there were identifiable bodies.

From the wreckage of the cruiser, it was impossible to separate bodies let alone identify individuals. Someone on Julian's staff had decided to dispense with normal protocols and hold a joint funeral for all who died in that inferno. Emperor, family members, bodyguard and crew alike. Instead of a single coffin, the remains of the cruiser were paraded through the capital to a stage in the center of the plaza where they would be cremated a second time.

It was, Chalwen grudgingly conceded, something Paul would have approved of. Nevertheless it was, in her opinion, a catastrophic error of judgment. The populace was being reminded forcibly of what they'd lost, of the enormity of this atrocity, particularly the young princes and princesses killed alongside the Emperor.

And they were angry.

This seemed a move calculated to inflame nationalist outrage. That wasn't obvious from the outside, but Chalwen's desktop was logjammed with reports of acts and threats against foreign business interests, particularly Firenzi-owned businesses.

After an orientation and a two-day crash course in the arsenal of tools and data sources available to Imperial Intelligence, Chalwen had been put to work. There was more training to come, of course, but she had enough to get started. Enough to be dangerous. It was scary, when she paused long enough to think about it, just how much ImpSec could pry into a citizen's life once they had you in their crosshairs. It was Chalwen's job to sift through the thousands of reports, delegating ones that looked like the actions of aggrieved but solitary individuals for the attention of local authorities. Many, though, had hallmarks of an orchestrated campaign of unrest. Those, she flagged for her superiors' attention.

For a long while she sat and gazed at the flood of information, wondering how Callum Steinway fared in all this mayhem. Had he fled already? His fears now seemed uncannily prescient. Part of her itched to call and check up on him, but his contact details and her faked identity had been hidden on her old notepad along with all the illicit tools she'd used to talk to The Hidden Light. All gone. Confiscated and swept clean by the paranoid Taraq Marand.

She felt that loss most keenly. To the outside world her life had been in the bodyguard, while her unseen life revolved around the subversive community of the Light. Both now taken from her. Yes, she could easily contact Henri directly through the comms network, but who might be listening in? She longed to hear how the investigation was going. Had they got anything useful out of Esme Sellick? More than that, she ached to hear a friendly voice, a change from the snobbish hostility in Civil Watch. But she daren't do anything to risk bringing a spotlight onto Henri's under-the-counter activities.

She was alone, cut off from Light business until she could re-establish contacts safely.

And so she patiently traced sources of communications, looked for duplicated phrasing across unrelated messages, trawled lists of suspects and contacts, catalogued subtleties in methods, looking for common threads.

There. She took a closer look at reports of arson in a textile warehouse on Bhotan. On its own, it could have been just a random incident, but ... she leafed through dozens of other reports from Bhotan ... a leaflet campaign in the same district whipping up public outrage, scathing opinion pieces in the local news feeds, a Firenzi business mogul embroiled in a corruption scandal that had conveniently come to light from a tip-off, followed suspiciously quickly by in-depth revelations of how local health services had been harmed by his actions. Nothing obvious made these items stand out from the background noise, except for the timing. It was as if someone kept asking themselves what's the most inflammatory thing that could happen *right now*?

In each case, Chalwen teased out connections, associates, lines of communication, to see where the trails converged. Eventually she reached dead ends that all her prying couldn't advance any further. But not before she reached one clear conclusion. These were not random local disturbances.

The strings were being pulled by someone here, on Magentis.

Year 8069, autumn

Taraq Marand looked up from his desk and frowned as Chalwen peered around the half-open door. "Yes?"

"Can you spare a few minutes?"

Taraq claimed to have an open door policy and to make time for his staff, but it always felt to Chalwen that he resented people putting that policy to the test. Or maybe it was just her. Either way, she was determined not to be put off this time.

She'd now spent weeks of mind-numbing, painstaking toil on a never-ending mountain of reports, some big, some trivial. The far-reaching tentacles of Civil Watch tapped into the activities of its populace, looking for hints of dissent or criminal activity. The vast majority of the reports were of no interest to ImpSec. She was panning for flecks of gold in a turbulent river of information.

With more training and growing experience, she'd developed better procedures to sniff out promising leads and identify relevant associations from the deluge. She'd passed dozens of case files on to Taraq, but seen no signs of the alarm bells that should by now have been ringing throughout the organization. At the very least, she'd have expected some more focused direction, maybe targets of interest or specific patterns of behavior to watch out for. Someone by now must surely have distilled her analyses, and presumably those from other analysts in the sprawling department, into more refined signatures of a well-organized foe eating away at the foundations of the empire.

But the silence from elsewhere in the branch was deafening. She was after answers, and if this ghastly little man didn't want his staff dropping in on him then he should shut his damned door like everyone else.

Without waiting for an answer, she slipped into the office and closed the door. He'd already drummed into her a paranoia of secrecy around any work-related conversation.

"More patterns. Same hallmarks as the rest. This time it's Evenia, Derrin, and Tigris."

"So?" Taraq's eyes bulged. "Submit the reports."

"I have. They'll be waiting for you in your workspace right now, but I wanted to ask about something broader than the details of any one report."

Taraq looked wary. "Okay."

"I know I'm still finding my way around here, but I wondered what's happening to the reports I've filed. These aren't isolated. I think there's a common source, which suggests a massive and well-organized conspiracy. Is anyone looking into this?"

"That's not something you need to worry about." He sniffed. "Just keep doing what you're doing. Leave the bigger picture to people with all the information."

"I *am* seeing a bigger picture, even from where I'm sitting. But if these are all going off to different people to look into, *they* may not have all the pieces."

Taraq gave her a frosty glare. "It's my job to piece things together, not yours."

Despondent, Chalwen slouched back to her office. The collection of news feeds she habitually kept showing on one wall had one theme in common today. The growing crowds in the plaza outside readying themselves for the spectacle of the coronation. Crown Prince Julian had survived attempts on his life, and attempts to oust him in favor of Ivan. Thank Space for small mercies. But the celebrations a few hundred yards away might as well have been on another planet. Once again, she should have been *there*, but instead she was here. Imperial Security never slept, and didn't stop for a planetwide public holiday either.

She had work to do. More connections to ferret out, no matter how pointless it seemed to her right now.

Then one news feed caught her eye. A niche channel devoted to serious political analysis. It stood out because it was the only one not showing scenes of adoring crowds. Instead, Grand Duke Ivan's face stared out at her.

A chill ran down her back at the smug expression. The Grand Duke seemed to have invaded her privacy, here in the heart of Imperial Security. She couldn't shake off the fleeting but powerful impression of a deeply personal intrusion, no matter how illogical that thinking might be. But the chill deepened as she cut in the audio and listened to the report.

Julian had appointed Ivan as his chief political advisor.

Chalwen felt sick to her stomach. She angrily shut off the news feeds and stumbled out of her office in search of a drink.

Wrath of Empire's lower hangar, tucked into the main hull beneath machinery spaces and forward of the plasma cannon, was usually reserved for VIP arrivals and departures. Visiting emperors, ambassadors, and heads of Families docked their shuttles and private yachts here. This hangar was usually off-limits to most crew members.

Today was a rare exception.

The hangar's few craft had either been moved to one side, or temporarily housed in the main hangar seven hundred feet above. The floor was cleared to make an impromptu theater for five thousand of the ship's crew. Today, anyone not on duty was down here watching a live stream of Crown Prince Julian's coronation on vast screens rigged up for the occasion.

It hadn't escaped Gregor that any of the crew could see the ceremony together with their choice of commentary on wall screens in the many messes and recreation rooms, or on their own scrolls and notepads. There was no logical reason for the captain to go to such lengths to bring the crew together like this, but there was something symbolic about the shared experience of such a momentous event.

Along with a handful of senior officers, Gregor leaned on the railing of a walkway twenty feet above the main hangar floor. A sea of heads stretched from one side of the hangar to the other, and from the temporary screens to the massive airlock doors at the far end. The screens themselves showed the Assembly Room in full imperial pomp, alongside views of crowded plazas in capital cities across the empire.

Gregor wondered what difference this would make to the tensions still rife throughout Skamensis worlds. He'd risked a couple of check-ins on The Hidden Light, but was in no place to help. The organization seemed to be purely on the defensive, using all its resources to head off the worst of the violence. A month since his brush with an angry mob, the back of his head still felt tender to the touch. The state funeral hadn't helped matters. What the heck did those fools on Magentis think they were doing? The navy should be patrolling the borders, but instead they found themselves bolstering local police forces against increasingly sophisticated attacks on foreign-held property, and increasingly caught in the crossfire when well-armed foreigners defended themselves.

While the mood today on distant Magentis seemed to be wall-to-wall jubilation, not surprising from state-controlled media channels, the atmosphere in the hangar was mixed. Yes, there was relief that they had an appointed leader once more, but any celebration was restrained, half-hearted.

A small knot of ratings directly below Gregor, half hidden from the hangar floor behind a cargo loader, muttered among themselves when Crown Prince Julian walked the length of the Assembly Room to ascend the dais at the far end. The group quickly dispersed when a uniformed ImpSec officer strolled past. From his vantage point, Gregor watched similar scenes play out while Julian swore the oath of office under the guidance of a hawk-faced judge. Suddenly, the use of the hangar made sense. Whatever the captain's own opinions on the matter, open disloyalty needed to be discouraged. Bringing the crew together on this charged occasion gave Imperial Security a chance to observe people's reactions. Gregor was sure there would be a few stern follow-ups.

Even Gregor, a long-time supporter of the old Emperor Paul, had mixed feelings. Grand Duke Ivan as emperor didn't bear thinking about, but Julian hardly seemed a better choice. Paul should have been on the throne for at least twenty or thirty years more, giving Julian a chance to learn and to prove himself. In fact, until today Gregor would have been hard-pressed to pick Julian out of a crowd. The Crown Prince had stayed out of the limelight, making few public appearances and those only as a bystander. Now here he was, front and center, an unknown quantity.

When the master of ceremonies called on the onlookers to greet their new emperor, the crowds in streets and squares on world after world yelled their approval in unrestrained joy. By contrast, a few muted cheers from the hangar floor were quickly silenced. For the most part, the crew looked on in sullen silence.

As the ceremony drew to a close, someone nudged Gregor in the ribs.

"C'mon," murmured navigation officer Jerve van Verden. "The oiks will be hitting the transit big time to get back to their posts."

Gregor left the railing and hurried after Jerve. "Our rank will get us a capsule ahead of the crowd."

"But how many of them will remember there's a ferret station on this level, and figure a couple flights of stairs will let them avoid the crush on the main deck?"

"Point," Gregor acknowledged, as Jerve hit the call button by the transit hatch.

"What did you make of all that?" Gregor asked while they waited.

"What?" Jerve asked. "The ceremony?"

"No. The new emperor."

The panel flashed orange, signaling an arriving capsule. Jerve glanced over his shoulder. Already, boots pounded on the companion-way nearby. As the panel turned green, Jerve hustled Gregor through the hatch and into the capsule. There was a brief sensation of move-ment while the capsule pulled out into the main tube, freeing up the station for the next customer.

Jerve frowned at the control panel as he punched in a destination code. "Officer's quarters?"

Gregor nodded agreement. It seemed like Jerve was stalling, choos-ing his words carefully.

"Don't want to sound disrespectful, especially today, but ... he's young." Jerve held up his hands expecting a retort. "I know he's the legal heir and all that, and I know there's precedent for someone his age taking the throne, but honestly, I'm worried."

"You'd rather see Ivan on the throne, then?" Gregor tried to keep the bitterness out of his voice. "You and most of the crew by the sounds of it."

"Can't say I care all that much for Ivan, either, but at least he's been 'round the block a few times."

"And," Gregor conceded, "he's got battle experience."

Jerve looked surprised.

"Led a battle group against di Brugui when they tried to push their boundary past the Scorpion nebula. He's always been hands-on in defending his holdings in the southern zone."

"I'd forgotten about that."

"That was years ago. Back in Empress Florence's heyday." Gregor shuddered.

"But that just proves my point. He knows how to defend the realm. That's the kind of experience we need right now, and Julian hasn't got it."

Gregor studied Jerve carefully. Talk like this skirted dangerous ground, but the two officers had known each other for years. They could respect each other's differences, and Gregor was confident none of this conversation would be repeated afterwards.

Not even to ImpSec.

Especially not to ImpSec.

Besides, Jerve seemed to be talking from a combination of fear and practicality. That wasn't a bad thing, it meant he was open to persuasion. A lot of the crew and many of the officers would follow Ivan without question, simply to bring back the glory days of the empire.

"Julian has good advisors, and would you really want to go back to how things were under Florence?" Gregor huffed. "I don't know what your own experience was like, and I know a lot of people did well under the old regime—"

"You don't have to remind me." Jerve's expression was unreadable.

"Not trying to pry," Gregor hastened to add. "As I say, some people had a better time of it than others, but believe me, that's where Ivan would take us given the chance."

"Regardless," Jerve growled, "Julian may be the emperor now, but he can only rule with the backing of the Assembly and the Admiralty, among others. Think about it! When push comes to shove, can an unknown youngster really command the loyalty of the navy? Would this ship follow him into battle?"

That stopped Gregor in his tracks. Jerve was right. Loyalty to the office only went so far. The occupant had to earn the right to stay there.

"My biggest fear is, if we go to war," the navigator whispered, "we're toast."

———————

With a pounding in her head, Chalwen downed three glasses of water and struggled to get dressed.

Huh! She hadn't noticed until now how tight her tunic was getting across the waist, but as she fumbled the buttons with shaking fingers the lack of room to work made itself felt. Dammit! She'd have to expand her wardrobe anyway. She was used to a lifetime in uniform, and her range of civvies was limited. And, apparently, shrinking.

The walking cane leaning up against the foot of the bed seemed to mock her. She'd tried the occasional day without it in the last two weeks. She hated the show of weakness it represented, but without it she struggled to get around. Stubbornness won out. The hangover would help distract her from the pain in her legs. Or the other way around. Either was a win.

She kept to the cool of the palace's underground passages and emerged in an internal lobby within the ImpSec building. Tea beckoned. One of the smaller canteens on the first floor offered a viciously strong brew with the best fruit pastries to complement it.

On her way through the building it was clear she wasn't alone in her suffering. Most of the people she passed walked gingerly, holding themselves as if their heads were made of glass. But she still had another headache to face that wouldn't be cured by liquid and sugar. She still hadn't fathomed what to do with the information she'd culled from that mountain of data, that the higher-ups in her branch seemed determined to ignore.

Clutching a thermos and carry box in one hand, leaving the other free to support her if her legs weakened, she almost collided with someone rounding the corner to the canteen. She lurched and gasped, momentarily blinded by the pain of an icicle stab up her thigh.

"Hey, nice to see you, too," a familiar voice said.

"Henri?"

"Where in Space have you been hiding this last month?"

"Busy," Chalwen mumbled. "And likely under close surveillance as the newbie, plus I ask too many awkward questions."

Henri snorted. "This is ImpSec. Everyone's under surveillance. You just need to know how to deal with it."

A giddy elation hit Chalwen, and she used her free hand to steady herself against the wall. "I wanted to contact you, but I'm pretty sure any calls I make will be monitored, and I've lost all the comms tools I had to contact the Light. I figured that in the eyes of the higher-ups any contact might draw unwanted attention to both of us."

"Fair point. We'll have to do something about that. Can you find your way around the building yet?"

Chalwen nodded, and Henri gave her a room number on the third floor. "Meet me there in half an hour." He glanced at the flask and box Chalwen was clutching. "Looks like you had the same idea. See you in a while."

In the solitude of her office, Chalwen managed half a cup of the scalding tea and one of the pastries. The rest could wait for later. That small infusion of taste eased the worst of the headache, and a weight seemed to have lifted from her that she hadn't even known she was carrying. Henri's was the first truly friendly face she'd seen in this building, and that brief contact had revitalized her beyond belief.

Half an hour to the minute, she navigated the labyrinth of halls and offices that made up Imperial Security headquarters. A door ahead of her opened as she approached. "Huh. That wasn't at all creepy!" She slipped inside and closed the door.

"Well, look how the other half live." Compared to Chalwen's cramped quarters, Henri's space was palatial. A clean and functional desk sat facing the door, similar to Chalwen's, but alongside there was room for a coffee table and a quartet of comfortable chairs.

Simone smiled a greeting from one of the chairs. "Hello stranger."

Henri beckoned Chalwen to sit while he fiddled with controls on the desktop.

Chalwen glanced at Henri, trying to decipher the twinge of misgiving that had caught her by surprise seeing Simone here. She and Henri had worked covertly together for as long as she could remember, partly through their connection to The Hidden Light, but they also shared secrets and acted as sounding boards for each other. It was all work-related, nothing intimate, but their bond was deeper than mere work colleagues. They'd shared dangers and saved each other's lives on countless occasions.

Now, it looked like Henri had taken Simone into his inner circle, someone Chalwen barely knew. Once again, the ground under her shifted.

Simone snapped her fingers and pointed to Chalwen's notepad. "Let's have it then."

"I said we'd get your communications difficulties sorted out." Henri nodded towards Simone. "She knows what she's doing. There are back channels that everyone in ImpSec uses to talk privately."

"It's unofficial"—Simone grinned—"and most newbies spend a year or so before anyone lets them in on the secret, but Henri vouched for you."

"Is it safe to be talking about this?" Chalwen handed her notepad over and lowered herself cautiously into a seat. She'd done more walking already than she'd planned to today, and regretted not bringing her cane.

"This office is secure," said Henri. "As in, secure even from snooping from within the organization."

Simone gave him a sharp look that Henri returned with bland innocence. "I guess the authorities aren't aware of that enhancement?"

"The highest authority in the land approved it."

This exchange brought a curious sense of relief. Henri was hedging. Chalwen wondered how much Simone knew, or guessed, and how far they could trust her. Although he was drawing a line, Henri was coming dangerously close to revealing secrets of The Hidden Light. She also wondered whether there was any prospect of her getting a similar office upgrade. She didn't trust Taraq not to be spying on her, and it made it difficult to conduct Light business.

Which brought her to the matter at hand.

"I'll be thankful to have a means of reaching you without being monitored. There are things going on across our space that I don't like the look of."

Simone's eyes twinkled as she glanced up from the notepad in front of her. "Talking about work outside your unit is a hanging offense. I hope you paid attention to the orientation."

Henri grinned. Although Simone was correct, it seemed she was joking rather than taking the rule book seriously.

Chalwen took a deep breath. Henri had given her none of the signs that said she should guard her tongue, and if he trusted this woman she'd have to trust his judgment. "You've probably seen reports of all the protests and civil unrest happening right across the empire. It's not just a coincidence of local agitation. There's a heap of evidence that everything is being organized from here. I found so many common threads pointing to Magentis, and reported everything back up the chain, but I don't know that it's being acted on."

Henri squinted at her. "Just because there's been no high profile arrests doesn't mean they've ignored it."

"But things are hotting up, out of control. Surely they'd have to put a stop to this? Reports are crossing my desk faster than ever and it's getting to the point where Assembly Members are openly talking about forcing Julian to declare war."

Simone said, "It does sound odd that they've not started counter-measures to limit the damage."

"I can't prove anything of course," Chalwen said, "but recently whenever I ask my supervisor about follow-up, he's looking worried. He's stopped giving me the sarcastic 'above your pay grade' answers and is simply evasive, but I get the feeling he's genuinely troubled."

"But not troubled enough to raise questions higher up the chain," said Henri. "There's a lot of people at that level who just follow the rules and keep their heads down. Don't ask questions, don't rock the boat."

"And," Simone added, "no offense, but Civil Watch is where Intelligence generally dumps its least imaginative people."

"So, are my reports winding up in some Intelligence graveyard or not?"

Simone looked thoughtful. "There are ways to trace a given document through the system."

Henri shook his head. "Whatever Chalwen writes will get incorporated into a new report, maybe a summary with analysis and recommendations, by her supervisor, and so on up the chain. Her original document will have stopped there, with no way of singling out the onward report."

"Unless ..." Simone paused, deep in thought. "Yes, that could work. If I give you some very specific wording to include, a few juicy sound-bites that might survive transcription and editing, I think I can follow the trail."

"Speaking of trails, what happened to Esme Sellick? I haven't been out that way since the funeral."

Henri grimaced. "We took her in. Her mind eventually turned to jelly under questioning."

Chalwen opened her mouth to speak, then closed it again as the implications of Henri's matter-of-fact statement hit her. She reviewed what she knew and suspected about Henri's skills, or at least those of his department. "So she was conditioned. She told us nothing?"

"Actually, she told us more than you'd think," Henri said. "The pattern of conditioning, the mental blocks used, the trigger words ... all that is like a signature. Every training school leaves its own unique mark."

"You can tell who she was working for?"

"Sellick was a PDC agent."

"PDC," muttered Chalwen. "As in the defense conglomerate? The ones behind the battle system that Paul was so angry about?" Chalwen sat back, absorbing the news. "Regardless of who she was working for, the fact that she had any kind of conditioning means she was working for *someone*. That alone is significant, because up until now she might have simply been an innocent party, even with those carryalls of hers being loaded onto the Emperor's craft where they had no business being. But add in the fact that she's clearly not an innocent civilian, she had to be part of that plot."

"And Sergeant van Buren being linked both to that event and the later attempt on Julian ..."

"That means PDC was involved in the assassination."

Chapter 34

It took another month of painstaking toil, seeding a range of carefully chosen words and phrases into her reports. Chalwen gritted her teeth and forced herself to patience. Simone had warned her this was a delicate game, a balance between finding phrases unusual enough to stand out, but not too odd to arouse suspicion. Many wouldn't survive the process of summarization, but hopefully some would get through.

Now, they met once more in Henri's office to hear Simone's findings.

"Your reports aren't being blocked by your supervisor." She got straight down to business. "He's packaging them up and passing them on as he should, and I think he really is concerned by the patterns you've uncovered. His own summaries highlight the suspicions of a deep-rooted organized campaign."

"So why isn't anything being done to follow up? Or is there something happening that's beyond my pay grade to know about?" Chalwen's tone was bitter.

Simone gave a sad smile. "I expect that's what Taraq Marand himself has concluded. He's not the most imaginative person."

"A career public servant," Henri cut in. "Keeps his head down, follows orders, keeps his nose clean."

"But he's wrong?"

Simone's expression turned grim. "Your reports, and those from one or two of your more perceptive colleagues, are being intercepted and deep-sixed by someone in Security."

"Security?" Chalwen stared at Simone. "That's not even in my chain of command." Not any longer, she thought sadly. The imperial body-guard came under the Security branch of ImpSec. It used to give her a sense of belonging, even though the bodyguard had very little to do with the rest of the branch, but no more.

"Do you have an ID?" Henri asked.

"A signals tech. Warran ap Meradan. Know him?"

Both Chalwen and Henri shook their heads.

"Me neither, but we soon will."

"Signals ..." Henri tapped his lips with a forefinger while he pondered. "He could be well placed to mess with surveillance ..."

"To cover for van Buren?" Chalwen asked. "Could this be another member of that cell?"

Simone shrugged. "If he can re-route documents without either sender or recipient being any the wiser, he must have the smarts and the necessary access, either legitimate or covert. Placement in the organization wouldn't have much to do with it by that point."

"So," Chalwen said, "do we pick him up and break his balls a bit?"

"Not that easy." Henri still looked thoughtful. "If he's part of van Buren's network he probably has the same deep conditioning as Esme."

"Meaning?"

"Meaning, the moment we pick him up, that conditioning will set up a load of mental blocks." Simone's face was grim. "He'd die before we get anything from him."

"What sets off the conditioning?" Chalwen was intrigued.

"Usually a combination of stress hormones and the right situational context. As soon as the agent is taken, the blocks get triggered."

"Can you dope him?"

"It can be done, but it's risky. Unless you catch him so quickly that there's not even a subliminal awareness."

"It's that fast?"

"Worse. Often it doesn't even need conscious awareness to trigger the response."

"So, we need to be more sneaky," Henri said. "Fortunately, knowing the conditioning regime used opens up some possibilities. I'll need to do a bit of research, but I think there's a vulnerability we can exploit."

———◆◆———

Chalwen took a deep breath. Her target was in sight, according to Henri murmuring in her earpiece. Chalwen couldn't see him. She was focused on the tray on her table, making a show of scraping various leftovers onto one plate while she bided her time. Her tray of lunch remains included half a cup of still-scalding tea.

The signals tech, Warran ap Meradan, didn't follow a set routine, but he did have some predictable habits. A covert check on his schedule told Simone that Warran had a busy day today with only a brief lunchtime break. On such days, careful observation over the past two weeks told them he always visited this particular canteen, the nearest to his workplace. And he was in a hurry, so he'd take the shortest route.

From the far side of the canteen, with a clear view of the door Warran always used, Henri whispered, "Chalwen, you're up in three ... two ... one ... *go!*"

Chalwen lurched to her feet, tray in hand, and turned to reach for the cane leaning against the back of her chair. Henri's timing had been impeccable. Warran barged right into her. She angled the tray so its contents would spill over him, rather than back onto her.

Her own reaction needed no faking as she sprawled backwards onto the floor with a yelp. Tray and dishes clattered down, hardly heard above Warran's own shriek of outrage turning to pain as the hot tea seeped through his shirt.

"Hey, are you okay?" An expertly-disguised Simone stood from the next table and placed a hand on Warran's arm.

He brushed it off angrily.

"Easy, man. Just trying to help." Simone grabbed a handful of napkins she'd left handy on her table. "Space alive, what a mess!" She handed the napkins to Warran. "Here, you best do the honors." She patted his arm, and while he started brushing off the worst of the food remnants she moved her hand up to his shoulder. "Come on. Let's get you away from these gawkers."

Chalwen started struggling to her feet, spluttering an apology.

"Hey, you clumsy oaf!" Simone stepped between Warran and Chalwen, and gave Chalwen a shove. "Stay down until you can control your feet." She turned back to Warran. "You need some help to clean up? There's a washroom just around the corner."

Straightening her tunic, Chalwen felt the used medipen Simone had dropped down her front. She worked it down to sit in a fold of her tunic, above the waistband of her pants. She'd fish it out and dispose of it as soon as she was out of sight. Damn! That was slick work. Chalwen hadn't spotted the medipen in Simone's hand, but she must have administered the drug. While Warran's attention was on the steaming stain spreading down his front, his eyes looked increasingly unfocused as the drug took effect. Chalwen looked down to hide a smile. As long as none of Warran's subconscious triggers had been tripped by now, the drug would suppress the mental pathways long enough for Henri's team to get to work.

"Say, do you have quarters nearby? Someone could fetch you a change of clothes, or I could find something to tide you over ..." Simone led the bemused Warran away from the canteen, keeping up a soothing patter.

Henri followed at a discreet distance.

Chalwen made a performance of hauling herself upright, using the chair and table as support. She apologized loudly and profusely to the canteen staff rushing over with mop and bucket, and insisted on dropping to her knees again to pick up the mess tray and dishes.

Anything to keep the room's attention on her, and away from the unfortunate Warran and his newfound companions now disappearing out of sight.

It was difficult, but she resisted the temptation to look in the direction of the doorway. She helped clear up the mess, made one last round of apologies for her clumsiness, and headed out the canteen through the opposite door. She burned with curiosity, but she returned to her desk and carried on as if nothing out the ordinary had happened. She was the one everyone would remember and she needed a rock solid alibi for the next few hours. Most especially, she couldn't afford to be seen associated with Simone or Henri right now.

Her hands shook. What were they thinking? Abducting an Imperial Security officer right in the heart of Imperial Security headquarters?

In all the plans and preparations and rehearsals for this operation she'd busied herself in the minutia, not letting herself think about the consequences.

Surely questions would be asked. An ImpSec employee couldn't simply vanish without someone noticing, and given the sensitivity of his position there would surely be alarm bells ringing and a full-blown investigation launched.

Henri had reassured her that this kind of thing happened from time to time. Foreign powers were always trying to infiltrate the vast bureaucracy of ImpSec. Sheer statistics said some of them were successful. The Bureau of Counterintelligence, Henri's agency, had its hands full sniffing out and dealing with infiltrators. There were procedures in place to silence the alarms when they needed to remove an unwanted agent without a fuss. 'Spring cleaning' they called it.

In fact, Henri said, his department found it easier to snatch someone silently from within ImpSec than a civilian off the street.

Chalwen shivered again and glanced nervously at the door.

Somehow, Henri's assertion didn't reassure her.

Chapter 35

Year 8070, winter

"You looked like you've done that kind of thing before." Chalwen scanned the rather ostentatious menu and settled on a simple lemon tea. She felt the tightness of her waistband and decided to forego a pastry, tempting though they looked. She'd bought new civilian clothes to fit, only a few weeks ago, but for some reason they felt uncomfortable today. Perhaps it was the unaccustomed walk in the afternoon mugginess of a Prandis early winter. Her shirt stuck to her back, and the waistband chafed.

"I've spent some time in the field," Simone said primly. "Not all networks and interesting data stores are accessible from a comfortable desk."

Simone, Chalwen and Henri huddled around a table outside Dognoty's, a brash new coffee shop a couple of miles from the palace and off the beaten track for imperial administration staff. Traffic and pedestrians hustled by on the other side of a rope barrier separating the seating area from the street. Most people passing by seemed to be clerks and tradespeople. Very little chance of them being seen together by anyone who knew them, and near the noisy street no chance of being overheard.

"I could see you had fieldcraft," Chalwen said. She turned to Henri. "So? It's been three weeks. Did you get further with this one?"

Henri pursed his lips and gave her a cryptic look. Crap! Their charade in the canteen had to deliver a specific drug before the signals tech's implanted conditioning put up its defenses. Even then it was dicey. Had they been too slow?

Then Chalwen noticed the slight twitch at the corner of Henri's mouth. "Dammit, Chargon! Quit messing with me."

The twitch turned into a grin. "The extraction team waiting in the washroom got him down to the basement in a matter of seconds."

"That's the trick with this kind of operation," Simone added. "Getting the target into a controlled environment in time to properly counter the conditioning. Your Henri's a talented guy."

"He's not ..." Chalwen spluttered.

Henri smirked. "We still had to go carefully. Even without deep psych conditioning he had standard training, and he knew what he was doing. It took a while to break him in a way that we were sure he was giving good intel, not just what he thought we wanted to hear."

"Break the shell but not the yolk," Simone said with a laugh.

A waiter approached to take their order. Chalwen simmered with impatience until he'd gone and they all leaned close over the table again. "So, what did you find?"

"Short version, he confirmed what we suspected. He was part of a small sleeper cell run by PDC. They carried out the sabotage of the cruiser."

"And," Simone said, "we have the whole interrogation captured and documented with a custody chain and practice methodology that will stand as valid evidence if needed."

Chalwen squinted at Henri. "You had a whole team involved. How far up the hierarchy is this known?"

"We're used to running operations fenced off from the hierarchy. We assume there are always elements in our own organization that can't be trusted, so it's a normal practice. I just went a little bit out on a limb to set it up. Also," Henri gave Chalwen a bland stare, "the operatives I chose can be trusted."

Chalwen nodded. She knew what Henri meant. They wouldn't all be Hidden Light members, the organization was too thinly spread for that, but everyone built a core team around them that weren't in on the secret, but who were thoroughly vetted. Like the bodyguard team she'd assembled. She quashed a pang. "PDC," she muttered. "This makes no sense. The conglomerates are in it for business. They'll influence policy any way they can to create a favorable landscape, but they don't interfere in politics writ large, and regicide comes pretty high up that scale."

Simone tilted her head. "True ... I don't know what to make of that either. They took a huge risk."

"You're not kidding. If this became known, they'd be wiped off the map."

"Well," Simone shrugged, "the Families would freeze them out but there's still profits to be made in the unallied outworlds. But ... what's interesting is, I've gone over records of the surveillance hacks at the palace in the days after the assassination. Most of them were extremely subtle and well-disguised. The rolling outages that covered the hideout down in the abandoned power room, for example, were done by a replicating program following a semi-random pattern with a core of fixed objectives."

"That," said Henri, "means that collection of outages were from the same source."

"And they had to be orchestrated by a team of people, maybe only a small team but bigger than this cell, covering each other's tracks. This was a sophisticated attack. An inside job by someone with a deep hold on our security organization."

Chalwen thought. "I sense there's a 'but', isn't there?"

Simone grinned. "But, the glitch under the family quarters when you caught van Bellin, and a few specific outages around the hangar on the day of the assassination, weren't the same work."

Chalwen's heartbeat thumped in her throat. She waited for Simone to continue.

"Those we traced back to signals tech Warran."

"Who is linked to van Bellin and PDC." Chalwen fought to keep the agitation out of her voice. "That much makes sense. He had the same conditioning and he covered van Bellin's actions, and hid the crew that sabotaged the Emperor's cruiser. But, you're saying the broader interference under the palace was someone else. There are two distinct parties involved."

"And neither of them are Firenzi," said Henri.

"And the PDC cell appears to be only a minor player in this whole episode." Chalwen finished the line of thinking she'd been dreading. "The Emperor needs to hear about this."

———————

After Chalwen, Henri, and Simone parted ways in the great plaza that fronted the Mosaic Palace, Chalwen stopped to catch her breath.

Late afternoon sun slanted across the facade, throwing the rhythmic progression of arches and windows into sharp relief. The severely symmetrical facade imposed a sense of order on the chaotic jumble of buildings peeping out above the galleries and bulwarks of the frontage. Above it all, the dazzling dome of the Green Throne Room soared four hundred and fifty feet into the sky and dominated the masonry hinterland.

Chalwen shook herself and lumbered into motion. She needed to see the Emperor.

That was an obstacle they'd never faced before. Emperor Paul had been the linchpin of The Hidden Light. With the covert comms packages on their scrolls and notepads, they'd always had ready and secure access to the Light, and hence to the Emperor.

Now Chalwen had lost her notepad with all its tools. There were more conventional ways, emergency contacts, to reach the Light, but they would never be as secure. Not that she needed to make contact herself. She'd already been over this endlessly with Henri. He was still trying to track down someone in the organization to re-equip Chalwen, but the point was moot. Emperor Julian didn't know the Light existed and there were no members inside the palace with regular access to him. Not since Chalwen had lost her position as head of his bodyguard.

She headed into the palace and, with a heaviness in her heart that caught her by surprise, she threaded through the jumble of buildings and limped up the steps to the guard house. The building held too many painful memories of a life she'd lost to an assassin's poison. Her regular medical check-ups revealed that the nerve damage had stabilized. She wouldn't get any worse, but the nagging pain and stiffness in her legs would be a lifelong companion. All she could do was grit her teeth and put up with it.

Chalwen paused in the doorway into the main operations room, conscious of all eyes turning her way. She nodded greetings to a few friendly faces, carefully ignored others, and plodded across the room to the rear hallway that led to the back offices.

Relieved to find Colonel bin Merrin's door ajar, she squared her shoulders and knocked.

The colonel looked up, startled to see Chalwen. "Lieutenant." He recovered quickly and hurried around his desk, gestured Chalwen to a chair, and carefully shut the door. "How are you?"

Chalwen glanced at the closed door. "Coping with a life-altering malady. Enough said. And you didn't choose privacy to ask after my health."

The colonel looked sheepish. "You're right. Of course I'm concerned for you. If there's anything I can do ..."

Chalwen barked a short laugh. "Create a position for a semi-mobile bodyguard, maybe?"

"But," the colonel said firmly, ignoring her interruption, "I am hoping you're here because you've made some headway in your inquiries."

For a few seconds Chalwen gazed blankly at him, then she remembered those nightmare moments trying to absorb the news of the Emperor's cruiser, and the colonel's indirect orders to find Julian's would-be assassins. In the intervening six months, while she'd been coming to terms with her change in circumstances, she'd been doing exactly that, but the colonel's desperate plea had faded in her memory.

With a twinge of guilt, Chalwen shook her head. "Sorry, but that's not why I'm here."

Yes it is, a rebellious voice insisted. But could she risk taking the colonel into her confidence? He'd always seemed unwavering in his support of the Emperor, but she and Henri had agreed they needed to keep their circle as small as possible.

"You're on the inside in Intelligence now." Colonel bin Merrin slumped back in his chair. "All I know is that the investigation's still ongoing. Anyone got any clues about what happened? Anything you can share with me?"

Chalwen shook her head again. "You must remember, I'm not part of the official investigation into the sabotage." Ignoring the disappointment evident in the colonel's face, she said, "I'm here to ask a small favor."

"Well, I did ask if there's anything I could do." The colonel gave a wry smile.

"I was hoping to speak to one of my old squad. Tara, maybe, or Wilder or Eve. Someone still close to the Emperor who can tell me off the record how he's bearing up. I'm just as starved of news as you are."

"Of course," the colonel muttered. "You were very close to the Crown Prince for years."

"I worry about him. He's still just a boy."

Colonel bin Merrin sighed, and tapped a stylus on his desktop. "I tried to keep as many as possible of your old squad on duty with Julian." He frowned at the desktop, then brightened. "You're in luck. Wilder just came off duty. He should be on his way to the guard house. I'll have him meet you outside on the riverside walk. If this isn't an official visit I assume you want to be away from prying eyes."

Chalwen thanked him and let herself out a side door, not wanting to run the gauntlet of curious stares in the main office.

The riverside path was shaded by a steep embankment that also shielded her from view. She sat on a bench to wait. Across the river, the Emperor's Meadow stretched into the distance with no sign of the city that spread beyond it. From here, you could easily be sitting in the middle of the country instead of in the heart of the capital of a star-spanning empire.

"Good to see you, Lieutenant."

Chalwen looked up as Wilder approached. Lieutenant. Yes, even though she was now retired from the imperial bodyguard, she still carried her old rank. A permanent reminder of the life she'd lost.

"The colonel said you wanted to hear how Julian's faring." Wilder sat on the bench next to Chalwen. "Of course, we both know that's a crock of horseshit."

A faint smile cracked Chalwen's morose features. Trust Wilder to see through the deception. To be fair, the colonel probably had, too. He wasn't stupid. And he was smart enough to know he needed plausible deniability for whatever Chalwen was doing.

"Of course I am concerned for Julian's welfare, but if you and the old crew are still on the job then I know he's in good hands. But I have information for him that won't reach him through any official channels."

"Is this about the assassination?"

"And events being stirred up across the empire."

"Isn't half of ImpSec already working on all of that?"

"I don't think the investigation is going to reach any useful conclusions. It's being hampered from the inside."

Wilder whistled. "Do you have evidence of that, or just a hunch?"

"We have evidence." Chalwen wondered how far she should go. Wilder didn't need to know much, only enough to convince him this was serious, and too much information could be dangerous. "We got one agent, and there's enough to tell us we don't know who to trust. I need to bypass the whole chain of command and bring the report direct to the Emperor."

"Access to the Emperor is hard to get." He snorted. "That's why we're here now, isn't it?"

Chalwen smiled.

Wilder sighed. "What do you need?"

"I need to deliver a report direct into his hands, so I know it's reached him unaltered. It can't be with any of his regular advisors present, and ideally nobody else would even know about the meeting."

Wilder squinted at Chalwen. "You know damned well that can't happen. Even when the Emperor is technically 'alone' he's still got his bodyguard nearby. They may not always be in the same room, but nobody can approach without the squad knowing about it."

"Okay, but I'd only want members of our old squads present. People I hand-picked and know I can trust." At Wilder's troubled look, Chalwen asked, "How many of the old crew are still with Julian?"

"Many of us are still here, but things have been shuffled around a lot in the last few months. Squads have been broken up and reformed."

Chalwen's heart sank. It was another painful reminder of the family members lost. She forced herself back to practicalities. "How bad is it?"

"There's a lot more guards around the Emperor now, and a much bigger pre-screening crew running ahead to clear the way. We've all been mixed in with the remains of the other Family bodyguards. There isn't a squad now that's entirely made up of Julian's old guard." Wilder lowered his voice to a disgusted whisper. "Some of them even have goons from the Grand Duke's guard mixed in."

Chalwen shuddered. "So, a meeting in secret is probably out of the question." She gazed across the sluggish river, lost in thought. "But ... the Emperor does hold private meetings all the time. Can you at least pass him a message without anyone noticing?"

Wilder frowned. "Should be possible."

"Tell him, Chalwen says there's trouble in paradise."

"We don't use those code phrases any more. We've got a whole new set."

"All the better. It won't be mistaken for anything from the current bodyguard."

Chapter 36

The waiting game preyed on Chalwen over the next week. Had Wilder managed to deliver the message? Would Julian respond? More to the point, would he listen?

Chalwen was painfully aware that it was five months since she'd last been in the same room as the Crown Prince. A lot had changed in her own life and, she grudgingly acknowledged, Julian himself had undergone even more dramatic changes. In all that time, she'd been completely out of touch with him. A growing, impressionable, vulnerable young man. Still only a boy. What pressures and influences had he been under in those months?

As days went by, a deepening unease gnawed at Chalwen. Julian had always looked up to his ambitious uncle. The older man had been a more constant presence in his life than his own father, and now he was one of the Emperor's innermost advisors. How much of Ivan's influence might have rubbed off on him? By now, the young Emperor would likely be very different from the scared and grieving Crown Prince she'd last known.

Not for the first time, she wished Lorenzo had agreed to take Julian into his confidence. One uncle's influence might help counterbalance the other's.

The summons finally arrived, a formal message through official channels demanding her presence in the Office of Deliberation. With a sigh of relief and a wry smile, Chalwen wondered what tongues this would set wagging. A direct communication from the Emperor would be flagged as an item of interest all the way up and down the ImpSec hierarchy.

She hauled herself from her seat and across the office. On an impulse, she grabbed the walking cane lying neglected in one corner. She rarely used it now, preferring to master the residual pain in her legs, but she decided it might serve to remind Julian of the times they'd shared.

She had the dubious satisfaction of seeing Taraq Marand and a pair of Chalwen's more stand-offish work colleagues huddled outside Taraq's office as she passed. They appeared to be in deep conversation, pretending to ignore her, but she felt their covert attention on her as she turned towards the stairs. The pretense was laughable. Nobody in this section stood in hallways to talk. The message gave no clues as to the purpose of the audience. All they knew was that such an invitation either signified immense privilege, or spelled fatal disaster. No emperor wasted time on bland middle ground.

Let them speculate.

Despite herself, a grin split her face then turned to a grimace as she took a stair awkwardly. Dammit. She needed to focus, and to rehearse one last time her planned approach to convince Julian of the danger he faced.

The trek from ImpSec headquarters and across the palace grounds seemed endless today, giving Chalwen ample time to consider all the ways this audience could go wrong. Once again she cursed the decision not to reveal The Hidden Light to Julian. Things had been so much easier under Paul.

And, she reminded herself yet again, Julian all these months on was now an unknown quantity. The pressures of his office will have shaped him in that time.

At last she arrived in the outer guest lobby to the Office of Deliberation, where she was invited to wait until the appointed time. She remained standing despite the electric jolts up her legs.

A uniformed usher showed her in. Julian sat behind his desk, arms outstretched and palms pressed downwards on the polished surface. Chalwen studied him as she advanced, trying to read some clue into the stern and regal mask. She stopped a few paces short of the desk and gave a short bow. "I am at your service, Magister Summis."

"At ease, Lieutenant. You know why you're here."

A tingle of unease brewed in Chalwen's stomach at his cool aloof manner.

"I'm afraid I have little time for niceties. Your message alarmed me. You have my attention."

Chalwen glanced around the office, pleased at least to note that Julian had dismissed the guards who were normally stationed at doorways. Emperor Paul occasionally held audiences with guests alone in here, but only on rare occasions. The gesture showed a great depth of trust. She felt reassured, but only slightly.

"Sire, you're right to be alarmed. I've made troubling discoveries that point to a widespread conspiracy against Emperor Paul, and against you."

"I take it all this goes back to the time you spirited me out of the infirmary?"

"It does."

Julian sighed. "Chalwen, you acted on your best instincts at the time. But our best investigators found nothing to show anything untoward happening inside the palace. Their conclusion is that you exercised judgement under pressure, and simply erred on the side of caution."

Chalwen's mouth hung open. She swallowed hard and fought to stifle an angry outburst. After all they'd been through over the years. And, she realized, her misgivings stemmed much further back, right to the days of the old Empress's funeral. But it was too late to backtrack, the damage was done.

"Obviously that's better than being wrong the other way around," Julian continued, "and I'll always be grateful for your dedication. And of course I'm glad you were just as alert when that assassin tried to poison me."

Chalwen tried to regroup. The attempted abduction was a sore point. The conspirators had covered their tracks so thoroughly even she was sometimes tempted to doubt her own memory. She needed to steer onto firmer ground. "That was just the starting point for deeper investigations. I've been working with colleagues in Imperial Security, and the findings are troubling."

Julian's eyes widened. "I didn't realize you were part of that investigation team."

"I'm not. Not the official team. A small group was commissioned to conduct a parallel investigation, coming at it from a different angle."

"I have to commend Imperial Security on its thoroughness, but this sounds like we can't trust our own people."

"That's the problem," Chalwen said grimly. "We don't know who can and can't be trusted, outside a very small circle. I'm told this is fairly normal for ImpSec."

"So," Julian said slowly, "what have you found?"

"All the public rumors spinning out of control paint the Firenzi as the villains." Chalwen took a deep breath. "The trails we've followed say the sabotage of your father's cruiser was carried out by agents working for one of the defense conglomerates, not the Firenzi. And alongside them, covering their tracks, was a more extensive network on our own staff. Again, nothing to do with the Firenzi."

Julian cocked his head to one side. "I'd be happy to hear Josef Firenzi isn't involved. I never got to meet him, but I know he and father were close. We're very close to war with them and everyone around me is convinced they're behind our troubles."

"There's more. Much of the civil unrest in the empire isn't random. It's being carefully stage-managed from here on Magentis. That line of inquiry *is* part of my official duties," she hastened to add, seeing Julian's skeptical look. "But those reports have been sidelined and buried inside Imperial Security. Someone doesn't want this to become known."

"You have evidence of all this? Evidence of cover ups and records being removed?"

Chalwen fingered the edge of her notepad, thinking about the package of reports she'd prepared to hand over. A chill tickled the nape of her neck. Julian wasn't buying it, and she wondered if any amount of evidence would convince him. Someone had been talking to him. His trust lay elsewhere, and suddenly Chalwen wondered if the two of them were truly as alone as they appeared to be.

She fidgeted, undecided. She badly wanted to convince Julian, but now she thought about it she wondered what he would do with the information. Take it to his advisors, who would be as hard to convince as he was?

And then there was Ivan. How would he react to this revelation? He was the dominant influence on Julian now, and it occurred to Chalwen that he had much to gain from the way events were turning.

Standing here now, she felt foolish thinking she could achieve anything this way. She'd grown so accustomed to Emperor Paul, someone with experience and sound judgment, who wouldn't be bullied by anyone, ready to view the evidence and make up his own mind.

Whatever she said here would be dissected by people all too ready to persuade Julian she was wrong.

The notepad with its hoard of documents felt like a ticking bomb in her hands. It would be a mistake to reveal too much of the hard evidence they'd secured. If the wrong people knew how far they'd progressed, they and their efforts would be quietly obliterated. She had to find a way to get this to someone who wouldn't be pressured or manipulated, someone in a position to take decisive action.

Quietly, she said, "There's a weight of things that don't add up, and gaps in the records, but the people behind it remain hidden."

"Chalwen, I've known you for most of my life. I know you mean well, but you've always been erratic. If you have findings that will hold water, report them direct through Commander Stanhope. I need to hear this from someone whose job it is to inform me of security threats."

————— ◆ —————

Ivan gazed hard-eyed at the former bodyguard on the wall screen as she hobbled from the office. He still remembered Lieutenant Bresk's suspicions about this one, but seeing her now, seeing how months on she still relied on a walking stick to get about, this woman couldn't possibly have been part of Josef Firenzi's jailbreak.

He shook his head in frustration. He had a special interrogation cell set aside for the perpetrators of that defeat, should they ever be identified. Meanwhile he'd been content to allow Bresk a free hand in pursuing his personal vendetta against his counterpart in the bodyguard, but somehow she was still causing trouble in her own bumbling way. And she'd come frighteningly close to uncovering the damaging truth. A link to a defense conglomerate and links to Magentis. How much did she really know, and how much was conjecture?

And on top of that, Julian had sent her to Stanhope. Ivan's jaw clenched. He'd specifically talked to Julian about hooking her up with someone firmly in Ivan's own payroll, so he could vet and edit whatever findings the former bodyguard might have uncovered. Stanhope was too independent-minded, and the Emperor was also showing occasional flashes of original thought.

With great care, Ivan calmed his breathing and settled his face into the genial mask of a loving uncle. As agreed, he joined Julian in the Office of Deliberation as soon as Lieutenant ap Gwynodd had left.

"Well?" the Emperor demanded as soon as Ivan appeared. "What do you think?"

Ivan considered the question. "I feel sorry for her."

Julian looked startled.

"I mean, she's suffered greatly in your service and the empire owes her a great debt of gratitude. She's unfit to remain as a bodyguard, but she seems entirely unsuited to intelligence work."

"I thought Security liked people with active minds." Julian frowned.

"When it's tempered by reasoned judgment. She was already jumping at shadows as a bodyguard."

"Are you talking about the incident in the infirmary?"

"Exactly so. Just think what the atmosphere of secrecy in ImpSec might do to someone with such an active imagination."

"All the same," Julian said, "I'd be dead now if she hadn't followed her imagination. Everyone else decided those surveillance gaps in the palace network were just technical glitches. Are you saying she's jumping at shadows again now?"

Ivan pursed his lips. It would be dangerous for him to side clearly one way or the other. He didn't want to lend any credibility to these claims, possibly leading to someone taking a closer look, but on the other hand it would be suspicious to appear too dismissive. "That's why I thought maybe a third party should be involved. Someone who isn't so invested in the work she's done." He paused, then decided to push his luck. "Sire, might I ask why you directed her to Stanhope?"

"He's the head of Intelligence. Who better?"

"I mean, it would seem extraordinarily presumptuous for a lowly analyst to go straight to the top like that."

"As opposed to talking to someone lower down the hierarchy, like you suggested?"

Ivan hesitated at the edge in Julian's voice. He realized he couldn't press the point further without drawing attention to his interest here. He shrugged.

"I don't know people lower in the hierarchy well enough," Julian continued. "I do feel I know Stanhope, and this matter could be nothing, or it could be of the highest importance."

———————

Still stinging from her failed audience with the Emperor, Chalwen met with Henri and Simone in one of the seedier inns near ImpSec, on the outskirts of Riversedge. Too downmarket for them to meet anyone they knew, but civil enough that a brawl was unlikely, it was a place where people routinely met for mildly nefarious purposes and the landlady asked no questions.

While they sat themselves at a heavy table with a polymer surface moulded to resemble real wood, Simone had surreptitiously swept the room for listening devices and pronounced the place clean.

They nursed tankards of strong ale and Chalwen recounted her meeting in a hushed voice. "The problem remains, how to bring this intelligence to someone who'll actually do something with it."

"The simplest solution is to do as the Emperor suggested." Henri's expression was unreadable.

Chalwen raised an eyebrow. "I don't know Stanhope like you do. Can he be trusted with this?"

"Probably. And that might have to be good enough. I'm struggling to think of anyone we can rely on with absolute certainty. What about your old colonel?"

"Bin Merrin? I believe he can be trusted, after all he did ask me to get to the bottom of the sabotage, but what would he do with information of this magnitude? He was probably imagining I'd pinpoint a small handful of perpetrators he could round up and hand over to ImpSec."

"And what we've got is bigger than anyone thought," Henri said glumly, "and implicates a large slice of ImpSec into the bargain."

Simone glanced down at her notepad and looked up, startled. "Check your alerts," she hissed to Chalwen.

Puzzled, Chalwen opened her own notepad, and grimaced. "I have a feeling the matter is being taken out of our hands." She looked sharply at Simone. "Wait! How come *you* know about this?"

Simone grinned. "I'm being assigned to observe and provide an independent analysis on your upcoming disciplinary hearing."

"Discipline?" Chalwen's cry momentarily silenced all other conversations in the gloomy common room. She glared around her until the suddenly-alert patrons returned to minding their own business. In a whisper she continued, "All I see is a notice to appear in Stanhope's office tomorrow morning."

Henri chuckled. "You haven't been with ImpSec long enough. That kind of invitation is code for trouble." He sobered. "I assume this must be related to you engineering a meeting with the Emperor."

"You mean Stanhope's mad because he thinks I've bypassed him?"

"Haven't you?" Simone asked innocently.

Chalwen shrugged. There was no answer to that.

"A more important question is, who told him? I doubt this came from Julian himself, so I assume you've pissed someone off by trying to go to the top. It may not be Stanhope himself who's angry, he could be responding to someone else complaining."

"I guess that's a lifeline I'm going to have to cling to." Chalwen looked helplessly at her two companions. "What do I do?"

Chapter 37

A very nervous Chalwen climbed the stairs to the fourth floor, where she was ushered into Commander Stanhope's inner office. There was no sign of Simone. Chalwen presumed she'd be watching unseen on a screen somewhere.

The commander gestured to a chair in front of his desk. Chalwen lowered herself gratefully into it, acutely aware of his keen scrutiny even as he lounged back in the appearance of relaxation.

Abruptly, the commander leaned forward, forearms on his desk in front of him. "When we last met, you only told me half your story."

Chalwen barely stopped herself recoiling at the sudden movement, but the shock kicked old training into life. The instant she realized there was no immediate physical threat, she assessed the situation as if she'd just startled an intruder. In a bodyguard's life, the psychology of conflicting goals was often more important than physical reactions, and keeping a clear objective view of the field of conflict was vital. Instinctive reactions could too easily escalate a situation instead of reaching a non-violent solution.

She narrowed her eyes. "I was hardly in here long enough. Half is an overstatement."

"So, an employee of mine is keeping secrets from me. Running operations of her own, presumably with unofficial help. Knowing that, how can I trust you?"

"I took information straight to the person who ultimately rules both our lives. I assume that's why I'm here now. The question is, Commander, can I trust *you*?"

Commander Stanhope blinked, then sat back. "Colonel bin Merrin was right. You *are* very direct and independent. I'm impressed you lasted as long as you did in Civil Watch."

A flock of starlings seemed to have taken flight in Chalwen's stomach. Past tense? So, she *was* on trial here and it sounded like judgment had already been passed. She mustered whatever defiance she had left. "There remains the question of trust, Commander, and it still comes back to the reason I'm here. Who told you about my meeting with the Emperor?"

"Direct *and* persistent. You're right. And you're wondering if I had someone spying on you." The commander inspected his fingernails. "Not so. You're here at the Emperor's behest."

That was unexpected. Chalwen had assumed someone had reported her unorthodox meeting to Stanhope, but she hadn't thought Julian himself might be behind it. "Did the Emperor lodge a complaint? If he was displeased, he has far more direct ways to make it known."

Stanhope wheezed a breathless laugh, and slapped the desktop. "Oh," he chortled, "you thought you were in trouble?"

"It had crossed my mind. My colleagues told me this had to be disciplinary in nature."

"Aah. My reputation at work." He winked. "And I think it would suit both of us to let everyone outside this office continue believing that. The Emperor had already directed you to see me, but I think he had a keen awareness of your independent nature and wanted to make sure you complied."

Chalwen gripped the armrest for support. Julian wanted her to speak to Stanhope, and went out of his way to make sure she did. He must have known she'd have misgivings talking to someone she didn't know. Then she recalled her sense in that meeting that they weren't alone. Could Julian have been guarding his tongue too? He'd sounded dismissive, but maybe he couldn't afford to show too much interest in what she had to say, so he'd briefed Stanhope in secret afterwards.

That was impressive reasoning for a youngster.

Chalwen opened up her notepad and gazed at it. The device seemed to burn in her hands with the incendiary report she, Henri and Simone had compiled. She was close to opening up to Stanhope, but still she held back. Ninety-nine percent wasn't good enough. She longed to consult with her colleagues. They'd know better what to make of Stanhope's words. "While I was with the Emperor, we were alone in his office but I had a strong impression someone was listening in."

Stanhope grunted. "Very likely. I know Emperor Paul held private audiences, but they rarely went unobserved."

"The thing is," Chalwen said firmly, "I believe the same is true today, and I would very much like to hear what your watcher might have to say about this conversation." She forced the pounding in her chest to calm down, certain that Stanhope would hear it in the sudden hush.

"I'm afraid your curiosity will have to go unsatisfied today," Stanhope grated out. "I will neither confirm nor deny any speculation on my working methods." His voice softened. "But I can understand your concern about revealing dangerous information to an unknown party."

A message flashed discreetly in one corner of Chalwen's notepad. "Clear to proceed." The fluttering in her stomach subsided and her heartbeat resumed a less life-shortening pace. Simone had understood her plea. She took a deep breath. "Before I say anything, what makes you think I have something worth listening to?"

"Thank Space we're back to questions I can answer. I've had calls from numerous quarters telling me to get rid of you."

"That doesn't sound like a resounding endorsement."

"The very pressure I'm under to silence you tells me you've hit something of importance."

Chalwen gazed at him. "You're saying they ... whoever 'they' are ... just made a tactical error?"

"If you had nothing, all they had to do was shut up and let you embarrass yourself."

"So it was a forced error, but still an error."

Commander Stanhope spread his arms wide in a theatrical shrug. "Now I need to see if they have something to worry about."

Stifling a tremor, Chalwen transferred the package of documents to Stanhope's notepad. He glanced down and leafed through the package.

"So, the summary is that the administration is riddled with people organizing against Emperor Paul, and now against his son. Have I read that right?"

Chalwen nodded. Her scalp crawled at the memory of her own involvement in just such a movement against Empress Florence. "I wouldn't call them traitors in the traditional sense. They just want someone else on the throne."

Stanhope gave her a sharp look. "We owe allegiance to the throne, whoever's on it. We don't get to choose. But ... I know what you mean." He leaned back in his chair and swiveled to and fro. "What you say is nothing new. Every branch of government has partisan interests, but this level of activism is new."

"That's just one layer," Chalwen said. "Fertile ground for the seeds that someone is sowing."

"Yes ... so far we have an assist and a cover up for the sabotage, stirring up a mob against a visiting Family head, and fomenting unrest across the empire. Seems like someone's trying to upset the status quo."

"That's the answer I came to."

"But a war with the Firenzi would harm the empire. How is that patriotic?"

"Harm, yes, but if we go to war, who do you think the Assembly would rather see on the throne?"

Stanhope tapped his teeth as he thought. "Yes, I see where you're going with this." He straightened abruptly and faced Chalwen again. "Thank you for bringing me this. Don't get impatient if you don't see immediate results. We have to be careful. I will brief the Emperor but with caution. I don't honestly know for certain who to trust even within his inner circle of advisors."

There's certainly one I know to steer clear of, Chalwen thought. For a moment, she wondered if Ivan himself might have any knowledge of what was going on. He stood to benefit, after all. She set the thought aside for now. There were more pressing questions on her mind. "You said 'we', but what do you want *me* to do?"

"Good question. How useful do you think you can be under the watchful eye of Taraq Marand?"

Chalwen's involuntary grimace seemed to answer the question.

"Thought so. And yet you've done remarkable work even within those constraints."

"I worked with the data I was fed." Chalwen shrugged. "I just didn't limit myself to being a cog in the conveyor belt."

"Hmmm. Just mind you don't wreck the entire conveyor belt, Lieutenant. Marand is a good officer. Not imaginative, but always remember a lot of intelligence work is tedious, detailed grunt work and people like Marand and his cohorts excel at it."

"So, I'm going back to keep up the good work?" The thought settled in Chalwen's stomach like last week's stew.

"No. I'm pulling you from Civil Watch and reassigning you to Sanitation."

"Sanitation?"

"It's where we dump our 'troublemakers'. Look on it as punishment, if you like. Your former colleagues certainly will, and they'll quite glee-fully conclude you got your just desserts. The truth is, Sanitation gets all the shit nobody else can handle."

"I'm guessing there's dirty work you'd rather most people didn't know about?"

"Something like that. I hope you're up for some intensive training. Handling shit without getting your hands dirty is a specialized skill."

———— • • ————

Chalwen gritted her teeth and did her best to ignore the smirks of passers-by as she packed her few belongings into a box. The sudden foot traffic outside her open office door was an oddity in the normally-quiet hallways in this section of the vast building. She hated being the object of gossips and gawkers like this, but Stanhope had advised her to make sure she was seen packing up in apparent disgrace.

That wasn't the only oddity. The packing box had already appeared in her office when she returned from her visit with Stanhope. That was efficient, even by Imperial Security standards. And the box had a des-tination label for one of the sorting offices in the building's basement, rather than directing the porter to deliver it straight to Chalwen's new workplace. To outsiders it would seem it was simply being held until she was assigned a new spot, but Chalwen suspected it was to conceal its true destination.

She gave one last glance around the bare office, and steeled herself to run the gauntlet of veiled stares and sneering whispers. Until just now she'd not heard of Sanitation, and she had no idea what she was getting herself into, but anything had to be better than the soul-crushing drudgery of Civil Watch. And she had a feeling there was more to Sanitation than most people knew.

This suspicion deepened when she followed the directions she'd been given. Room designations in Imperial Security headquarters followed a systematic pattern beloved of bureaucracies since time immemorial. In theory, given a room number you could find your way there even in an unfamiliar part of the building.

The sub-basement room Chalwen arrived at proved to be a front. The locked door opened when sensors recognized her implanted passkey to reveal an empty office. A door at the rear opened as soon as she closed the first door behind her.

Now the rest of her directions made sense. Down a flight of stairs and along a hallway. Chalwen hesitated only a fraction before pushing open the second door on the left as instructed. Stanhope's secretary had been very precise and unusually emphatic. The hairs on Chalwen's neck prickled as she stepped through. The corridor she'd been in would make an effective kill box to deal with unwanted visitors. And it seemed this obscure branch of ImpSec took its privacy very seriously. She'd passed through at least three passkey-locked security cordons to get this far. Excessive, even by ImpSec standards.

This place was an enigma within an enigma.

The door behind her snicked shut with an ominous finality. Chalwen took in her surprising surroundings, a comfortable reception area with low tables, easy chairs, and a samovar steaming quietly on a sideboard. She flinched and backtracked. Her gaze had skimmed over a woman on the far side of the room who seemed to blend into the background.

Simone smiled. "Welcome to Sanitation."

Chapter 38

Year 8070, spring

Weeks of intensive training left Chalwen feeling that the more she knew, the more there was to learn. Simone, she soon realized, had a talent for fieldcraft and a breathtaking genius for both setting up and bypassing electronic security. The trouble was, Chalwen was a dunce in those matters. She finished her sessions with Simone frustrated and feeling stupid.

"Not to worry," said ever-patient Simone. "You'll find your specialty soon enough."

Chalwen was passed from one teacher to another through the shadowy world of Sanitation, some with more success than others. At least the grueling program had its upsides. It got her out of Civil Watch, and Chalwen held out hopes that she could find a niche here where she could do something useful. Her office, Simone had promised her, was secure from intrusion. Sanitation did indeed take secrecy very seriously. Best of all, Henri had found someone to re-equip her with the comms tools to properly rejoin The Hidden Light. She no longer had to rely on secondhand news from Henri.

The Light had been busy in Chalwen's absence, countering the spreading blight of unrest and outright insurrection that she'd uncovered. They'd even embarked on a growing number of field operations to neutralize some of the most troublesome local agitators. The fighting spirit of her rescue mission lived on. Along with the efforts of ImpSec themselves, now that Boris Stanhope had introduced his colleagues to evidence of an organized conspiracy, it seemed they were turning the tide.

And so, with some trepidation, Chalwen once again found herself summoned to Commander Stanhope's office.

The commander seemed to be in a jovial mood as he greeted Chalwen. "So, how's my new cleaning lady making out?"

"I feel useless," Chalwen said. "It seems to me you'd be better off putting me back in some desk job crunching data."

"Yes, yes." Stanhope flapped his hands dismissively. "There's a lot of specialized disciplines you'll never properly get the hang of. We put our recruits through the mill anyway to see what sticks."

"You're expecting people to fail?" Chalwen's mind went back to all the security drills Colonel bin Merrin used to throw at her.

"We expect people to absorb whatever they are capable of," Stanhope growled. "Adjust your perspective."

Chalwen nodded, chastened.

"My observers agree with you on one thing, though," the commander continued. "Your place is crunching data, just not in the narrow way you were doing in Civil Watch. You already showed you have a nose for patterns. What if you had access to better, more complete sources?"

"Sources? You mean intelligence data? Field reports?" Chalwen's pulse quickened.

"Archive records. Surveillance. Political and economic analyses," Stanhope added. "Whatever you decide you need."

"To what end?"

Stanhope sighed. "Don't make me regret the effort we've put into you. I told you at the start, Sanitation deals with the crap no one else can handle. We have offices upstairs full of people dealing with all the routine stuff. Yes, to regular law enforcement we all seem like a bunch of secret squirrels working on confidential stuff behind the scenes, but all that is relative. Even within ImpSec there are layers of secrecy."

"The basement is a fortress within a fortress."

"You got it. While most of ImpSec deals with routine security matters begging a routine response, Sanitation picks up the most delicate assignments, often looking into our own people."

"I thought that was Internal Affairs?"

"Again, there's the difference between confidential and secret. Internal Affairs investigates matters that are merely confidential. People out there know someone's screwed up, even though the details of the investigation stay behind closed doors. Sanitation looks into matters that nobody outside even knows exist. I said we handle what no one else *can* handle, either not sharp enough, or not cleared for the necessary sensitivity."

"You seem to have more faith in me than all your trainers." Chalwen's head spun.

"I'm just asking you to do what you seem to do best. Sniff out trouble."

"I don't really sniff out trouble. It seems to find me. But that was when I was out in the field, not behind a desk."

"I know. After his twelfth anniversary celebration, the Emperor is flying out to Chevinta to accept an honorary doctorate."

Chalwen raised her eyebrows at this abrupt change in tack.

"No, it's not common knowledge yet." Stanhope seemed to have misinterpreted her confusion. "But it won't be a surprise. It's a tradition for the university freeworld to admit imperial rulers to their ranks in this way." He scowled. "I assume they think this kind of toadying will keep them in the ruler's good books."

"There's no serious threat to their neutrality or freeworld status, is there?"

"Hard to imagine any concerns anyone could have. As long as they keep turning out world-class academics and keep sharing the results of their research without bias, their standing is safe with the Families. And the Families would quickly unite to turn on any outworlder who broke the treaty."

It was Chalwen's turn to scowl. "Seems to me that favoring the imperial family, even just with empty honors, could be more dangerous to them than helpful."

"I believe they find ways to curry favor with the other Families, too. No, I'm not concerned about their impartiality." He speared Chalwen with a sharp and unwavering gaze. "That's not why I brought the matter up."

Chalwen met his gaze. "Are you worried the trip might offer another opportunity to remove Julian?"

Stanhope waggled a hand. "It's a risk, but he has a good bodyguard. All the same, I'm thinking I need someone independent and sharp-eyed close to the Emperor."

Grand Duke Ivan Skamensis took his place at the polished cherry-wood table, and noted with satisfaction how the others there deferred to him. In this room, as political advisor to the Emperor, he technically ranked equal among the other members of Julian's inner circle. In practice, his blood relationship to the old emperor and to the Empress Florence set him apart, and he sensed a wariness close to fear among his less well-connected colleagues.

That was understandable. Most of them were from Paul's old Council, whom Julian had kept in place. They were steadfast in their moderate views and well aware of Ivan's passionate adherence to traditional values of duty, regardless of cost, as well as his reputation for ruthlessness. Yes, they were afraid, but they could also not be discounted. Nobody got to this level without their own streaks of determination and resources, along with at least *some* distasteful but necessary acts. Right now, Ivan was treading carefully through a minefield of opposition.

There were a few rays of sunshine. The frail old diplomatic advisor could be helped into the afterlife at any moment of Ivan's choosing. Ivan was already grooming a suitable successor, who would be Julian's obvious choice when the time came. And against all the odds, Grand Admiral Gabriel bin Jovin was still in place after the Maestro affair. With Bernie Fischer's behind-the-scenes help, enough scapegoats had been found within the Admiralty to delay Emperor Paul's retribution until the point became moot. And in the confused aftermath of the assassination, all records of Paul's displeasure had been quietly removed. The Grand Admiral wasn't exactly a supporter of Ivan, but he was shallow and blinkered enough to be manipulated. That made him almost as useful.

As for the rest of the Council, Bernie's staff had spent months compiling dossiers on each, seeking out weaknesses and points of leverage. Assets working under duress were more dangerous and unpredictable than true supporters, but on the plus side it would be less of a loss when it came time to clean up loose ends.

He savored the feeling of power as other members of the Imperial Council waited for him to sit before seating themselves in the sumptuous cabinet room next to the Office of Deliberation. The good mood evaporated when Boris Stanhope entered the room with that bloody ex-bodyguard in tow. Ivan narrowed his eyes but otherwise gave no reaction. Interesting that she seemed to have ditched her walking stick now. Ivan wondered if maybe that had been an act after all.

The Chief of Intelligence loomed over the table. "I believe some of you may already know Lieutenant Chalwen ap Gwynodd. Formerly a member of the imperial bodyguard, she is now part of my organization."

The lieutenant stood at ease, to one side and a pace behind Stanhope, and acknowledged surprised greetings with terse nods.

"Lieutenant ap Gwynodd will be deputizing for me day-to-day as security intelligence liaison to the Emperor."

"All very well, but what's she doing *here?*" the Grand Admiral demanded. "This is a meeting of the Emperor's Council."

"She can hardly act as liaison without full knowledge of the inner workings of the imperial administration." Stanhope's mild tone acquired an edge of tungsten steel. "This arrangement has the Emperor's blessing."

Well, damn. Ivan would be having words with Bernie Fischer about how he'd missed *this* arrangement.

Any further discussion was cut short as an usher threw open the far door and Emperor Julian strode to the head of the table.

Everyone scrambled to their feet and gave short bows, waiting for Julian to open the proceedings.

An hour later, after an unusually quiet and uninteresting agenda, Julian announced, "The final matter today is my upcoming absence."

Like flipping a switch, creeping boredom jolted to alert focus. Suspense hung in the air like ozone. The Emperor's choice of traveling companions was seen as a sharp indication of someone's standing in the Council. Whether that was true or not, whatever practical factors weighed in his decisions, the choices of who traveled and who stayed would be analyzed to death for weeks to come. Regardless of any objective reality, perception was everything.

"I'll be gone a total of eight weeks, mostly travel time."

Despite his self-assurance, Ivan found himself holding his breath. He forced himself to relax. He and Julian had been almost inseparable for years. His berth was assured. He scanned the anxious faces around the table, wondering who would be honored and whose egos would be dented today.

"I will be taking a bodyguard and minimal staff, together with Commander Stanhope's intelligence liaison. This is a routine trip to accept a purely ceremonial honor from Chevinta. My advisors, especially economic, diplomatic, and political, are better placed here on Magentis to keep things moving and to deal with the Assembly in my absence."

His words were met with interminable seconds of stunned silence.

"You're not taking political or diplomatic representatives, and yet you need a security advisor?" Ivan could barely keep the rage out of his voice.

"Security *liaison*, Sire," Stanhope responded smoothly. "And before anyone presses the matter further, I shouldn't need to remind anyone at this table that Imperial Security *never* discusses its reasoning ... other than to sworn members of a grand inquiry, of course."

Stanhope chuckled at his own joke. Nobody else cracked a smile, least of all Ivan.

Of all the old Council members, Boris Stanhope showed no awe or fear of Ivan, neither of his family connections nor his reputation.

Of all the old Council members, Boris Stanhope had just promoted himself next in line for pre-emptive retirement.

———•◆•———

Barely controlling himself, Ivan strode from the cabinet room and through corridors of the adjoining senior staff offices. Rage clouded his vision as he slammed through the far doors out into the crowded courtyard by the concert hall. Only a finely-honed sense of self-preservation among the servants and functionaries prevented a collision. Enough sanity returned for Ivan to note the avenue opening up ahead of him as people scurried out of his path. He slowed, realizing he'd hoped for some confrontation that would give him an excuse to fry someone on the spot.

He badly needed to damage something.

Ivan thumbed his lapel transmitter. "Bernie. Guard hangars. Twenty minutes." Without waiting for a reply, he switched channels and snapped orders to the barracks watch officer in the far corner of the palace.

By the time a puffing and sweating Bernie Fischer arrived at the walled landing field, Ivan paced restlessly alongside a *Hammerhead* two-seat fighter that a ground crew readied for flight. Ivan nodded to the crew captain as they disengaged the last fuel line and withdrew. To Bernie, he growled, "Get in."

An hour later, the fighter banked and twisted at a heart-stopping pace through the Freetha badlands, a million square miles of weathered wastelands north of Prandis.

Ivan piloted recklessly, skimming canyon floors, relying on adrenaline-fueled reflexes to navigate a route past whatever obstacles appeared around blind corners. Finally the steep-sided canyon opened into a miles-wide gash in the parched landscape. The far wall rose sheer in the distance, guarded by ranks of buttes and slender pillars five hundred feet high, remnants of eons of weathering.

With a harsh cry, Ivan loosed bursts of particle beams at three pillars a mile ahead. Direct hits on all three, the flanking towers stood firm but the middle one slumped then toppled with a satisfying rumble and shower of house-sized slabs.

Ivan hugged the ground, heading straight at the collapsing heap, only pulling up at the last second. He took grim satisfaction in Bernie's white-knuckle grip on the armrest next to him as a river of rock and dust rolled beneath them. Ivan exhaled a shaky breath, then circled the fighter and landed atop a nearby rock pillar scarcely wider than the length of the craft. Silently he opened the canopy, extended the built-in ladder and climbed down, signaling to Bernie to join him.

Pale and shaking, Bernie clung to the ladder and huddled on the ground. He looked at once relieved to be on a solid surface, yet mesmerized by the edge of their perch scant feet away. Safety was a relative concept.

Disdaining the precipitous drop at his feet and the fitful dust-laden gusts tugging at his robe, Ivan surveyed the damage he'd wrought. Ochre clouds rolled across the valley floor, coating the waters of a meandering river carving a path through the desert. Faint thunder echoed still from the opposite cliffs.

The anger remained, but finally penned back in its cage, back under control after this visceral release of tension. Ivan turned to Bernie. In a low and dangerous voice he said, "I don't enjoy being blindsided in cabinet meetings."

New fear flickered in the depths of Bernie's eyes. After the piloting display just now, he'd wonder if maybe Ivan was mad enough to toss him off the edge. Ivan let his uncertainty fester a while.

A touch of color returned to Bernie's cheeks. "Then you'd best decide what you're going to do."

Ivan raised an eyebrow.

"Either dispense with my services or enlighten me."

Ivan scowled, leaving Bernie in suspense a few seconds longer, but inwardly he was relieved to see Bernie showing some fight. He hadn't broken his Private Secretary. Such people were hard to replace. "I learned today that the Emperor is only taking a minimal staff to Chevinta, along with Stanhope's new lackey."

"That's ... unusual. Ooh!" Bernie's face lit in a broad grin. "So *that's* what's got you mad. He didn't choose *you*. Got your nose put out of joint, and in front of all those lowlifes too." He rubbed his hands together. "So what doesn't young Julian want too many people seeing?"

"My thought exactly." Reliving the pointed snub, Ivan ground his teeth together. The few square feet of rough sandstone didn't give him room to pace, his usual outlet for excess energy. "We need to find out what the little weasel is up to."

"Given Chevinta's jealous attitude to client secrecy, we won't get a direct look at what he's doing. It will all be down to circumstantial clues."

"Do we have assets there who'd know what to look for?"

Bernie used the ladder to haul himself to his feet. He looked thoughtful but one hand still clung tight to the nearest rung. "I'd want to be there in person. Who knows what clues might turn out to be relevant?"

"Good point. Officially, I'm supposed to remain on Magentis, although"—Ivan tapped his lips with his forefinger, deep in recollection—"there were no explicit orders on that point. The exact instructions covered who the Emperor *was* taking to Chevinta with him. The other advisors are simply to keep things ticking over. I reserve the right to decide how and where to achieve that."

"All the same, while we can't be held liable for other people's wrong assumptions, it wouldn't do to advertise your real whereabouts."

"Agreed. Prepare *Kirov* for a trip. Destination classified."

"Officially, routine drills and maneuvers to keep the crew battle ready." Bernie pouted. "Dangerous world out there. You never know what nasties the Grand Duke's personal yacht might run into. Got to stay on our toes."

Now fully in control again, Ivan's mind raced. Chevinta lay in a large wedge of unaligned territory between the rimward ends of Skamensis and Firenzi space. May as well make the most of this trip. "Contact Scipio. If he can meet us at Chevinta, it's time for another private conference. We need new ways to turn up the heat."

"Consider it done."

As Ivan reached for the ladder to board the fighter he said, "One more thing. It's time we dusted off Operation Ghost Town."

Bernie blanched, then recovered. "Ghost Town. We never thought we'd go that far. We already have so much of ImpSec under our thumbs. It will take time to put assets in place, and of course I need a list of targets."

"Understood. But our young Emperor is getting far too independent for my liking. When the time comes, I need to ensure Imperial Security is one hundred percent in my hands."

Chapter 39

S imone led Chalwen through the basement labyrinth deep beneath the Intelligence quarter of the building. "Pray you're never admitted here as a house guest," she whispered as they entered an observation room.

Two wardens, the first uniformed people Chalwen had seen inside Sanitation, looked up from their consoles. The senior, a rotund man with greying hair and a straggly beard, nodded at Simone. He pointed to the nearby wall, which came to life.

On a floor to ceiling screen, so clear they seemed to be standing in the same room, signals tech Warran ap Meradan lounged in a swivel chair that was bolted to the floor. He was reading something on a scroll. A table beside him held the remains of a meal. A bed, wash basin and toilet seemed to be extruded from the far wall. Although the room was sparse and clinical, Chalwen raised an eyebrow at the apparent comfort of his quarters. She'd lived in barracks more basic than this.

Simone must have expected her confusion. "We're not some backwoods outworld here. Besides, every little privilege he gains here gives him so much more to lose. Never underestimate the power of the humble carrot."

"You questioned … interrogated … him, and broke him."

"You're expecting to see signs of disfigurement? Maybe a missing limb, or at least digits?" She laughed, a sunny and musical sound at odds with their grim surroundings. "Our techniques are harsh. Yes, they include physical pain, but a large part of it is psychological and the use of appropriate drugs. The only lasting damage is mental."

Chalwen spared Simone a sidelong glance before turning her attention back to Warran.

"And we are still working on him. Of course, his days are numbered. He can't be allowed to leave and he is still a traitor."

"Of course." Chalwen stared at the young man, who seemed unconcerned at his plight. "What will you do with him?"

Simone chewed her cheek. "Ultimately, that's up to the commander, but I suspect there'll be no publicity around this one. A quick execution. He's probably luckier than he has any right to be."

"I need to talk to him."

"Any idea what you're looking for?"

Chalwen pursed her lips. "Not exactly. Trying to tease out something that's bugging me. I won't have much time to follow our investigations now I'm assigned back to the Emperor." An understatement. Chalwen had hardly seen anything of Simone or Henri recently, and she was only getting busier as the Emperor's visit to Chevinta approached. But something in the back of her mind threatened to distract her from her official duties. "You and Henri will have to keep that going, but I can't leave this loose thread dangling. Something about the sabotage doesn't feel right. I just can't put my finger on it."

"Hoping hearing things first hand might jog something loose? Then go talk to him."

Simone's matter-of-fact manner reassured Chalwen. She'd been worried that she couldn't explain herself properly. "Is it safe?"

"He'll give you no trouble," Simone reassured her. "And I'll be watching from here."

For a moment, Chalwen wondered how much could go wrong in the seconds it would take Simone to reach her. In the past, she would have always figured on being able to look after herself. Her physical safety hadn't even occurred to her, but she was no longer the person she once was. Then she mentally kicked herself. Cells like this would surely have remote operated safeguards. Simone was staying where she could intervene most effectively if needed.

"Actually, I meant you've put a lot of effort into making him compliant. Is there any risk I might accidentally undo some conditioning you've managed to set up?"

"Nothing we can't repair."

The younger of the two wardens appeared at her side, startling Chalwen. He must have been paying closer attention to their conversation than she'd realized. "If you'll follow me, Lieutenant."

Simone gave her an unfathomable look. "Good luck."

The guard led Chalwen through a series of locked doors and into a long corridor. He pointed to a door. "If he should cause trouble, drop to the floor. We'll handle the rest."

She opened the door.

Warran ap Meradan looked up and his eyes widened in recognition. The door hissed shut behind Chalwen. She was committed.

"Well, I wasn't expecting *this*, but then, surprise visits help pass the time in here."

Chalwen stepped closer and noticed for the first time there was a second chair at the table. Simone said they were still working on him. Did they sometimes question him right here in his cell? She pointed to the chair. "May I?"

He gave a languid wave. "So, I was wondering if the walking stick and clumsiness was part of an act. Good for you to turn an affliction into an asset."

His mind seemed sharp and his gaze missed nothing, but his whole body, the half-hearted wave and the way he slouched, gave the impression he was battling impossible weariness. Drugs? What kind of cocktail were they using to keep him compliant?

"I know you've been debriefed at length, but I like to hear people's stories first hand. Tell me how you managed to slip past security and nobble an imperial cruiser."

"Simple operation." Warran smiled, far too eagerly. Like a puppy craving attention. "A few guards to distract. A few cameras to point elsewhere at the right time."

Chalwen shuddered at the knowledge and planning he so glibly dismissed. How did they know which guards and cameras would open up enough of a window to work without arousing suspicion?

"How many of you were there?"

"Not many. You already know all this."

"Humor me." Chalwen attempted a welcoming smile. She wondered how a conditioned undercover agent could be made to talk so freely.

"Heather was the boss. Got orders and materials from outside. Inside, there was me, a guard, a groundsman, and a maintenance tech."

"That's it?"

"All I ever knew."

Somehow Chalwen believed him. "Could you have had other help on the inside?"

"Didn't need it. We had it all sewn up between us."

"And the attempt to poison the Crown Prince?"

"Loose ends. He missed the flight." He sounded bored, then his head jerked. He struggled to stop it lolling to one side while he studied Chalwen more closely. "You were *there!* I saw you on the cameras just outside the dead zone. Came out of nowhere. How did you get there so fast?" His glance at her legs completed the unspoken question.

"I was fit and healthy then, before the poison did its work." Her voice was flat.

He gave a small and bitter laugh. "Nothing personal. You were just in the wrong place at the wrong time."

Silence stretched for long seconds. Warran let his head slump to his shoulder, a vacant smile on his face. Chalwen's heart thumped as she struggled to her feet and stumbled to the door. She'd finally pinpointed what had been troubling her.

Back in the observation room, Simone joined her and they made a hurried exit. Chalwen messaged Henri to make sure he was in his office. Simone gave her a puzzled look but refrained from asking questions when Chalwen took an elevator instead of stairs. She was too impatient to allow herself the luxury of stubborn pride.

Breathless, they arrived to find Henri wearing an anxious frown. He checked his office security without a word while Chalwen slumped into the nearest chair.

"That hideout we found down in the disused power room," she gasped. "We thought it had been used by the saboteurs, as a hideout and preparation area. But that makes no sense. From the recent debris it looked like the room had been occupied by at least a dozen people."

"But there were only a handful in the PDC cell." Henri was quick on the uptake. "And they were all sleeper agents. They had no need of a hiding place."

"Plus," Chalwen continued, "the surveillance blackouts that hid the room were caused by someone else. Not that cell. Simone had already pointed that out, but I missed the significance until now." She cursed. "We were all so focused on the assassination itself, and we assumed the PDC cell was simply getting some unasked-for help, maybe to make sure they succeeded, but that doesn't explain the hideout."

"Crap," Henri said.

"Space alive." Simone's eyes widened. "While the Emperor's cruiser was being sabotaged by Warran's crew, something else important was happening in the palace at the same time. Something we've completely overlooked."

Chalwen dimmed the lights in her subterranean office, and stirred a spoon of honey into a mug of hot black tea. She usually took tea unsweetened, but today she needed more of a boost.

In accordance with the coded summons delivered that afternoon, she tapped into her encrypted channel to The Hidden Light. The face of her notepad remained blank. While she waited, she took a sip of scalding tea, then leaned back in her chair with her legs stretched out and the notepad on her lap.

Eyelids drooped.

A swirl of thoughts clouded her mind like autumn leaves. So many things spinning out of control. The act of regicide nine months ago had been conclusively tied to the defense conglomerate, Philip Drayson Coolidge. Normally that would have been enough for the Emperor to take action, but that whole plot was entangled in more sinister intrigues that infested the whole imperial administration. The deliberate sowing of discontent, the secretive activities within the palace, the attempts to lynch another Family head. They didn't know how far the corruption went, or how high up the food chain. Given the reach and power of the murky opponents, they were led by someone near the top, hence the caution. You didn't shake the tree if you might get clobbered by a falling branch.

And, somewhere buried in the middle of all that, the puzzle of the hideout beneath the palace. The purpose there remained a mystery. It hadn't been linked to anything harmful and yet Chalwen was sure it was of vital importance. It was a glaring anomaly, and the timing alongside the assassination couldn't be a coincidence.

A chime from the notepad jerked Chalwen from a doze. She struggled upright and fumbled the notepad onto her desk. A frown. Only Shadowland showed in the list of people present. He usually joined once other members were assembled.

"It's just the two of us this evening, Chalwen. Let's dispense with codes."

That he knew this was evening to Chalwen didn't fool her. She had no idea where in space he called home, if indeed he had such a thing as a fixed home, but she could be certain he was nowhere nearby.

Was he?

Who knew, with Lorenzo.

"This is an unusual meeting, Lorenzo. How can I help?"

His laugh set her at ease. "Less formality, for starters. We've been through too much together for reticence."

His face appeared on the notepad. Chalwen stared in shock, then added a visual feed from her end.

"That's better. It's been too long since I actually saw the people risking their lives for our cause."

The face gazing out at her through the comms feed had aged since she'd last seen him. Deep lines framed his eyes and mouth, but hazel eyes still gazed at her with piercing intensity. He sported a close-cropped beard, black with a sprinkling of grey. Interesting. There were few places in Skamensis space where facial hair was commonplace, and surely he'd be looking to blend in. That reaffirmed Chalwen's belief that he was far away.

Lorenzo smiled and said, "I wish to discuss the purpose of the Emperor's visit to Chevinta."

"That's public knowledge. He's receiving a symbolic honor from the university."

"And the part that's not public knowledge?"

A shiver ran up Chalwen's spine. She'd spent so many waking hours on preparations for the visit, so many precautions to keep the real, unspoken purpose hidden. To hear someone speak of it outside the immediate circle around the Emperor came as a visceral shock. She gathered her composure and said, "I can't possibly comment on anything beyond the public purpose." She softened her bland tone to add, "Not even to you."

Lorenzo grunted. "Fair enough. I'm not asking you to compromise your loyalties by revealing anything you shouldn't. I'll make it easier for you. I know he's set up a meeting with Josef Firenzi, with hopes of easing the tensions between the Families."

Some of the tightness drained out of Chalwen's shoulders. She should have known Lorenzo would be aware of the empire's innermost secrets. "And without asking you to compromise anything on your side, I'm going to guess that you've been smoothing the way to make that meeting happen."

It made sense. From the moment Boris Stanhope and Julian had brought her into their confidence, she'd wondered how someone so young and inexperienced could have made such an approach successfully. She'd spent long evenings trying to fathom who among Julian's advisors could have helped him. The answer had been staring her in the face the whole time.

Lorenzo shrugged. "I don't need to discuss the meeting itself. The fact that it's happening at all is the important part. That's why I needed to speak with you. In light of this knowledge, I'm prepared to reconsider my decision of a few months ago."

"You mean, you're coming out into the open?"

"I'd hardly call it that. But I think it's time to let the Emperor know he's not walking this road alone."

"How do you plan to do that?" Chalwen was already running through the difficulties of getting to see or even talk to the Emperor without a host of people knowing about it. Another thought struck her. "You're going to introduce him to The Hidden Light, but do you plan to introduce yourself?"

Lorenzo was family. Family that Julian didn't even know he had. How would he react to a long-lost uncle suddenly appearing on the scene?

"I know it will be risky. I'm still working on a way to manage this, and I know I'll need help on the inside. Keep your comms open. I'll be in touch."

It seemed the meeting was over, but Chalwen was reluctant to cut the connection. Seeing Lorenzo's face rather than a disembodied and distorted voice brought back so many memories. Not always good ones. In the time of Empress Florence, they'd seen and done things that Chalwen would rather forget, but those were the times they lived in. They'd survived, and seen the glimmers of sunshine on the horizon.

Lorenzo, also, seemed lost in distant thoughts. What was going through his head? Was he reliving shared memories, or looking to the future? Chalwen shifted her posture to ease the ever-present ache in her legs. She was painfully aware that their paths had diverged over the years. So much had happened to her that Lorenzo had not shared, and she realized she knew nothing of his present life. It was probably best that way. But they still worked to a common purpose.

Cherishing this rare moment of connection, she said, "Lorenzo, you've seen what can be achieved when we have a dedicated force. Look at how you've kept the diplomatic channels open despite the disturbances. What if the imperial administration could be manned openly by people with such loyalty?"

Lorenzo smiled sadly and shook his head. "I can think of two reasons right away why that wouldn't be the solution you think it is. The most obvious is the sheer impossibility of what you have in mind. We are a force numbering fewer than five thousand, thinly spread. Even with this number, we are always at risk of someone infiltrating or turning a member's loyalty. Imagine trying to screen and maintain the loyalty of the entire public service."

Chalwen grimaced, feeling foolish. She already knew how hard it had been recruiting even a handful of people she could trust to form the squads of Julian's bodyguard. She'd been carried away by the thought of the power this group wielded, working totally to a common purpose.

"Apart from practicality, though, there's a more subtle and serious reason any such thought should be discouraged. You, Chalwen, should be able to figure it out. Think back to our early days."

Chalwen shuddered. "We had to work in secrecy, to put the brakes on Florence's ambitions."

"And we were only able to do so precisely because the imperial service and military contained diverse views, even if those views were only held in private. Imagine if a ruler like Florence had at her disposal an unswervingly loyal administration."

With a sick feeling in her stomach, Chalwen thought about the secretive forces she'd seen at work, both in the palaces and within Imperial Security. Forces clearly opposed to Paul's reforms, hankering for the old ways. "Ivan is already half-way there," she whispered. "We have to protect Julian."

Chapter 40

"Chevin Secundus, Sire." Captain Harman Galliano pointed to the bright yellow star separating from the background clutter and growing visibly on the main screen on the bulkhead of the command deck. Heavy cruiser *Merciless* dropped into realspace a few seconds later. Screen optics dimmed the star's fury to a pale yellow orb. "Chevinta isn't visible without magnification yet. We'll be two hours braking and making our approach in the primary's gravity well."

Chalwen eyed the adjacent tactical plot, noting with relief the rest of the escort appearing in space around them.

Julian leaned on the railing separating the captain's command bridge from the dense warren of alleys and equipment pits set a few feet below. The expanse of floor between them and the far bulkhead forty feet away was a seething hubbub of orders, questions, acknowledgements and reports, each station an oiled cog in a complex war machine. From this vantage point, the watch officer had a clear line of sight to the presiding officer in each section from helm to comms, from engineering to deck management, from weapons to defense.

The width of the far bulkhead carried a spread of displays, including the main screen Captain Galliano indicated. But it seemed Julian, like Chalwen, was more interested in the abstract detail of the tactical plot than the meaningless real world view.

"I see Chevinta there," he said. "No planetary defenses showing? Can that be right?"

Chalwen suppressed a grin. The captain had misjudged, thinking a twelve-year-old boy would be more distracted by a pretty picture than technical readouts.

As usual, Doctor Vicky stepped in with a learning opportunity. "Sire, recall our talks about the Freeworlds."

Talks, Chalwen thought, not lessons. Doctor Vicky was a master diplomat as well as a learned tutor. Julian's expression settled into a bland mask while he thought. That was new. Doctor Vicky must have been coaching him to do away with the boyish scrunch of his face when he concentrated. Chalwen eased herself into a more comfortable position, shifting her weight from one aching leg to the other.

"Freeworlds are guaranteed independence by imperial charter," Julian stated at last, "and recognized by all the Families."

"And why would the Families do that?" Doctor Vicky prompted.

"To become a Freeworld, you have to provide something, usually a valuable service or some unique expertise, that the Families agree should be held in trust for everyone's benefit equally."

"That's right, Sire. So the Freeworlds are parties to treaties that all the Families are bound to honor. There's more to it that we haven't got around to covering yet, for example they are typically barred from fielding a military force, hence the lack of defenses."

"It helps," Chalwen added, "that Chevinta still holds the master keys to the comms nodes that its technicians developed five thousand years ago. Anyone threatening them, Family, Freeworld, or outworld, will find themselves isolated from the rest of civilization."

"I thought Chevinta was a university world."

"Its faculties include a lot of practical research and innovation." The tutor gave Chalwen a warning glare. "It doesn't build or market anything, that's part of its charter terms, but it does hold knowledge."

* * *

From the relative comfort of his stateroom on *Kirov*, Ivan, Bernie and Scipio watched *Merciless* take up orbit around Chevinta. Ivan's scalp crawled at the thought of military-grade sensors sweeping the planet and surrounding space.

As if sensing his unease, Bernie waved at their surroundings. "One of the advantages of choosing a small ... small-ish ship for a personal yacht. May not have the home comforts of something bigger, but you can land. And shelter in a shielded hangar."

"All right, Bernie," Ivan growled. "I know the theory, but theory is impersonal. It's a different matter when your own future hangs in the balance. I'd find it hard to explain my presence here, in hiding."

Scipio turned from the display on the wall and opened the drinks cabinet on the other side of the room.

Bernie quirked an eyebrow at the Firenzi noble then said to Ivan, "We're fine. We're transmitting the signature of an outworld freighter, and your personal comms are being routed through encrypted channels back to Magentis, so as far as anyone knows, you're still there." He shrugged. "Just not accessible in person."

"Seems to have enough home comforts to keep a gentleman happy," Scipio said as he poured himself a generous measure of Eloon liquor. He settled in a couch next to the cabinet and raised the glass in salute. "We could be here for some time."

They studied the orbiting warship for signs of activity. After half an hour, Bernie broke the silence. "Our safe anchorage didn't come cheap, mind. The planetary authorities are used to hosting nobles and other VIPs in secret, and hiding their presence from each other, but they expect premium rates for their executive service."

"Of course they do." Ivan's tone was as dry as his throat. He reached for a decanter of iced juice and wondered how long they'd have to play this waiting game. "And that same secrecy makes any kind of remote surveillance impractical."

"Hence the need for boots on the ground." Bernie finished the well-worn argument with a grin. "It's fortunate I had the makings of a network of contacts already in place."

"Let's just hope it's worth it."

"I just hope I've cast my net in the right pond."

Ivan raised an eyebrow. It wasn't like Bernie to express uncertainty like this.

"I discovered that the Emperor isn't landing in the administrative capital, like you'd expect."

"Where then?" Ivan rarely pried into the details of Bernie's machinations, trusting his aide to exercise judgment and keep him informed of anything vital, but this tidbit startled him. From the depths of interstellar space, a planet looked deceptively small. A pinpoint on a tactical display. But if they didn't know Julian's point of landing, that pinpoint suddenly became vast on an inhuman scale.

"Secret, and knowledge beyond my reach in the limited time available, although there's a short list of likely spots. I've covered the most obvious candidates, but young Julian could surprise us yet. We won't know until his shuttle de-orbits."

"Well, at least we didn't meet here on false suspicions." Scipio drained his glass and refilled it. "Clearly there's something happening more than a degree ceremony to pamper a royal ego. Any idea what?"

"The Emperor is getting support from somewhere," Bernie's tone grew serious. "As far as I can tell, Stanhope is Julian's strongest ally. And he's up to something, but I haven't been able to break past the secrecy. ImpSec's just one bloody big onion. Layer after layer."

"You have a large stable of contacts buried throughout," Ivan said. "Surely *someone* must know something."

"Contacts, yes. Widespread, yes. But not everywhere. Some corners remain too deep, and cutting through the layers sometimes makes me want to weep."

Ivan said mildly, "Weep? I pay you to *bleed*." He was only half joking.

"Does it matter?" Scipio sneered. "Yes, bloody ImpSec's managed to keep the lid on the rabble-rousing your misinformation machine's stirring up, but I'm taking the program up a notch or five."

"Armed Firenzi transports landing on Skamensis worlds," Ivan murmured. The thought made him uneasy, but the logic was compelling. "Julian will have to respond in kind."

Scipio pantomimed a hurt look, with his hands crossed over his heart. "All in the name of protecting our own interests when your local forces fall short." The sneer returned. "If Julian doesn't match force with force, the Assembly will take matters into their own hands. The voters will see to it."

"Look." Bernie pointed to the screen. "Game on."

The ground-to-orbit shuttle dropped from *Merciless's* forward hangar. On the view screen, Chalwen caught a fleeting glimpse of the bulging dome of the lower beam battery before darkness engulfed them as they passed into Chevinta's night. The cruiser was nothing but an emptiness in the starscape above, the planet an even more unfathomable blackness below, broken by a few lonely dustings of light.

A half hour passed in idle talk until they dropped low enough to enter atmosphere and white noise outside the hull made conversation difficult.

Dawn broke ahead as they descended. Chevinta in daylight was as unimpressive as in the dark. Barren tans and russets stretched to the horizon. On a closer look, the landscape was slashed with a network of glittering lakes and patches of green. Chalwen checked their altitude and calculated that some of them must be substantial oases.

It seemed as if Doctor Vicky was following Chalwen's thoughts. "Unsuitable for large scale farming," she said. "Few natural resources."

"Nothing to fight over," Chalwen added. "Ideal for a Freeworld. Plenty of stone for building, though."

Finally, the shuttle banked and dropped sharply. Ahead, a smudge on the horizon grew to reveal itself as another oasis of greenery surrounding a mile-wide expanse of water. From close-up, Chalwen saw the green was ringed by a broader swathe of buildings that blended into the surrounding desert.

They landed at one of dozens of small landing fields scattered amongst the buildings.

"Curious," said Julian, as they stepped from the ramp onto a laser-cut rock surface. "Why so many fields in one small city? And look at all the air traffic! Is that because they're so spread out?"

"The population on Magentis is spread out across the planet's surface too," his tutor said.

"But Magentis has a road network. Most travel is purely local. I didn't see any roads leading out as we flew in."

Well observed, Chalwen thought. Doctor Vicky nodded encouragement.

"Okay. Do they not have settlements other than these cities built around the lakes? If the nearest place you'd want to reach is hundreds of miles away I guess it's easier to fly than build a road all that way. Ah. Here's our welcoming committee."

A small convoy of ground cruisers swept out to meet them. The bodyguard fanned out and Chalwen scanned the flat-roofed buildings hemming them in on all sides. The nearest lay a hundred yards away across the empty field. Her scalp crawled and she was glad Wilder was in charge of the Emperor's protection. Despite the dozens of potential sniper hides in the jumble of walls and roofs surrounding them he seemed at ease. He would have been in contact with local security forces and briefed on their surveillance and point defenses.

A tall and solidly-built man in a plain green tunic and pants stepped from the leading car, flanked by two officials. He bowed to Julian. "I, the chief provost of this humble seat of learning, welcome you to Philosophy and Jurisprudence."

With calm assurance Julian said, "Thank you, Provost Stark, for your hospitality."

"I am deeply sorrowful that you declined the offer to receive you in the Celebration Plaza with all the pomp befitting a royal visitor."

"I'm sure there'll be time enough for ceremony later in the week. I do appreciate your discretion in allowing me to land without fanfare. I need time before my presence becomes official. Has my guest arrived?"

"Guests, Sire."

"Guests? Plural?" Julian glanced at Doctor Vicky, puzzled. "Who else am I supposed to meet?"

The provost gave a worried look at the group assembled behind the Emperor. "Did I misunderstand?"

Chalwen stepped forward. "No misunderstanding, Chief Provost. Your information is correct." To Julian she said, "Sire, there was a late addition to your schedule. A matter of honor."

After only the briefest hesitation, Julian nodded understanding at the code phrase. "I see. Thank you, Lieutenant. In which case I think we should get going. This week is going to be busier than I thought."

They all climbed into one of the middle cars, while the provost and his attendants resumed their place in the front car. The space was cozy but comfortable. Chalwen was uneasy that the whole escort was confined to a single car, but again Wilder didn't question the arrangements. The reason became clear as they set off. Through darkened windows,

Chalwen noticed cars peeling off in twos and threes into the labyrinth of side streets.

Decoys.

Fifteen minutes later, the remains of the convoy swept through a series of archways into a shaded courtyard.

A woman in a green robe met them. "Provost Stark conveys his greetings. I am to extend our fullest hospitality. Please to follow."

She ushered the party into a long room. Windows down one side were screened to admit a mellow wash of sunlight while affording them privacy from outside. Tables to one side carried a spread of delicacies.

"Please to avail yourself of refreshments and comfort while under my humble roof."

"A Chevinta safe meeting house," Doctor Vicky whispered to Chalwen. "I believe we're in good hands."

"We'd better be," Chalwen whispered back. "The Emperor isn't the only important guest here today. Many people would ransom their grandmothers to know who's under this roof together." She eyed the procession of alcoves opposite the windows, and the elaborately molded ceiling. Paintings in the alcoves, statues, a tinkling fountain in the center of the floor ... the room was a security nightmare, but Chalwen placed her faith in the Chevinta obsession with guests' safety and confidentiality.

"Your first guest awaits behind yonder door, Sire." The woman glanced at Chalwen. "Are you the one with knowing of the meeting protocols?"

"I am, Honored Housekeeper." In her preparations for today, Chalwen had studied the proper etiquette. Meeting house caretakers held a revered position in Chevinta society.

"Then I leave the proceedings in your hands." The housekeeper pressed her palms together with a short bow, and left without further explanation.

Chalwen drew Julian to one side. "Sire, I'm asking you to trust me now more than ever before."

Julian looked puzzled. "Chalwen," he murmured, "I've trusted you with my life for as long as I can remember. What can possibly beat that?"

"As your chief bodyguard, I was entrusted with the Crown Prince. Now I'm asking you to entrust the Emperor and the empire to my judgment." She paused there and solemnly caught the Emperor's eye.

His eyes flicked briefly away as the true importance of her request sank in, then he gazed squarely back and nodded. "What do you want?"

"We must leave the rest of our escort here."

Julian opened his mouth, but whether to question or to protest, Chalwen didn't wait to find out. "Yes, that means your bodyguard and advisors. It must be just the two of us going through that door, or there will be no meeting."

"You ask me to leave myself completely vulnerable, in a strange town on a strange planet."

"Unfortunately, yes. Once through that door, our communicators will not work. There will be no way to summon your bodyguard if you feel threatened."

"Can you give me some idea what the reward is for such a risk?"

Chalwen smiled. He was learning. "You have assets in the empire that you know nothing about. Those assets helped your father in setting up the Conclave. I know it never took place, but it was close, and Emperor Paul couldn't have hoped to get that far on his own."

Julian's eyes and mouth formed silent 'O's. Then a look of calculation replaced the boyish wonder. "Those assets have continued working, haven't they? Even if I refused this meeting, they'd continue on my behalf?"

Chalwen hesitated, then nodded.

"Then why would I need to expose myself to risk, leaving my bodyguard behind?" His face creased in a wry smile. "This is a test, isn't it? This goes against everything you ever taught me."

"No test. No trick." Space alive! Chalwen hadn't been ready for *this* line of thinking. And yet, it was entirely in keeping with the youngster's training. What she was asking was beyond ridiculous and went against a lifetime of conditioning. She longed to be able to include at least Wilder in the meeting, but the Light had only survived as long as it had through precautions going way beyond paranoia.

If she'd thought about it, maybe she could have had Wilder vetted ahead of time. It would have eased Julian's reluctance, but it was too late now. She sighed. "You're right. If we turned away now, the people the other side of that door would continue as before. But it's my belief you'd benefit from being able to draw directly on these assets. And, there is a … personal … element to this meeting."

"You set this up, didn't you?"

"I had a hand in it. I believe it to be for the best."

Julian chewed his lip for a moment. "The odd thing is, I trust *you* absolutely. It's just that your request is so odd I feel like I'm failing in some way by agreeing. Huh! If I'm making a fool of myself, so be it. How do you think Lieutenant Wilder will take it?"

Chalwen glanced down the room to where the squad leader directed the bodyguard in conducting a systematic scan of the room. Wilder caught Chalwen's eye and gave a barely-noticeable nod. Chalwen grinned. Wilder had already been briefed by his Chevinta counterparts.

"It won't be a problem. Come on."

They stepped through the door the housekeeper had indicated, and found themselves in a small windowless room. The door sighed softly shut behind them. A few moments later, a faint click from the door opposite told Chalwen that hidden security had confirmed only the correct people were present.

"Julian," she whispered, breaking protocol, "this meeting will I hope be joyful, but it will be hard too. Prepare yourself."

He paused, then nodded and squared his shoulders. Every inch an emperor, straight-backed and stern, he threw open the door and strode through.

A solitary figure stood across the room, peering through the screen shielding a window.

Chalwen's pulse thudded in her throat. *After all these years.* "Sire, I'd like you to meet the man who helped your father come so close to realizing his ambitions for lasting peace between the Families, and who's been helping you this past year."

Lorenzo Skamensis turned slowly to face them. Julian gasped. The family resemblance to Paul and Ivan was clear. Julian looked from Lorenzo to Chalwen and back again. "What is this, Chalwen? *Who* is this?"

It took Chalwen a few tries before she could find her voice. "This is a man exiled before you were born, and erased from the imperial records."

Julian gaped. A glimmer of understanding crossed his face, battling with puzzlement. "There have always been stories. Father sometimes spoke of a brother he'd lost, but I assumed he meant you'd died."

"Not yet, though that's not for want of trying." Lorenzo gave a twisted grin. "You still have family besides your uncle Ivan."

Chalwen could see the realization take hold. It washed over Julian like a cloud over the face of the sun. His eyes dimmed and his shoulders slumped. His whole posture sagged and Chalwen wondered if he was going to collapse.

She started forward to catch him, but Lorenzo held up a hand. Gently, he placed his hands on Julian's shoulders. "Your father would have introduced us, in time. When he felt you were ready."

The words seemed to pull Julian out of his daze. "Father knew about you?"

Lorenzo nodded. "We've been in close contact all through the years. The two of us, standing opposed to Florence and Ivan."

"But Grandma Florence made my father emperor, not Ivan."

"A late change of heart. But even then, Paul and I decided it was better for me to stay in hiding. Hedging our bets, I suppose."

Julian straightened and nodded. Weak with relief, Chalwen turned to the nearest window. While they talked, she gazed through the slats of the screen at the street outside. There was little foot or vehicle traffic in sight, but the air above buzzed with small craft. It was the same on the streets she'd seen on their tortuous drive here. Maybe this was simply a residential or academic district, but she wondered at the lack of obvious commerce in this town. Chevinta, it seemed, ran to its own rules.

She wondered also what the rest of their companions next door were making of the Emperor's absence. Hopefully Wilder would be able to convince them that all was well. The bodyguard squad would take his lead, she had no worries on that score, but Doctor Vicky would be going frantic. Chalwen smiled at the sudden image of the fiercely protective tutor taking the bodyguard to task about dereliction of duty.

She turned back to the room behind her, and found Julian and Lorenzo had seated themselves and were still in earnest conversation across a coffee table.

"I would love you to meet my own children one day. A girl and a boy. They're a bit younger than you. They have a good life, but sometimes it pains me that they'll never understand their real heritage."

"Does this mean you'll come back to Magentis?"

Lorenzo shook his head sadly. "Brother Ivan has no knowledge of my whereabouts, or he'd have me killed."

"Sire," Chalwen said, "you took a risk leaving your guard behind to step into the unknown. You must understand Lorenzo is taking as much of a chance in agreeing to this meeting."

"Even a confirmed sighting of me alive would be dangerous," Lorenzo added. "As far as Ivan's concerned I dropped out of sight and haven't been seen or heard of since."

"Does he think you're dead?"

Lorenzo pondered the question. "He has no reason to think that, and he's not a man to make rash assumptions. But he has no reason to think I'm still alive either. And if he knew how actively I was helping Paul he'd move planets to find and silence me." He chewed the inside of his cheek. "All I can say is that I haven't crossed into Skamensis space in fifteen years."

Abruptly, Julian stood and paced the floor, agitated. At last he stopped and faced Lorenzo. "You've been here, behind the scenes all along. Including the last year since my father's death. In all that time, you stayed hidden from me. That had to be deliberate. So why show yourself now?"

Lorenzo and Chalwen exchanged glances. "You're correct, Julian," he said. "I was waiting. I needed to see which of my brothers you intended to follow." He looked at Chalwen again and shrugged. "These are times of great tension. There's pressure on you to go to war with the Firenzi and yet you're meeting with him in secret."

Julian looked stunned. "That ... how ...?"

"The meeting is highly confidential," Chalwen cut in. "You're wondering who leaked the information."

"You?" Julian's hurt look stabbed Chalwen in the tenderest core of her mind. How could he flip from trust to suspicion so readily?

"There was no leak," Lorenzo hastily broke the awkward moment. "Who do you think worked with a deeply suspicious administration to smooth the way for your meeting?"

"I'm being an idiot, aren't I? I'm glad Doctor Vicky isn't here to see me now."

"You've had a huge shock," Chalwen said. "I hope in time it will be a happy one, but it *will* take time to sink in."

Lorenzo coughed. "Back to the question of timing, your own actions decided that."

"This meeting with Josef?"

Lorenzo nodded. "That told me you'd made up your mind."

———•+•———

"Interesting." Bernie Fischer threw off a dusty cloak revealing a sweat-stained tunic and loose slacks. A blue and orange sash tied around his waist marked him as a student of philosophy. "As we said, there is more to this trip than receiving an honorary degree. The Emperor has met in secret with at least two persons or groups of persons unknown."

Ivan stared. "You mean you can't even tell how many people he met with?"

"Only that there were two separate meetings. The other parties went to great lengths to keep their origins and identities under wraps. The same measures that are protecting us ..." He shrugged. "Excellent security cuts both ways."

"But you managed to get *something*."

"I had someone in place in the city the Emperor visited. She persuaded a member of the catering staff in the faculty conference center to observe. He was assigned to the Emperor's party. Luck of the draw. Would have been more informative if he'd attended to the people Julian was seeing, and of course he wasn't allowed in the meeting room at the same time as other guests."

"Did he plant a listening device?"

Bernie gave an expression that said 'are you serious?'

Ivan sighed, resigned. "They swept the room and found it."

"As I said, excellent security. He did make discreet inquiries of others in the building, but they either knew nothing or were saying nothing." Bernie looked around the stateroom, perhaps wondering if he could leave his grimy cloak somewhere. He settled for folding it carefully over one arm. "I had boots on the ground with a number of surveillance teams around the meeting house. Analysis of traffic in the neighborhood in the hours leading up to the Emperor's arrival gave few clues. Vehicles are unmarked, and they use decoys, but pattern analysis led us to deduce the two separate meetings."

Ivan gazed at the tactical repeater screen. There was *Merciless* drifting overhead again. Ships coming and going. Freight and commercial craft from all corners of human space. The university Freeworld was a popular hub of academia. And ... he looked closer. "I suppose it would be too much to hope we can draw a direct link, but this is too big a coincidence. There is a large Firenzi presence in orbit. Navy. Not the makeup of an offensive fleet, more like an escort for someone of great importance."

"Interesting. How long have they been up there?" Bernie tapped his teeth with a fingernail while his other hand manipulated the desktop. "We didn't see them when we arrived because they were in a long holding orbit. They closed in about the same time that *Merciless* arrived in-system."

"That definitely can't be coincidence," Ivan gritted out. "He's meeting with Family Firenzi."

"And," Bernie said after a few more minutes of work, "some of the units up there are the same ones that accompanied Josef Firenzi to Magentis. Do you think Scipio knew of this?"

"Maybe not. Josef's been freezing him out of a lot of his dealings recently." A slow rage built up in the back of Ivan's mind. "So, Julian's picking up where his father left off."

"If that's so, how did he arrange that without either of us noticing?"

"And how in all Space did he get that far that quickly?"

"He couldn't have. Not without help. We suspected Paul had a network of support entirely separate from the official bodies. Could he be using that same network?"

"Again, how? Julian had hardly anything to do with government until about a year before Paul died. Surely he couldn't have been handed control in that time, and at such a young age?"

"And yet, the pattern of obstruction is similar. Look at how our program of civil unrest got derailed. I know ImpSec pulled out all the stops tracing the cells co-ordinating efforts—"

Ivan shuddered. They'd only managed to cut the lines of communication just in time to avoid them being traced right back to the source.

"—but they always managed to appear in the wrong place at the wrong time, and I don't credit ImpSec with all that success. They had backroom support, and I'm not sure they were even aware of it."

Ivan's jaw dropped. "That would explain it. Maybe the network exists, but Julian doesn't know about it."

"Hmmm. Wonder what such a network might look like." Bernie hummed to himself while he thought. "Something like that would need a lot of co-ordination. Communications."

"But heavily encrypted. You'd never tap into it." Ivan narrowed his eyes at Bernie. "Would you?"

"Unlikely. But that may not be necessary. Simply the fact that A is talking to B can speak volumes without knowing *what* they are talking about."

Ivan knew his expression showed his skepticism.

"Oh, it's technical." Bernie flapped his hands dismissively. "Suffice to say, a widespread network like that should show distinctive patterns of connections between end points, and some correlation in activity in time with real world events."

"Do you have the access and tools to spot something like that?"

"I don't." Bernie grinned. "But there are some sympathetic folks inside ImpSec who do."

Chapter 41

Year 8070, summer

The call to the main briefing room came in the middle of the ship's night. Gregor hustled in, still fastening the top of his service fatigues. The room was already half full and more officers crowded in behind him. He was thankful to note urns to one side where serving staff were pouring tea into mugs ready to be picked up, and more servers had just deposited platters of hot food. Copious quantities of protein and carbs. This could be their last decent meal for a while.

Captain Borodina waited impatiently until the servers had left and the doors were sealed. "Encrypted alert from the deep space net around Stour," she began without preamble.

"That's right on our doorstep," senior navigation officer Jerve van Verden noted. "We've been patrolling near here for three weeks. Is that a coincidence?"

"We had intelligence of Firenzi movements in the neighborhood, so we've been positioning ourselves to cover a couple of possible targets. Stour was the most likely, given the Firenzi trading interests there."

Gregor grabbed a mug of tea and lined up for food. Unless someone sounded general quarters, they clearly had time to plan their action. "If this is following recent patterns," he called across the room, "the Firenzi will be moving in to protect their own people's assets."

"Your point?" The captain scowled.

"On other planets, they've arrived on the scene before too much harm was done."

Captain Borodina's expression told him he had two seconds left to make his point.

"They'd never get there in time unless they had intelligence days in advance of a threat to those assets."

"I think I see where Commander Pavlenko is going with this, Captain." That was Anya Schevchenko, the diminutive head of ship-board Imperial Security. Gregor shuddered. He hadn't wanted to draw himself to Anya's attention. To Gregor, she said, "An astute person might wonder what intelligence the Firenzi had access to that we hadn't. Or, alternatively, why would we not get there ahead of them?"

Gregor shrugged. Anya had nailed it.

"The answer is, we do have an idea of where foreign assets might come under threat, and we do follow up on those reports, just as the Firenzi do. But with several hundred active reports at any one time, the trick is to guess which one *they'll* respond to."

Or, thought Gregor, you could just hand those reports over to local forces to stop the trouble brewing in the first place. He held his tongue. Comments like that could be seen as criticism, and ImpSec did not take criticism willingly.

"So we have Firenzi intruders heading to Stour for some vigilante policing," someone called from behind Gregor. "Will we be in time to head them off, and what about local forces?"

"Limited," Anya said. "Two destroyers in orbit, ground-based forces standing by to intercept landing craft. They can't hope to blockade the whole planet, but neither can we allow other Families to carry out their own police action on our turf."

The captain cleared her throat. An unmistakeable danger sign. "We'll be in-system in three hours. We have that time to assemble teams and prepare briefings. Best estimates are that the Firenzi will be at least four hours making their approach from their last known location on the edge of the system."

"I guess we don't have anything more precise?" Jerve van Verden asked. "And we'll also need time to approach from far enough out in the gravity well."

Gregor loaded up a plate and took a seat at the long conference table. He had burning questions but he'd already pushed his luck far enough. The surveillance on his tablet still spooked him, and Anya's gaze had lingered on him too long at the end of their exchange. Things would become clear soon enough.

"We'll enter the system as close in as safety margins allow, and upstream." The captain nodded to the navigation officer. "And our secondary drive beats the shit out of any small craft. Relative velocity in-system?"

Gerve van Verden consulted a scroll in front of him. "Three point one percent light." He looked up. "That's fast. Was that planned too?"

The captain gave a satisfied smile. "Good enough. We'll need maximum braking on secondary to close for combat, but that's fast enough to hit them by surprise."

The navigation officer scribbled hasty calculations on his scroll while the captain turned to Gregor and to the hangar deck officer beside him. "I need two squadrons of fighters ready to scramble as soon as we reach orbit, and both primary and secondary weapons hot and ready."

"If they follow the pattern we've seen," Gregor said, "they'll be light and fast. Drop squads armed and equipped for urban conflict to cordon off the assets, put down the civilian protesters, then fade into the woodwork." He frowned. "What kind of role does a *Sword* play in all this?"

"You're right. They'll have dropped their payload before we can get there, so that's up to the local forces to handle. Our job is to make sure they don't get away."

———•———

At general quarters, the combat operations room simmered with controlled tension. Red lighting gave the crew's faces a demonic air as they stared at consoles. The pervasive hum of the warship's machinery was muted behind sealed double blast doors. Ventilation hissed with locally scrubbed and recycled air that quickly dried Gregor's mouth.

Gregor strapped himself into the command chair at the heart of the operations room, and brought up his command and tactical consoles.

This was not a drill. The thought chilled him. It must have been years since Violet last fired in anger. The secondary armament, arrays of particle beams encircling the main battle platform and directed by teams of gunners over to his left, had been used many times in minor border skirmishes. Those beams alone could easily have overwhelmed the small craft reported by the far-flung sensor net, but they were precision weapons. For this ambush, Captain Borodina had ordered a show of blunt force.

Nut, meet sledgehammer.

To Gregor's right, a small army of engineers tended the cranky complexity of the primary plasma cannon. All that city-wrecking firepower lay in the hands of a solitary gunner, a skeletal man who looked too frail to wield such a weapon. But his hand was steady on the tiny control joysticks, and his eyes had the piercing, unwavering look of a raptor stalking prey.

Thankfully, and Gregor in moments of paranoia double- and triple-checked this fact, Maestro remained disengaged. This was a purely human operation.

"Dropping to realspace," Gregor announced as data flowed on his command console. They still had a long wait while the ship closed in from the shallows of the star's gravity well. As per standard operating procedures they were coming in ready for action as if this were a hostile system. The handful of small craft they knew about were perfectly capable of interstellar travel, so there was no need to expect a mother ship nearby, but they could have backup lurking at the edge of the system out of sensor range.

In the protective cocoon of ship's gravity, their bone-breaking deceleration was only apparent in the navigational readouts on the tactical plot. The still-distant planet of Stour was nothing more than a dot for most of the two-hour descent.

"Plot still clear," Gregor muttered. "Looks like they came in unaccompanied after all."

"Or there could be forces too far out to spot." Una looked unhappy. "There's our destroyers, but low orbit is clear."

"Local control must have grounded all traffic when the Firenzi appeared."

"Surely that'll tip them off?"

"Maybe not. Clearing the skies would be a natural response to hostile forces, so there's no reason they'd be aware there was a bigger firefight imminent. Sure, they'll know they've been spotted but they must have known they couldn't hope to approach without tripping an alarm somewhere."

In the last few minutes the planet ballooned to fill half the screen with heart-stopping speed, slowing in the last few moments as the ship shed the remains of its relative velocity.

"Hah!" Gregor said, studying the plot. "We got a break. Bandits have landed on the far side."

"As long as they're shut out of the satellite network, they'll be blind." Una's voice was calm and level, but Gregor caught an underlying edge of jubilation.

"They are," he confirmed. "We've got all-round data access. They're limited to line of sight."

He skimmed reports on the command feed. "Fighters are away."

A constellation of green dots swung away from *Wrath* and swept around the curve of the planet.

"Bandits lifting." The intercom spoke calmly in Gregor's ear. "Intercept flight will chase them our way. Take them out."

Gregor gave his gunnery officer a hand signal. "Take them out, aye. Give us helm." A crawling sensation across his skin told him the primary cannon was warming up for action.

"You have the helm," the voice in Gregor's ear announced. "Intercept flight will remain hull down past the horizon. *Spiteful* and *Sherpa* remain in high orbit blocking bandits from a direct ascent. Try not to cook them."

"I have the helm," the gunnery officer confirmed. "Friendlies identified and flagged for avoidance." He eased a joystick to one side and the vast warship rolled in response. *Wrath of Empire* crabbed sideways on to the planet, lining up her underbelly with the distant horizon and the unsuspecting enemy still out of sight.

"Firing, firing, firing in three ... two ... one ..."

An unseen hand seemed to stretch the skin across Gregor's forehead.

On an external visual, *Wrath* painted a swathe of lavender across the sky too brilliant to look at without heavy filters.

Gregor tensed, momentarily convinced the gunner had fired too early as the plasma bolt grazed atmosphere and arrowed towards the horizon. But he saw immediately that the seasoned weapons master had judged the shot perfectly. The atmospheric graze smeared the bolt across a widening path, casting a net too broad for the Firenzi craft to avoid. One by one they sped into the trap that had been sprung unseen and unexpected. Fireflies caught in a blowtorch.

Gregor focused on technicalities. "Readings," he snapped at the spotting crew. "I want a count of debris flares. Tactical, confirm IDs on all remaining blips. I don't want a bandit slipping past."

"Stand by, weapons," the bridge intercom announced. "Comparing tallies with reports from local control. Helm remains with you."

"Helm with us, aye," Gregor responded. To his battle crew he said, "Standard three-sixty sweeps until ordered to stand down. Eyes everywhere, including skywards."

Finally, the command channel announced, "Ground control confirms six bandits were identified inbound. Spotters tally six hits. Airspace clear. Stand down and return helm to bridge."

"Returning helm to bridge, aye," the gunner acknowledged.

"Nice shooting," Gregor said. "It takes skill to control the spread of the beam like that."

"I'd like to see some fucking AI come up with a move like *that*," Una whispered beside him.

Cool down checks took an hour, even though they'd only fired a single shot. They'd stood down from general quarters, and this part was well-worn routine. Gregor and Una had little to do while the team under them ran through their procedures and checklists.

Beside him, Una hissed.

Gregor glanced over her shoulder and gasped. "This real time?"

"A live feed from one of the local news channels."

"That street looks familiar." At least, part of it did. Even after a year, Gregor recognized the brash tavern on the corner. Smoke billowed from buildings further down, including the coffee shop and the cafe where they'd stood up to an angry mob. "Did the bandits do this?"

The report cut to other scenes of conflict elsewhere in the city. Street after street looked like a war zone.

Una brushed a tear from the corner of her eye. "Hard to say." With angry strokes of her stylus on the desktop she pulled up more newsfeeds as well as military reports.

"No. Can't be," Gregor said. "They landed miles away and formed a cordon around a garment factory. This looks like citizens taking reprisals into their own hands." Chicken and egg, Gregor thought. Which was cause, and which effect? Mob attacks businesses, business owners defend their turf, enraged citizens take revenge, and so it goes on.

"And yet," he mused, "all the media opinions are saying outright the Firenzi are responsible."

Una crossed her arms, clearly struggling to contain herself. "They *are*, dammit. They sent a raiding party into our space."

Gregor's mind went back to the events of a year ago. He fingered the back of his skull where remembered pain nagged him. "What would have happened if we hadn't been at the restaurant when that mob attacked?"

Una shuddered. "I don't know. Do you think they'd have stopped at a few broken windows?"

"Maybe, maybe not. Either way, there was no one else within shouting distance to help, was there? Raids like this aren't the answer, but maybe they wouldn't have to if our own forces kept better order."

Gregor glanced over his shoulder. The nearest crew members hastily turned back to their checklists. A cold sweat beaded Gregor's forehead. These men and women were trained professionals. Within the confines of the weapons bays and operations room, with alarms sounding and tactical data flooding the ranks of consoles, he trusted them utterly. But he could never ignore *Wrath of Empire's* true sympathies.

Chapter 42

The mood in the quiet corner of Dognoty's coffee shop was a curious blend of optimism and worry while Chalwen debriefed Henri and Simone on the Emperor's meeting with Josef Firenzi.

They huddled close over a small table and kept their voices low, while Simone constantly scanned for eavesdropping devices. The lunchtime hubbub drowned out their words outside of their immediate circle. Dognoty was making a name for himself, and the coffee shop had grown popular among palace staff in recent months. This increased the chances of being seen by someone they knew, but since Chalwen's transfer away from Civil Watch, the three of them had decided there was no reason to keep their association hidden. Now they were simply three colleagues out for lunch.

"It was their first meeting in person," Chalwen said, "and the two of them spent a lot of it alone together. Advisors and bodyguards, including me, kept at arm's length. I'm only reporting what little I was party to, and what I gleaned and deduced after the fact. Simple summary is, both leaders right now are looking for a peaceful settlement, despite all the crap flying around."

Henri looked thoughtful. "Paul and Josef were unusually close, for heads of rival Families. Do you think Josef's banking on Julian following his father?"

Chalwen nodded. She didn't mention how Lorenzo had reached the same conclusion. Simone knew nothing about The Hidden Light. Chalwen would bring Henri up to date on *that* development separately.

"Fine," Simone said, "but how does that square with the armed incursions that we know *are* the Firenzi?"

"Good point," said Henri. "Any idea what Josef had to say about that?"

"Only that he acknowledged the origin of the raiders, but denied they were acting on his instructions. I think he has internal problems of his own to deal with."

Simone glanced back at her notepad. "What? Similar to whoever's been stirring shit across our own territories?"

"As long as you believe him," Henri said, "that means, just like Julian, Josef Firenzi is dealing with someone high up in his administration trying to undermine him. On our side they're doing a damned good job of it, too. The public unrest is close to getting out of control. A large part of ImpSec's still chasing down links, homing in on whoever's pulling the strings here."

With a grimace, Simone said, "Trouble is, the trails are going cold. We're not seeing as many of the highly-targeted and orchestrated campaigns that caught your eye in the first place."

A ground car rumbled along the narrow street outside, parting crowds with impatient blasts on its horn. "So," said Chalwen, "they might be winding up that line of attack. Either it's served its purpose, or the countermeasures are putting them off."

"Either way, I think our window is closing. And enough damage has already been done." Henri tapped the tabletop restlessly. "In fact, it seems there are enough anti-Firenzi groups out there now, organizing themselves locally, that they don't need to pull strings from here any more. It's got a life of its own. As I said, out of control."

Chalwen suppressed a snarl of frustration. "Julian should be saying *something* in public. More than the bland appeals for calm that his public statements so far have stuck to."

"And say what?" Henri shook his head. "*We* have the evidence that the Firenzi had nothing to do with the assassination, but it's all inference based on conditioning methods. It won't hold up in the court of public opinion. If Julian comes out right now and points the finger elsewhere it won't make any difference. Not unless he can stem the misinformation *and* stop the Firenzi attacks at the same time."

"A vicious circle," Simone said, bitterly. "And it's not just public opinion. The Assembly is seriously considering bringing a motion to force Julian to declare war."

"Okay," Chalwen said slowly. "Those public campaigns make Julian's hold on the throne precarious. Seems all the more reason to expose what went on in the palace that day. I've been out of touch for weeks but I'll bet the official investigation still hasn't drawn any conclusions?" Her companions' expressions confirmed her suspicions. "What about your own work. Any progress?"

"Well," Henri started, "we know the assassination itself was planned by PDC, but there was something else going on here alongside that. Something to do with the hiding place you found in the old power room." Henri and Simone exchanged glances. "Go ahead," Henri said. "This part was your work."

Simone shrugged. "It's not much, and I don't know how it helps, but I re-analyzed the surveillance glitches from the day of the assassination, and I spotted something we missed at the time."

Chalwen's heart thudded and she leaned closer in.

"Here's the puzzling part. The PDC assassination plots were hidden by one pattern of surveillance outages, both around the hangar and then under the residence. We know the hideout was concealed by a second, entirely separate smokescreen. So, guess which pattern covered the party sent to snatch the Crown Prince from the infirmary?"

Chalwen stared at Simone. "You're going to tell me it was the second?"

Simone nodded.

"That makes no sense. Julian was supposed to be on that cruiser. He should have died alongside everyone else. I can understand PDC wanting to tidy up a loose end, and they *were* behind the poisoning attempt, but you're saying they *didn't* try to snatch him from the infirmary?"

"As I said, I don't know what to make of it. All I can say is that the crew that came after you and Julian in the infirmary had nothing to do with PDC."

Chalwen shook her head. "There's too much happening all at once. Where do we start?"

"Take stock," Henri said. He held up his hands and checked off points on his fingers as he spoke. "PDC take out the Emperor and family. But there's also an unknown player in the mix, purpose unknown."

Chalwen said, "Persons unknown are stirring up trouble between us and Firenzi, at first through the media, then escalating with Firenzi vigilantes."

"With extreme prejudice, in some cases," Henri added, checking off another finger.

"Could that be PDC as well?" Simone wondered. "They stand to gain from any conflict."

Henri sniffed. "Could be any number of factions that thrive on confusion. All I can see is people want conflict, and presumably this would favor Ivan as emperor in place of Julian. The Assembly would support that in a heartbeat if things tipped over the edge."

"Meanwhile," Chalwen said, "Julian knows it wasn't Josef. He's trying to avoid war and build some kind of alliance, but all behind the scenes so far because the Assembly would have a fit if they had any idea what he was up to."

"This is worrying," Henri said. "It won't take much more provocation on either side to start a full-scale war."

"So." Chalwen toyed with the handle of her cup. "Where do we turn next?"

———— ✦ ————

"We've had too little time together like this in the last year."

Morning dew glistened on bottlebrushes lining an overgrown trail through the Imperial Meadow. Muted hoofbeats clopped on hard-packed earth. Ivan rode alongside Julian, their bodyguards forming a watchful cordon out of earshot.

Julian seemed distant this morning. "It feels like a lifetime ago you were showing me the hidden secrets in this park."

Ivan couldn't argue with that. "A lot has happened. Great tragedy. Great change. In a sense, the person you were then *was* a lifetime ago."

"I never imagined being an emperor was so much work." Julian gave a long sigh that twisted into a strangled groan. "What am I going to do about the Firenzi?"

Ivan glanced sidelong at Julian, but the Emperor seemed to be musing to himself, not really expecting an answer. They'd arrived at Julian's favorite lookout. He gazed across the wetland meadow with the open pavilion in the distance.

"My father had good relations with them. Between our two families, we held the rest of the Accord together for centuries. Yes, there's always conflict but never all-out war, and the Families band together to keep the lawless outworlds under control."

"And now the Firenzi are the enemy."

"You know as well as I do that my father was not killed by the Firenzi."

Ivan grimaced. There was no denying the evidence stacked up by Boris Stanhope. "I know that, Sire, but the people out there don't want to believe it."

"They make up their own truth"–Ivan had never before heard such bitterness in the young Emperor's voice–"and there's nothing I can do to set them right. Stanhope says we can't reveal what we know about the assassinations."

Ivan counted himself among those who'd dearly love to learn all that Stanhope knew. He'd revealed enough to convince the Emperor's closest advisors that the evidence pointed away from Josef Firenzi, but how much was he keeping to himself? Had he made the connection to Honorina Philip? Did he suspect a connection closer to home? Could he make the leap to Ivan's own involvement? That would explain his refusal to allow the details to be put on public display until he was ready to nail Ivan to a burning post.

"So it's left up to me to convince people of Firenzi innocence, without showing them another villain to hate instead." Julian turned pleading eyes on Ivan. "What can I say? What can I do?"

Ivan pretended to consider the question while deciding how best to deflect the conversation away from any really helpful advice. "People need to see evidence. Is there a way to persuade Stanhope to release something?"

He suspected Stanhope knew as well as he did that no facts would change peoples' minds. Not now their hearts were set in their beliefs, firmly tied to emotions that no simple truth would shake.

Julian shook his head. "I've tried that. I need help from my other advisers."

Ivan sighed. "All in good time, but out here"—he gestured to the sweep of green around them—"I'd like to think that I'm not your political advisor. I'm just your uncle, and it sounds to me that you need family right now."

The pained look Julian gave him startled Ivan. The boy seemed to have aged ten years since his trip to Chevinta. Something profound had affected him, and neither Ivan nor Bernie had gleaned any further insight into his mysterious visits under the planet's cloak of jealous secrecy. He longed to question Julian about that trip, but in the month since Julian's return Ivan had long since exhausted all avenues of innocent inquiry. Any more pushing would arouse suspicion.

Maybe Bernie's contacts would dig up something useful yet. Meanwhile Ivan had other levers to pull. "I feel I could be more help to you, if you'd let me. Beyond my official duties, that is."

Julian quirked an eyebrow.

"There's a lot of day-to-day matters that rob you of time and energy to truly govern. A good leader knows how to use the people around him to best effect."

"Father always used to remind me there could only be one emperor."

"You must lead the Assembly, obviously. The people and their representatives need to know who their emperor is." And where to lay blame when things go tits up. "But I can be of use behind the scenes, making sure your wishes are put into practice."

When Julian frowned, Ivan hastily added, "Remember, I'm familiar with the machinery of government. More than I think you realize. I sat alongside your grandmother for years before you were even born. Many of the edicts that came from her office actually came through me under her seal."

"Really? I find it hard to imagine her needing help to rule."

Ivan gave a small laugh. "She projected strength and unstoppable energy, but that took its toll. In private, she was starting to feel her age. Anything I could do to ease her burden, I did gladly."

Julian's shoulders straightened. "You're right. I need to concentrate on the Firenzi problem, but there's so much distraction every day."

Ivan smiled encouragement. The rumors and riots orchestrated by Bernie hadn't lit the flames hot enough, and Imperial Security had been damned effective in putting out the fires, so Scipio was doing his part.

The disgruntled Firenzi heir had resources of his own. The guerrilla fighters dropped into centers of population had been his idea. Always, of course, with the visible aim of protecting Firenzi-held assets from the ravages of an embittered and vengeful and lawless population.

The collected media channels were having a field day flipping between pearl-clutching outrage at the violations of sovereign space and sympathy for the victims of local vigilantes. Everywhere, there were human, personal stories splashed across wall screens, of devastated families who'd been part of the local communities for generations, carefully offset by scenes of debris-strewn streets and massacres of rioters by the intruding forces. People no longer knew who to believe, and their anger turned more and more towards their ineffectual government.

It didn't help that the Firenzi protection squads had hit the mainstream media while Julian was away from the capital. The timing had been perfect.

"And now there's the spate of disappearances."

Ivan looked sharply at Julian then hastily looked away. Feigning a casual tone he said, "That's new to me. What kind of disappearances?"

Julian morosely nudged his horse into an amble down the slope towards the valley floor. "Yet more bad news. I guess this has just come up in private security briefings so far."

Ivan wondered whether Julian would elaborate. He didn't want to seem too curious, yet his mind burned with frustration. He curbed his impatience and let silence do his work for him.

As Ivan hoped, after only another minute of riding Julian said, "Merchant vessels have gone missing. Just one or two at first, enough not to stand out from the usual dangers of travel, but it's getting to the point where people will notice a trend."

With his heartbeat thudding and his mouth dry, Ivan didn't dare to speak. This was more than he'd agreed with Scipio. What was the rebellious noble up to? They were trying to hit a delicate balance, enough tension and unrest to force a discontented population to demand proper leadership. But attacking civilian vessels was an act of war. That was a dangerous and slippery slope. What in Space was Scipio playing at?

Or, a cold hand clutched Ivan's heart, was it Scipio?

He knew one person for sure who'd be wholeheartedly behind a full-scale war. The bloodier the better.

———•——

The main canteen at the heart of the battleship's crew accommodation operated around the clock. Even in the quiet of ship's night, there would be people coming off watch ready for sustenance before hitting the rack. But this was early evening and the place was heaving.

The vast food factory contained three separate serveries surrounded by a network of seating areas to serve twenty thousand meals a day. Gaping blast doors gave a sense of openness from one side of the vast space to the other. Voices rivaled the clatter of mess trays, and both vied with heat and spice and a kaleidoscope of motion to assault all the senses at once.

One feature of the canteen was both a blessing and a curse. Men and women of all ranks mingled here freely.

Gregor Pavlenko collected a tray of rice and lamb kofta and set off in search of a table with a free seat among a crowd of talkative crew. The blessing ... this was prime stalking ground for the news-hungry in search of gossip.

He'd just spied a likely feeding ground when a cheerful voice at his elbow derailed his plans. The curse ... you never knew who you might run into.

"I hope you're not trying to avoid me, Gregor." Security chief Anya Shevchenko cut in front of him and steered him to a small table against the bulkhead. "You and I need to chat."

Without making it too obvious, Gregor scanned the aisle for a plausible escape route.

"What do you make of these Firenzi incursions into our space?"

The question, the tone, oozed innocence, but Gregor knew better than to assume any kind of innocence here. Had an unguarded comment been reported back to ImpSec? "I've heard rumors." Gregor kept his manner brusque. It didn't do to annoy the local ImpSec head, but he didn't want to get talking either. Who knew what pitfalls a conversation with Anya might conceal? "You'd be in a much better position to tell me if there's truth in any of them."

"Oh, come on, Gregor. Play with me." She grinned.

Gregor winced. The secret surveillance on his notepad still haunted him. He'd been careful ever since discovering it, but he couldn't escape the feeling of living on borrowed time. And Commander Anya Shevchenko never played.

"It bugs the hell out of me," she continued. "Hit and run squads landing on our planets and assaulting our citizens. How do you feel about that?"

She sat and smiled up at Gregor. He felt trapped. There was no way to leave without appearing suspicious. She was a colleague and of equal rank. He had no plausible reason to avoid her.

Other than the knowledge he had from The Hidden Light. Knowledge of the underground running battles across imperial space with cells of agitators stirring up nationalist fever and vigilante actions.

Knowledge he had no business possessing.

He scowled and sat. "You know damned well I pay no attention to rumors. Whatever's going on out there has nothing to do with me until I have a target to point something big at."

Anya laughed. "I'll make it easy for you. Question for question. I just want a different perspective on the news, and most of the crew are scared to talk to me." She pouted.

"I wonder why," Gregor growled under his breath. "Okay, you want to trade? But your answers must be honest. I'm not prepared to walk out of this conversation feeling I've just been verbally butt fucked."

"Deal!" Anya's grin broadened. "And as a token of goodwill, you get to start."

"Okay." Gregor collected his thoughts while taking a mouthful of food. "Rumors vary from one-off attacks by pirates, to an all-out invasion. Where do these attacks really sit on that spectrum?"

Anya chewed her lip. "It's a long way up from isolated attacks, but falls short of outright invasion. It seems to be a consistent pattern of very targeted incursions."

"Targeted?"

"Oh, no." Anya laughed. "My turn. How are your crew feeling about this?"

"Angry. They want a straight-up fight with an enemy they can see. So, back to these strikes. You said 'incursions', can you explain what they're trying to achieve?"

"They seem to be defensive in nature. Landing forces to protect people and assets. Not an obvious precursor to an all-out assault. Now, all this is happening in civilian territory and I'm guessing some of the crew have families affected by these incursions. How do they feel about that?"

Gregor wondered if she meant the crew members, or the families back home. He decided to hedge. "People are worried. It seems nowhere is safe, and they're wondering what the Emperor is going to do about it. As we're being honest, I have to say that people are getting as angry with our own administration as with the attackers."

Anya narrowed her eyes. Gregor's palms turned clammy. This discussion was straying into dangerous territory. He remembered it was his turn. "Do we know for sure Family Firenzi is behind this?" He hastened to add, "As opposed to some faction within their administration or someone else entirely."

"Oh, Gregor, I do believe you tried to sneak more than one question in there."

Gregor gave her his best innocent look. "It's a question with nuance."

"Okay, I'll let you off with that. We are sure it's Firenzi forces, but how officially they're sanctioned isn't clear."

Gregor was spared further questions by a shrieking alarm. A call to general quarters. Both of them were on their feet, meals forgotten, before the sound had a chance to properly register.

———————

Three hours later, Gregor stared at the relayed visuals on his console in the combat operations room. They'd send a search party to board the burned-out hulk, but with a sickness in his stomach Gregor knew it would be a worthless gesture.

The merchantman hung in space like a gutted fish, floating in a halo of wreckage glinting in *Wrath of Empire's* floodlights. Specks caught like dust in the beams still drifted outward. In the cold depths between the stars, the sphere of destruction would expand for geological ages, spreading and thinning with nothing to disturb it.

"Four light years. Practically in our laps, and we're still too late," he muttered.

"We could have been sitting right on top of them," Una Spelze hissed through clenched teeth, "and we'd still have been too late. Look at the burn patterns. This was fast and overwhelming."

"But not fast enough to stop them sending a distress call." Gregor studied the wreckage more closely. He knew the profiles of classes of warship across the navies of all six Families, but civilian craft were too numerous and varied in layout to remember them all. This design was unfamiliar, and any external markings had been burned off during the attack. "This is a big one. They'd want to take out primary drive first to stop it simply hopping, then the comms arrays. Look. This one had a large secondary array on the opposite side to the main."

Una studied the visuals from the shuttle as it approached and looked for a point to dock. "If the attacker had to maneuver to take out both arrays that would explain how they managed to send off a call. But that suggests just one vessel did all this damage. And how in Space did they get caught like this? You can't intercept a hopping ship. They must have dropped into realspace for long enough ..."

"Which means either a breakdown, or a rendezvous."

They sat for a few minutes, listening to occasional reports from the sensor team still scanning surrounding space for threats or targets. Eventually Gregor broke the silence. "Who did this?"

"That blast spread on the starboard quarter. Look at the size of it. That was the work of a capital ship, at least as heavy as our *Implacable*-class."

"The only Firenzi ships that fit the bill are *Enforcers*," Gregor whispered.

"You're assuming it's Firenzi?" Una lowered her voice to match. Speculation like this could be dangerous.

"We're sitting in the buffer zone between us and them. The only systems here are a few Freeworlds, and they don't field navies. There's di Brugui to the south, but they have nothing comparable."

Sourly, Gregor watched the shuttle nose closer to the wreck and listened to the comms chatter. They were still at general quarters, battened down and alert for trouble, but the aggressors would be light years away by now.

Finally, a piece of information made Gregor swear. "The command deck survived the initial attack. Intruders boarded and blew the compartment. Killed the bridge crew. Burned out the storage core and secondary nodes."

Una frowned. "No witnesses and all sensor records destroyed. They didn't want to be identified."

Gregor had to wet his lips twice before he could talk. "They left the cargo. This wasn't piracy. They're hitting our supply lines." He frowned at the latest data on the command channel. "This isn't as simple as it appears. This victim was a Firenzi-registered ship."

Chapter 43

Year 8070, autumn

Placing a case of beer on the corner of her desk, Chalwen sank into her chair and rubbed her eyes with the heels of her hands. She sighed, straightened, and cracked open the first bottle.

Since she'd last spoken to Henri and Simone, nothing new or useful had turned up. The empire was on the verge of war, and with war it seemed inevitable that Ivan would steal the throne from Julian. The Assembly was ripe for a motion to declare Julian unfit to lead the battle. All it needed was for someone to pull the trigger, and maybe they already had. Defenseless ships on both sides were disappearing, mostly without a trace although a couple of distress calls had been picked up. So far, both Firenzi and Skamensis security forces had managed to contain the extent of the problem, but it was only a matter of time.

The mood of the population had been expertly steered and the strings of the puppet masters expertly hidden. ImpSec had spent the last year trying both to contain the unrest and to trace the source of the poison. To no avail.

Now, fortified against a long night ahead, Chalwen was trying another angle.

She was going back to the days immediately following the assassination, before the more sophisticated campaigns began. Someone had seeded rumors of Firenzi involvement. Someone had had access to internal reports on the cruiser's destruction, and someone had leaked information on the whereabouts of the Firenzi entourage.

Maybe in those early days, someone hadn't been quite so careful at covering their tracks.

Yes, at the time Colonel bin Merrin had assured her that ImpSec was trying to pinpoint the sources, but they were also busy with the Emperor's assassination still raw on their minds, not to mention the attempt on Julian's life. Rabble-rousing and endangering a foreigner, even a Family head, would hardly merit the same attention.

The bottle clinked as Chalwen set it down. With a sharp and fragrant mouthful swilling around her tongue, she pulled up files of reports from the ImpSec archives.

———— • ————

Gregor stared at the screen. One clenched fist bounced on his armrest. "It's so damned *random*."

"That's another five in the last month, after that first Firenzi freighter." Una Spelze looked sick. "Three of our own, and two outworld-registered. Yeah. Random."

No one else in the operations room spoke. The warship sang its endless chorus of machinery. All eyes were on the screen and the destruction bathed in *Wrath's* floodlights. A scene now all too familiar.

"Apart from the Firenzi merchantman, none of them got off a distress call." That was the part that Gregor still couldn't get over. "They simply drop off the grid."

A pair of shuttles slid into view, heading for the gutted merchant ship. Gregor knew it was hopeless, but they went through the motions anyway.

Una shook her head. "And by the time we home in on their last known location and set up a search pattern along their flight path, all we find is a wreck. No survivors. No records."

And nothing to fight, Gregor thought bitterly.

"This still looks like the work of a single attacker," Una whispered. "I've been plotting the attacks across time and space. Looks like a single track looping around our borders."

Gregor eyed Una. That was good initiative. "The only warships able to kill a large merchantman so fast would be a *Sword* or an *Enforcer*."

"And all our *Swords* are accounted for."

Simone poked her head around the door to Chalwen's office. "You found something?"

Chalwen closed her eyes and massaged her forehead with her fingertips. She nodded. It was the cause of long and sleepless nights, first worrying that she'd be proven wrong, all her efforts wasted. Then she started freaking at the thought of being proven right.

At last, the burden was too much to bear alone. She needed a second opinion. Normally she'd turn to Henri, but a hunch told her she needed Simone's analytical insight this time.

She gestured at her desk. The surface was smothered in a confused mass of circles, lines and annotations in Chalwen's tiny and untidy scrawl.

Simone blinked, and stared at Chalwen.

"You know how we've been trying to track down who's pulling the strings, organizing all the protests and riots?"

"We keep running into brick walls." Simone grimaced. "They're covering their tracks too well."

"Yeah. So I wondered if they were as careful in the early days. It's always bugged me, who leaked forensic details of the incendiary used to down *Nightwish*, and who turned the mob onto Josef Firenzi."

Simone narrowed her eyes. "You're assuming that's the same people?"

"Seems a reasonable assumption. Anyway, I've scoured the comms archives and all the deep-dive forensic logs I know how to use. Broadcasts, messages, public posts, quotes. Unmasking the players behind the writing. Account details, geospatial markers, timestamps, looking for connected threads."

"Seems like some of your training rubbed off."

Chalwen huffed. "The advanced stuff is beyond me, but I do have a fair measure of common sense. Anyway"—she gestured at the desk— "this is the map I've made up. The rumors about Firenzi guilt, and later about Josef's whereabouts on Magentis, were seeded from these five channels." She pointed out two fringe news channels, a political analysis show, a local sports celebrity's profile, and a well-known political fundraiser and lobbyist.

"It all exploded from there, and soon gets impossible to trace forward because now everyone's talking about it. At the time it felt like the rumors came out of nowhere, but I hunted for the earliest reports I could find. Hundreds of them. Every thread I followed back from mainstream sources seems to connect to one of these. This is the seat of the fire."

"But who lit the fuze?"

"Exactly. Here's where the trail gets murky. You can see where I changed the lines from solid to dotted. Mostly there are no direct electronic trails, so I'm now looking for indirect connections. Associates, business partners, membership of the same clubs, funding, lobbying on behalf of ... you know the drill."

"Apply some hard core set theory, fuzzy logic, probabilities, mapping association strengths ..." Simone trailed off. Her eyes seemed to focus on one corner of the picture.

"Yeah. Look at this nexus. Tell me if this makes sense."

Simone gazed long and hard at the sprawling network of lines on the desktop. Her face, normally pale anyway, turned pure white. Eyes glowed a startling hazel underlined by a sprinkling of freckles standing stark against her skin.

Not for the first time, Chalwen wondered about her background. Firenzi ancestry? Or maybe di Brugui? Chalwen longed to introduce Simone to the The Hidden Light. She was formidably talented, but no matter how dedicated she seemed to be to ImpSec there was always the nagging question of true loyalties. Without access to the full resources of ImpSec's background researchers she couldn't take the chance. Simone was so good, she could easily be a double agent.

Thankfully, Simone asked no questions, and seemed unfazed by the enormity of what Chalwen was asking her to consider. She simply settled down with her own notepad and trawled data sources with her own arcane collection of tools.

Ignored in her own office, Chalwen wandered out to Sanitation's well-stocked pantry. An urn was always on the go. No matter the unsocial hours, catering staff kept a steady flow of tea, coffee, and pastries. She returned with a laden tray.

Simone was still deep in furious concentration. She reached absently for a lemon slice when Chalwen set a plate in front of her.

An hour later, Simone sat back and pushed her notepad away. "You're right. This all stemmed from the Grand Duke's office."

Chalwen gaped, lost for words. She'd hardly dared trust herself when the clues first pointed this way, which is why she'd spent hours checking and re-checking her analysis. Now, to hear it spoken aloud by someone else knocked the breath from her lungs.

"Did you have any idea the trail would lead here?"

Chalwen shook her head, still too shocked to speak. It felt too unreal. She realized she'd honestly been expecting Simone to find a flaw in her reasoning. She'd been bracing herself for another lecture on statistical validity and probabilistic non-binary logic. Granted, she didn't like Grand Duke Ivan, his politics, his methods—though nothing untoward had ever been proved. But to stoop to outright treason?

Once again, her own past history haunted her. In his own way, wasn't he as justified in opposing Paul as she and Paul had been when working against Florence? She pulled her mind back from that dark and bottomless rabbit hole and realized Simone was still speaking.

"Thing is, you haven't yet pinned it down to any one individual in the office. In theory it could be any one of dozens of people."

"And Ivan himself?"

"Impossible to say."

Chalwen wasn't sure what to make of that. On the one hand, you'd think that someone like Ivan would know what was going on in his own office, and yet Chalwen, Henri and Simone themselves were living proof that people pursued their own agendas behind the backs of their superiors. Once again, she felt she was treading on quicksand.

"We'll need to pull some of these close contacts in for questioning. I can't see ImpSec dropping this bombshell without a rock-solid case. That means physical evidence, witness statements and confessions, to back up the electronic trails."

"We can bring Henri into this." Chalwen fought to gather her wits. "Not sure who else to trust with this kind of crap. I can't see us doing this on our own, though. I suppose we'll need some more labor-intensive detective work, too, to prove some of these connections."

Simone nodded. "Surveillance, eavesdropping, interviewing people on the periphery."

"I'll have to brief Stanhope and pray to all Space that he doesn't flip out on me."

"Not just yet," Simone said. "This is all circumstantial, nothing here he can take action on. We'll assemble the evidence first." To Chalwen's skeptical look, she said, "Hey, this is what Sanitation's for, remember?"

Chapter 44

Visibly agitated, Emperor Julian strode back and forth across the emperor's dressing room. A muted clamor of raised voices filtered through the doors leading into the Assembly Room. A hush, then a roar of applause.

"The Assembly will demand strong action," Ivan said, taking advantage of the few moments of relative privacy. No busybody tutors or other advisers within earshot for once, but it was natural for Julian to keep his political advisor close to hand for a meeting with the Assembly. "Military action. They won't sit still for anything less."

"Commander Stanhope was very clear. We *know* Josef Firenzi didn't sanction any of this."

Ivan wiped a hand across his eyes, feigning weariness. "You know that. I know that. *They* don't." He gestured to the closed doors.

"We can't go to war on the basis of a lie. I won't have it."

"Then prove the lie. Bring them around. That's your *job*," Ivan growled.

A spark of anger flashed in Julian's eyes. Good.

"What we have won't satisfy *them*." Julian's voice dripped scorn. "They're so riled up now, no words will do. We need to bring the real culprits forward before they'll be happy."

"Bring the evidence you have. It'll take time to explain, but you have to trust your elected officials to do their jobs."

Through thick wood panelling, the Clerk's voice barely registered above the din, struggling to bring order to the proceedings.

Julian rolled his eyes. "Reason? With that lot?" He shook his head. "Stanhope has dozens of inquiries going on right now. It's sensitive. If I reveal the evidence we do have, it'll warn the people we're trying to nail. We'll never bring my family's killers to justice."

He nodded to the waiting usher, who threw the doors open. The thunder of a hundred angry voices hit like a physical blow.

"As your political advisor," Ivan hissed in Julian's ear, "I'm telling you you *must* inform the Assembly. If you don't do as I say, they'll force it out of you anyway."

Julian said nothing as he marched through the door, but his shoulders bunched and his fists clenched. Ivan suppressed a smirk as he followed the Emperor out onto the floor of the Assembly Room and took his seat in the advisors' gallery to one side.

Expectant hush blanketed the room as the Clerk acknowledged the presence of the Emperor. Julian strode to the throne, but remained standing in front of it. After a pause, when it became clear Julian wasn't about to say anything, the Clerk motioned the standing Assembly Member to continue.

The young and ambitious Member for Tigris Plateau gave Julian a perfunctory bow and Ivan a slight nod. So, he was the one rabble-rousing so effectively just now. One of Ivan's puppets, oily, persuasive, and hard as tungsten carbide.

"So glad the Emperor could spare the time to join us," he said. "Maybe we can finally hear first hand how he proposes to deal with the Firenzi aggressors."

The Member sat with a look of triumph and a roar of approval from the surrounding throng.

A glance around the vast chamber confirmed the importance of this session. Ivan couldn't see a vacant seat in the chamber. That had to be a record. The media and public galleries were also packed, standing room only, and Ivan knew these proceedings carried in real time to billions of homes across known space.

"I came here to persuade you away from this madness. Both sides are being played." Julian's voice sounded plaintive compared to the seasoned orator.

"More sniveling appeals for calm?" The Member for Tigris Plateau was on his feet again. He glanced at the Clerk, who signaled him to proceed. "Our ruling family murdered, attacks on our own soil and in our sovereign space—your father would never have tolerated this. Florence certainly wouldn't."

Julian's eyes widened, his face paled, but he gave no other sign of how that reminder must have hurt.

At a nod from the Clerk, another Member stood. "We must act." The elderly man's voice was gentle, pleading. "We've lain back and taken these affronts for too long. If we don't crush Family Firenzi *now*, the other Families will see our weakness and crush *us*."

"I will not sign a declaration of war against the Firenzi." Julian folded his arms and faced the room. "Family Firenzi were friends and trusted allies to my father, and to me. They are not the enemy."

"Prove it!"

The cry echoed off the distant walls and ceiling, swelled and repeated in a torrent of sound as Assembly Members and public alike yelled their frustration.

Three loud cracks cut through the bedlam as the Sergeant at Arms smacked the butt of his ceremonial spear on the floor.

Julian's face purpled, his mouth twisted in a snarl. "My father's killers will be found, tried, and executed," he shouted. "I won't reveal anything that would jeopardize investigations."

Ivan could barely contain his elation. This was going better than he'd hoped.

Into the shocked hush, the Clerk intoned, "The Assembly recognizes the Member for Stour Coastal."

A portly woman stood and faced the throne. "I fully understand where the Emperor's heart lies. I, for one, do not need to see what muck ImpSec may have raked up."

Ivan's heart pounded. What was she up to? She sounded to be on Julian's side. Her tone and smile friendly and placating.

"We know the raids on our towns stem from the Firenzi," she continued. "Nobody has bothered to deny that. Now our shipping is under attack. Defenseless merchantmen." The friendliness evaporated. Her voice rang harsh and strident across the chamber. "All this talk of proof and the assassination is outdated and irrelevant. Yes, we want the

Emperor's assassins caught, but right *now* we need security inside our borders. Emperor Julian has his eye only on the first, not on the second."

A murmur of agreement rose like thundering surf. As the sound peaked and dwindled she spoke again, this time oozing concern. "This is understandable. Emperor Julian suffered a great tragedy at a tender age. It's only natural for that to be his overriding concern. That is why this Assembly must take matters into its own hands regarding the security of the imperium."

This was it. Ivan found himself on the edge of his seat. The veteran Assembly Member had called the mood in the room and rode the wave with practiced ease.

"I call for an emergency motion to bring our forces to full readiness, and to exercise our prerogative to take pre-emptive action to secure our borders."

———— ◆ ————

Chalwen managed a stiff-legged but steady pace through the palace grounds with Henri at her side. She gritted her teeth. "That whole steaming heap of shit-stirring started within days of the assassination."

Henri stared at her. "You're right. And yet what you've unearthed shows real sophistication. That would have taken time to arrange."

"That's what I thought. Surely the wheels must have been turning *before* the assassination."

"We know the assassination itself was a PDC effort, but all that"– Henri waved in the general direction of the ImpSec building half a mile behind them, and by implication the mess of analysis on Chalwen's desk that she'd shared with Simone, and now Henri–"came from a group inside the palace."

They skirted the hexagonal Fountain Court with its splashing water features and manicured rose beds. Chalwen paused by the senior family offices fronting one side of the courtyard. "We already know from the distinct styles of electronic interference there was a second group involved. What if they knew of the plot and had plans of their own? Something beyond PDC's goals?"

"You're getting back to that basement hideout, aren't you?"

"Seems too much coincidence that there'd be a *third* group plotting at exactly the same time."

"Point. So what next?"

"Chase down those leads." Chalwen turned and hobbled up a wide flight of stone steps and into the cool of the office. "Someone's brought us to a war footing, and this is the closest we've come to the seat of the fire. Simone is using the few we can trust in ImpSec to do the plod work."

"Makes sense." Henri lowered his voice. "If you're tying this back to someone on the Grand Duke's staff—"

"We need solid evidence or Ivan will trample us into a gooey mess. I know. But it's too damned slow, so we're going to rattle some cages and see who squawks."

Henri glanced at the doors Chalwen steered them towards. A look of understanding crossed his face. "What do you need from me?"

"Your presence. Just look menacing."

Chalwen's cane clacked an angry announcement as they marched from carpeted hallway onto the hardwood floor of the Grand Duke's staff office. A receptionist glanced up from his desk and started to rise as Chalwen plodded past. His protests died on his lips under Henri's withering glare.

A murmur of conversation faded away, leaving nothing more than the faint creak of furniture filling the hush. Neatly-groomed clerks gazed at Chalwen and Henri from two dozen desks arrayed with geometrical precision either side of an aisle down the center of the room. Polished oak doors near the windows at the far end led into the sanctums of the Grand Duke's Private Secretary, and of the Grand Duke himself.

Chalwen tucked her cane under one arm. She made a show of consulting her notepad and making a few annotations, before plodding to a more ornate desk occupying a prime spot by the windows. The snooty and elegantly coiffured man behind the desk tried to look down his nose at Chalwen, but his gaze kept flickering past her shoulder to where Henri lurked, silent and predatory.

"Harald Scorf." The ice in Chalwen's voice snapped his attention back to her. The Grand Duke's personal staff were accustomed to being treated with utmost deference. They'd have no answer to an unthinkable intrusion like this.

"Yes?" A waver in his voice revealed his inner turmoil.

"Huh!" She consulted her notepad again. "You look after all external relations for the Grand Duke. That would include handling media as well as lobbyists and commercial contacts."

"What's this about?" He recovered quickly. The Grand Duke didn't surround himself with milksops.

Chalwen ignored the question. "Would I be right to assume that any messaging the Grand Duke wishes to put out there would go through your hands? That would include covert and off-the-record messaging as well as above-board channels."

"You know damned well I won't discuss the Grand Duke's business."

Chalwen nodded as if he'd revealed a profound truth, and wrote more notes.

"This is outrageous. I'll call ..." His voice trailed off.

"Please," she said. "I *am* security. I trust you have no plans to leave the capital in the next week? There will be further questions."

The man spluttered. "Who in all of Unity do you think you are?"

"My deepest apologies, you are absolutely correct. I'm forgetting my position as a senior Imperial Security investigator." She smiled sweetly. "That was of course meant to be an order not a question." The smile vanished. "Be available when we need you."

Out in the hallway, Chalwen chuckled. "Man, that felt good. Hope you're ready for more harassment. We've got a diplomat's office, a judge, and a media mogul to shake down this afternoon."

Henri gave her a puzzled look. "What in Space was that about? Do you really think that stylus jockey back there handled the kind of material we're looking for?"

Chalwen grinned. "Not for a moment. That wasn't the point. But whoever *is* the string-puller in there will now wonder what the heck we know to go barging into Ivan's lair like that. Simone is standing by to see which lines light up."

An emergency security motion, Ivan reflected, as he crossed the Fountain Court from the Assembly Room to the family offices. Not quite a full declaration of war, but close enough. It would provoke an escalation from the Firenzi. The Assembly had taken the initiative out of Julian's hands, and they were only a step away from a motion of competence.

He felt a twinge of regret for the ordeal he was putting his nephew through. But, he steeled himself, it was necessary for the good of the empire.

A *competent* emperor could have spent the last weeks working behind the scenes, pulling strings, calling favors, making promises. Or Julian could have summoned a select committee of the most die-hard skeptics to be sworn in and shown the most sensitive of ImpSec's findings. They could have been convinced to bring enough Members around to stave off rash action. Even today, Julian could have promised a strong enough stance to placate the war hawks without tipping over into full-on war.

There were so many avenues open to a seasoned and competent ruler. Julian would learn in due course, after all Ivan still needed an heir once his own rule was done, but the boy would have to wait his turn.

Ivan was so close.

He reached his office and reviewed messages waiting for him from his staff, including a complaint from his media relationships manager.

All sense of wellbeing evaporated. Rage blinded him.

Bloody ImpSec!

Chapter 45

Year 8071, winter

W*rath of Empire* ran silent deep in Firenzi space, or as close to silent as a large warship ever went.

Gregor lounged in one corner of the primary operations room, set just behind the main command deck. He was technically off duty, but, like everyone else in the room, he carried gloves and a flash hood tucked into the belt of his utility overalls. He picked at a tray of food from the nearby ready room servery. On this months-long tour of duty behind enemy lines, there was no such thing as off duty. This operations room had been set aside for senior officers with suitable clearance to stay informed of any news without cluttering up the command deck itself.

The chances of being spotted in interstellar space were next to nonexistent, yet the support fleet remained alert in a state of high readiness—one step down from general quarters—at the rendezvous point. The nearest star lay two light years distant, the nearest inhabited world over fifty.

Ships routinely broadcast a unique signature to the nearest comms relay through the multidimensional folds that surrounded real space. This constant broadcast kept them hooked into the galactic network. In theory, nobody but Imperial Security could track the whereabouts of one of the Emperor's ships, but encryption could be broken, a risk they couldn't take. So comms were now shut down leaving them effectively blind and deaf, other than brief glimpses of the outside world brought to them by a steady stream of scout ships reaching out to the network at random intervals and at a safe distance from the rendezvous.

The same conditions that made discovery virtually impossible also worked against their mission: scouting for Firenzi fleet movements for hints of an invasion massing on the border. The chances of stumbling across a fleet in a volume a hundred light years cubed were about the same as picking the right grain of sand from a beach. And of course, a whole army of imperial cryptographers and comms analysts was working around the clock to glean insights into Firenzi movements through the comms net, but anything important would be running silent just as they were.

Instead, they relied on indirect clues, such as the covert monitoring of the main Firenzi naval bases and supply points.

A ripple of excitement ran through the room. "*Chancer* just checked in," one of the senior lieutenants called out.

"Where from?"

"Main naval base at Havel."

They waited an agonizing half hour while *Chancer* reported to Ivanka Borodina as the senior captain in the task force. Word had spread and the room was soon crowded with, as far as Gregor could tell, every off-duty officer on board. At last, the frigate's second officer appeared on the wall screen, free to discuss any findings that hadn't been deemed classified.

Captain Borodina knew her officers and those from other ships would exchange gossip to supplement the official reports cleared by the local ImpSec branch. Rather than drive it underground and provide a breeding ground for speculation, she believed in acknowledging the inevitable and making it above board. A well-informed senior company could make better tactical decisions. And bringing the gossip out into the open allowed ImpSec to better monitor the chatter.

"Our mission wasn't to observe directly," *Chancer's* officer was saying. "Of course, we did as a matter of SOP, but we're trying to keep a stable population of passive spy drones to monitor movements in and out of the base."

There was a rumble of agreement around the room. Use of drones was a standard tactic to limit the risk to warships.

"For the last month, we've been losing drones as fast as we can deploy them. But the Firenzi are even sharper now. They must have extended their own deep space network. We may be off the comms net but a ship puts out electromags as soon as it pops into realspace."

"How quickly were they onto you?"

"Twenty minutes at most. Not enough time to get a good look at Havel itself, and things got hot before we deployed more than forty drones. They must have a really dense grid."

"A grid with a few light minutes' spacing? That's a lot of sensors."

Something nagged at Gregor. "Presumably you hopped between drop-off points?"

"Sure, it's a quick drop and go, on to the next point."

"In which case with each hop you multiply the chances of appearing at least once near a sensor. Maybe the network isn't quite as dense as all that."

"All the same, we can't hang around long enough to be really useful."

And, thought Gregor, every time you dropped into realspace, you'd leave a ripple behind that would be picked up by sensors eventually. They'd triangulate your drop-off points and have a good chance of spotting the drones. No wonder you're losing them so fast.

"You didn't have much time in realspace," Gregor said, "so no real clear look at Havel itself, but you must have seen *something*."

"Yeah, here's the thing. You're right, we couldn't observe the system properly, but on a superficial scan it seemed almost empty."

"Why would that be?" someone across the room wondered. "That's a major base."

Icy fingers touched Gregor's spine. "It means they've emptied out the base. If we see the same pattern elsewhere it means they're assembling somewhere in deep space. Massing for an assault."

———•◆•———

The windowless room felt stifling despite the high ceiling, bright lights, and a whisper of ventilation barely audible beneath the babble of voices.

Emperor Julian sat at one end of the long table, flanked by the heads of the Admiralty and the diplomatic service. Half-way down the table, Commander Boris Stanhope presided over a small army of intelligence aides and analysts.

Maybe that was it, Chalwen mused, the sense of oppression. The weight of intellect seated opposite her was positively overwhelming, and the discussion too rarefied for mere mortals like her.

She glanced down the table at Julian. As if he sensed her attention, he looked up from the scroll on the table in front of him and flashed her the briefest flicker of an eye-roll. Nothing, she hoped, anyone else in the room would have noticed. That settled it. If the Emperor didn't care for abstruse explanations of communications theory, path analysis, and node associativity, then she wouldn't either.

Behind Boris, Grand Duke Ivan sat against the wall facing Chalwen, looking as sour as ever. Though maybe his obvious ill temper was the result of being relegated to the periphery, invited to this meeting as little more than a courtesy. Yes, Chalwen thought with an inward smile, that would piss him off.

"Enough of the theory, Commander Stanhope," Julian talked over the senior analyst, and addressed the Chief of Intelligence directly. "You have no need to impress me that your department knows its job, so if you please, can we have the layman's version now?"

The analyst looked flustered. Had he been showing off, or even trying to talk down to the young emperor? For a moment Chalwen wondered if he would try to continue with his lecture. He was saved from his indecision when Boris rose to his feet. The analyst plonked himself down with such obvious relief that Chalwen realized he'd been genuinely perplexed by Julian's interruption. Space alive, he really thought he'd been talking in plain terms. All the same, through the dense jargon Chalwen noted the similarities between the analyst's work and her own research into the rumor mill. The techniques, looking for patterns and connections, were similar. Only the underlying data was different.

"As you wish, Sire," Boris said. He paused a few moments to collect his thoughts. "We've been observing unusual communications over the last year. Of course, with so many billions of messages flowing through the interstellar relays every minute, it's hard to tease out signals of interest from the background noise. But ImpSec analysts *are* good at their job, as you noted so astutely, Sire, and they are on the lookout for signs of communications that don't want to be noticed."

"And they've found something."

"Indeed. The messages themselves are heavily encrypted, of course, probably with layered protocols, and fragmented and routed through different networks ..." He paused and coughed at a sharp glance from the Emperor. "We'll continue working on breaking the keys, but I don't hold out much hope of getting at the actual content of individual messages."

"Then what use is all this analysis?"

"Even without being able to read the messages, the patterns themselves are revealing, as are changes in the flow over time."

Chalwen found herself nodding as he explained.

"We've homed in on a few thousand key nodes that crop up repeatedly and which seem to form a stable network, along with many thousands of incidental branches."

"Okay." Julian leaned forward and propped his elbows on the table. "There must be millions of networks like that across space. Local governments, trading networks ... what makes this one special?"

"Both the furtiveness and the spatial and organizational spread. What we're seeing is typical of a dispersed network of agents collaborating, and the build up over time points to plans developing and coming to a head. Soon."

"Fair enough, but why is this a matter for this group?"

"I'm coming to that. The lines of connection are complex, but a major nexus is here on Magentis, and there's an even bigger nexus centered on Eloon."

"Eloon?"

"Here, Sire." One of the Intelligence aides pointed to the star chart. "A moderately prosperous world in the northern quarter of Firenzi space."

"We believe we are looking at a network of spies and agents spread across our own territory with tentacles into all the other Grand Families. The endpoints are as heavily obscured as the messages themselves, but they appear to include major merchant and manufacturing entities, heavy industry, arms and defense, government, and our own military."

This drew a gasp from the Admiralty chief.

Julian frowned. "You're not here just to present clever data. I assume you've also drawn some conclusions from all this."

The Intelligence chief nodded, and looked troubled. "We are already in a state of emergency, and close to war with Family Firenzi. I believe we are looking at a pre-emptive strike in the making."

"That's a big statement to make."

"This pattern is what I would expect to see from a network of spies seeking out intelligence such as fleet movements and points of weakness on our side, and funneling the data back to a central point. The fact that the central point is on a nondescript planet in foreign territory, but right in the middle of a network of bases close to our border is what makes me suspect a possible invasion." Stanhope paused for a deep breath. "The most obvious target is the Cutler Drift."

"The Cutler Drift?" Julian's voice was a strangled cry of outrage.

From where she sat at the edge of the room, Chalwen couldn't read the chart spread out on the table, but every child was taught the map of civilized space. She could clearly picture the region they were discussing. An offshoot from the main body of Skamensis space, three hundred light years across, and home to nearly a quarter of the systems directly controlled by Family Skamensis. The Cutler Drift had always been vulnerable, with vast walls of dust and dense thickets of stars forming a natural barrier to navigation, all but cutting it off from the main body of Skamensis space.

It was also closest to the borders with Firenzi space. Chalwen could see why it made an attractive target. A rich enough prize without risking a full frontal assault.

"What is the state of our defenses in that region?"

"Three *Swords* currently on patrol." Grand Admiral Gabriel bin Jovin sweated as he consulted the scroll in front of him. "Plus five heavy cruisers and numerous smaller craft ready to deploy from Cendithor."

He hummed to himself, forehead creased in concentration. At last he seemed to reach a decision. "I also have a *Sword* and support units managing a fleet of scouts inside Firenzi space near there. All the incursions we've suffered must be coming from somewhere, so we've been looking out for signs of offensive preparations."

"And ...?" Julian demanded.

"No direct observations to report as yet. The task force is running silent so we're not in direct contact with them. I'm expecting a report later today."

The Grand Admiral looked back to Stanhope. "Could this be a feint? Something to draw our forces away from the real objective?"

Boris shook his head. "The traffic is too dense and carried on for too long to just be a smokescreen. And there was no guarantee we'd ever have found it. A diversion's no good if it's never seen. No. The pattern we're seeing is legitimate and serves a purpose."

The Grand Admiral grimaced. "Doesn't mean someone won't take advantage of any holes we open up in our borders." He studied his scroll intently. "With your approval, Sire, we'll keep five *Swords* back to cover the rest of our territory. No major system should be beyond a two-week flight. And I'll call up all reserves of scouts and other light craft to set up a deep early warning blanket. I don't think one of the Families could launch an assault without ImpSec noticing, but there's a few outworld warlords who might take advantage while our attention is elsewhere."

———————

As Ivan climbed the stairs from the secure briefing room to his own office, the cool marble of the balustrade under his palm seemed to cool his own thoughts. During the briefing, he found it hard to control his expression while a multitude of possibilities tumbled through his mind. Now, in the luxurious hush of the senior imperial family office building, an almost religious quiet broken only by the rhythmic hiss of his feet on thick carpet, his muddled mental landscape came back into sharp focus. The initial rush of agitation passed, and his analytical mind functioned once more.

Imperial Security were worried about patterns of traffic that they assumed signaled an assault on Skamensis space. Ivan saw something entirely different. The pattern exposed by ImpSec matched exactly the kind of activity Bernie Fischer was looking for.

This looked like the support network that had been thwarting Ivan for so long. He schooled himself to patience. Looks might be deceiving, and he might be mistaken. But it was too much of a coincidence to ignore. In chasing down their own ghosts, it was possible that ImpSec had inadvertently exposed the agonizing thorn in Ivan's own side.

His mouth tightened, the long corridor with its priceless collection of paintings, tapestries, and sculptures, blurred. With the imperial family and all heirs out of the way he should have been sitting on the throne eighteen months ago. That plan had been thwarted by an over-ly-alert bodyguard, and his progress ever since had been hampered time and again by unseen hands. Worse, everywhere he looked, that smug bodyguard kept showing up.

He'd been patient for too long. His frustration threatened to boil over, but he had to hold himself together a while longer. His ambitions were almost within reach.

Bernie had warned him that someone in ImpSec was getting uncomfortably close. That unforgivable intrusion and veiled threats to his own staff, and even some of Ivan's more streetwise political and business contacts had seen subtle signs ... watchers lurking on street corners, people asking questions about seemingly innocuous matters, minor acts of official harassment. Fury again threatened to overwhelm him. Insufferable.

Wherever they were operating from lay beyond even Bernie's reach. Somewhere in Stanhope's part of the organization. That was all he could tell for sure.

That bloody lieutenant had something to do with his setbacks, he knew it. And with ImpSec sniffing far too close, the time for caution had ended. He needed to act now with overwhelming force to bring the situation back under control.

Even an all-out war with the Firenzi was by now a small price to pay. It was inevitable now anyway, thanks to Honorina Philip's unasked-for interventions in deep space. Ivan was not a gambling man, but he had no hesitation in rolling the dice when the situation called for it. He knew his next moves were a risk. In gambling terms, he was going all in.

A chill ran up his spine at the enormity of what he had in mind. The risk was great, and the collateral damage unprecedented. But when Ivan set that against the alternatives, he knew it was the best hope he had of setting his future back on course.

One ray of sunshine brightened Ivan's dark world. Julian was over-whelmed with the crisis exploding on his borders, too busy to look after more mundane matters. In desperation, he'd signed over authorization codes that allowed Ivan to act directly on his behalf.

The naive youngster didn't fully appreciate the gravity of what he'd done. Ivan had persuaded him that it was perfectly normal practice to delegate imperial powers in this way. With those codes, nobody other than Julian himself would know that orders issued by Ivan hadn't come direct from the Emperor.

It was clear that Julian trusted Ivan to act behind the scenes. In fact, that unofficial delegation was what had gained Ivan admittance today to what was supposed to be purely a security briefing on the Firenzi situation. Ivan's scalp crawled at the thought of such serendipity. He might otherwise never have learned of the key to eliminating once and for all the heart of the Emperor's secret network.

Eloon. Who'd have thought it? Setting up a secret headquarters operating from Firenzi space was an inspired move. Risky, but breathtakingly audacious. That had Paul's fingerprints all over it, and Julian had clearly inherited the machinery, whether he realized it or not.

When he reached his suite of offices, Ivan dismissed the handful of staff still there and closed the outer door. He carried out his usual sweep for listening devices and engaged countermeasures, then he summoned Bernie Fischer.

The necessary orders to deal with Eloon would take time, but then it was finally time to do some serious house-clearing.

Chapter 46

Year 8071, spring

"The Emperor is expecting you in the Office of Deliberation directly after breakfast."

The call had come from the Emperor's administration office. Some flunky Chalwen couldn't quite place by name, even though the snotty arrogance of the voice should have been memorable. She frowned. "That wasn't in my diary."

"Then it's just as well I reminded you."

Chalwen bit back a snarky retort at the smug tone. She could hardly be reminded of something she'd never known about. But she *did* know it was pointless to argue, and the Emperor could summon anyone at any time without a need to justify himself.

"I'll be there."

Chalwen glanced down at her wrinkled clothes, and pushed herself away from her desk. There was no sense of the passing hours deep in the sub-basements of Imperial Security headquarters. She could go days at a time without seeing sunlight. She checked there was still enough of the night left to make it worth hitting a real bed before her appointment. How many days had it been?

Until the call had broken into her thoughts, she hadn't realized just how tired she was. While Simone's team delved into their investigations into the Grand Duke's office, sometimes with subtlety and sometimes rattling more trees to see what fell out, Chalwen painstakingly assembled the fragments into the first glimpses of a picture.

She needed to be presentable for the Emperor, and at least somewhat rested. The quickest route to the staff quarters took her through the labyrinth of tunnels under the palace. The safest too. In her past life, Chalwen considered being accosted by vagrants or drunks in the streets around the palace as nothing more than an annoyance. Her manner discouraged all but those too inebriated to be really harmful, and she used to be able to look after herself. Now, she wasn't so sure. The poisoned nerves in her legs limited her workouts, and being deskbound played havoc with her fitness.

At least she still refused the lure of elevators to carry her up to ordinary basement depth, even if the climb now left her breathless as well as aching. And she was going days at a time without resorting to the use of a cane.

A bright-lit carpeted corridor stretched in either direction at the top of the stairs, turning at the ends to form a half-mile loop through the main basement level. The only signs of life at this hour were around the entrance to the security operations room to her right, a round-the-clock hive of activity. She crossed into a smaller hallway and past a guard station. Sets of locked doors opened when they detected her passkey. The last one thunked closed behind her, and she was out of the ImpSec secure zone and into the warren under the palace.

The air here was several degrees warmer, and sweat beaded on Chalwen's face at the sudden temperature change. She longed for a proper shower, then bed.

In the distance, a porter slowly pushed a wheeled bin along the service corridor. As she got closer, a prickle of unease tugged at Chalwen. There was something familiar about the man, about the way he hunched over the handle of the bin as he shuffled along. She couldn't quite place him, but she was sure he wasn't any part of cleaning or maintenance crews.

She reached for the stud of her lapel transmitter. Her finger never made contact. A jolt like cold electricity froze her. The floor rose to meet her, but darkness claimed her before she hit. Her last thought was that she finally recognized the porter. He was one of Lieutenant Shan Bresk's crew, Ivan's bodyguard.

———— • ————

"I recognize this planet," Una murmured. "See the main land mass with three circular seas?"

Gregor squinted. Wispy cloud obscured much of the surface, but straggly lines of green and beige showed through in sweeping arcs enclosing patches of blue deepening to black.

"That's pretty distinctive. That's Eloon."

Gregor cocked an eyebrow at Una.

"There's no military targets here," she hissed.

"Unless the Firenzi navy is massing nearby, but I see nothing on the tactical plots." Gregor suppressed a shiver of unease. "We've been sent here for a reason."

The massed fleet, now comprising seven *Swords*, lurked on the fringes of the system, an ominous scatter of icons on the tactical plot. Fingers of ice crawled up Gregor's spine. With no opposing navy nearby, a force of *Swords* had only one purpose holding station a light hour out from a defenseless planet.

A document appeared on his desktop, tagged with a "priority" flag. Gregor stared at it, frozen into immobility.

"Sir ... Commander!"

Una's voice broke through the fog that seemed to have buried him. "We have battle orders."

Gregor's hands seemed to belong to someone else, moving of their own accord to enter the authorization codes necessary to unlock the document.

He stared in shock at the contents. The headings were clear, the source of the orders unambiguous. This had come direct from the Emperor himself. But the contents of the orders were unreadable.

"There's a second layer of encryption," he gasped. He exchanged looks with Una.

She swallowed. "Then this is the highest level directive. An action that will put us on a war footing."

Gregor's mind was racing. He remembered these secrecy protocols from training exercises, but never expected to see them used in anger.

Both Una and Gregor turned at a cough behind them. An Imperial Security officer stood over them, flanked by four guards. Their weapons were drawn and ready. Gregor became aware of a deathly hush in the combat operations room.

"If you please, Sir." The officer's voice was polite but uncompromising. "Load the orders, and I'll provide the code for full decryption."

Numb, Gregor had no alternative. If he refused, he'd be executed on the spot and Una would have to take his place. This was a burden he refused to lay on anyone else. His mind screamed misgivings as unfeeling fingers on autopilot dropped the file into Maestro's waiting portal.

The officer entered his own codes and locked the tactical objectives, now readable, into the system.

Gregor stared at the mission objectives. Beside him, Una gasped and let out a tiny cry, hastily muffled.

Even the surly ImpSec officer cursed under his breath. "That's it, then," he muttered as the confirmation set of orders entered by the First Officer on the command deck matched. "I wouldn't like to think what those poor buggers did to deserve this."

Nothing, Gregor thought. Nothing warrants this.

Full planetary Cleansing. Gregor still couldn't believe what he was seeing. All human settlements, and total destruction of the ecosystem. This was the scenario that Maestro's automated system had been designed for. Orders that a human might baulk at carrying out.

Orders given by an emperor he had trusted.

There had to be a mistake.

Gregor tried to appear casual as he stood and picked up his notepad. "Take the hot seat for a minute, Lieutenant. I need a few moments' privacy before the engagement starts."

Una Spelze frowned up at him. Gregor hope the sweat running down his cheek wasn't too noticeable. He staggered slightly, his vision blurring, as he made his way to the ready room at the back of the operations center. He entered the nearest washroom and bolted the door.

It took three tries, furiously wiping sweat from his jittery hands, before Gregor succeeded in opening the secure comms package on his notepad. He entered the access codes and engaged the direct line to his Hidden Light colleagues.

It took an age for the comms link to come live. Gregor was dimly aware of a furious pounding on the door.

"Firenzi planet Eloon targeted for Cleansing. Repeat, Firenzi planet Eloon targeted for Cleansing. Alert civilian population and find the Emperor. There must be a mistake."

Electrical discharges crackled behind him. The door slammed open. Gregor turned, holding his notepad in front of him like a shield.

The first bolt shattered the notepad.

The second ...

Fire burned through Chalwen's limbs. Clarity returned. And pain. She didn't try to open her eyes just yet, but instead took stock of her injuries. The effects of the drug washed away and the pain dwindled to a dull ache from bruises all over her body, but, she concluded, it was all superficial. The results of her fall and likely some rough handling since.

How in Space had they managed to snatch her like that, in the heart of the palace? And how had they known where she'd be? She stifled a gasp at the obvious thought. That call from the Emperor's office. There was no audience this morning, and the call had not come from anyone on his admin staff.

"Come on," a voice growled nearby. "You've had the antidote. You're awake. Quit playing around."

Chalwen cracked open an eye and groaned. A more careful self-check told her she was tied to a chair.

It was cold. Dry air wafting past her cheek brought a whiff of ancient dust. She must still be in the palace. Her passkey would be recorded if they'd tried to take her out through any of the controlled gates. Unless, she shivered at the thought, they had access to tamper with gate records.

Blearily, she glanced sideways to find the source of the voice. She recoiled at the closeness of the leering face. A name finally surfaced. She had only ever heard him referred to as Stewie. One of Ivan's worse thugs, nimble despite his stooped and awkward appearance, and famed for his skill with anything sharp.

"His Lordship will be pleased to finally see the back of you," he said.

His oily voice churned Chalwen's stomach. "What the fuck would Ivan want with me?"

"Doesn't take kindly to people getting in his way."

That confirmed Chalwen's suspicions. The rot in the palace went all the way to the Grand Duke. Someone behind her hissed. Seems they also recognized Stewie's slip.

"Aw, give over, Beth. This one's troublemaking days are done." The casual malice in his tone chilled Chalwen.

"You're both right, of course," a cheerful voice on Chalwen's other side announced. "She's not talking to anyone outside this room, but I'll be the one to say if and when we relax protocols." Ivan's fixer, Bernie Fischer, strolled into view. "But the damage is done, so we're all out in the open. Stewie, we'll be having words later about that little mistake."

Stewie's face paled.

"But," Bernie continued, "you can redeem yourself by how well you apply your skills to the good lieutenant here. Think of it as a teensy bit of extra motivation." He turned back to Chalwen and leaned close. In a conspiratorial tone he whispered, "Of course, a man shouldn't need external motivation to pursue his passion, now, should he?"

To stem the terror threatening to numb her, Chalwen tried to take stock of her situation. She had vital information for Simone and Henri, but how to get it there? She'd already tested her bonds and found them firm. She couldn't be sure with her limited range of vision, but the chair leg felt cold against her calf. Metal. Not good. May be heavy and likely not breakable.

Aside from Stewie and Bernie in front of her, there was at least one person, Beth, behind her. In her extreme peripheral vision there also seemed to be someone else standing silent and watchful a few feet away. Chalwen decided that was probably it. A hit squad like this would be as small as possible to limit the chances of discovery or of someone leaking information. Not that it mattered unless she could somehow free her hands.

The lapel of her shirt was torn where someone had ripped out her comms. No chance of reaching the transmit stud with her chin.

"You sly dog!" Bernie's eyes widened in mock amazement. "You're conducting a situation check. Even restrained like this you're looking for a way out." His manner turned brisk and businesslike. "You've been a right royal pain in the ass, and you're stubborn as all hell. I know it's

ImpSec's job to pry, but you're proving too darned good at it. I wonder just how much do *you* know?"

So, they were going to question her. She still had time to string this out and look for an opening.

Bernie shrugged. "Well, my curiosity will have to remain unsatisfied. His Lordship looks forward to seeing Stewie's handiwork. He expects to see proof that you've been suitably punished for all the trouble you've caused him."

Goosebumps ran up Chalwen's neck. This was revenge, not an interrogation. She pulled against her bindings once more.

Bernie tutted. "All in good time, of course. He's the other side of the planet right now, well away from events unfolding in Prandis. Speaking of which, I am needed elsewhere, so I'll leave you in my team's capable hands."

With Bernie gone, Stewie smiled and dropped an electrician's toolbox on the floor in front of him. He seemed to be taking his time, savoring the moment. Chalwen was sure the box didn't hold a typical tradesman's tools.

She flinched at a pair of sharp cracks that echoed from the shadows. In front of her, Stewie jerked and spasmed. Behind her, a muffled thud suggested another body hitting the floor.

The mysterious figure moved. Although Chalwen craned her neck she couldn't get a good look at ... him, she decided from a glimpse of his build before he crouched behind her. Her heart thumped. A whisper of steel.

"Shock rounds."

Puzzlement turned to understanding. "Non-lethal, and won't trigger detectors like a beam pistol would."

"It'll keep them quiet for maybe fifteen minutes. Now I'm going to free your hands. Don't do anything stupid."

"Why?" Even as she spoke, she realized the question could be read different ways. Especially with her reputation for doing stupid things.

"Tungsten," he murmured.

Hairs on Chalwen's neck stood on end at the sound of her Hidden Light code name.

"Dovecote," he added. "I recognize you from the Josef jailbreak. I didn't share my real identity, too risky, but I admire those of you who did." He sliced the industrial tape binding Chalwen's wrists.

"How did a member of the Light get mixed up in this lot?"

"Long story. Stanhope tasked me with getting close to Ivan's crew, but now I need to disappear. Friends will be along soon, and there'll be too many awkward questions if I'm found here."

"Friends ...?"

"I know you work closely with Hawkwind. I messaged him with your location."

"Henri ... Look, you don't need to leave. You could be useful still, and we can hide you."

He gave a quiet chuckle. "My cover's blown now. I show my face anywhere in Prandis I'm a dead man, but I think it was in a good cause. I need to leave town, maybe get off-planet, before the people I've been mixing with catch up with me. They know I was part of this squad, so they'll ask questions when I'm found to be missing. I can hardly wander back to them and say 'Hey, look, I got away!' Whatever you're doing, you must be hitting some nerves. Keep it up."

A knife dropped into Chalwen's lap. She recognized it as her own, presumably removed along with anything else useful when they brought her down here. By the time she'd freed her legs, she was alone.

But not for long.

She had rummaged through Stewie's toolbox, ignoring assorted implements that had nothing to do with electricity, and some that very definitely did. She found a roll of heavy duty tape and was in the process of binding Stewie's hands when a whisper of stealthy footfall on stone startled her.

Chalwen heaved a weak sigh of relief when Simone entered the pool of yellow light cast by a pair of free-standing glowtubes. "That was quick."

Simone took just a moment to flick her gaze around the room before she relaxed and lowered a small stun pistol similar to the one Dovecote must have used. "I have an analyst receiving reports of all surveillance glitches, no matter how small. This one fit the profile of the interference prior to the assassination, so it rang alarm bells. Then Henri got an anonymous tip."

Three more people followed Simone into the dim-lit cellar. Chalwen recognized one of them as being a member of Sanitation. That helped ease some of the tension stringing her up like garroting wire. Even though she didn't know the other two, they all worked as a team, scouring the area for threats and evidence.

"You seem to have things under control," Simone said, "but clearly you had help."

"Long gone. Sorry. Where are we?"

"Deep under the Assembly Rooms, beneath the legislative archives. Level fourteen, if I counted correctly."

Simone surveyed the scene again and turned her attention to their captives. Chalwen had finished binding Stewie, and one of her team was securing the woman Stewie had called Beth. "Looks like these two are still in the land of the living. They'll wish they weren't, soon enough. Wonder if we'll get anything useful out of them."

They were starting to regain consciousness. One of the rescue team casually stunned them again. He raised an eyebrow at Simone's quizzical look. "There's a cart down the hall and a working service elevator a hundred yards away. They'll be easier to handle as raw meat rather than walking trouble."

Simone shrugged. "You know what to do with them." While the clean-up crew bundled the comatose prisoners into the wheeled bin that Stewie had been pushing, Simone turned to Chalwen. "You seem to've had a lucky escape."

"You were on your way." Chalwen's attempt to make light of the situation wasn't fooling anyone. "I was hoping they'd let slip some more information while they questioned me."

"All the same, how come you had help on the inside?"

"Happy coincidence. Stanhope has people infiltrating Ivan's network. One of them happened to be in the right place. I'm not complaining." She tried to stand, and her legs buckled under her. She collapsed back to the floor and gathered her strength for another try. "I did learn one thing. Ivan's pet fixer was here, in person."

"Fischer?"

Chalwen nodded. "And Ivan himself is pulling the strings." She massaged her legs. Damn! Whatever drug they hit her with could be reacting with her poisoned nerve endings. "I'll need some clean clothes and my stick, then we need to wake the Emperor. There's something big going on. Fischer mentioned events in progress."

With Simone's help, Chalwen struggled through the underground maze to the staff quarters. She sat on the edge of her bed while Simone rummaged in her closet for a change of clothing. She was just shrugging into a clean tunic when an orderly hammered on the door and burst in without waiting for an answer.

"Lieutenant ap Gwynodd?" he gasped out between gulps of breath. "The Emperor is calling for you. Imperial warships are attacking a planet in Firenzi space."

"Wha ... ?" Chalwen tried to untangle the words. For a moment they were a meaningless mush in her mind, then they sprang into shocking clarity.

With hands seemingly on autopilot, she finished buttoning her tunic while she quizzed the orderly.

"A distress call came in twenty minutes ago," he said. "We have comms analysts verifying the source."

"The Emperor?"

"Talking to the senior fleet captain as we speak." As Chalwen pulled on boots he added, helpfully, "In the imperial quarters."

Thankfully not too far. The dump of adrenaline dulled the pain in her legs, but she grabbed her cane anyway and sprint-hobbled to the door and down the stairs of the staff quarters.

The chill of the desert night snatched her breath away and a sharp stab like ice ran up her leg. The imperial quarters loomed ahead. Bright lights obscured the stars and washed out the inky night sky above her.

Somewhere up there, someone was starting an interstellar war.

Not for a moment did she believe this was the young Emperor's doing.

She sprinted up flights of stairs, ignoring the protest of damaged nerve endings by counting each step and each landing as she went. Guards saluted as she past, but she barely acknowledged them.

A few feet from the door to the Emperor's bedchamber, Chalwen slowed her pace and calmed her breathing. An ashen-faced guard at the door nodded recognition and pushed open the door for her.

Chalwen hobbled through, relieved to see Doctor Vicky already there, as well as Colonel bin Merrin and Boris Stanhope. The latter had brought with him a grey-robed member of his Intelligence staff. Not someone Chalwen knew. ImpSec had a whole building full of anonymous agents who were never seen outside their lair except in his presence.

Emperor Julian strode back and forth at one end of the bed, his voice a tightly-controlled monotone as he talked to a sharp-featured woman in captain's uniform flickering life-size on the wall screen.

"What are you doing in Firenzi space?" Red and gold robes flapped open around him as he paced.

A fraction of a second's delay as the signal traversed the network of intra-space comms relays. "Orders from the Admiralty, Sire."

Julian shot a furious glare at Chalwen. "There you are! You were in the briefings. Am I mis-remembering something? My orders were to secure our border and scout for fleet movements, not mount an incursion." He turned back to the captain. "I'll have someone's head for this, but right now why are you launching an attack? We are not at war. Damned close, but not yet. Until now."

The captain looked confused. "The Cleansing order came directly from you! It was under your seal, and doubly encrypted. We had no sight of the content until after the ImpSec commander here had applied a secondary key. He assured me the orders had to come straight from the Mosaic Palace."

Cleansing? Chalwen's legs weakened under her and she gripped her cane until her knuckles cracked. Had she really heard that right? Cleansing. All signs of life wiped clean from a planet's surface.

Someone on the command deck behind the captain called out, "Two minutes to next target."

Next target? The attack was already under way. Chalwen caught Doctor Vicky's eye. The tutor seemed close to collapse. "Which planet?" Chalwen whispered.

"Eloon." The answer came out as a frightened squeak, but it confirmed Chalwen's assumption. Eloon. A moderately prosperous world. How many millions of people were being killed right now?

"Well, cancel the order! Call off the attack." Somehow, Julian's tone was still icy calm, but a wild desperation had crept into his eyes.

"The commands are locked into our battle system. I need a countermanding order from you to return control to my officers."

"I just gave you a damned order!" Julian's voice broke in frustration.

"No, I mean an order in an imperial fleet message form that we can deliver to the battle system."

Chalwen's heart sank. "I thought Emperor Paul had stopped all work on those kinds of systems," she muttered to herself.

"I have the forms here, Sire." The intelligence officer had been working furiously on her notepad the whole time. "Captain, I need the original order number from the package you received."

Chalwen gave the officer an appraising stare. Not some mindless flunkey at all, the young woman seemed unflustered by the world-shattering events she was party to. Instead, she talked and moved with cool efficiency. Still anonymous, though. Chalwen didn't recognize her, which was odd because her pale complexion was unusual in Prandis.

The captain rattled off a string of letters and numbers from off-screen, which the intelligence officer repeated to her. "Here, Sire, sending to your scroll. You need to sign it and I'll transmit it."

An anxious minute passed while the officer and Emperor conferred. All the while, a running tally of destruction sounded in the background from somewhere on the distant warship's command deck.

The captain reappeared, looking relieved. "We have the message packet. Thank you, Sire." She turned to face someone out of view. "Distribute this to all units in the fleet. Top priority."

The atmosphere in the room eased noticeably. Julian's mouth twisted. "Well, that's that. But this is still a disaster of the first order. There will be an Imperial Board of Inquiry to answer questions on where these orders came from. I regard this as an act of treason."

The Emperor sank onto the edge of the bed in little more than a controlled fall.

"But first, I'll need to meet with the diplomatic corps immediately and figure out how to stop this spiraling into all-out war. Captain Borodina, presumably we have detailed intel on Eloon. I need an estimate of civilian casualties."

The captain seemed not to have heard. She was in heated discussion with someone off-screen. "That's not possible," she barked. "Try again."

"Same result," the unseen officer reported. "Authorization mismatch."

Julian turned grey. "What do you mean, authorization mismatch?"

The captain glanced back and forth between the Emperor and something to one side. She looked flustered. "The system recognizes you as Emperor Julian Skamensis, but there's something in the encryption headers that doesn't match the original order. To all intents and purposes, it's as if the order was given by—and can only be countermanded by—a *different* Julian Skamensis."

"That's not possible."

A cynical portion of Chalwen's mind wondered why people kept claiming things were impossible, despite the evidence in front of them.

Boris frowned. "Unless someone else has access to the authorization codes of the Imperial Seal."

Julian and Chalwen exchanged looks. A shock of understanding flashed between them. *Ivan.*

"Regardless," Julian protested, "it's still the same seal, the same codes."

"But," the young officer said, "if someone else used the Seal, the embedded biometrics from your passkey would be different. Depending on how tightly the order was bound to personal identity, that could make all the difference."

"Is there no higher level authority I can use to override the orders in place?"

"The Imperial Seal is the highest authority in the empire."

"Back doors?" asked Chalwen. "Emergency protocols, in case the Emperor is incapacitated?"

"We've already tried everything we can think of," the captain said.

"Errm …" Doctor Vicky hesitated at the sudden focus on her. "This is a bit theoretical, but what about line of succession?"

Boris looked thoughtful. Chalwen had no idea what the tutor was suggesting, and was glad when Julian's questioning stare showed he was as much at a loss.

"If the person who issued the order dies," Doctor Vicky added, "the successor would be able to countermand it."

"Hah!" Boris's short-lived outburst startled Chalwen. "Nice try, but I can't see a way to make that work. In normal circumstances, with a true succession, you're right. But the order would need to be accompanied by a legal declaration of death and succession. In this case, how can Julian succeed himself?"

"Or, to put it another way," Julian said, "how do we prove the death of someone who doesn't exist? I'd slit his throat myself if that's what it takes."

"No. The only solution is for the imposter to issue the countermanding order in person."

"Where is the Grand Duke?" Cold fury edged Julian's words.

Colonel bin Merrin coughed. "Stalking a Grant's Stag in the Chensing wilderness. The hunting lodge confirmed they set out this morning by air cruiser then on foot. Both the Grand Duke and his security detail are out of comms reach."

How convenient, Chalwen thought. And that was fast. The colonel must have come to the same realization that she had.

"I can send a flyer out to their location and have him in comms contact within the hour."

"We don't have an hour," the warship captain announced from five hundred light years away. "And I fear it's already too late to make any real difference. All major cities and large towns have been destroyed. The fleet is maneuvering for a final broad sweep to burn the countryside."

"Can you not disable the ship while we figure out an answer?"

"What do you think we've been doing all this time?" the captain snapped. She visibly shook herself. "Forgive me, Sire. As soon as the legitimacy of the order came into doubt, I and every captain in the fleet realized we couldn't wait for a counter-order. We started doing exactly as you just suggested."

Julian gazed blankly at the wall.

"The main weapon bay is not accessible under battle conditions. I already have teams of engineers physically disconnecting power lines in. But the connections are redundant and the weapon bay itself has backup capacity. And the ship's drive is just as hard to disable, at which point we fall out the sky."

"Are you saying you really have no control over your own ship?"

"With due respect, Sire, large warships are intentionally hard to cripple. All these systems were designed not to be bypassed, in case a captain and crew objected to an imperial decree."

Finally, the captain faced the comms screen once more. Her face was lined, and monsters haunted the depths of her eyes. "Mission objectives complete. We have command of the ship once more. It is done."

Julian shook himself, as if from a deep sleep. He turned to look each person in the eye. "I've no doubt you will leave here with questions in your mind, and you will hear rumors and speculation in the days to come. The memory of what happened here you will take with you to your graves." He looked back at the comms screen. "Captain Borodina, this imperial command applies also to everyone on your ship who was privy to this last hour of consultation. Imprint this on your memory and do not stray from this version of events."

There was a long silence.

"Emperor Julian Skamensis ordered a Cleansing." He swallowed, and a tear clung to his cheek. "And the records will show that is *exactly* what happened."

A heavy mist rolled across the slope of the mountain, deadening the splashing of water in the valley below. Ivan narrowed his eyes, imprinting on his memory the distant outline of the stag before it vanished behind a grey veil.

Carefully, he turned to meet the eyes of his ruddy-faced local guide. With small hand signals he asked if the mist was likely to stay.

An hour, maybe two, the guide signed back. Ivan glanced skywards. A diffuse circle of blue hovered, faded, then reappeared. Yes, he could see this burning off in time. The guide spread a waterproof blanket, the fabric designed to minimize the sound of rustling. With slow movements, Ivan unslung and set down his composite bow, and settled cross-legged on the blanket. In this visibility the stag might stay put. The hunt was still on. All he needed was patience.

Patience out here on this mountainside Ivan was well-practiced in. Here, and a hundred wildernesses like it. But patience was harder to come by in the wider hunt unfolding in parallel across the light years. Ivan's breath caught in his throat as plans paraded through his mind. Committed. Unstoppable. Events he'd set in motion would be coming to a head about now. A move of overwhelming aggression that the Firenzi couldn't possibly ignore. Julian would guess where the attack had come from, but he could never admit it. Even if he did, who'd believe him? Any attempts to disavow the actions carried out in his name would be easily spun into a tale of craven avoidance, or negligence, or incompetence.

And once the second part of Ivan's play came into effect, with Operation Ghost Town in motion and ImpSec's Chief of Intelligence disgraced, Julian's weak grip on his own administration would be laid bare before the Assembly. The atrocity now unfolding would be seen to be a hideous mistake. This time, they'd have to act.

A crash in the distance, then silence. From long experience, Ivan knew the stag had sensed their presence and bolted. He stifled a pang of disappointment and exchanged looks with the guide, who shrugged.

That just about summed it up. This hunt had never been about the kill, after all. With no further need for stealth, Ivan stood. He did a mental calculation. He'd been in hiding long enough; it was time to rejoin civilization.

———————

Chalwen ran a hand through her hair. Shock would come later, along with grief, anger, and a constellation of raw emotions, but it was too much to process right now. A cold and calculating intensity washed over her. She glanced at Boris Stanhope, then turned to Julian. "Sire, I'm going to clear the room. There is a matter of imperial security we need to discuss."

A glimmer of understanding lit Stanhope's eyes as Chalwen ushered everyone out.

Colonel bin Merrin looked set to protest, especially when Chalwen signaled Skinner, the squad leader on duty this evening, to clear even the bodyguards.

"Colonel," she said, "I'm in no position to give you orders but I believe Commander Stanhope will confirm my request that no one else can be privy to the conversation we need to have with the Emperor."

Colonel bin Merrin glanced at the Commander, who nodded.

When the three of them were alone in the bedchamber, Chalwen sank wearily into the nearest chair.

"Lieutenant," Stanhope snapped, "this is a security breach of the highest order. If the Imperial Seal has been compromised I need to launch a full investigation without delay."

Good. He'd understood the real issue here. A planet full of dead people was a tragedy, but the safety of many planets hung in the balance. The first, they could do nothing about, but the second was very definitely in need of addressing. "The Seal has been compromised, but I don't think an investigation will be needed." She turned to Julian. "Will it, Sire?" she added gently.

Julian grimaced and locked eyes with Chalwen. She held her breath, willing him to remember his training and hoping to Space and beyond that Doctor Vicky had also instilled the honesty and accountability she needed to see now.

For a moment, all Chalwen saw was a terrified young boy, then he straightened and the Emperor stood before them, hard and commanding. "You're correct. I gave the Grand Duke authority to act on my behalf. I see that was a big mistake, but what's done is done."

Stanhope's jaw dropped.

This wasn't the right time to go into details of how Ivan had persuaded Julian to hand him such power. It went against everything he should have known, as emperor. But then, she reflected, Julian had been thrust into the role too soon and under traumatic conditions, and he'd had no one with experience of all the pitfalls to teach him any better.

Add to that the admiration the youngster showed his uncle, and she could easily see Ivan making light of this surrender of power. Hell, she could imagine him convincing Julian it was standard practice. With all the hours the two of them spent alone together, who would be able to advise him differently?

She made a mental note to speak to someone on the security side of ImpSec about this kind of vulnerability. The office of emperor should come with an instruction manual. But to more pressing matters, she said, "This cannot be allowed to become known. People need faith in the integrity of the Emperor's word."

Glancing between Chalwen and Stanhope, Julian seemed to have finally grasped the enormity of what he'd done. He swallowed, then squared his shoulders once more. "Commander, there is no mystery here. The fault is mine, so you can turn your energies to first securing the Seal, issuing me with new authentication codes, and then ensuring no record remains of the confusion over countermanding the Cleansing order."

Chalwen wondered how much longer the young emperor could keep up the brave front he was putting on. When she left this room, she'd seek out Doctor Vicky and Marcus Tyee to keep Julian close company. As Emperor he had a job to do, a role to play. Many of the people around him did too, and would only show their official faces in his presence. But right now the thirteen-year-old boy on the throne needed friends as well.

Stanhope had recovered from his shock and now looked thoughtful. "I will have to take a small team into our confidence on this—"

"For starters," Chalwen interrupted, "I know of two people within the division who can be trusted totally."

Stanhope speared Chalwen with a fierce look, then his shoulders sagged. "I'm guessing these are people you've already worked with on your various investigations. So be it. It's a start. Fleet comms and ships' logs will be tricky but can be addressed with care. We'll have to do something about the fleet message packets and their encrypted biometrics."

"I guess they could be corrupted to hide the mismatch?"

"That leaves the comms from this end. All communications from the Emperor are automatically filed in the research archives."

"No records," Julian repeated. "Not even in the secured archive."

"You understand what you're asking?" Stanhope's eyes bulged.

"I'll have to stand in front of the Assembly and announce that I've put down a real threat to our borders. There can be nothing to contradict that claim."

Space alive, Chalwen thought, this youngster had actually been thinking several moves ahead the whole time. "That's why you declared ownership of the order." She nodded, eying Julian with even deeper respect. Somehow, in the depths of an unimaginable crisis, he'd realized the path he needed to tread. Chalwen had seen the determination in his eyes when he'd issued his final orders to the people in the room and in the distant fleet. At the time, she'd put it down to an immature need to be seen to be in control, but now she saw it was the only way he could hope to keep control of the empire through the days to come. The people and the Assembly needed to know without a shadow of doubt who was in charge.

The hunting party toiled on foot down the long shoulder of the mountain. Lush green and scattered thickets of trees were broken by slate grey outcrops and escarpments where the highlands stepped down in rough terraces to an expanse of glistening wetland. They followed a barely-perceptible trail tracing a safe course along the treacherous slope. The fog had long since cleared, leaving blue sky slashed with heavy clouds that promised a drenching by nightfall.

As they rounded a knoll, the party's grounded air cruisers came into sight. Unease clenched Ivan's stomach. Alongside his personal cruiser sat a squat troop transport in imperial livery. He was expecting an emergency summons back to Prandis once the fireworks started, but they could have simply sent a message to Ivan's crew. The presence of a military escort suggested an altogether higher level of urgency.

Or they could simply be providing air cover to protect the Grand Duke in what must now be tense times. He tried to relax. There was no point trying to second-guess how people in the palace would be reacting.

Ivan showed no undue hurry as they descended the last quarter mile. He cast a critical eye over the camp his servants had set up alongside the hunt's cruisers in his absence. His own tent sat opposite a long ridge tent where the servants would bunk. Making the third side of a square, an open-side pavilion sheltered several camp tables. In the middle of it all, a fire pit already flamed and crackled.

But there was clearly something amiss. A full squad of troops, not part of Ivan's contingent, patrolled the wilderness camp. Ivan's own crew eyed them with outright hostility, and the troops' weapons were held in readiness.

A lieutenant strode out to meet Ivan. After a moment's recollection Ivan placed him. Javarro. One of the old Crown Prince's guard. Now promoted, apparently. "What's all this about, Lieutenant? I was planning on another week out here, so you must have good reason to interrupt my hunting." Inwardly, his thoughts roiled. Why would a member of the imperial bodyguard be tasked with the duties of a messenger?

"My apologies, Sire, you're to accompany us immediately." The lieutenant's tone held no contrition. On the contrary, his manner was unnaturally brusque for addressing a noble of Ivan's standing. Anxiety knotted his guts with renewed force. Something had gone wrong.

"Is there trouble at the palace?" Ivan fought to keep the growing panic from his voice, although some show of concern would be natural given the unusual circumstances.

The lieutenant didn't answer, but simply gestured to the rear loading ramp.

Ivan shrugged and said to his hunt master, "Clear up here. I think the outing is over." Feigning nonchalance, he climbed aboard and strapped into one of the jumpseats at the front of the troop cabin. Within seconds, the visiting contingent had also boarded and the transport leapt into the air.

Well, no standing on ceremony. Things must be desperate at the palace.

Ivan pulled a notepad from an inside pocket of his jacket and activated its comms. He always made a point of staying out of reach of distractions while hunting, and this time his habitual practice played into his determination to be well away from the danger zone. There was no practical danger, but perception was everything in the public eye. When the Emperor ordered an atrocity, the Grand Duke wanted to be visibly distanced from the decision.

The sky outside darkened from ultramarine to silky black as the troop carrier looped high around the planet in a dizzying suborbital hop.

He frowned, then checked his notepad more carefully. Comms was being blocked. He glanced up and locked eyes with Javarro, sitting facing him at the other end of the troop cabin. The lieutenant wore a faint and knowing smile.

A furious protest died unspoken. The escort would be acting on the orders of the Emperor. Ivan seethed, anger slowly giving way to the chilling realization that he was now a prisoner, physically helpless in the company of a hostile guard, and blocked from electronic communications.

There was no point descending into panic, though it was a battle to keep himself on the right side of sanity.

Ivan gave the lieutenant a contemptuous look, settled back into his seat and closed his eyes. He had no thought of sleep, however. For the two-hour-long flight, he reviewed all the scenarios he and Bernie Fischer had mapped out, and rehearsed his lines of defense. If his comms had been working Bernie could have given him a coded summary of where they stood, but he lacked that luxury. He just had to be ready for all eventualities.

With a numbness in her heart, Chalwen secured her office and set up the encrypted comms that would connect her to the hastily-convened meeting. She knew that, elsewhere in the building, Henri was doing likewise.

Anxiety preyed on her. After such a monumental disaster she'd been expecting Lorenzo himself to summon The Hidden Light, but the coded message had come from one of the small group of administrators who managed the organization's security. The woman's voice had sounded strained. Not surprising, given the scale of events unfolding.

Her mind quailed again at last night's memories. A Cleansing. Even Florence in her heyday had never brought that ultimate sanction to bear.

Full-on war. Between Skamensis and Firenzi for sure, but something on this scale would drag in the other Families. Formal protests from all quarters were already flooding the diplomatic office. And the Assembly would certainly judge that Julian lacked the experience to steer the empire through such perilous times. They'd have no choice but to invoke a Declaration of Competence and appoint Ivan in his stead. It felt inevitable. The empire had been skirting that cliff edge ever since Paul's death, and now they seemed to be flying over the precipice on the wings of a hurricane.

While she knew this meeting of the Light was vital, it all felt too late. This was the kind of atrocity the group was supposed to guard against, but they'd been focused on the wrong aggressor. She should be with Julian right now. That was where the real battle of words was about to happen. Right now, he was closeted with his best diplomatic team preparing to face Josef Firenzi's righteous wrath.

At least he was armed with the hastily-assembled intelligence data showing the depth of the Grand Duke's treachery. It was a slender hope that the Firenzi head would keep his fleet his own side of the border long enough to figure out a diplomatic solution.

The one detail they'd carefully excluded from the briefing material was the involvement of the automated battle system and the false use of the Imperial Seal. Josef Firenzi didn't need to know that. They just had to convince him that it was an act as much against the Family Skamensis as against his own people, and that the perpetrators would be suitably punished.

"I think we'd better start." A voice on the comms startled Chalwen out of her dismal thoughts. "No knowing how many members to expect right now."

It sounded like an aside to one of the meeting administrators. Where was Lorenzo?

"You'll notice that we've carefully excluded the Emperor himself from this meeting."

Chalwen puzzled at the apparent hostility in the admin's tone, then she decided she was being overly sensitive. Of course, they'd know that Julian would be too busy trying to rescue an impossible situation to deal with The Hidden Light.

"What was Shadowland thinking, introducing him to our group so young?"

Crap! Chalwen hadn't been imagining it.

"I was against it from the start. Now he knows about us, how long before he ferrets us out? What kind of tyrant have we taken in?"

"What are you talking about?" Chalwen couldn't keep the outrage from her voice.

"Tungsten, right? You're close to the Emperor. What in Space is he up to?"

"Right now? Trying to stop a no-holds-barred war machine in its tracks, that's what."

"I heard he used the Imperial Seal. He gave the order."

Chalwen's heart sank. "You've been misinformed." Even to her own ears, the denial sounded feeble.

"The order was forged." That was Henri's voice, calm and assertive. "It didn't come from the Emperor, but he has no choice other than to own it. He'll accept responsibility in a public address this morning. I don't know how he plans to spin it to avert a war, but that's the only stance that will hold Skamensis space together."

So, Henri had heard something about Julian's instructions to the witnesses last night. Chalwen hadn't had a chance to discuss events with him. Stanhope must have briefed him already, to start work on covering the damning trail.

"A Cleansing," someone moaned. "Hasn't been heard of in decades ..."

"Centuries."

"Not in living memory, anyway. The Emperor's weapon of last resort against planetwide insurrection."

"What sort of person would give such an order?"

"What about the people who pulled the trigger? The people in those warships who pointed their cannon at cities and wiped them off the map?"

Chalwen ached to tell the true story, to convince them of Julian's innocence. She bit the inside of her cheek to stop the words from blurting out.

"A member on board one of the warships got off a brief message. We alerted ground authorities and broadcast a warning to whoever was listening."

"What good did that do?"

"I'm told a few hundred, maybe a couple of thousand, people evacuated before the fleet hit."

"How? They couldn't have been seen or they'd have been gunned down."

"The fleet allowed them to escape. Standard practice. Let a few witnesses live to tell the rest of the population what happens to worlds that defy the Emperor."

A quiet voice broke the stunned silence. "Eloon was Shadowland's base of operations."

Chalwen felt the bottom drop out of her world. After several attempts to force out the words past the sudden lump in her throat, she finally voiced the question they were all hanging on. "What about Shadowland himself?"

A long silence.

"No word."

The admin who'd opened the meeting spoke. Even through the distortions of light years of travel through comms networks, Chalwen could hear the iron control in the woman's voice. "Torremis, the planetary capital, was the first target. Shadowland was there."

"There's more." Another of the admins, a man who sounded weighed down with age and grief. "Our own members have been singled out in the last twenty-four hours."

"What do you mean?"

"There are at least six I was able to positively confirm that have died in suspicious circumstances. Many more have gone silent and are unaccounted for. Someone's identifying and silencing us."

"How can that happen?"

"Someone must have managed to trace our network activity, don't ask me how, but they may be using statistical analysis to follow connections to comms end points."

"Imperial Security," an anonymous voice spat. "They're the only ones with the reach to do something like that. The Emperor *must* have turned against us."

"Then we're all in danger," the original admin said. "I suggest we avoid meeting in any group larger than ten at a time until we can deal with the threat."

Before the meeting broke up, Chalwen felt compelled to make one last plea. "I know it's hard to tell facts from fiction right now, but I need everyone here to be clear about one thing. This was not Julian's doing. I was there in the imperial quarters while the attack was happening. There was no mistaking the horror when he saw what was happening, and he did everything in his power to stop it."

She breathed a sigh of relief when Henri chimed in. "And the attacks on our members are devastating, but they're proof that we've been effective. We've supported the Emperor against a plot bigger than anyone could have imagined. But that means we're all targets and our comms network is vulnerable. The admins are right. We need to go dark for a while."

"What do we do in the meantime?"

"Stay alive." Henri's voice was bitter.

Chalwen broke the connection and eyed the cabinet in the corner of the office where a small stash of beer lay in reserve for a long night or a rainy day. She had a feeling beer wouldn't cut it today.

Lorenzo, gone.

And he had a young family. Presumably gone too, in the hellish conflagration of man-made starfire. Her eyes glazed over. Without conscious thought, she opened out an electronic toolkit on her desk surface.

Eloon. Population one hundred and five million yesterday. Zero today. But the planet administration had kept good records, still present in semi-public archives on the Firenzi capital world.

Of course, ImpSec had numerous covert pathways into a greater depth of information than was readily available to the general public. Using them was risky. These access points had been sniffed out and carefully preserved. If anyone was alert in the Firenzi Special Service they might spot Chalwen's intrusion, but she was past caring by now.

A morbid fascination took hold as Chalwen assembled what little she knew of Lorenzo. He wouldn't be living under his real name, of course, but things like age and physical characteristics were an innate part of him. Never mind his previous life in imperial space, she brought up a mental picture of the Lorenzo she'd met only months ago on Chevinta. Painstakingly she added dribbles of information to the search and narrowed down the list. Still too many people to trawl through, tens of thousands and any one of them could be Lorenzo.

Squeezing her eyes shut, Chalwen replayed that meeting in her mind. Children. A boy and a girl he'd said. Younger than Julian, but not by much. She guessed a possible age range and narrowed the list down further. Assume married and with spouse still part of the family. He hadn't said one way or another, but it seemed like a reasonable working assumption.

Finally, in desperation, she added in his name. Surely he wouldn't be using it, but the alternative now was to examine each of a list still thousands strong. Okay, not the Skamensis part, that would be too reckless, but how many Lorenzos could there be?

And there he was. The image in front of her was unmistakably Lorenzo. How the hell had he stayed hidden so long under such a flimsy disguise?

Now she had him, she had his family too.

A family man. Chalwen would never have believed it. Yet there they were. And the resemblance was unmistakeable, especially the boy. That could easily have been Julian a few years ago.

What kind of woman could have snared him? Curious, Chalwen brought up her record and immediately hit an Imperial Security flag. A person of interest. What? With growing dread, Chalwen pulled up the ImpSec file. Once again, the ground under her seemed to shift. Had Lorenzo known about his partner's associations?

She rubbed her eyes. A furious hammering on the office door almost toppled her from her chair. "What the fuck ...?"

The moment she released the locks, Simone tumbled through. "You need to come, quickly. Stanhope's dead."

———⋆•⋆———

Ivan scowled out the window at a flawless sky. Somewhere beyond the walls of the inner gardens, palace life continued as normal. Midday sun glared off the dome of the Green Throne Room, dominating the view from his quarters.

His prison.

A sense of unreality still gripped Ivan after his unorthodox transfer from the wilds of Chensing to the capital city. His slim grasp on sanity wasn't helped when they landed directly in the secure hangar adjoining the imperial quarters. Normally reserved for small air cruisers, the hangar this morning had been cleared of all other craft to make room for the bulky troop transport. That was unheard of, as was his rough manhandling through the building to his private quarters.

No explanations had been offered, no words exchanged other than terse commands.

Left alone, Ivan had checked his suite inch by inch. All ways in and out had been locked, even the windows. All means of communication removed. He wondered what this signified.

Some form of accusation had been among the scenarios he and Bernie had anticipated and planned for. Even if he didn't disclose Ivan's unprecedented access to the Imperial Seal, Julian himself would know Ivan had ordered the attack, that much was certain. How he would react to that knowledge was unpredictable.

Going public and hanging Ivan out to dry was always a possibility, but that would bring Family Skamensis crashing down. Ivan was banking on Julian keeping a more level head than that.

A more private vengeance was more likely, but, Ivan reasoned, he'd now be incarcerated deep under ImpSec headquarters. In that event, he still had a couple of safeguards to fall back on.

But here he was, a prisoner although held in his own quarters rather than some dark sub-basement. This was an unexpected twist. What did it mean?

A glimmer of a smile crept across his face. *The Emperor didn't know what to do with him.* This wasn't one of the scenarios he and Bernie had thought through, and the hesitation, keeping options open, showed a much greater maturity and level of control in Julian than Ivan had expected.

It meant the Emperor could be bargained with. Ivan was still in the game.

A knock at the door. At least his jailers still observed some niceties. At Ivan's command, a guard entered with a tray. "Lieutenant Bresk sends his compliments, Sire, and thought you might be hungry."

Ivan watched as the man crossed the room to a small alcove away from the windows and set the tray down on a side table. Not the main table near the windows, which would have been an obvious place to sit in comfort. Curious.

The guard busied himself setting dishes and silverware out, and depositing platters and serving spoons on the table. Two items caught Ivan's eye that were not part of a standard dinner service. A portable sonic damper the size of a teacup, which the guard activated, and a thumbnail-sized communicator.

At a glance from the guard, Ivan strolled over and studied the table.

"This alcove is a surveillance blind spot," the guard murmured. "The damper will only suppress quiet conversation in a three-foot radius so keep your voice down." He pointed to the comms unit. "Tuned to a non-standard and encrypted channel direct to the Lieutenant. The best we could arrange at short notice."

A phalanx of guards barred the way to the fourth floor. Simone spoke quietly to the sergeant in charge. He didn't look happy but he waved them through.

"You must teach me how you do that," Chalwen whispered as they passed through the reception area. "They won't open up a crime scene like this to just anyone who wanders past."

For once, Simone's usual cheerful manner had deserted her. "Very few people know what Sanitation actually does, which suits us well. And people like to fill the gaps with wild imaginings. Let's say, I could have threatened him and his family with banishment to the fisheries of Chensing and he'd believe it."

"You didn't, though?"

"Didn't have to. Stick around with us long enough and people will simply choose not to get in your way when you look determined enough."

As they stepped into Stanhope's inner office, Chalwen had to fight down a reflexive gag. The air was heavy with the reek of cooked meat and voided bowels.

Up close, Boris Stanhope looked like he could be sleeping. His face was almost untouched, but his head lolled back against the headrest of his chair affording anyone entering the office a clear view of the charred hole in the underside of his jaw. The back of his skull was missing. A palm-sized beam pistol lay on the floor under his chair.

Chalwen studied the body, the desk, and the perimeter of the office. She reached for the sliding door that led out to a rooftop terrace, but caught herself just in time. She looked quizzically at Simone, who shook her head.

"I'm keeping on top of investigation findings in real time. So far only the first sweep to secure the scene. That one is locked and hasn't been disturbed."

"Main office door? Other ways in?"

"All locked when security arrived on the scene. They had to get override codes to gain access."

"This is recent. I assume the pistol emission tripped alarms?" Chalwen lowered herself to her knees, struggling against spasms in her shins, but managed not to touch anything. She studied the angle of the shot, neatly aimed to fry the brain stem. She held her hand close to the weapon discarded on the floor, curling her fingers into a grip the right size, then held her empty fist to her own neck. "An awkward angle, and he must have had a steady hand."

"No last-minute flinching, but not an impossible shot."

She beckoned Simone to help her back to her feet. A stylus lay on the desktop alongside a brief sentence in Stanhope's crabby handwriting. "I was wrong." Chalwen grunted. "Wrong about what?"

"Who knows? We'll trawl his logs and records to see what else he might have left behind."

"I can't believe it, but it looks very much like a suicide." Chalwen sighed and shook her head.

"And I'm going to hazard a guess that the official investigation will reach that conclusion."

"But you're not buying it?"

"All the physical evidence we just ran through can be faked. That just leaves what we know about the man himself, and in my opinion that trumps any amount of evidence I don't trust."

Feeling helpless, Chalwen scanned the room once more. "There will be visual records from surveillance, especially out in reception."

"What's the betting those records will reveal nothing?"

When Chalwen didn't answer, Simone said, "Okay, I've seen enough. Let's let the professionals get on with their jobs."

Chapter 49

This part of the ImpSec basement still gave Chalwen goosebumps. She and Simone stood in the same observation room from which they'd studied Warran ap Meradan so long ago. The wall screen showed a similar cell, but this time the center of the room was dominated by a padded gurney to which a naked body was strapped.

Bernie Fischer.

A part of Chalwen enjoyed a grim satisfaction at this turnaround in their respective fortunes, but seeing the man in this state gave her the shivers. "Is he asleep?" she whispered, despite the thick walls separating them from the cell.

"Being held in a hybrid state. Dreaming. And believe me they're not happy dreams."

"Drugs?"

"A carefully balanced cocktail. We're steering his mental state, but the raw material that's tormenting him is all his own work."

"Has he said anything useful yet?"

"Only what we got from our first round of questioning last night, and a lot of that's reading between the lines. We know he's the key to Ivan's network, and there's a load of plots in flight right now. Stanhope was just the start."

Frustration burned behind Chalwen's eyes. "We could be sitting on a time bomb. We need to find out what he knows, and fast."

"It will be days yet, before we can get anything reliable out of him. You can't rush this process."

"Let's call it what it is." The room swayed and Chalwen reached for the wall to steady herself.

"Yes, it's torture." Simone's face was unusually grave. The freckles dusting the bridge of her nose stood stark against her skin as she chewed her bottom lip. "It has a history going back to earliest records of humanity. All regimes have used it, either openly or secretly, but results have often been mixed."

The depth of weariness in Simone's voice had nothing to do with the timeless futility of wresting secrets from reluctant subjects. Chalwen looked closer and saw for the first time the grey smudges under her eyes, and the tinge of red in the whites. Chalwen shook her head. "People will say anything to make it stop, so they'll say whatever they think you want to hear."

"Our approach isn't as blunt as 'tell us and we'll stop.' It's a form of conditioning to tell the truth, no matter how unpalatable."

"Does that actually work?"

"Better than you'd think, and one heck of a lot better than any other technique we know of."

"Did he have anything to do with Stanhope's death?"

"Of course he did, but actually proving the link is going to take patience. There's something else I haven't had a chance to share with you yet. The comms analysis Stanhope presented to the Emperor, the network that highlighted Eloon, was sound." An edge of bitterness crept into Simone's voice. "But as for some of the later intelligence that pointed to an invasion force being readied ... we now have clear evidence it was either flawed or falsified."

"Falsified?" Chalwen gaped, the naked body on the screen momentarily forgotten.

"Expertly done. It took a real deep dive to pick up inconsistencies in document headers, but once we knew where to look it all unraveled."

"You've been busy these past few hours." Another thought struck Chalwen. "What prompted you to look in the first place?"

Simone's expression hardened. "Stanhope's death. Apparent suicide, and the note. I know where you're going. This was meant to be discovered, but I think it was meant to take a while longer. Maybe coming to light *after* Julian addressed the Assembly."

"A trap for the Emperor? So that confirms Stanhope's death was staged, too. What do we do with this? Julian needs to know, but how will it look when he stands in front of the Assembly and says he destroyed a planet based on fictitious intel?"

"And if he stands by ImpSec and insists the attack was justified, what's the betting someone is ready and waiting to leak the fact that the intelligence was crap?" Simone leaned against the wall. "I'm on my way to brief Jevriel Tollini, but I thought you'd want to speak to the Emperor yourself."

"Tollini? Head of Counterintelligence?" Chalwen pictured Henri's boss's boss. Crotchety, but competent from what she'd heard.

"I think he'll be a good Chief of Intelligence, but he has a lot of catching-up to do."

"Meanwhile, how many other assassins are on the loose with a target in their sights?"

Leaning closer, Simone murmured, "A lot of senior people in the administration are watching their backs right now."

"You said there were plots already in flight. Do you think we ourselves have anything to worry about?"

Simone regarded Chalwen steadily. "They already snatched you once, so you're obviously on the hit list."

"But maybe that shot is spent. Would Fischer have had time to arrange another attack before you picked him up?"

"Maybe, maybe not. I'm sorry, Chalwen, only time will tell. We don't know how far his network reaches, or how far ahead he planned."

Network. The word tumbled a cascade of facts clicking into place, and suddenly her own personal safety became unimportant. The room swayed again, and this time she stumbled towards the guard console and the safety of a solid chair beneath her. She ignored Simone's worried look, and buried her face in her hands. The network ... Eloon ... of course it was real.

Despite the depth of their failure just becoming apparent, the irony didn't escape Chalwen. The Hidden Light, a widespread and stable network of people across space. Imperial Security had spotted them and jumped to all the wrong conclusions, and in the process led Ivan to the heart of the organization that had thwarted him for so long.

They'd led the might of the imperial navy to Lorenzo's hiding place.

A renegade member of the imperial family, an exile, a fugitive, hiding on Eloon.

In Firenzi space.

"They took a swipe at you, and missed." Cool fingers closed around Chalwen's, and eased her hands away from her face.

Chalwen's cheeks burned as she realized Simone had mistaken her reaction. She managed a grim smile. "With you and Henri at my back, they'd be stupid to try again. Sorry I frightened you just then. One of these days maybe I'll be able to explain properly."

But the leaden feeling in her gut told Chalwen that she'd never fully accept what had happened last night. The most powerful of the Emperor's supporters, targeted by the very administration he'd spent his life helping.

Lorenzo, gone.

———————

All the way from his quarters, through the family offices and to the Office of Deliberation, Ivan felt unbalanced like he was walking a tightrope. Maybe he was, figuratively. At last he'd been summoned into the Emperor's presence and he knew his future hung in the balance. This might be just the first in a series of meetings, but he was under no illusions that any victory simply kept him in play for the next round. Just one mis-step would finish him.

More disturbing, his mental imbalance seemed to be making itself felt in a very physical sense. As he descended stairs, he slid his hand along bannisters to steady himself. Along hallways whispering with distant conversations, the solid floor beneath his feet seemed to undulate like he was walking on water.

He'd used the smuggled communicator to check in with Lieutenant Bresk. The news was mixed, maybe stoking Ivan's disorientation. On one hand, the teams Bernie Fischer had briefed in advance were doing their work. Most of them. Stanhope was gone. Other thorns in his side would soon follow. But the infuriating lieutenant had somehow escaped the trap laid for her, and most troubling of all, Bernie himself had vanished.

Ivan hoped he was simply laying low after setting all the pieces of Ghost Town in motion, but an emptiness in Ivan's gut told him that something more serious had happened.

A spasm of real fear gripped Ivan as he wondered if some drug had been slipped into his food. Would they resort to such tactics to keep him off balance, or even to make him more compliant? Somehow he couldn't see Julian being so devious, but Julian wasn't the only one he had to worry about.

His escort kept an unusually close cordon around him, and there must be advance guards clearing the way. The office hallways were never this empty, but at least he wasn't being manhandled like before.

As he was ushered through outer offices and lobbies and into the Office of Deliberation itself, his escort melted into the shadows. Emperor Julian sat behind the polished desk, alone in the room. Ivan noted the absence of the usual guards and attendants around the perimeter.

The Emperor motioned Ivan closer. He slid a disc the size of a saucer across his desk and tapped a button on its edge. A yellow light blinked slowly in the middle for several seconds before turning a steady green. A blue light slowly orbited the green.

"I've dismissed my guards, and ordered all the usual surveillance and recording equipment turned off. As far as imperial archives are concerned, this meeting never happened."

Ivan studied the device on the desk with curious amusement. "And yet you feel the need for additional scanners and a broad band jammer. A high-end model. It will take ImpSec maybe fifteen minutes to break the encryption and sneak past the jamming?"

Either the Emperor had genuinely set up a totally private conversation, which suggested he was about to be frank with secrets that only he and Ivan could share, or he was trying to lull Ivan into sharing with an unseen audience.

The jamming device itself could be a clever fake. A hologram on the surface suggested it was genuine, but you could never be entirely sure. It occurred to Ivan that there had to be a more foolproof way to assure a visitor of their privacy. Tongues would never be truly free while the threat of eavesdroppers remained.

Ivan stood patiently in front of the desk while Julian lounged back in his chair.

"You've placed me in a very awkward position, Uncle."

Aah, play the family card. Did he imagine that earned him some kind of concession? Ivan cocked an eyebrow, refusing to be drawn into saying anything too soon. Let the youngster show more of his hand.

"You let me believe Empress Florence had shared access to the Imperial Seal ... that such an action was routine."

Ivan wondered whether he should say something, but he realized Julian hadn't openly confessed anything. Damn! The youngster really had been learning this last year.

"It took me until now to realize you never actually said as such. You just let me hear what you wanted me to." The raw bitterness in Julian's voice tore something in Ivan. He swallowed and hastily tamped down the pain in his chest. There were bigger things at stake than his fondness for the boy he'd stood by for so many years. Not least, Ivan's own survival, and the future of the Skamensis empire.

"Only you could have used the Seal in my absence."

There it was. An unambiguous admission. This conversation really must be private. A knot between Ivan's shoulders began to relax.

"I used the Imperial Seal for the good of our people."

"So ..." Julian looked thoughtful, but Ivan could see the effort it took him to control himself. "You don't deny ordering a Cleansing?"

Ivan spread his hands. "What would be the point in that? Unless you shared access to the Seal with someone else."

"This is something I would never have allowed. You must know that."

There it was, a flash of raw anger showing. Angry youngsters could always be trusted to run with impulse rather than clear thinking. The Assembly would see a boy emperor hopelessly out of his depth. All he needed was a bit more goading, and Julian would be ready to lash out, to find a scapegoat.

"I make no apologies." Ivan squeezed as much patronizing superiority into his tone as he could manage. A grown-up admonishing a witless child. "There was a very clear threat to our security, a conspiracy of monstrous proportions sniffed out by your own security organization. Armed raids on dozens of our own planets, and evidence of a large-scale imminent attack. I did what any emperor would have done."

"You are not emperor."

The ferocity of the shout startled Ivan. He fought to suppress his triumph. He'd hit a sore spot, and reminded Julian of the supposed rationale for the Cleansing. A defense that would crumble under closer inspection. "And yet you delegated me the authority to act on your behalf. I don't recall any constraints being agreed on my discretion in support of your rule."

"This atrocity is hardly supporting me. As I said, you've put me in an awkward position, and now I have to limit the damage somehow."

"Sire, the action may be distasteful, but it was necessary. Times like this demand a strong ruler, someone who will not flinch from unpleasant decisions."

Julian stared at Ivan, breathing hard. Somehow he brought himself back under control. His manner and tone turned to ice. "You know, Uncle, I'm glad to find there are *some* things we can still agree on. Now, you will return to your quarters. I need to prepare myself to address the Assembly."

Chapter 50

Chalwen limped out of the first floor stairwell and paused to one side of the imposing central corridor running through the heart of Imperial Security. She massaged her thighs, hoping to relieve at least some of the ache in her legs, but she really needed a hot bath and copious pain meds. Stubbornness compelled her to still take the stairs rather than succumbing to the lure of effortless elevators, but she wished to Unity she'd remembered to bring her walking cane today.

As she pushed herself away from the wall, ready to brave the chaos of scurrying bodies thronging the hall, a voice from behind startled her. "Dangerous times, eh, Lieutenant?"

Chalwen stiffened and turned.

"Maybe you were right to see conspiracies around every corner." Taraq Marand, her old boss in Civil Watch, peered at her. There seemed to be no resentment in his tone, just concern and a nervousness she'd not seen in him before. His bulging eyes seemed to be trying to dart in all directions at once.

Suppressing a surge of alarm, Chalwen said, "Not sure I follow you. There are *always* conspiracies, but which one in particular are you talking about?"

Taraq's eyes widened, a feat Chalwen wouldn't have believed possible. "You haven't heard? I suppose it's not common knowledge yet. Early days." He chewed his lip. "You know the Emperor asked Jevriel Tollini to take over from Stanhope?"

Chalwen nodded, swallowing against a sickening feeling in the pit of her stomach.

"Jevriel's dead."

Chalwen stumbled and leaned back against the wall. Her mind raced. That might explain why she'd not been able to contact Henri before she left her office. She'd been hoping he'd join her in the Assembly Room this morning for the Emperor's address.

"What happened?" She managed little more than a strangled gasp.

"Just dropped dead in his quarters. Natural causes, we were told, but nobody's buying it. They had a cone of silence around the whole affair since he was discovered, but the news is leaking out."

Chalwen's mind was torn. There would be another investigation. Maybe Simone was already there to read what the official team would be reluctant to see, and she couldn't see Henri allowing himself to be shut out of proceedings. She gritted her teeth and made up her mind. They'd share reports later, but right now she needed to be with the Emperor before his pivotal speech to a hostile Assembly.

She grabbed Taraq by the arm and leaned on him as she pushed away from the wall once more. "Come on. I take it you were on your way to the Assembly?" She didn't give him a chance to answer. "We can talk on the way. Tell me everything you know."

Together, they headed towards the sunshine spilling in through the foyer fifty yards ahead.

Taraq grunted under Chalwen's weight. "When he accepted the post, Jevriel sent his family away from the capital. I think he knew he'd be in danger."

"Presumably he had a protection detail."

"Of course. But we're not in the habit of posting guards actually inside someone's bedchamber."

"So he died in his sleep?"

"Obviously the medics are screening for poisons. That's about all that makes sense if you suspect foul play. There were no physical signs, no hint of a struggle."

Still leaning some of her weight on Taraq, with her free hand Chalwen squeezed the bridge of her nose. "Another locked room mystery."

Taraq gave her a puzzled glance. "Another ...?" His mouth formed an 'O'. "So you already know the next part then?"

It was Chalwen's turn to look confused.

"Haav Mesteer was summoned to the Office of Deliberation last night," Taraq said, "but has since vanished."

"Last night, so after Jevriel was found?"

"Yes. I assume the Emperor is desperate to find a replacement for Stanhope."

"But Mesteer? From Border Security? Wouldn't your own boss be a more obvious successor, after Jevriel?" Chalwen scrunched her face in concentration. Her understanding of the many divisions and branches in ImpSec was still a work in progress, along with the strengths and personalities of the more senior members.

Mutely, eyes darting from side to side as they emerged through the main doors and into the sunlight of the grand plaza, Taraq shrugged. He helped Chalwen down the steps to street level.

He stopped to catch his breath. "Not so strange, really, and the Emperor has his own criteria I suppose. People he knows best, and trusts. People who'll be loyal."

"Would Tammy fit that description?" Chalwen hadn't dealt directly with Tammy Hopewell, Taraq's boss. She had little information to go on.

"I believe so, but right now she's doubled the guard around her office, and installed new security. She hasn't stepped out of her office today except to tell the Emperor she's not currently interested in a promotion."

Chalwen stared at Taraq. "She's trying to take herself out of the line of fire."

"She doesn't scare easily, believe me, but she's scared today."

"It's like there's a hit list of anyone Julian might put into Stanhope's seat," Chalwen mused. "Anyone who might pick up where he left off."

"So, you don't believe that suicide crap either?"

Interesting. It seemed a lot more people than she realized doubted *that* story. But the news Taraq had revealed held her attention. There simply wasn't time between one killing and the next. It took research and planning to weasel past ImpSec security, and that took time. The killers hadn't been waiting for Julian to designate a replacement, they must have already decided their targets and laid plans in advance.

She stopped, and almost fell when Taraq continued walking. Chalwen pointed back up the steps. "Tammy has good reason to be scared, even now. This was all set in motion before today. They *do* have a hit list and they're not waiting for Julian to act. Get back in there and make sure she understands that just because she refused the Emperor doesn't make her safe."

Taraq gulped. "You really think so?"

"It's not just about who's replacing Stanhope. Someone is targeting anyone the Emperor might consider for the post. *Anyone* who'd be trusted and loyal. Go!"

After a moment's hesitation, Taraq turned and scurried back into the building. Chalwen hoped he'd be in time. If the assassins could get to Stanhope in his office, no one was safe. She studied the glass and stone ImpSec facade, wondering what more secrets lay back there, then shook her head irritably and limped across the plaza towards the main palace gate.

As she walked, the back of Chalwen's neck crawled. Was she still a target, or was that kidnap the only attack lined up against her? She wondered also about Henri and Simone. Were either of them in the crosshairs? And who else back there might be in danger?

She fingered the communicator on her collar and tried contacting Henri again. No response. However, she did manage to raise Simone, who sounded unusually flustered over the comms channel.

"Sorry, Chalwen, I decided it was best to keep you out of the mess here."

"Mess? You mean Jevriel Tollini and Haav Mesteer?"

"Ah. You heard. Well, we knew we couldn't keep the lid on that for long."

"Dammit, Simone, you brought me in on Stanhope, why shut me out now?"

"Orders. Sorry. My boss is bringing people in by invitation only."

"And I'm not good enough yet? Or not to be trusted?"

"Not that. Never that. But your place is with the Emperor right now, and I knew you'd want in. But you can't afford to get distracted."

"I just sent Taraq Marand back to warn Tammy Hopewell she's still in danger, even though she turned the Emperor down."

"Space, Chalwen, you reached that conclusion fast, but we're already onto that. We're fighting a war of assassins here."

"I only just left the building, it all seemed pretty normal."

"That's the point. Assassins don't work out in the open."

"And Henri?"

"Safe, and leading the tech analysis here. We've got most of the rats out of the system now, so they're running out of places to hide. Meanwhile, we both have places to be."

Despite the spring sunshine, Chalwen felt cold inside as she approached the looming portico and returned the sergeant's salute at the main gate.

There was an all-out but invisible attack on Imperial Security in progress, but that was nothing compared to the battle that lay ahead. She gritted her teeth and hurried her steps through the crowded vestibule and towards the Assembly Room. With Jevriel gone, the Emperor wouldn't yet know about the forged intelligence. If he spoke publicly now, he would be walking into a political disaster.

Back in his quarters, Ivan found a large wall screen in his sitting room had been activated. The screen was being controlled from somewhere outside his room, whether on the Emperor's instructions or something Lieutenant Bresk had arranged, Ivan couldn't tell. Right now, it showed a news feed from inside the Assembly Room.

The vast auditorium was almost empty. Puzzled, Ivan checked the time. The planned announcement was almost due, and by now the rows of Members' desks should have been filled. Surely no one would miss such a momentous occasion.

The reason struck Ivan when the camera angle panned to show the overhead displays of Members joining the meeting from afar. The remote displays were full. Most politicians were already in deep space, fleeing the capital to rejoin their constituencies.

A shiver of anticipation ran down Ivan's back. The empire really was ready for war. In his mind, he rehearsed his speech to persuade the frightened Members to entrust the safekeeping of their future into his hands rather than Julian's. He had enough sympathetic Members in his pocket ready to call a motion of fitness at Julian's first sign of weakness, and to demand Ivan's presence on the floor of the Assembly Room.

The view shifted again and, while the floor of the room was deserted, the public viewing galleries were packed. Even so, the usual bedlam that preceded a session of the Assembly was curiously absent today. All eyes were on the far end of the room, and the doors leading from the emperor's dressing room.

Ivan found himself pacing his quarters, tense and hardly daring to breathe as the hour approached. All his schooling in patience failed to calm his growing agitation as seconds crawled by. The hush in the Assembly Room was unreal. Everyone present must sense they were about to witness a once-in-a-lifetime event.

Finally, the team of officials filed silently out and took their places. Without fanfare, Emperor Julian Skamensis followed them and stood in front of the throne. The Sergeant at Arms called for order, a redundant gesture in the expectant hush, and the Clerk of the Floor intoned, "The item of business before the Assembly today is an extraordinary address from His Imperial Excellency, the Essence of Unity, Emperor Julian Skamensis."

Ivan frowned. Surely an occasion like this demanded more ceremony, more observance of millennia-old protocols. Julian should have waited to be announced so he could make a more imposing entrance. He seemed to be showing his inexperience. All the better for Ivan, though he'd find the boy's inevitable humiliation painful to watch.

Julian shuffled his feet, gazing at the floor in front of him. The silence deepened. For a moment, Ivan wondered if the youngster had completely lost his tongue. He must surely know he faced an impossible battle to justify what had happened.

Then the Emperor looked up and gazed across the expanse of tiered seats. He seemed to ignore the empty ranks where the Assembly Members were conspicuously absent, and instead focused on the public galleries. The look in his eye chilled Ivan to the core.

When he spoke his voice was quiet and firm, carried effortlessly across the ancient hall by acoustic pickups.

"Over the last year, the people and planets of Family Skamensis have suffered repeated attacks on our citizens and our property."

An angry muttering swelled around the room.

"I know people have been demanding a response from me, and many of you think I've failed you, abandoned you."

The anger rose to a murderous growl. What the heck was he playing at? The Emperor could never afford to show this kind of weakness. But a nagging doubt quelled any sense of triumph on Ivan's part. Julian was working to some game plan here.

"In reality, my administration has been fighting an underground battle within our own borders, against conspirators determined to force us into a state of war." Julian's voice shook with his own outrage, cutting off the protests from the galleries. It seemed his passionate outburst had caught everyone by surprise. "War is profitable for a privileged few. It is *devastating* for those of you who have to fight it." Julian gestured to take in the packed galleries. "I refused to squander your lives, and the lives of your families, on the whim of a few traitorous profiteers."

With his mind reeling, Ivan wondered if Julian could possibly be referring to Honorina Philip? Surely not. The conglomerate executive was too wily to leave any trails linking her to her activities.

"I'm sorry that I've appeared preoccupied, and seemed unable or unwilling to show the strength you called for, but that time is past." He paused and drew himself straight. "Know now that, as Emperor, I have claimed my right under the Trown Plains Accord to meet unprovoked aggression with overwhelming force."

Ivan's heart thudded in his chest. He couldn't believe what he was hearing.

"Imperial Security uncovered an extensive network of resistance organized from the planet Eloon, in Firenzi space. You've all heard rumors, but I stand before you today to confirm that the night before last, heavy units of the imperial navy assembled over Eloon and carried out a punitive strike."

Dammit! Far from making excuses or casting blame, the little imp was *claiming credit* for Ivan's strike.

Into the shocked hush, Julian whispered, "Let it be put on record here and now that, for my part, matters between Family Skamensis and Family Firenzi have been squared."

The full meaning of Julian's words sank in. More importantly, Ivan realized what the Emperor *hadn't* said. There was no mention of an invasion force, no reference to the intelligence that would justify such a strike ... until it was revealed to be a myth.

Silence weighed heavy for several seconds while the audience also grappled with the Emperor's words. Then a handclap cracked through the air. Another, and another, quickly building to a thunderous tide of approval.

Ivan staggered back from the screen and groped behind him for the edge of a seat. His legs buckled. With scant regard for anyone who may be eavesdropping, Ivan palmed the communicator and rested his chin on his clenched fist as if deep in thought. "Bresk?" he whispered. "Are you following the broadcast from the Assembly?"

"Affirmative," came the murmured reply. "It's not following the expected script."

"Damned right it's not."

As the applause died down, the Clerk announced, "The Floor recognizes the Member for Sethridge Townships South."

Ivan tensed. This was one of his loyal followers.

"What of the reports that the purpose of this assault was to head off a full-scale invasion of Skamensis space?"

The Member was trying to tempt Julian into the trap, however hopeless it now seemed. After the public reaction just now, the politicians would be weighing their own popularity. It was one thing to drag down a weak figure enmeshed in a ghastly mistake, quite another to take shots at someone who'd hit such a popular note. And Julian must have been briefed to avoid this poisoned cup. "The Assembly Member will forgive me if I decline to be so liberal with confidential sources of intelligence."

Dammit. The youngster had not only sidestepped the question, but he'd managed to issue a sly rebuke at the same time.

"Nor will I comment on the rumors that have plagued our citizens regarding any possible Firenzi involvement in the assassination of Emperor Paul and others of my family. All I will say is that the culprits are known to Imperial Security and they have nowhere left to run."

Ivan had heard enough. He needed to deploy his last safety net. "Operation Newsroom," he murmured into his fist.

"Newsroom, confirmed."

More questions followed, but Ivan was barely listening.

"I stand by my earlier statements," Julian was saying. "We had evidence of a conspiracy stemming from Eloon, and the Cleansing was ordered in retaliation for the many raids we've already suffered, both on our own planets and in shipping lanes."

One shock piled on another had numbed Ivan. The mention of the assassination was only just registering. Had they really uncovered the source of that plot? Bernie's contacts throughout ImpSec reported the investigation had come nowhere close to the truth. How was this possible? Was it a bluff? Maybe so, but right now the public was lapping it up. Julian was untouchable … for now.

"You may well debate whether the response was proportionate to the crimes. If Members wish to bring forward a motion of censure then I will of course co-operate with any inquiry, but I stand by my claim that I gave the strong response that this Assembly and my own people have been demanding for months."

Of course you did, Ivan thought bitterly. And that final flourish was an open challenge to Ivan's supporters. Act now, if you dare. But they were all politicians first and foremost, none of them ready for a duel.

A grudging smile twisted Ivan's lips. He'd been beaten this round, but he still had a trump card to play, and he would remain a force to be reckoned with.

———— • • • ————

Chalwen lounged in the lower corridor of the guard house, watching the door to Lieutenant Shan Bresk's office. At last, the door slammed open and Bresk emerged yelling, "Stokes! Where the fuck are you?"

He hesitated when he saw Chalwen, alone in the corridor. He glanced past her shoulder to the small ready room beyond.

"Corporal Stokes is busy." Chalwen inspected her fingernails. When Bresk pushed past her into the ready room, she added, "As is the rest of your squad."

Lieutenant Bresk whirled, his walnut complexion turning the color of old brick. "What is going on, ap Gwynodd? You know you're living on borrowed time, don't you?"

Chalwen shook her head. "It's our turn to do some spring cleaning. You and I are going to have a little chat about Operation Newsroom."

Bresk's hand dropped to his holster. He froze when a voice behind his shoulder purred, "That would be a *very* bad idea."

Lieutenant Bresk's eyes darted back and forth, taking in the four grey-clad figures that had materialized silently around him. Their lack of obvious weapons was somehow more intimidating than any overt show of force.

Simone reached from behind him and slipped the beam pistol from his grasp, then quickly frisked him for more weapons.

One of her colleagues from Sanitation administered a drug to keep the dangerous bodyguard subdued, and the trio led him down to the basement corridors, leaving Simone and Chalwen alone in the strangely quiet guard house.

"You caught his conversations?"

"Oh, yes." Simone chuckled. "We couldn't break the encryption on his link to the Grand Duke, not in time, anyway, but the presence of the link itself is clear and we snooped audio from both rooms." She sobered. "Not that it gave us much to go on. His conversation with Ivan was brief and cryptic."

"Who did Bresk contact afterward?"

"That's where we lose the trail. He didn't talk to anyone suspicious. Just placed an advert in one of the local 'for sale' columns. It's possible someone will respond, but my guess is it's a one-way instruction, posted in a public place."

"A trigger." Chalwen sighed. "So, we're back to the game of patience. Any luck with Fischer yet?"

Simone's mood darkened further. "It's too soon to get anything useful from him, and I think we're running out of time."

"Too right. Ivan still has something up his sleeve. He's set something in motion. Bresk was just the messenger but Fischer must know about it."

"That's not what I meant," Simone muttered. "His health is failing, and our best medics have no clue what's going on. They don't think they can keep him alive more than a couple more days."

Chalwen gaped. "Could Ivan's crew really get to him? In the heart of Sanitation?" The thought filled her with dread.

"Let me worry about that. I'm off upstairs to brief the colonel, and you said you needed to return to the Emperor."

Chalwen grunted. After Julian's successful address to the Assembly, Chalwen had insisted on apprehending Bresk in person. She felt she was owed that pleasure. But Simone's words haunted her all the way back to the Office of Deliberation. The triumph soured. Damn Ivan!

———•◦•———

Chalwen arrived breathless and sweating. The usher in the outer office put a finger to his lips as he cracked a side door open. Chalwen eased herself into the main room, meeting the Emperor's angry sidelong glance with an unapologetic stare of her own. Dealing with Lieutenant Bresk had taken longer than she'd expected, but she was damned if she'd feel guilt at indulging herself in his arrest. It wasn't as if Julian didn't have enough advisors around him already, and there was precious little Chalwen could do to counsel him on *this* meeting.

Julian, looking flustered, turned back to the floor-to-ceiling wall display, where it sounded like he was being given a severe dressing-down by the head of the Firenzi Family.

She did feel a tiny twinge of guilt when she heard the tail end of the tirade that Julian was gamely weathering. Even if she had no wisdom to offer, she could at least offer emotional support. She was relieved to see Doctor Vicky and Marcus Tyee standing to one side, out of Josef's view. There was also the frail diplomatic advisor, Ivana bin Durin, whose advice Julian would be leaning on most of all.

Chalwen surreptitiously scanned the room and was shaken to realize there was no one here from Imperial Security. Julian couldn't have appointed another Chief of Intelligence yet. Maybe she should have been here after all.

She must have stepped further into the room than she meant to, into view of the comms screen, because Josef's angry speech tailed off into silence.

"I know you," he said at last. A pale-faced officer stepped into sight and whispered in Josef's ear.

"Colonel Damra Chort." Chalwen saluted. "Congratulations on your promotion."

"Out of uniform, Lieutenant?"

"Retired from the service." Chalwen indicated her cane. "Now advising the Emperor on matters of security."

Josef snorted. "You should stick to bodyguarding and jailbreaking, because your intelligence services have dropped us into this damned mess." His tone softened. "But I and Margerite owe you our lives."

"The threat to you and your entourage in Henriss was all part of the same plot to pit us against each other. Both Families been played, and the rot runs both deep and high."

"Even if I can accept there was a galactic conspiracy," Josef said, "with Eloon at the heart of it, that doesn't justify wiping out a whole population."

Julian coughed. "I've stood in front of my people and declared a rightful act against Firenzi aggression. There's no way I can go back on that, or reveal it was a rogue element in our own ranks. In my own Family. The Skamensis dynasty would be through, and I don't need to paint you a picture of the mayhem that would follow." Although he looked like he wanted to collapse, Julian managed to speak with steady assurance. Once again, Chalwen saw the Emperor emerging from the shadow of the young boy. "You ask about justification. I don't believe there were any clear yardsticks written into the Trown Plains Accord to guide us on what is and isn't a justifiable premise."

"The Accord is thousands of years old!" Josef looked incredulous. "Drawn up in barbaric times, to place limits on conflicts that were threatening to wipe out humanity altogether. Its provisions were tame by those standards, but it has dozens of entitlements that no one in their right mind would try to exercise in these more civilized times. You're not seriously resting your case on some ancient technicality?"

"Nevertheless, that document still lays the legal framework for the Families to act. Or do you propose setting it aside?" Although Julian's voice was little more than a whisper, the threat it contained was all too real.

With a grudging and brief nod, Josef said, "My legal advisors acknowledge that you may *technically* have the right, but it's not for certain, and it would be by the most tenuous of flimsy arguments. Morally, no one here will accept it."

"It was more than simple conspiracy," Julian said. "*Technically*, you've been harboring a known traitor and fugitive."

"You can trot out as many fugitives from justice as you like," Josef huffed. "That still leaves the response out of all proportion to the crimes.

Only a direct act of war would come close, and no civilian conspirators would ever have the power to send our fleet into your space."

"And yet," Julian said grimly, "Firenzi forces have made repeated raids on our populations. Did that happen with your official sanction?"

Josef gave an irritated flick of his hand. "We've been over this, back on Chevinta. A few renegade captains, which we've managed to stop. That doesn't come close to the kind of provocation I'm talking about."

"Not all fugitives are equal in the eyes of imperial justice."

Josef opened his mouth, then slowly closed it again, giving the Emperor a wary look.

"I'm talking about my uncle, Lorenzo Skamensis." Julian's voice caught for a moment. "He was hiding on Eloon."

Josef Firenzi goggled at Julian. "I had no idea Lorenzo was still alive."

"That puzzles me. You see, he had settled with a wife and children. Jasmina Skolax."

Was that a flicker of alarm in Josef's eyes? Chalwen was glad she'd stumbled on this piece of intelligence. It pained her that Lorenzo was being painted as a traitor, but it looked like it might help in dealing with Josef.

"You should know the name. Jasmina was a minor noble in the Firenzi hierarchy."

"I know of her. But there are thousands of noble families scattered across our worlds. I probably even met her at some point, I'd have to check my records, but I know nothing of her situation or her family arrangements."

"She was also an undercover agent for the Firenzi Special Service." Julian's voice could have cut battleship armor. Chalwen was impressed with the training he'd retained, and she could see Doctor Vicky's influence all through this meeting. "I simply cannot find it in me to believe that the Service was not fully aware of exactly who an agent of theirs had hitched herself to."

The long silence in the office that followed was heightened by faint sounds outside. The call of collared jays counterpointed the distant tramp of marching boots muffled by the armored windows.

When it was clear the Firenzi head had no answer, Julian said, "Josef, I'm offering you a way out. Your senior Cabinet will need to see proof that Lorenzo was operating a clandestine network out of Eloon, I get that, but with them on your side you can bring the public around. Acknowledge a fair exchange of blows, and we both keep our honor more-or-less intact."

"More-or-less? I watched your address just now. Seems to me you came out ahead."

"While people's blood is up, they'll cheer me on, but there *will* be a reckoning. This wave of support will fizzle out when it really sinks in exactly what we've done. I expect the calls for war to die down, and I'll be the scapegoat on my side when questions of overreach start getting asked. I'm asking you, as a long-time ally and broker for peace, to accept a similar blow to your pride."

Silence hung thick in the air. Chalwen hardly dared breathe. Julian, Doctor Vicky, Marcus Tyee and Ivana bin Durin stood like statues, staring at Josef. Even the guards stationed around the office, normally detached and impassive, showed sharp interest in the patriarch's response.

Finally, Josef grimaced. "I need to take back to my Family something more than an Emperor's righteous wrath. Can you convince your population that the Firenzi had nothing to do with the Emperor's death? The attacks on Firenzi holdings need to stop."

Chalwen eased herself out of view and sagged against the nearest wall, fearing her legs would give way. The nearest guard, one of her old squad, gave her a questioning look and moved to leave his post. Chalwen gave a tiny shake of her head, and turned her attention back to the two Family heads.

"Those attacks were being fueled by the same people responsible for Eloon," Julian said. "That network is broken and I'm dealing with the ones responsible." His stance relaxed, and he started pacing in front of the wall screen. "I do expect the Assembly to take me to task for over-reacting. I'll swing that around to a motion for suitable reparations."

The hard lines of Josef's face softened. "Don't expect the price to be cheap."

"I don't think anything can honestly make up for what happened between us. What happened was unforgivable, but it's done. It's our job to stop this sinking into something even worse."

Chapter 51

Ivan fought to conceal his anxiety as he faced Julian across the broad desk in the Office of Deliberation. Past Julian's shoulders, subdued lighting glittered on the cascades of the Fountain Court beyond the windows, and dispelled the chill night.

Nothing lessened the cold seeping into Ivan's bones. This was it. This audience would decide his fate. What resources did he have still at his disposal? First Bernie Fischer and now Shan Bresk had broken off contact. His guard had been changed and had proven immune to bribes, pleas or threats, so he'd been cut off from the outside world since Julian's address to the Assembly. He had no idea how interstellar affairs were going these past days. In that one brief speech, the Emperor seemed to have the Assembly on his side, but they only spoke for Skamensis space. What was happening beyond those borders? Were they at war? After toasting a planet, the Firenzi should be up in arms, but, frustratingly, Ivan could glean no hint from anyone's talk or manner.

The lack of any useful information filled him with dread. He had to pray his last message to Bresk had reached its destination. The only other person present in the office today was Lieutenant ap Gwynodd, still maddeningly alive. That fact plunged him even deeper into despair. If Bernie's preparations had failed in this regard, what else had gone awry?

Minutes ticked by, each an eternity, while Julian stared silently at his uncle. The nephew Ivan had been so close to seemed a stranger now. He tried and failed to read Julian's expression, his mood. Was that anger twisting his lips, or disgust?

When he finally spoke, Julian's voice was low and dangerous. "You need to understand that you're finished in this Family. I'm keeping you under close arrest, no contact except through guards I appoint, while I decide what to do with you."

Ivan raised an eyebrow, allowing himself a touch of optimism. Although Julian's pronouncement sounded dire, Ivan focused on the last part. Clearly his fate wasn't settled yet. "I stand by what I said when we last met. I did what was necessary for our empire, our dynasty. You're angry, and rightly so, but that will pass. You brought the Assembly around, and you need to stand by what *you* said. Do you think this crisis will just blow over if you offer me up as a scapegoat?"

"Scapegoat? I can't picture the Assembly standing for outright treason. You admitted as much."

Ivan's scalp crawled. That private meeting days ago may not have been private after all. "Not everyone will see it that way." His mind raced as he grasped for arguments to head off this line of thinking. "You've seen how the media, the populace, will make up their own truths. Announce my arrest and see what public unrest really looks like."

Julian sat back. He appeared dumbstruck as he processed Ivan's words, but a look of calculation sharpened his gaze, quenching the glimmer of triumph Ivan had started to feel. Julian shook his head in disbelief. "You think I'm just talking about the Cleansing, don't you?"

Ivan's thoughts switched track of their own accord. Not Eloon? Then what?

"I know you've been acting against the peace process from the start. Using the media. Organizing unrest and acts of aggression to rally opposition. All treasonous acts."

Each accusation stabbed home like an assassin's blade. And, Ivan belatedly realized, he'd just indirectly admitted his own hand in that unrest. But Julian and ap Gwynodd seemed not to have noticed his slip. Not that it made any real difference. So this was what Stanhope had been holding on to.

"You tried to make me look weak in front of the Assembly," Julian continued. "I knew you wanted the throne for yourself, but I never imagined you'd sink so low."

There was no answer to that. Ivan let the silence draw out while he desperately cast around for lines of defense. They had Bernie. It shouldn't be possible, but they must have broken him. It was the only thing that made sense. Bernie was too paranoid to commit any of his arrangements to any physical or electronic record, but his mind held an encyclopedic knowledge of all Ivan's covert affairs.

Before Ivan could come up with anything to say, Julian buried his face in his hands. When he looked up, there were tears in his eyes. "We know who killed my father, my family."

"That was not me." Ivan felt weak.

"But you stood by and let it happen. You sought to profit from it. And when I didn't die along with the others, you tried to dispose of me to clear the way to the throne."

Something didn't add up there. Maybe they hadn't broken Bernie after all. He knew the attempt on Julian's life was nothing to do with Ivan. Maybe ImpSec's investigations had been more thorough than Ivan had been led to believe, just not quite thorough enough. He eyed ap Gwynodd suspiciously, then turned back to the Emperor. Whatever Julian believed, it couldn't end well for Ivan. Julian was simply stalling, putting off the inevitable.

Ivan realized he'd also been stalling. He had one card left to play, but it was a dangerous and unpredictable weapon. All the same, this was a time for last resorts. He took a deep breath. "There is something you need to see. Then you can make your mind up what to do with me."

It seemed that Julian was ready with an angry retort, but something in Ivan's tone made him pause.

"There is a document in your workspace." Ivan wished he felt as confident as he forced himself to sound. If Bernie's specially-assigned task force had failed him, he had nothing left to bargain with. He gave the Emperor guidance to a secure location in the palace network, and a key to unlock the document waiting there.

Julian stared at the desktop. Silently, he signaled ap Gwynodd to look.

At first she didn't react. Maybe she thought she was looking at archive images of Lady Miriam and her children, but she'd see there was something off about them.

"Is this from the time of Grandmother's funeral?" Julian whispered.

Ap Gwynodd shook her head. "At a glance, I thought that was you and Matthew in front."

"But the *older* boy is Matthew. I can see that. And I don't remember that room or this picture being taken."

"He's too old, though, and if that's Matthew, that has to be Jonathan."

"That can't be."

Ap Gwynodd's mouth hung open. She staggered back and leaned against the windowsill overlooking the Fountain Court. "The hideout under the palace." She glared daggers at Ivan. "That was your doing."

Ivan nodded.

Julian gaped at the lieutenant. "What are you talking about?" Clearly, he hadn't made the deduction yet, or was struggling to accept it.

"One of the leads we followed brought me to a room in a disused machinery space. It had been occupied recently. I thought it was some-thing to do with the crew that killed your father, but it was used to hold the family until they could be moved out of the palace." Her legs trem-bled with the effort of holding herself upright. "I missed the meaning of it at the time, and then the assassins, what was left of them, tried to poison you. Everything that happened after that pushed the hiding place out of my mind until much later."

"Sire," Ivan said gently, "your family is alive. This image is proof of that."

"Do you believe this man?" Julian hissed to ap Gwynodd. Ivan shud-dered at the venom in his expression. "My family really is alive?"

Ap Gwynodd looked like she was about to be sick. "We'll need more than a single image. Something that can't be faked. But," she whispered, "I think this will prove to be genuine."

"Emperor Paul is dead, make no mistake about that." Ivan's tone was flat, devoid of emotion. "But I couldn't let them kill the rest of the family. I saved them."

"You mean you stood by while someone killed my father, and turned it to your advantage." Julian's tone was glacial.

Then a sickening premonition emptied Ivan's mind. Would Julian make the connection? Time slowed, and he watched realization cloud Julian's face with the weight and inevitability of an approaching sandstorm.

"You meddled in the assassination plot to pull my family out. That means you could have saved my father too, but either you left him to die or you ordered his death. Either way, his death is on *your* head."

Ivan's eyes flashed. "I genuinely wanted the family to come to no harm. My brother was a legitimate mark, part of the power games we all play, but I made it clear that the others were off limits."

"You showed me those hides in the Meadow." Julian sounded thoughtful, but Ivan could see the pain in his eyes. "Was that just for show, knowing I was about to die?"

Ivan shook his head. "That was before I knew of the assassination plot. But it was obvious Emperor Paul was making too many enemies in high places. It was only a matter of time. The empire was never going to survive his policies of appeasement, so, yes I took precautions to advise you and try to safeguard a line of succession."

"And then a better opportunity came along." The venom in Julian's voice burned. "If I hadn't fallen off Coal, what would have happened to me?"

With a deep sadness, Ivan said, "You were meant to go into a comfortable exile with the rest of the family." The sadness threatened to swallow him. He knew, finally, that he'd lost the one relationship he'd truly valued. There could be no forgiveness, only survival. He steeled himself and his tone hardened. "Now, their future depends on your actions. I suggest we sit down and negotiate."

Epilogue

Honorina Philip leaned forward, not caring that she looked eager and hungry. Despite her physical limitations—even the effort of shifting her bulk on her couch raised her heart rate—she was a predator. Her ship, *Bringer of Tears*, was an extension of herself and there was nothing so fearsome in all known space. Not even a *Sword* could match her.

Besides, there was no one here to observe apart from Honorina's retinue of guards, and they would neither judge nor tell. They'd been medically and electronically enhanced for combat. In the process, something of their humanity had been stripped out. One day, maybe, battlefields would swarm with engineered armies like this, but that day was generations away yet.

Meanwhile, the wall opposite showed the plot of a laden merchantman skimming through the dimensional folds of realspace, making nanosecond appearances like a stone skipping the surface of a lake.

It was a well-known fact that battles in space always happened in the gravity well close to a planet or star, where it became too risky to engage a ship's primary drive. Anywhere else, and opponents could simply flee as soon as the tide turned against them. There was no known way to force a battle out in open space. Apart from the encrypted comms signature all ships put out, there was no known way even to track a hopping ship, let alone force an engagement.

Nothing known to the Families, the freeworlds, the pirates and out-worlds, that is. Of course, the defense conglomerates kept the best tech to themselves. They maximized profits by dribbling improvements out like misers, keeping opposing navies finely balanced, no one side ever getting a decisive advantage. Civilization was a precarious host, and the conglomerates milked it carefully.

But *Bringer of Tears* could track a ship through the trail it left in folded space, like an old-fashioned ship's wake. This defiance of known facts was something that PDC kept to themselves for now. The time wasn't yet ripe for maximum profits, and every use of the technology carried a risk of premature discovery. Honorina Philip chose to look on her current work as essential field trials.

It galled her that she'd resorted to intercepting Ivan Skamensis all that time ago, and leaving witnesses behind, but the need had been urgent at the time. She'd argued long with her partners on that point, after the fact. She'd always based her life on asking forgiveness rather than permission, and even then only rarely. She was sure, though, that the risk was small. Ivan was too blinkered to guess at the truth. He'd assume that they'd simply broken his ship's encrypted comms signature and followed that.

This time, as with other attacks in recent months, there would be no witnesses. The Emperor was dangerously close to patching things up with Family Firenzi, but mistrust between the two populations made the situation precarious still. Ivan had failed, so it was up to her to nudge the fragile peace over the edge and into profitable war.

"Torpedo armed and ready," the captain announced. "Targeting solution prepared and locked in."

Honorina Philip paused to savor the moment. This was another argument that she'd have to face soon, but the dividends to be reaped from her judicious interference in galactic affairs would win her partners around in time.

Once you could track a hopping ship, it was possible to target it with a specially-designed weapon. The weapon didn't even need a warhead. It consisted solely of a small hopper drive, tuned for a short burst of extreme speed. All it needed was for the torpedo's drive to interfere with and cause a small wobble in the target ship's drive field. The ship's safety systems would shut it down, leaving the vessel vulnerable to a traditional assault.

"Stand down, Captain."

Honorina looked up, startled at the familiar voice of one of the other partners. "Amelia! This is an unexpected honor." Her mind raced. How had Amelia bypassed the usual comms protcols? Why had the bridge channeled the call here without consulting her first?

"We held an emergency board meeting." Along with his nasal tones, the image of Jarvis Coolidge appeared on the wall alongside Amelia Drayson.

Honorina's mind blanked for a moment. "I never received notice of a meeting."

"You've been hard to reach in recent months. Flying dark." Amelia's smile could have curdled milk. "As we had a quorum, we chose to proceed anyway."

Honorina narrowed her eyes.

"Your activities over the last year have placed PDC into something of a crisis. We had to discuss emergency measures to limit the damage."

"We already discussed my meeting with Ivan Skamensis," Honorina squawked. "And my present activities can't be traced back to us."

"I'm not talking about your ill-advised gallivanting across space. I'm talking about PDC's involvement in regicide."

Honorina's heart stopped for several seconds, before resuming a frantic thudding in her chest. The heat in the room seemed to have cranked up ten degrees. She tried to speak, but no words came.

Jarvis smoothly filled the gap. "The Emperor presented clear evidence, but he has chosen not to pursue us through the courts."

"Huh?" Honorina's wits seemed to have deserted her.

"Too slow and uncertain. He has other avenues to exact retribution."

"We have been blacklisted." The smile vanished from Amelia's lips. "None of the Families will deal with us."

"Or any of our partners or subsidiaries," Jarvis added, in tones smoother but no less venomous. "That is not good for business."

"The Emperor wants our heads."

"But we persuaded him to settle for yours."

Honorina stared, wide-eyed, as the guard in front of her leveled a beam pistol at her. The guard's face was hard and emotionless.

There was a hiss of steel behind Honorina, and a flash in her peripheral vision.

The room spun ...

————•——————

Given her preoccupation over the last two years, it could have been worse, Chalwen reflected. The barricade of plant debris at either end of her hidden retreat had deterred intruders and provided a natural bulwark against new growth that might have choked the gates. Inside the walls, brambles and vines had swamped her paths and beds but their grip was fragile still. No match against a determined assault.

It would be a long slog, especially when every step still pained her, but at times she could almost ignore the electric jolts up her shins when she cleared a new corner to reveal the outlines of the garden plan she'd so lovingly laid out.

Besides—she struggled to bend forwards to ferret out the shallow roots of a runner—she needed the exercise. There were only so many wardrobe upgrades she was prepared to put up with.

Her favorite quince had died, neglected, but other plants could be coaxed back to health. The packing crates she and Henri had sat on had rotted at the corners and were close to collapse, but Chalwen rejoiced as she pulled a thicket of vines away from her small aluminum table. She brushed off the worst of the debris and leaned against it to get her breath back.

Since Ivan's bombshell, things had gone eerily quiet. She, Henri, and Simone still carried on their semi-official investigations, as official as anything Sanitation ever did, but any clues to further unravel the Grand Duke's network were maddeningly sparse. Bernie Fischer died of a mystery ailment as Simone had feared. The palace medics had been helpless to intervene. And for all his bluster, Shan Bresk knew nothing of importance. He was simply Ivan's muscle, not trusted with any real information.

The rest of the network had vanished into the palace's ancient woodwork.

The atmosphere inside ImpSec headquarters was one of dread. It felt like a disease still stalked the hallways, ready to pick off unsuspecting victims at will. The high profile assassinations of senior officials were bad enough, but somehow word had leaked out about Fischer's death in custody.

Staff were used to people occasionally vanishing into the depths of the basement, but it was understood that was a matter of internal housekeeping. Sanitation was scrupulous in their research, and everyone knew those who vanished did so for a good reason. But the unwritten rules of engagement had been breached. Here was an outside party slipping past their defenses with impunity, picking off loyal staff. And it was unheard of for a 'guest' of ImpSec to be killed off *prematurely*, right in the heart of the building.

Everyone was rattled, wondering who would be next.

Meanwhile, Julian had closeted himself away from all his advisors, even Chalwen, while he thrashed out some kind of working arrangement with his murderous uncle.

She'd been shaken by the revelation about Julian's family, perhaps more so than Julian himself. The seemingly-superfluous hiding place deep under the palace had been an anomaly. Yes, she and Henri had puzzled over its meaning. Yes, they'd realized there had been something else going on that day, but they'd failed to piece the jigsaw together. And now, Ivan had an unbreakable stranglehold on the Emperor.

Failure weighed heavy on her.

And so, to give her mind a break from bashing itself senseless against unseen obstacles, Chalwen had returned to her tiny derelict garden.

There, she'd found some measure of peace and perspective. With each patch cleared, each discovery of a treasured shoot still fighting for life, her mood lifted. Things could have ended up far worse. Millions of pointless deaths preyed on her, but they'd averted an even bigger catastrophe. The destruction of Eloon had shocked the Families into silence with a foretaste of the manyfold devastation full-on war would bring. Relationships with Josef Firenzi would be strengthened, given time.

Ivan's treachery may never become public knowledge, but the fate of Honorina Philip, the original architect of all this destruction, would echo through palaces and boardrooms alike as a salutary lesson to those who thought to meddle in the affairs of the Families.

A rustling at the northern gate caught her attention. Could that be Henri, looking for her? He was the only other person who knew about this retreat. A muffled curse, a boyish voice. Not Henri. Chalwen stood, alarmed, wondering if she should escape through the other gate before she was seen, but before she could move, Julian pushed past the edge of her barricade.

At Chalwen's puzzled glance past his shoulder, Julian said, "My bodyguard is standing guard outside. I wanted to talk to you alone."

Chalwen checked her lapel to reassure herself that her communicator was still attached. "You only had to summon me and I'd have been at your side."

Julian ignored the comment. He gazed up at the ivy-clad building towering over them, then around the perimeter of the narrow space. He strolled the few square yards Chalwen had managed to clear, studying the outlines of order still visible beneath wild encroachment. "You've claimed this space before, haven't you?"

"A long time ago. I was making good progress, until your father's death. We've all been a bit busy since then."

"You have a big task on your hands," Julian said. "Why aren't the palace gardeners looking after this place?"

"The perils of an over-efficient bureaucracy." Chalwen grinned at his obvious confusion. "People develop a willful blindness to even absurd anomalies. This little corner doesn't exist on any official records, and people trust the record above the evidence of their own eyes."

Julian turned his back to Chalwen. He looked deep in thought, and the bunch of his shoulders said he was tussling with what to say. Clearly he hadn't come to discuss gardening, but whatever the reason for his visit, it was troubling him.

"Pure logic says I should put the needs of the empire ahead of the well-being of five individuals."

The catch in his voice tore at Chalwen. She scratched the back of her head. "If you were able to follow cold logic to that extent, you'd no longer be the Emperor I serve. I assume the Grand Duke has been negotiating for his life."

"Is it really a negotiation when one party holds a sword to the neck of the other?"

"As long as *something* is staying the sword hand, there must be room for negotiation. Have you reached some sort of conclusion with the Grand Duke?"

"Obviously he's demanding his own safety and freedom."

Julian turned when Chalwen spluttered, and his mouth twisted in a bitter smile. She couldn't form words, but her outrage was clear enough.

He shook his head. "I don't see any way around that, but any freedom will have its limits."

"The fact that he's still breathing is an offense." She sighed. "But I don't see a way around it either."

"I don't know whether to call it a deadlock, or an agreement. Ivan knows I can't touch him without condemning my family. But I'm still an emotional teenager. I managed to convince him that if he tested my patience too far I'd throw the unholy mother of a tantrum and destroy everything. If the true version of events got out, neither of us would survive the fallout. He knows that too."

Chalwen mulled this over. "So, your only real bargaining chip is the threat to go nuclear?"

Julian nodded.

"That will buy you time, but it won't work forever. One of these days he'll call your bluff, when he sees you've got past the impetuous and dangerously unpredictable stage. When your head is clear, you'll realize you have too much to lose. You'll blink first."

"So I need to use that time wisely."

"We need to find some vulnerability, so you have a useable weapon to hold to his throat in return."

"You have an idea?" Julian's boyish eagerness would be comical if the situation wasn't so dire.

"I honestly don't know what that would look like." Chalwen spread her hands helplessly. "His hold on your family will always protect him from direct harm, but we have to make sure it's a shield only, not something he can use to any further advantage."

"So you understand my position." Something in Chalwen's words seemed to have lifted a weight from Julian's shoulders. "I knew you would. That's why I'm here."

The weight seemed to settle on Chalwen instead.

"I needed to talk privately with you but I chose not to summon you to come to me. Instead I came to you, because I have something big to ask of you. There's a senior position in my organization that's proving hard to fill."

With growing dread, Chalwen said, "You're talking about Head of Intelligence. You have several good people ready to step in. Right now it's got a reputation as a death warrant, but we've got the situation in HQ under control."

"Have you, though?"

Words of reassurance died on Chalwen's lips. "Sort of."

"You'll get there. But to your other point, yes I have good people who could do the job. That's no longer good enough. This appointment is now about more than qualifications. You know the situation with Eloon, and with Ivan. I don't want to share that knowledge with anyone I don't need to."

"But, Sire, I've failed you time and time again. All this time I've been two steps behind Ivan and his conspirators, too late to save your father, too late to save Eloon."

"Two steps behind Ivan, maybe, but how many steps *ahead* of everyone else in ImpSec? Who first spotted the trouble in the palace when everyone's eyes were on the Traplinki coast? Who uncovered the poisoner under my quarters? Who realized Josef Firenzi was a target?"

"I've been lucky."

"Trouble finds you. You told Stanhope yourself." Julian laughed at Chalwen's expression. "Yes, he shared secrets with me. That was his job."

"All the same, how the heck can I fill his shoes, with all his years of experience? What in Space do I know about running an organization like that?"

"If it helps you deal with your feeling of worthlessness, you can look on it as my least worst option."

"Hah! That's more like it."

"I need someone to take the heat so the rest of my staff, the ones already refusing this poisoned chalice, can get on with *their* jobs. That will be my official line. Your role will be to keep the wheels oiled and stay out of their way. By the time they realize they can come out from hiding, you'll have established yourself."

Chalwen eased back to prop herself up again on the edge of the table. Stress, she decided, didn't help her nerves. "You want me to let the division heads do what they know best. Meanwhile, there's still the problem of the Grand Duke."

"With the resources at your disposal, I expect you to clean up ImpSec and then work out how to fence him in. Limit his power. I can't have him thinking he can dictate terms to me."

"Cleaning up ImpSec alone would be the task of a lifetime. That and the palace administration are still riddled with people who'd turn against you in a heartbeat. All it takes is a word from Ivan." Weariness leached through Chalwen's limbs. She squeezed her eyes shut then shook her head irritably. "It galls me that we can't punish him properly."

"He should burn for treason." Julian kicked at a pebble, dislodging it from dry soil. "And yet I'm not sure I could sign the order. There's another empty threat in his favor."

"It's not all one way. He went to great lengths to remove your family from the firing line, which tells me there are limits to his ruthlessness."

"But was that for them, or for his own benefit?"

Chalwen pondered. "If he'd let the plot run its intended course, he'd have been the only one left to take the throne. He didn't have to intervene. He really does care for them, like he does you. I suspect the danger may not be as absolute as he'd have us believe. Just like your own threats against him, he's making a threat he'd be hard-pressed to carry out."

"While he still holds my family, I can't take that chance. We can push each other, test each other's patience, but neither of us can push too hard."

"For now, his power is broken. Yes, I'll take on ImpSec for you and root out the corruption. For a man like Ivan, that's probably a worse punishment than torture and death." Chalwen gazed around her tiny private realm. She should probably alert the palace groundskeepers to their clerical oversight. It looked like she'd have little time to give this plot the attention it deserved.

Julian bared his teeth. It was not a smile. "He may have escaped with his life, but he'll come to regret it."

"As for your family"—a hard glint crept into Chalwen's eyes—"we'll find them. All the resources of ImpSec and The Hidden Light are available to us. Ivan will have left a trail somewhere, and he must have a holding facility somewhere. And staff and guards. You can't hide something like that forever."

Ivan paced the deep carpet of his office spanning the top level of Greyspire. Beyond tinted windows lay the comforting familiarity of Devonia's landscape, but even this spectacular panorama couldn't calm his inner turmoil.

Stukker had assured him there had been no visitors prior to Ivan's arrival. No strangers sniffing around to install unwanted surveillance equipment. And everyone in the weeks since then were known to him and their entourages carefully vetted. That would have to be good enough. Ivan could no longer trust the security measures surrounding him in the Mosaic Palace, or even on board *Kirov*. He'd rebuild his defenses in time, but for now this was the only place where he could be assured of privacy.

Abruptly he turned on his heel to face the only other occupant of the room. Scipio Firenzi lounged with his feet propped up on a coffee table. He swirled a ruby red Tigris Gamay around his glass and scowled at Ivan. "You took a risk asking me to come here. Both ImpSec and Special Service will know we've met."

"You flatter yourself," Ivan said, drily. "You're just one in a procession of visitors. I've retreated from the lights of Magentis to lick my wounds, where I'm entertaining a long list of allies from all quarters. Of course they'll scrutinize you, but as far as the Emperor is concerned I'm doing my bit to make amends and build bridges with Family Firenzi."

"You think he'll believe that?" Scipio snorted.

"Of course not. But for now I'll give him no reason to claim otherwise."

"So, you're repenting past misdeeds and becoming a new man?"

"That is the face I'll put to the Emperor behind closed doors. After all, even though the wrong Skamensis is on the throne, we're still family. In public, of course, I have nothing to atone for. What really happened around Eloon, where the order really came from, is known to only a few people."

"I thought a whole bridge crew witnessed the Emperor's attempts to countermand the order."

"Memories are malleable. Especially when all records tell a different story. People will eventually spin their narratives to match what they read." At Scipio's gape of disbelief, Ivan added, "Oh, yes. ImpSec have amazing powers of fiction when they're suitably motivated. And my own people in the organization put their backs into making sure the fiction was thorough and convincing. I have as much interest as Julian in keeping my involvement hidden."

"You still have people there?" Scipio's eyes widened in mock amazement.

Ivan nodded, though the question pained him. There were too few left, too few he could still access. Especially with Bernie gone. Speaking of whom ... "Your laboratories produce an amazing range of untraceable poisons."

"Glad to be of help. I hear the Emperor finally appointed a Head of Intelligence who hasn't met with an untimely end."

"Sadly true, and she's as much of a nuisance as she's ever been." And still too damned inquisitive for comfort. "Unfortunately she's too well protected, and I no longer have the resources to deal with her." Not yet. That pleasure would come, Ivan swore to himself. Never mind thwarting his attempts to take the throne, his grudge with ap Gwynodd had become personal. Through her meddling, she was the one responsible for the irretrievable rift between him and Julian.

A flicker of disappointment crossed Scipio's face. He really did like a good bloodbath.

"Now, I did have a serious purpose in inviting you here."

Scipio set his glass down and dropped his feet to the floor, suddenly attentive.

"Are you sure you're still in the clear with your own people?"

Scipio snorted. "Josef suspects nothing. He still takes me into his confidence, as much as he ever has. And my own activities were distanced enough no one can trace them back to me. So, you have a favor to ask, obviously."

Ivan swallowed his anger. He liked people owing *him* favors, not the other way around. But his own power would take time, maybe years, to regain. Meanwhile ... "I have some assets to relocate."

"Assets?" Scipio squinted at Ivan.

"They are vital to my continued life and liberty, and they're no longer safe in Skamensis space."

Light dawned in Scipio's eyes. Ivan was as sure as he could be that it was safe to speak openly here, but it didn't hurt to be circumspect, even if only to keep Scipio in the habit of caution.

"These ... assets," Ivan continued, "will need careful looking-after. I can supply some loyal guardians, and considerable funding, but I wonder if some carefully-chosen people from your side might jump at the chance to hold Family Skamensis over a barrel."

Scipio scowled, and Ivan swore he could see the thought processes at work as the other man pondered. "There will need to be an engineering project to house these assets. Funding, manpower and supplies will need to be channeled carefully to avoid tracing."

"In the past, my own network would have been able to handle matters like that." Ivan heaved an inward sigh of relief that the Firenzi noble wasn't baulking at the task they were discussing. "But it will take me years to re-establish my connections and ensure they remain free from contamination." Especially, Ivan thought sourly, with the added scrutiny I'll be under from that bodyguard-turned-chief.

"Have no worries on that front." Scipio looked thoughtful, then he smiled. "I believe some prime real estate has recently become available. A whole deserted planet should afford ample hiding places for a small holding facility."

Afterword

More about Shayla's world

For a behind-the-scenes dive into the worldbuilding for this story, visit my website:

https://www.iansbott.com/shayla-s-world

The site contains a wealth of detail about the Shayla Carver universe – maps, pictures, terminology, technical information and more.

A final word from the author

If you've enjoyed reading a book – any book, not just this one – please consider leaving a review where other readers can find it.

One of the greatest challenges Indie authors face is gaining visibility in the immense marketplace of online publishing. Indies can't hope to compete with big publishers for shelf space or advertising copy or magazine column-inches. Our visibility to readers, our ability to be found, rests on ranking algorithms at online stores. Those algorithms rank books on sales and reviews.

You've got this book in your hands. You've already made me happy. The best way to make me even happier is to leave an honest review wherever you bought the book, or on a readers' forum where you hang out.

Thank you!